Praise for the work of Diana Norman

"Resplendent with historical details, filled with beautifully crafted characters, and kissed with a subtle touch of romance, Norman's tale is historical fiction at its best. Makepeace is so irresistibly indomitable, readers will relish every moment of her unforgettable adventures."
—Booklist

"Cracking historical novels." *—Daily Mirror* (London)

"Drama, passion, intrigue, and danger, I loved it and didn't want it to end ever." *—The Sunday Times* (London)

"It's all good, dirty fun shot through with more serious insights into the historical treatment of women and, perhaps, in its association of sex, sleaze, greed, and politics, not so far removed from present realities after all." *—The Independent on Sunday* (London)

"Quite simply, splendid." —Frank Delaney, author of *Tipperary*

Praise for
The Serpent's Tale

"Captivating medieval mysteries...[featuring] Adelia Aguilar, a woman brought up as a free thinker and schooled in Italy to perform autopsies. In *The Serpent's Tale*, which continues this exciting series, the focus is on Henry's contentious queen, Eleanor of Aquitaine, whose agile mind, strong will, and vibrant personality make her a formidable adversary for her royal spouse. This excellent adventure delivers high drama and lively scholarship from its heroine's feminist perspective." *—The New York Times Book Review*

"An impe... ...ost foul, regal intrigue, ...*tainment Weekly*

"A complicated mystery turns into a political maelstrom.... [Franklin] brilliantly captures the heated tension between king and queen, evoking jealousy as the root of political and personal turmoil."
—Los Angeles Times

"An enjoyable romp...A warm, promising continuation of the series."
—Kirkus Reviews (starred review)

"Set in twelfth-century England, Franklin's mesmerizing second historical delivers on the promise of her first, Mistress of the Art of Death. Franklin...brings medieval England to life, from the maze surrounding Rosamund's tower to the royal court's Christmas celebration, with ice skating on the frozen Thames. A colorful cast of characters, both good and evil, enhance a tale that will keep readers on edge until the final page."
—Publishers Weekly

Praise for
Mistress of the Art of Death
WINNER OF THE ELLIS PETERS HISTORICAL DAGGER AWARD

"Great fun! Franklin succeeds in vividly bringing the twelfth century to life with this crackling good story. Expertly researched, a brilliant heroine, full of excellent period detail."
—Kate Mosse, New York Times bestselling author of Sepulchre

"[A] vibrant medieval mystery. Outdoes the competition in depicting the perversities of human cruelty. Adelia is a delight, and her spirited efforts to stop the killings...add to our appreciation of her forensic skills. But the lonely figure who truly stands out in Franklin's vibrant tapestry of medieval life is King Henry—an enlightened monarch condemned to live in dark times."
—The New York Times

"[A] terrific book....Fascinating details of historical forensic medicine, entertaining notes on women in science (the medical school at Salerno is not fictional), and a nice running commentary on science and superstition, as distinct from religious faith,...a historical mystery that succeeds brilliantly as both historical fiction and crime-thriller."
—Diana Gabaldon, The Washington Post

DIANA NORMAN

Taking Liberties

BERKLEY BOOKS, NEW YORK

THE BERKLEY PUBLISHING GROUP
Published by the Penguin Group
Penguin Group (USA) Inc.
375 Hudson Street, New York, New York 10014, USA
Penguin Group (Canada), 90 Eglinton Avenue East, Suite 700, Toronto, Ontario M4P 2Y3, Canada
(a division of Pearson Penguin Canada Inc.)
Penguin Books Ltd., 80 Strand, London WC2R 0RL, England
Penguin Group Ireland, 25 St. Stephen's Green, Dublin 2, Ireland (a division of Penguin Books Ltd.)
Penguin Group (Australia), 250 Camberwell Road, Camberwell, Victoria 3124, Australia
(a division of Pearson Australia Group Pty. Ltd.)
Penguin Books India Pvt. Ltd., 11 Community Centre, Panchsheel Park, New Delhi—110 017, India
Penguin Group (NZ), 67 Apollo Drive, Rosedale, North Shore 0632, New Zealand
(a division of Pearson New Zealand Ltd.)
Penguin Books (South Africa) (Pty.) Ltd., 24 Sturdee Avenue, Rosebank, Johannesburg 2196,
South Africa

Penguin Books Ltd., Registered Offices: 80 Strand, London WC2R 0RL, England

This is a work of fiction. Names, characters, places, and incidents either are the product of the author's imagination or are used fictitiously, and any resemblance to actual persons, living or dead, business establishments, events, or locales is entirely coincidental. The publisher does not have any control over and does not assume any responsibility for author or third-party websites or their content.

PRINTING HISTORY
HarperCollins U.K. hardcover / February 2003
Berkley trade paperback edition / November 2004

Library of Congress Cataloging-in-Publication Data

Norman, Diana.
        Taking liberties / Diana Norman.—1st pedigree pbk. ed.
            p.   cm.
        ISBN 978-0-425-19815-5
        1. United States—History—Revolution, 1775–1783—Prisoners and prisons—
Fiction.   2. Great Britain—History—George III, 1760–1820—Fiction.   3. Prisoners
of war—Family relationships—Fiction.   4. Americans—England—Fiction.
5. Female friendship—Fiction.   6. Women—England—Fiction.   7. Devon
(England)—Fiction.   8. Smuggling—Fiction.   9. Nobility—Fiction.   10. Widows—
Fiction.   I. Title.

    PR6064.O73T34   2004
    823'.914—dc22

                                                                                    2004046310

PRINTED IN THE UNITED STATES OF AMERICA

15   14   13   12   11   10   9   8   7   6   5   4

To my friend and agent, Sarah Molloy

Chapter One

As the immediate family and the priest emerged from the crypt in which they had delivered the corpse of the Earl of Stacpoole to its last resting place, his Countess met the gaze of the rest of the mourners in the chapel and saw not one wet eye.

Which made it unanimous.

Perhaps, for decency, she should have paid some of the servants to cry but she doubted if any of them had sufficient acting talent to earn the money. For them, as for her, the scrape of stone when the tomb lid went into place had sounded like a gruff, spontaneous cheer.

Nevertheless, she satisfied herself that every face was suitably grave. The lineage of the man in the crypt was ancient enough to make William the Conqueror's descendants appear by contrast newly arrived; there must be no disrespect to it.

Despite twenty-two years' sufferance of many and varied abuses, the Countess had never encouraged a word to be spoken against her husband. Under her aegis, existence had been made as tolerable as possible for those who lived and worked in his house; floggings had been reduced, those who'd received them had been compensated and she had learned to employ only servants too old or too plain to attract sexual assault. But in all this she had refused to exchange confidences or criticism with any. The man himself might be vicious, but his status was irreproachable; if she could distinguish between the two, so must others.

A snuffle from behind the Countess indicated that her daughter-in-law at least was indulging the hypocrisy of tears. Yes, well.

Perhaps she should have acceded to the King's suggestion and had the service in Westminster Abbey but . . . *'They're not putting me alongside foreigners and poetic bloody penwipers. You see to it, woman.'*

The air of the chapel was heavy with incense. Heat from the closely packed bodies of the congregation rose up to stir hanging battle banners emblazoned with the Stacpoole prowess for killing people. The day outside being dull, only candlelight inclined onto walls knobbly with urns and plaques, increasing her impression that she and the others were incarcerated in some underground cave.

They'll bury me here. Beside him. *Beloved wife of* . . .

Even without the veil, the suffocation would not have shown on her face which long training kept as still as the marble countenances of Stacpoole effigies around her.

Nearly over. The priest intoned the plea that their dear brother, Aymer Edmund Fontenay, Earl of Stacpoole, might be raised from the death of sin into the life of righteousness—though not as if he had any hope of it.

A last clash from the censers.

'Grant this, we beseech thee, O merciful Father, through Jesus Christ our mediator . . .'

Outside, on the gravel apron, her hand resting on her son's arm, she paused to take in the air. The gardens of Chantries had never been to her taste: too artificial, more Le Nôtre than Brown—the Earl had seen little use for nature unless he could set his hounds on it—but today her soul sailed along the view of knotted parterre, fountains and lake to the utmost horizon of Bedfordshire. She was free.

Fred North bumbled up to her, bowing and blinking his weak little eyes, apologizing. She hadn't noticed him in the congregation; it appeared he'd arrived late. 'My deepest apologies, your ladyship, and my sincerest commiseration.'

'Thank you, Prime Minister. It was good of you to come.'

So it was; a less amiable man would have pleaded the war with America as his excuse to stay in London. Perhaps, like so many here today, he'd wanted to assure himself that her husband was safely dead. The Earl of Stacpoole had been among the tigers of the poor man's government, harrying him into standing up to the Americans against his inclination to conciliate. 'Feeble Fred,' the Earl had called him. *'I told him: it's castration that rabble needs, to Hell with conciliation. And the German agrees with me.'*

Always 'the German', never 'His Majesty'.

As they went along the terrace, the mourners were reduced to a train of grey and black Lilliputians against the vast frontage of the house.

She was allowed to go first up the steps but in the hall there was a bustle as her daughter-in-law came forward, taking Robert's hand and her new precedence to lead the procession into the State Dining Room for the funeral meats.

Of course.

Again, Diana's face showed nothing but its usual boredom. Her daughter-in-law had the undeniable right to display to the gathering that she was now mistress of Chantries, though a better-bred female might have waited until the corpse of its former master was a little chillier in its grave. Alice, however, was not well bred, merely moneyed.

The new Countess was aged twenty and the Dowager nearly thirty-nine, but their appearance narrowed the difference. Alice Stacpoole was the shorter by a head, muddy complexioned and a slave to fashion that did not suit her. Diana Stacpoole, on the other hand, had skin and hair the colour of flax; she might have worn sacking and it would have hung on her long, thin frame with helpless elegance.

She could also have been beautiful but lack of animation had settled the fine bones of her face into those of a tired thoroughbred. Enthusiasm for any creature—a dog, a servant, her own son—had brought reprisals on them and, for their sake, she had cultivated an ennui, as if she were bored even by those she loved. It had been a matter of survival.

Marriage to Aymer, Earl of Stacpoole, though it was his third, had been represented—and accepted—as an honour to a sheltered, sixteen-year-old girl, the desirable joining of two ancient estates; yes, he was her senior by twenty or so years but charming, wealthy, still in need of an heir; she owed the match to her family.

She never forgave her parents for it. They must have known, certainly suspected; the first wife had been a runaway and subsequently divorced, the second a suicide.

After the first year, she'd seriously considered following one or other of her predecessors' examples but by then she was pregnant, a condition which, as her husband pointed out, made her totally subservient. Kill herself and she killed the child. *'Run off and I'll hunt you down.'* He had the right; the baby would be taken from her to be at his mercy in its turn.

She could have given way and become a cowering ghost in her own home but she found defiance from somewhere. The man waxed on terror; she must deprive him of it. As a defence she appropriated boredom, appearing to find everything tedious, complying with the demands of his marriage bed as if they were wearisome games rather than sexual degradation, earning herself thrashings but withstanding even those with seeming indifference.

It was protection not only against her husband but *for* him; in the sight of God she'd taken him for better or worse, his escutcheon should not tarnished by any complaint of hers.

Nor her own. Though by no means as long as the Stacpooles', the Countess's ancestry was equally proud. After a somewhat dubious foundation by Walter Pomeroy, a ruffian who, like Francis Drake, had charged out from Devonian obscurity to fling himself and a large part of a mysterious fortune at the feet of Elizabeth, thereby gaining a knighthood and the Queen's favour, the Pomeroys had conducted themselves with honour. Young Paulus Pomeroy had refused to betray the message he carried for Charles I though tortured by Cromwell's troops. Sir William had gone into exile with Charles II. At Malplaquet, Sir Rupert had saved John Churchill's life at the cost of his own.

The wives had been equally dutiful; happy or miserable, no

breath of scandal attended their marriages. Like them, the Dowager threw back to the Middle Ages. Had the Earl been a Crusader, his absence in the Holy Land would have provided his Countess with blessed relief from abuse yet she would have defended his castle for him like a tigress until his return. In this disgraceful age, other women might abscond with lovers, run up debts, involve themselves in divorce, travel to France to give birth to babies not their husband's, but Pomeroy wives gritted their teeth and abided by their wedding vows because they had made them.

One's married name might belong to a ravening beast but the name was greater than the man. For Diana, true aristocracy was a sacrament. One did not abandon Christianity because a particular priest was venal. It was the bloodline that counted and its honour must be upheld, however painfully, with a stoicism worthy of the Spartan boy gnawed by the fox. Better that Society should shrug and say: 'Well, the Countess seems to tolerate him,' rather than: 'Poor, poor lady.' One held one's head high and said nothing.

Such public and private dignity had discommoded Aymer, put him off his stroke. Gradually, a spurious superiority was transferred from him to her that he found intimidating—as much as he could be intimidated by anything—and even gained his unwilling respect. After that, like the bully he was, he turned his attentions to more fearful victims so that she was spared infection by the syphilis that caused his final dementia.

By then she'd plastered her hurts so heavily with the appearance of finding things tiresome that its mortar had fused into bone and blood. The naive young girl had become static, a woman who moved and spoke with a lassitude that argued fatigue, her drooping eyes seeming to find all the world's matters beneath her, thus making people either nervous or resentful at what they interpreted as disdain. If they'd peered into them closely they might have seen that those same eyes had been leeched of interest or warmth or surprise by having looked too early on the opening to Hell. Nobody peered so closely, however.

Under the influence of the 1770 malmsey and the Earl's absence, his funeral party threatened unseemly cheerfulness. Instead of sitting in her chair to receive condolences, the Dowager Countess circled the great room at her slow, giraffe-like pace to remind the more raucous groups by her presence of the respect due to the departed.

There was a hasty 'We were remembering, your ladyship . . .' and then reminiscences of Aymer's japes, the time when he'd horse-whipped a Rockingham voter during the '61 election, when he'd thrown his whisky and cigar at Jane Bonham's pug because it yapped too much, causing it to burst into flame, the time when . . . Endearing eccentricities of the old school. 'We won't look on his like again.'

There was necessity for only one verbal reproof. Francis Dashwood was being overloud and humorous on the subject of her husband's last illness—*Dashwood* of all people—and met her arrival with defiance. 'I was saying, Diana, the pox is a damn hard way to go.'

The Dowager Countess hooded her eyes. 'For your sake, my lord, one hopes not.'

She passed on to where Alice was exciting herself over the alterations she proposed for Chantries. '. . . for I have always thought it sadly plain, you know. Robert and I plan something more rococo, more *douceur de vivre* as the French say, more . . .' Her voice trailed away at the sight of her mother-in-law but she rallied with triumph. 'Of course, dear *Maman*, none of this until we have altered the Dower House *à ton goût.*'

The Dower House, the overblown cottage on the estate that Aymer had used as a sexual playroom for his more local liaisons. She had never liked the place. Robert and Alice were expecting her to set up home in it—the conventional dower house for the conventional dowager—no doubt to spend her days embroidering comforts for a troop of little Alices and Roberts. Extend twenty-two years of imprisonment into a lesser cell.

'Make it nice for you, Mater,' Robert said.

'Thank you, my dear boy.' This was not the time to discuss it, nor did she want to hurt him, so she merely said gently: 'We shall see.'

He was, and always had been, her agony. It had been a mistake to have the baby in her arms when Aymer strode into the room after the birth; it should have been in its cradle, she should have pretended indifference, complained of the pain of its delivery. Instead, she'd been unguarded, raw with an effusion of love. Immediately, the child had become a hostage.

She had failed her son, could have failed him no more if she *had* run off; he'd been taken away from her: a wet nurse, a nurse, a tutor, school—all of them chosen to distance her from the boy and put his reliance on the caprice of a father who'd both terrified and fascinated him. Her mind trudged round the old, old circular paths. Should she have stood against Aymer more? But revenge would have been visited on the boy as much as her; warring parents would have split him in two. Yet what had she been to her poor child? A figure drifting mistily on the edge of a world in which women were cattle or concubines.

By the time she'd achieved some definition of her own, it was too late; both son and mother were too distanced from each other for the relationship that might have been. Individuality had been stripped from the boy, not a clever child in any case, and he'd opted for a mediocre amiability that offended no one and proved impossible for his mother to penetrate. She'd tried once to explain, said she'd always loved him, was sorry . . . He'd shied away. *'Can't think what you mean, Mater.'* Now, here he was at twenty years old, a genial, corpulent, middle-aged man.

And devoted to his wife. Whatever else, the Dowager Countess could have crawled in gratitude to her daughter-in-law. In this sallow, jealous little woman, Robert had found refuge and clung to her like ivy to a wall, as she did to him.

The couple talked to each other always of things, never ideas, but they talked continually; they were happy in a banality in which Diana would have been pleased to join them if Alice hadn't kept her out so ferociously that Robert, once again, was taken from her.

Yes, well.

Tobias was at her side. 'A methenger for Lord North, your ladyship.'

Alice almost elbowed her aside. 'What is that, Tobias?'

'Methenger at the door, your ladyship. For Lord North.'

'I'll see to it.' She bustled off.

Tobias hovered. 'A letter came today, your ladyship,' he said, in a low voice. 'Addrethed to the Countess. Her ladyship took it.'

Diana said lazily, 'Lady Alice is the Countess now, Tobias.'

'I think it wath written before hith lordship died, your ladyship. It wath for you.'

'Then her ladyship will undoubtedly tell me about it.'

Tobias was the most trusted and longest-serving of the footmen but even he must not imply criticism of Alice.

'Diana, don't tell me you're retainin' that balbutient blackamoor. Never could see why Aymer kept him on. Niggers look such freaks in white wigs, in my opinion. And the lisp, my dear . . .'

Diana's raised eyebrow suggested it was unwise of the Duchess of Aylesbury to include 'freak' and 'wig' in one sentence, the edifice on her grace's own head being nearly a yard high and inclined to topple, making her walk as if she had the thing balanced on her nose.

Actually, it was typical of Aymer, on finding that Tobias's blackness and lisp irritated his guests, to promote him to the position of head footman and thereby confront visitors with his announcements.

It was also typical of Tobias that he had kept the place by sheer efficiency. Poor Tobias. Alice and Robert, not having the assurance with which Aymer had flouted social taste, would undoubtedly get rid of him.

North was coming back. Normally those in the room would not have noticed his entrance but they did now. He had a paper in hand and greyness about the mouth. She didn't hear what he said but the reaction of those who could told her what it was; the man might have been releasing wasps into the room.

He made his way to her to kiss her hand. 'Forgive me, your ladyship. I must return to London. The French have finally come in on the side of America and declared war.'

It had been inevitable. She said coolly: 'We shall beat them, my lord. We always have.'

'No doubt about it, your ladyship.' But he looked older than he had a few minutes before.

She heard Dashwood talking unguardedly to Robert in his loud voice. Dashwood was always unguarded. 'Bad enough shipping supplies to our armies already, now we've got the damn French to harry us as we do it. I tell you, Robert, our chances of beating that lawless and furious rabble have grown slimmer this day.'

The Dowager was shocked. Locked away in looking after her husband, she had paid scant attention to the progress of the war, assuming that mopping up a few farmers and lawyers, which was all that the population of the American colony seemed to consist of, would be a fairly simple matter. That the war had already lasted two years must, she'd thought, be due to the vast distances the British army had to cover in order to complete the mopping up. That the rebels could actually win the war had not crossed her mind.

She glanced enquiringly at Lord George Germain who, as colonial secretary, was virtually the minister for war.

'Y'see, ma'am,' he said, 'we were countin' on Americans loyal to King George bein' rather more effective against the rebels than they're provin' to be.' He saw her face and said hurriedly: 'Don't mistake me, we'll win in the end, but there's no doubt the entry of the French puts an extra strain on the Royal Navy.' He brightened. 'There's this to be said for them, though, their entry into the war will give it more popularity with our own giddy multitude. They've always gone at the frog-eaters with a will.'

There was also this to be said for the news: it cleared the room. Nearly everybody in it had a duty either to the prosecution of the war or a protection of their investments.

She was enveloped in the smell of funereal clothes, sandalwood from the chests in which they'd been packed away, mothballs, stale sweat, best scent and the peculiarly sour pungency of black veiling. The gentlemen raised Diana's languid hand to their faces and dropped it, like hasty shoppers with a piece of fish; her female peers pecked at her cheek; inferiors bobbed and hurried away.

No need to see them to their carriages, that was for Alice and Robert now.

She was left alone. It was an unquiet, heavy room. On the great mantel, a frieze looted from Greece preserved death in marble as barbarians received the last spear-thrust from helmeted warriors in a riot of plunging horses. The red walls were noisy with the tableaux of battle, Blenheim, Ramillies, Oudenarde, Malplaquet. Mounted Stacpoole generals posed, sword aloft, at the head of their troops, cannons fired from ship to ship at Beachy Head and Quiberon Bay.

And now France again. It had been no platitude to assure North it would be beaten, she was sure it would be, just as America would be; Aymer had always said that was what France was for, to be beaten by the English. '*One Englishman can lick ten bloody Frenchman. And twenty bloody Americans. And a hundred bloody Irish.*' Though it was taking overlong to force America's surrender she accepted his precept, just as she'd accepted his right to tyrannize his fiefdom through right of blood even while she abhorred the tyranny itself.

I'm his creature, she thought.

She walked to the windows to try and recapture the uplift of freedom she'd felt on leaving the chapel but the horizon beyond the lake marked a future she did not know what to do with.

As Countess of Stacpoole, Aymer's hostess, charity-giver, political supporter to his Tory placemen, his loyal behind-the-scenes electioneer and, at the last, his nurse, she had at least known employment. All gone now.

She took in deep, hopeless breaths. She should be smelling roses, there was a neat mass of them below the terrace, but she couldn't rid the stink of decay from her nostrils. Since his death they'd burned herbs but, for her, the odour of that jerking, gangrenous body still haunted the house, like his screams.

His reliance on her had been shameless, demanding her presence twenty-four hours of the day, throwing clocks and piss-pots at doctors, even poor Robert, shrieking that he wanted only her to attend him—as if their marriage had been loving harmony.

As if it had indeed been loving harmony, she *had* attended him twenty-four hours a day; expected to do no less. For three months she had never set foot outside the suite of rooms that were his.

His nose had already been eaten away, now he'd begun to rot, new buboes appearing as if maggots had gathered in one squirming subcutaneous mass to try and get out through the skin. Before his brain went, he'd begged absolution from the very walls. Only the priest could give him that; her place had been to diminish his physical suffering as well as she could, and she and laudanum had done it—as much as it could be done.

She'd thought she could watch judgementally the revenge inflicted on his body by the life he'd led, but she had been unable to resist pity, longing for him to die, for his own sake. Her thankfulness at his last breath had been more for his release than hers. Then had come the scurry of funeral arrangements.

And now to find, after years of expectation of freedom, that Diana, Countess of Stacpoole, had died with the husband she loathed. *Beloved wife of* . . .

I'm nothing without him. That was the irony. He'd defined her, not merely as his Countess, but as upholder of his honour, soother of the wounds he inflicted, underminer of his more terrible obsessions. He'd been her purpose, even if that purpose had been amelioration, sometimes sabotage, of his actions. Years of it. She had no other. Thirty-nine next birthday and she was now of no use to a living soul except to vacate the space she'd occupied.

She heard screams and in her exhaustion turned automatically to go back to the sickroom but, of course, they were Alice's. In view of the news from France, Robert, like a good courtier, should return to his place by the King immediately and Alice was lamenting as if her husband were off to battle rather than a palace.

'*Maman, Maman,* come tell him he mustn't leave or I shall go *distraite.*'

Yes, well. Alice liked an audience for her hysterics. Was being an audience a purpose? No, merely a function. She left the room to perform it.

To humour his wife, Robert said he would not go until tomorrow; the King would understand he had just buried his father.

Even so, Alice did not see fit to recover until late evening; the advent of France into the war causing her to see danger everywhere. 'You must ask the King to give you guards. John Paul Jones will try and capture you, like he did the Earl of Selkirk.'

Alice, thought the Dowager, must be the only young woman who had not found that most recent raid by an American privateer a tiny bit thrilling. The papers had made much of it in apparent horror but the ghost of Robin Hood had been called up and, as always with the English weakness for daring, Mr Paul Jones's brigandage was taking on a hue of romance.

Robert said: 'My dear, the raid was a failure.'

Alice refused comfort. John Paul Jones, a Scotsman who'd joined the American side, was scouring his native coast to take an earl hostage. Robert was an earl. *Ergo*, John Paul Jones was out to capture Robert. 'True, the Earl was absent on this occasion but his Countess was *menaced*. He took her silver service.'

'I heard he returned it,' the Dowager joined in. 'In any case, we may comfort ourselves that Robert will be in London and not in a Scottish castle exposed to the sea. Mr Jones is hardly likely to sail up the Thames to get him.'

Alice was not so sure; she was enjoying her horrors. It wasn't until late evening that she remembered the letter and handed it to her mother-in-law.

'You will forgive me for overlooking it, Mama. It carried my title of course . . . *so* peculiar, sent on from Paris, not that I read it . . . the *impudence*, I wondered to show it to you at all but Robert said . . . who *is* Martha Grayle?'

Martha.

Salt and sun on her face, bare feet, a shrimping net, terracotta-coloured cliffs against blue sky . . .

Careful not to show haste, the Dowager turned to the last page to see the signature and was caught by the final, disjointed paragraph. '. . . you are my long hope, dear soul . . . I am in great fear . . . as you too have a son . . . Your respectful servant, Martha Grayle (née Pardoe).'

She looked up to find Alice and Robert watching her.

Deliberately, she yawned. 'I shall retire, I think. Good night, my dears.'

'But will you not read the letter?' Alice could hardly bear it.

'In bed perhaps.' Alice had waited to give it to her, she could now wait for a reaction to it. The whirligig of time brought in its petty revenges.

Joan was nodding in a bedroom chair, waiting to undress her, but when the areas that couldn't be reached by the wearer had been unbuttoned and unhooked, Diana told her to go to bed. 'I will do the rest myself.'

'Very well, my dear.'

'Joan, do you remember Martha Pardoe?'

'Torbay.' The old woman's voice was fond.

'Yes.'

'Married that Yankee and went off to Americy.'

'Yes.'

'Happy days they was.'

She couldn't wait for reminiscence. 'Good night.'

With her mourning robes draped around her shoulders, the Dowager picked up the letter that had circumvented the cessation of mail between rebel and mother countries. Somewhere on its long journey from Virginia to France to London to Bedfordshire it had received a slap of salt water so that the bottom left-hand quarter of each page was indecipherable.

Martha had penned a superscription on its exterior page, presumably with a covering letter, for the unknown person in Paris who'd been charged with sending it on to England: 'To be forwarded to the Countess of Stacpoole in England. Haste. Haste.' Martha had been lucky; from this moment on there would be an embargo on general mail from France, just as from America; the letter had beaten the declaration of war by a short head.

The fact that Martha had written only on one side of each of her two pages indicated that, however personally distressed, she was in easy circumstances; paper of quality such as this was expensive.

She'd begun formally enough:

Respectful greetings to Your Ladyship, if I am so Fortunate that your eyes should see this letter. Of your Gracious Kindness forgive this Plea from an old acquaintance who would make so Bold as to remind Your Ladyship of glad Times in Torbay when you and she were Children undivided by sea or War. Pray God may resolve the Conflict between our Countries. I shall not Weary you with Remembrance, loving though it is to me, but Proceed to the case of my son, Forrest Grayle, who is but eighteen years old . . .

Here the water stain obscured the beginnings of several lines and Martha's writing, which had begun neatly, began to sprawl as agitation seized her so that making sense of it caused the Dowager's brow to wrinkle. She got up from the dressing-table stool and went to the lamp on the Louis Quinze table to turn up the wick, unconscious that she was doing so. '. . . such a desire that all may have Liberty as has caused Concern to his . . . nothing would satisfy but that he Volunteer for our navy . . . John Paul Jones in France to take possession of a new vessel built there . . .'

Now the relief of a new page, though the penmanship was worse and punctuation virtually nonexistent.

O Diana word has it the *Sam Adams* is Captured and its Men taken to England and imprisoned for rebels while I say Nothing of this for it is War yet there are tales of what is done to men captured by King George's army here in the South as would break the Heart of any Woman, be she English or American . . .

Here, again, the interruption of the water stain.

whether my husband would have me write, but he is dead these . . . I beseech you, in the name of Happier days, as you are a Mother and a . . . will know him if you remember my Brother whom you met that once at . . . the Likeness is so Exact that it doth bring Tears every time I . . . you can do if you can do any Thing for my boy in the name of Our . . .

Here the writing became enormous: 'For you are my long hope, dear soul . . . I am in great fear . . . as you too have a son . . . for our old friendship . . .' Slowly, the Dowager smoothed the letter flat and put it between the leaves of the bible lying on the table.

Yes, well.

She could do nothing, of course. *Would* do nothing. As her daughter-in-law said, the letter was an impertinence. Martha had expressed no regret for her adopted country's rebellion; indeed, supposing her own interpretation to be correct, the woman had actually referred to the American fleet as 'our navy'.

If the boy Forrest—what like of name was that?—is so enthusiastic to get rid of his rightful King, let him enthuse in prison as he deserves.

Somewhat deliberately, the Dowager yawned, stepped out of her mourning and went to bed.

Seagulls yelping. Petticoats pinned up. Rock pools. Martha's hair red-gold in the sun. The tide like icy bracelets around the ankles. A near-lunacy of freedom. The stolen summers of 1750 and 1751.

The Dowager got up, wrapped herself in a robe, read the letter again, put it back in the bible, tugged the bell-pull. 'Fetch Tobias.'

Too much effort, Martha, even if I would. Which I won't. Too tired.

'Ah, Tobias. I've forgotten, did his lordship buy you in Virginia?'

'Barbadoth, your ladyship. Thlave market. He liked my lithp.'

Another of Aymer's japes, this time during his tour of his plantations; he'd sent the man back to England with a label attached to the slave collar: 'A prethent from the Wetht Indieth.' It was sheer good fortune that Tobias, bought as a joke, had proved an excellent and intelligent servant.

'Not near the Virginian plantations, then. Tobacco and such.' She had no idea of that hemisphere's geography.

'Only sugar in Barbadoth, ladyship.'

'Very well. You may go.'

She was surprised at how very much she'd wished to discuss the letter with Tobias, and with Joan, but even to such trusted people as these she would not do so; one did not air one's concerns with servants.

Diana went back to bed.

She got up and sat out on the balcony. As if it were trying to make up for her discontent with the day, the night had redoubled the scent of roses and added new-mown grass and cypresses, but these were landlocked smells; the Dowager sniffed in vain for the tang of sea.

She had long ago packed away the summers of '50 and '51 as a happiness too unbearable to remember, committed them to dutiful oblivion in a box that had now come floating back to her on an errant tide.

They had been stolen summers in any case; she shouldn't really have had them but her parents had been on the Grand Tour, there was fear of plague in London, and the Pomeroy great-aunt with whom she'd been sent to stay had been wonderfully old and sleepy, uncaring that her eleven-year-old charge went down to the beach each day with only a parlour maid called Joan as chaperone to play with a twelve-year-old called Martha.

Devon. Her first and only visit to the county from which her family and its wealth had sprung. A Queen Anne house on the top of one of seven hills looking loftily down on the tiny, square harbour of Torquay.

She listened to her own childish voice excitedly piping down years that had bled all excitement from it.

'Is this the house we Pomeroys come from, Aunt? Sir Walter's house?'

'Of course not, child. It is much too modern. Sir Walter's home was

T'Gallants at Babbs Cove, a very old and uncomfortable building, many miles along the coast.'

'Shall I see it while I am here?'

'No. It is rented out.'

'But was Sir Walter a pirate, as they say, Aunt? I should so like him to have been a pirate.'

'I should not. He is entitled to our gratitude as our progenitor and we must not speak ill of him. Now go and play.'

But if she was disallowed a piratical ancestor, there were pirates a-plenty down on the beach where Joan took her and allowed her to paddle and walk on pebbles the size and shape of swans' eggs. At least, they looked like pirates in their petticoat-breeches and tarry jackets.

If she'd cut her way through jungle and discovered a lost civilization, it could have been no more exotic to her than that Devon beach. Hermit crabs and fishermen, both equally strange; starfish; soft cliffs pitted with caves and eyries, dolphins larking in the bay: there was nothing to disappoint, everything to amaze.

And Martha, motherless daughter of an indulgent, dissenting Torbay importer. Martha, who was joyful and kind, who knew about menstruation and how babies were made (until then a rather nasty mystery), who could row a boat and dislodge limpets, who wore no stays and, though she was literate, spoke no French and didn't care that she didn't. Martha, who had a brother like a young Viking who didn't notice her but for whom the even younger Diana conceived a delightful, hopeless passion—delightful because it was hopeless—and would have died rather than reveal it but secretly scratched his and her entwined initials in sandstone for the tide to erase.

For the first time in her life she'd encountered people who talked to her, in accents thick as cream, without watching their words, who knew no servitude except to the tide. She'd been shocked and exhilarated.

But after another summer, as astonishing as the first, the parents had come back, the great-aunt died and the Queen Anne house sold. She and Martha had written to each other for the next few years. Martha had married surprisingly well; a visiting American who traded with her father had taken one look and swept her off to his tobacco plantations in Virginia.

After that their correspondence became increasingly constrained as Diana entered Hell and Martha's independent spirit conformed to Virginian Anglicanism and slave ownership. Eventually, it had ceased altogether.

The Dowager returned to bed and this time went to sleep.

In one thing at least her son resembled her: they were both early risers. Diana, making her morning circuit in the gardens, saw Robert coming to greet her. They met in the Dark Arbour, a long tunnel of yew the Stuart Stacpooles had planted as a horticultural lament for the execution of Charles I, and fell into step.

The Dowager prepared herself to discuss what, in the course of the night, had gained initial capitals.

But Robert's subject wasn't The Letter, it was The Will.

She knew its contents already. Before the Earl's mind had gone, she had been able to persuade him to have the lawyers redraft the document so that it should read less painfully to some of the legatees. Phrases like 'My Dutch snuffbox to Horace Walpole that he may apply his nose to some other business than mine . . . To Lord North, money for the purchase of stays to stiffen his spine . . .' were excised and, at Diana's insistence, Aymer's more impoverished bastards were included.

Her own entitlement as Dowager was secured by medieval tradition—she was allowed to stay in her dead husband's house for a period of forty days before being provided with a messuage of her own to live in and a pension at the discretion of the heir.

As he fell into step beside her, she knew by his gabbled bonhomie that Robert was uncomfortable.

'The Dower House, eh, Mater? It shall be done up in any way you please. We'll get that young fella Nash in, eh? Alice says he's a hand at *cottages ornés*. We want you always with us, you know'—patting her hand—'and, of course, the ambassador's suite in the May-fair house is yours whenever you wish a stay in Town.'

'Thank you, my dear.'

'As for the pension . . . Still unsteady weather, ain't it? Will it rain, d'ye think? The pension, now . . . been talking to Crawford and the lawyers and such and, well, the finances are in a bit of a pickle.'

The Dowager paused and idly sniffed a rose that had been allowed to ramble through a fault in an otherwise faultless hedge.

Robert was wriggling. 'The pater, bless him. Somewhat free at the tables, let alone the races, and his notes are comin' in hand over fist. Set us back a bit, I'm afraid.'

Aymer's debts had undoubtedly been enormous but his enforced absence from the gaming tables during his illness had provided a financial reprieve, while the income from the Stacpoole estates would, with prudence—and Robert was a prudent man—make up the deficiency in a year or two, she knew.

'Yes, my dear?'

'So, we thought . . . Crawford and the lawyers thought . . . Your pension, Mama. Not a fixed figure, of course. Be able to raise it when we've recouped.' He grasped the nettle quickly: 'Comes out at one hundred and fifty per annum.'

One hundred and fifty pounds a year. And the Stacpoole estates harvested yearly rents of £160,000. Her pension was to be only thirty pounds more than the annual amount Aymer had bequeathed to his most recent mistress. After twenty-two years of marriage she was valued on a level with a Drury Lane harlot.

She forced herself to walk on, saying nothing.

One hundred and fifty pounds a year. A fortune, no doubt, to the gardener at this moment wheeling a rumbling barrow on the other side of the hedge. With a large family he survived on ten shillings a week all found and thought himself well paid.

But at five times that figure, she would be brought low. No coach—fortunate indeed if she could afford to keep a carriage team—meagre entertaining, two servants, three at the most, where she had commanded ninety.

Beside her, Robert babbled of the extra benefits to be provided for her: use of one of the coaches when she wanted it, free firing, a ham at salting time, weekly chickens, eggs . . . 'Christmas spent with us, of course . . .'

And she knew.

Alice, she thought. Not Robert. Not Crawford and the lawyers. This is Alice.

Ahead, the end of the tunnel framed a view of the house. The mourning swags beneath its windows gave it a baggy-eyed look as if it had drunk unwisely the night before and was regretting it. Alice would still be asleep upstairs; she rarely rose before midday but, sure as the Creed, it was Alice who had decided the amount of her pension.

And not from niggardliness. The Dowager acquitted her daughter-in-law of that at least. Alice had many faults but meanness was not among them; the object was dependence, *her* dependence. Alice's oddity was that she admired her mother-in-law and at the same time was jealous of her, both emotions mixed to an almost ludicrous degree. It had taken a while for Diana to understand why, when she changed her hairstyle, Alice changed hers. A pair of gloves was ordered; similar gloves arrived for Alice who then charged them with qualities that declared them superior.

Diana tended old Mrs Brown in the village; of a sudden Alice was also visiting the Brown cottage in imitation of a charity that seemed admirable to her yet which had to be surpassed: 'I took her beef tea, *Maman*—she prefers it to calves'-foot jelly.'

Yes, her pension had been stipulated by Alice. She was to be kept close, under supervision, virtually imprisoned in genteel deprivation, required to ask for transport if she needed it, all so that Alice could forever flaunt herself at the mother-in-law she resented and wished to emulate in equal measure. Look how much better I manage my house/marriage/servants than you did, *Maman*.

Nor would it be conscious cruelty; Alice, who did not suffer from introspection, would sincerely believe she was being kind.

Dutifully, the Dowager strove to nurse a fondness for her daughter-in-law but it thrived never so much as when she was away from her.

No. It was not to be tolerated. She had been released from one gaol, she would not be dragooned into another.

The Dowager halted and turned on her son.

He was sweating. His eyes pleaded for her compliance as they had when he was the little boy who, though hating it, was about to be taken to a bear-baiting by his father, begging her not to protest—as indeed, for once, she had been about to. Let it be, his eyes said now, as they had then. Don't turn the screw.

If it were to be a choice between offending her or Alice or even himself, then Alice must win, as his father had won. He would always side with the strong, even though it hurt him, because the pain of not doing so would, for him, be the greater.

So protest died in her, just as it always had, and its place was taken by despair that these things were not voiced between them. She opened her mouth to tell him she understood but, frightened that she would approach matters he preferred unspoken, Robert cut her off. Unwisely, he said: 'If you think it too little, Mama, perhaps we can squeeze a bit more from the coffers.'

Good *God*. Did they think she was standing on a street corner with her hand out? All at once, she was furious. How dare they expect that she might beg.

'Thank you, Robert,' she told him with apparent indifference, 'the pension is adequate.'

He sagged with relief.

Oh no, my dear, she thought. Oh no, Alice may rule my income but she will not rule me. She had a premonition of Alice's triumphs at future gatherings: 'Did you enjoy the goose, *Maman*?' Then, *sotto voce*: 'Dear *Maman*, we always give her a goose at Michaelmas.' Unaware that by such bourgeois posturing she reduced herself as well as her mother-in-law.

Oh no. I am owed some liberty and dignity after twenty-odd years. I'll not be incarcerated again.

So she said, as if by-the-by: 'Concerning the Dower House, it must be held in abeyance for a while. I am going visiting.'

He hadn't reckoned on this. 'Who? When? Where will you go?'

'Friends,' she said vaguely, making it up as she went, 'Lady Margaret, perhaps, the De Veres . . .' And then, to punish him a little: 'I may even make enquiries about Martha Pardoe's son, Grayle as she now is—I believe you saw the letter she sent me.'

He was horrified. 'Martha's . . . ? Mama, you can't. Involving oneself for an American prisoner? People would think it . . . well, they'd be appalled.'

'Would they, my dear?' He always considered an action in the light of Society's opinion. 'Robert, I do not think that to enquire after a young man on behalf of his worried mother is going to lose us the war.'

She *was* punishing him a little; he should not have been niggardly over her pension but also, she realized, she was resolved to do this for Martha. It would be a little adventure, nothing too strenuous, merely a matter of satisfying herself that the boy was in health.

'Well, but . . . when do you intend to do this?'

This was how it would be—she would have to explain her comings and goings. And suddenly she could not bear the constraint they put on her any longer. She shrugged. 'In a day or two. Perhaps tomorrow.' To get away from this house, from the last twenty-two years, from everything. She was startled by the imperative of escape; if she stayed in this house one day more it would suffocate her.

'Tomorrow? Of course not, Mama. You cannot break mourning so soon; it is unheard of. I cannot allow it. People would see it as an insult to the pater's memory. Have you taken leave of your senses?'

'No, my dear, merely leave of your father.'

She watched him hurry away to wake Alice with the news. She was sorry she had saddled him with a recalcitrant mother but he could not expect compliance in everything, not when her own survival was at stake. People would think it a damn sight more odd if she strangled Alice—which was the alternative.

I shall go to the Admiralty, she thought. Perhaps I can arrange an exchange for young Master Grayle so that he may return to his mother. Again, it can make no difference to the war one way or the other. We send an American prisoner back to America and some poor Englishman held in America returns home to England.

Odd that the subject of John Paul Jones had arisen only yesterday. Had not Jones's intention been to hold the Earl of Selkirk hostage in order to procure an exchange of American prisoners? Goodness gracious, I shall be treading in the path of that pirate. The thought gave her unseemly pleasure. She stood at the edge of the yew-scented Dark Arbour, marvelling at how wicked she had become.

When had she taken the decision to act upon Martha's request? *Why* had she taken it? To outrage her family in revenge for a niggardly pension? Not really. Because of the picture Martha had tried to draw of her son? If she understood it aright, Lieutenant Grayle had a physical likeness to his maternal uncle.

An image came to her of Martha's brother, a young man in a rowing boat pulling out to sea with easy strokes, head and shoulders outlined against a setting sun so that he was etched in black except for a fiery outline around his head.

Dead now. He'd joined the navy and one of Martha's letters had told her he'd been killed aboard the *Intrepid* during the battle of Minorca in 1756. She'd put the mental image away, as with the other memories of her Devon summers, but its brightness hadn't faded on being fetched out again.

His nephew had 'such a desire that all may have Liberty', did he? Well, she might enjoy some liberty for herself while procuring his. It would give her purpose, at least for a while.

But, no, that even hadn't been the reason for her decision. It was because she owed Martha. For a happiness. And the debt had been called in: '. . . as you too have a son . . .' Because Martha agonized for a son as she, in a different way, had agonized for hers. Perhaps she need not fail Martha's son as she had failed her own.

Then she stopped rummaging through excuses for what she was going to do and came up, somewhat shamefully, with the one that lay beneath all the others, the one that, she realized in that second, had finally made up her mind.

Because, if she didn't do it, she'd be bored to death.

She stepped out from the arbour into sunlight and walked across the lawn towards the house to tell Joan to begin packing.

Chapter Two

Two hundred and fifty miles north of Chantries, Makepeace Hedley was also about to receive a letter from America. Since it had been sent from New York, which was under British control, its voyage across the Atlantic had been more direct, though no quicker, than that of the one delivered to the Countess of Stacpoole the day before.

As with most of Newcastle's post, it was dropped off at the Queen's Head by the Thursday mail coach from London and was collected along with many other letters by Makepeace's stepson, Oliver Hedley, on his way to work.

Further down the hill, Oliver stopped to buy a copy of the *Newcastle Journal* at Sarah Hodgkinson's printing works.

'Frogs have declared war,' Sarah yelled at him over the clacking machines, but not as if it was of any moment; the news had been so long expected that she'd had a suitable editorial made up for some weeks ready to drop into place in the forme.

Oliver read the editorial quickly; its tone was more anticipatory than fearful. Wars were good for Newcastle's trade in iron and steel, and mopped up its vagrants and troublemakers into the army. True, the presence of American privateers, now to be joined by French allies, meant that vessels sailing down the east coast to supply London's coal were having to be convoyed but, since the extra ships were being built on the Tyne and Wear, it was likely that the area's general prosperity could only increase.

Nevertheless Oliver detected a note of uneasiness in the editorial. It spread itself happily enough on the subject of French perfidy but was careful not to cast similar obloquy on the cause the French were joining. The Frogs were an old enemy and if they wanted war Newcastle was happy to oblige them. America was a different matter—on that subject the town was deeply divided. Indeed, when the proclamation of war with America had been read from the steps of the Mansion House two years before, it had been greeted with silence instead of the usual huzzas.

A strong petition had been sent to the government by the majority of Newcastle's magistrates offering support in the prosecution of the war but the burgesses, under Sir George Saville, had sent an equally strong counter-petition deprecating it. And Sir George was not only a popular man, he was also an experienced soldier.

'It's civil war,' he'd told Oliver's father, 'and no good will come of it. For one thing, we can't maintain a supply line over three thousand miles for long.'

'For another, it's wrong,' Andra Hedley had said.

At that stage, the majority of Americans would have forgone independence—indeed, still regarded themselves as subjects of King George III—for amelioration of the taxes and oppressive rules of trade which had caused the quarrel in the first place. 'But they'll not get it,' Andra had prophesied. 'The moment them lads in Boston chucked tea in t'harbour, Parliament saw it as an attack on property and yon's a mortal sin to them struttin' clumps. No chance of an olive branch after that.'

And he'd been right.

Oliver put the mail and the newspaper in his pocket as he went down the hill in his usual hopscotch fashion to keep his boots from muck evacuated by mooing, frightened herds on their way to the shambles. Under the influence of the sun, which was beginning to roll up its sleeves, the strong whiff of the country the animals brought with them would soon be overlaid by the greater majesty of lime, smoke, sewage and brewing. Coal- and glassworks were already sending out infinitesimal particles of smitch that, without the usual North Sea breeze—and there was none today—would add another thin layer to the city's dark coating.

He hurried past new buildings noisily going up and old buildings equally noisily coming down, past clanging smithies and factories, past street-traders and idlers gathered round the pumps, all of them shouting. Weekday conversations in Newcastle-upon-Tyne had to be conducted at a pitch which suggested deafness on the part of those conversing. A lot of them *were* deaf, especially those (the majority) who spent their working lives in its foundries, metal yards and factories with their eardrums pounded by machinery that roared day and night. Consequently, they shouted.

Clamour reached its climax at the river, Newcastle's artery. Cranes, coal rattling into the cargo holds of keels, ironworks, ship-yards, anchor-makers . . . But, as he walked along the Quay, the cacophony assaulting Oliver's ears was overridden by his step-mother's high, feminine, gull-like squawk twisting through it like a Valkyrie swerving through battling soldiers to reach the dead.

There was always something. Today a careless wherry carrying pottery upriver had knocked into one of Makepeace's keels and caused damage—luckily above its waterline.

She was staving off the wherryman's murder at the hands of the keel's skipper by holding back the keelman with his belt and remon-strating with the offender at the same time.

'Whaat d'ye think ye're playin' at, ye beggor, tig 'n' chasey? Ah'll have ye bornt alive, so ah wull. Howay ta gaffor an' explain yeself, ye bluddy gobmek. Hold still, ye buggor'—this was to the keelman—'divvn't Master Reed telt ye 'bout tuen the kittle?'

Oliver shook his head in wonder. Tyne watermen were renowned for their ferocity; this skinny little woman was dealing with savages in their own language and subduing them. While a new spirit of philanthropy was bringing charity, education and Sun-day schools to Newcastle it had seemed impossible that such enlightenment could touch the dark souls of those who worked on its river. His stepmother, however, had forced the men who shipped her coal to join a benefit society, the Good Intent, where godliness, rules and, in the last resort, fines were having a favourable effect on their swearing, drinking and fighting. The popular Newcastle maxim that keelmen feared nothing except a lee shore had been altered to: 'Nowt but a lee shore—and Makepeace Hedley.'

The wherryman having been dispatched to the Quay to report to her rivermaster, and the keelman, sulkily, to his repairs, Makepeace waved to her stepson and came ashore to kiss him.

Possibly the richest woman in Northumberland, she resembled what her mine manager called 'an ambulatin' sceercraa'. Her long black coat was old and the tricorn into which she bundled her red hair even older. She'd told Oliver once that femininity was a handicap in a masculine world; to be accepted by other coal-owners as well as by her subordinates she had to play a *character*. Men liked to make a mystery of business, she said, and the fact that any woman of intelligence could master it maddened them. But as long as she seemed an oddity, she said, men didn't resent her intrusion, or no more than they would resent a male competitor; she was merely a quirk of nature, an act of God, to be accepted with a resigned shrug. Eccentricity, she said, was sexless.

He supposed she was right. Newcastle had a surprising number of successful female entrepreneurs—the printer from whom he'd just bought his newspaper among them—and he wouldn't want to bed any of them.

Nevertheless, Oliver appreciated beauty and was offended by his stepmother's aesthetic crime. Not that Makepeace was beautiful; she was approaching forty and her red hair was beginning to sprout the occasional strand of grey, but, dressed up and with a prevailing wind, she could look extremely presentable. Her smile, when she used it—and she was using it now as she came towards him—was better than beautiful, it was astounding.

He owed a great deal to this woman, not just his father's happiness in marriage but the wealth brought to them all by her accidental ownership of the land on which coal was now being mined on a vast scale.

For Makepeace and Andra Hedley, their unsought meeting was

the stuff of legend, to be recalled again and again: she, a benighted American-born widow with only a title deed won at the gaming tables to her name, asking for shelter at the moorland house of Andra Hedley, a widower, equally impoverished but with the knowledge to capitalize on her one asset.

Together they'd exploited the rich seam of coal that lay beneath her land. Thanks to her, Andra, a former miner himself, had been able to build a village for miners that was a model of decent living.

Thanks also to her, the Hedley shipping office here on the Quay was a new and graceful building, employing clerks who worked in the light of a great oriel window that ran three storeys from roof to ground. And thanks to her, he, Oliver, had been raised from the position of a young lawyer with few clients to the directorship of one of the biggest mining companies in Newcastle, able to own a fine house and fill it with fine things.

More than that, this stepmother had been prepared to love him from the first, and he'd come to love her.

Lately, though, he'd begun to fear that her means were becoming her ends. The difficulties and setbacks she'd faced in a crowded life had given Makepeace the right to admire herself for overcoming them but now the determination that had enabled her to do so was becoming overbearing. Her boast that she spoke her mind was more often than not a euphemism for rudeness. She expressed an opinion on everything and showed little respect for anyone else's. She was in danger of becoming an autocratic besom.

Missing Dada, Oliver thought. The harshness he'd noticed in Makepeace had become prevalent in the three months since Andra Hedley had taken himself off to France to work with the chemist Lavoisier on investigating the properties of air.

Oliver knew himself to be more than capable of running the shipping end of the Hedley enterprise—very much wanted to—and his uncle Jamie, Andra's brother, was equally capable of overseeing the mining operation up at Raby. Makepeace, however, refused to give up control of either and was exhausting herself and everybody else in the process.

His father and only his father, as Oliver knew, could have made her take a holiday—nobody else would dare—but since Andra was not there and she missed him badly, his absence merely added to her self-imposed burdens and her tendency towards despotism was compounded.

Her smile faded as she closed in. 'What?'

'It's war, Missus. The French have declared.' He took her hands and she clutched them for support.

'And no word from your dada, I suppose.'

'No. At least, I don't think so . . .' He was, he realized, holding an unexplored bundle of the day's mail under his arm and together they hurried into the office and up to her room to riffle through it.

There was no letter from France. And now there wouldn't be; the ports were closed for the duration of the war.

Makepeace began striding up and down the room. 'I told him. Didn't I write that mule-headed goober? Come home, I said. There'll be war, I said. You'll get fixed like a bug in molasses. You wait 'til he gets back, I'll larrup that damn man 'til he squawks . . .'

When she wasn't scolding her employees in broad Northumbrian, Makepeace could speak English without an accent but in times of distress she reverted to pure American.

Oliver sat down while she tried, through rage, to dissipate a worry he considered needless; it was inconvenient that Andra Hedley should be in Paris at such a time but he was in no danger. The position held by the people he was with would ensure nothing happened to him.

Sun coming in through the great window provided the rare luxury of warmth to a spartan office, its new oak panelling still undarkened by the Newcastle air. Apart from an escritoire with its pigeon-holes neatly docketed, there was a table, only one chair—it was to his stepmother's advantage to make her visitors stand while she sat—and a good, but worn, Isfahan rug on the floor.

Oliver started sorting through the letters while Makepeace raved on: 'I'll go fetch him myself, that's for sure. I'll get one of the colliers to take me over to . . . to . . . where's somewhere neutral?

Flushing, I'll go to Flushing and get a coach to Paris and drag him home. I'll give that goddam Frenchman . . . what's the name of the bugger? Lavabo?'

'Lavoisier.'

'I'll give him gip, him and his experiments.'

'Missus.' Oliver's voice was gentle.

'What?'

'I doubt the pair of them are even aware war's been declared. They're scientificals, they'd not notice a thunderbolt. Even if Dada does know, he won't think it's important compared to what he's doing. If he can find a way to stop explosions from fire-damp . . .'

She quietened. 'I want him home, Oliver.'

Did she think he didn't? His father was one of those rare people whose very presence made one feel safe, possibly because Andra Hedley wanted everybody to be safer, especially those who worked in coal mines. As a child, Oliver had learned that he had to share his father's attention with his father's obsession to find a way to neutralize the gases that caused underground explosions.

Now Makepeace was having to do the same. Correspondence with the French chemist who'd discovered oxygen had drawn Andra to France, convinced that the disastrous coming-together of gas and flame might be overcome if he could understand the properties of the air that carried them.

'We all miss him, Missus,' Oliver said, 'but he'd be worse off crossing the Channel than staying where he is. So would you—a collier'd be taken by the privateers quicker than spit. Then there's the borders, they'll close those. And the Dutch and the Flemings ain't any too fond of us just now, what with the navy stopping their ships . . .'

'What's to do then?' She was irritable.

'Howay, lass,' he said, imitating his father. He got up to put his arm round her. 'The war can't last much longer.'

'Be over by Christmas, will it? *Another* Christmas? We've damn well had two already.'

He'd never quite known where she stood on the war; his father was all for granting America her independence, and so was he, but Makepeace never joined their discussions. Perhaps she agreed so strongly that it didn't need saying, perhaps she had reservations—it was American patriots who had driven her out of Boston. But on one thing she never wavered: America couldn't be beaten. 'King George ain't going to hold that country if it don't want to be held.'

Oliver wasn't so sure; viewed from the industrial ramparts of Newcastle the ill-equipped farmers who made up General Washington's army appeared as men fighting for a medieval inheritance. This, however, was not the time to say so. He sought inspiration, and found it.

'Ben Franklin,' he said.

Andra Hedley and Benjamin Franklin had become mutual admirers when they'd met in London before the war began and hostilities between their two countries had not lessened their regard, nor had their correspondence ceased when Franklin moved to Paris to become America's agent in France. It was Franklin, indeed, who'd put Andra in touch with Lavoisier.

'Oliver, you ain't the cabbage-head you look.' He'd won his stepmother's approval. 'Diplomatic channels, that's the ticket. They won't stop those. I'll get young Ffoulkes to contact Ben and set up a lazy . . . what is it?'

'Laissez-passer.'

'One of them. Get him back under a flag of truce. We'll have him home quicker'n Hell scorches feathers.'

While she elaborated on the matter, he turned back to the mail and saw that in their haste they'd overlooked the letter from New York.

Wordlessly, he held it out and she snatched it from him.

Of the many surprising facets to Makepeace Hedley, the one Oliver found most incomprehensible, was her relationship with Philippa, her daughter by her first marriage. Early on, when the child was seven years old, Makepeace had allowed Philippa's American godmother, Susan Brewer, to take the girl home with her to Boston. Philippa hadn't come back; it seemed she didn't want to.

The opening of hostilities between America and Britain had caused a hiatus in news of both Susan and Philippa and this, alongside the fact that most of the fighting was in Massachusetts, had—somewhat late in the day—awakened Makepeace to her daughter's danger.

She'd had to be restrained from sailing off across the Atlantic in one of her coaling fleet's vessels in order to see what was happening for herself. Undoubtedly she would have done, except that word came in time to say that Susan and Philippa had left Boston and were safely settled in British-held New York.

Oliver watched his stepmother flop onto the oriel sill to read a letter that had, from the look of it, undergone a rough passage. She'd taken off the dreadful tricorn and her hair had escaped from the cap beneath so that the sun turned it into a hazy, auburn frame around her head. He felt a second's jealousy on behalf of the mother who'd died giving birth to him. Could she have competed in such variety with this woman?

'Oh, Oliver,' she said, looking up, 'they're coming home. Susan don't reckon New York to be safe any longer. They'll be here. Susan sent this by the mail packet but they were going to sail for England right after she wrote, almost immediate.'

Her pleasure demanded his, yet Oliver thought of the Atlantic, the thousands of miles of sea that had become the battleground of two navies, now to be joined by a third.

'Um,' he said.

'No.' She shook her head. 'No, it's all right. Listen . . . "You will remember Captain Strang and the *Lord Percy* . . ."' She looked up: 'That's the frigate brought Susan and me and my first husband to England, a sound craft she is, and Strang's a fine captain.

' "She sails for London on Friday and Philippa and I with her. The *Percy*, you will remember, is a dispatch carrier and Captain Strang assures me he has no orders to give battle but will make for England as speedily as may be so that, with God's mercy, I shall deliver your daughter safely to you in six weeks." '

Makepeace blew out her cheeks. 'Phew. *That's* a relief.'

Her stepson saw that happy memories of the *Lord Percy* made the vessel invulnerable as far as she was concerned. 'Good news, Missus,' he said. 'When's she due?'

'Most any day.' Makepeace scanned the last page. 'Strang'll drop anchor in the Pool like he did before. Maybe I can go meet . . .'

She whimpered. Her face bleached so that her freckles looked suddenly green. Oliver took the letter from her hand before it could drop. Beneath a bold, curly signature, 'Your devoted friend, Susan Brewer', was a date. 'March 2, 1778.'

He met his stepmother's appalled eyes, went to his knees and held her against him. 'It don't mean . . . very well, the letter's been delayed but in that case perhaps so's the *Percy*. There's maybe another letter floundering around the seas somewhere telling us she'd changed her mind, maybe Strang couldn't take the two of them after all, maybe Susan decided to wait for better weather.'

But . . . four months, he thought; Susan should have written again, there should've been news one way or another in four months.

Makepeace didn't hear him. She was being assailed by certainty. God had drowned her daughter. Philippa and Susan had set off from New York and not arrived. Somewhere on the voyage, the *Lord Percy* had gone down.

It seemed inevitable now, as if she had known it in advance and allowed it to happen. Because of all the years she had let pass without seeing Philippa or summoning her home from America, God had chosen the ultimate punishment.

I didn't go to her. I didn't fetch her back. Andra wanted me to, but I didn't.

It was as if her daughter had been calling to her across the Atlantic in a voice that she'd been too busy to hear, allowing it to be subsumed in work, her marriage, the birth of other daughters.

Guilt snatched at a rag to cover itself. She didn't *want* to come back; she wrote she'd rather stay with Susan in America.

The small figure of her daughter at their last interview in London stood in front of her now, as clear as clear, listening to her explain that Aunt Susan wanted to return to America and that Betty, who had been Makepeace's nurse as well as Philippa's, would be going too. They wanted to take Philippa with them—the child was the apple of their eye, they had looked after her while Makepeace was busy—and Makepeace was giving the child the choice.

A plain, grave little girl with Philip Dapifer's long face, his sallow skin and hair, but without the humour that had made her late father so attractive. As she'd considered, she'd looked like a small, studious camel.

'Would you be coming too, Mama?'

'No. I have things to do in England. I must go up North again soon.'

So much to do. Well, there *had* been. She'd still been struggling to adapt to the loss of Philip and gain wealth from the coalfield she'd won so that she could beggar the two people, one of them Philip's divorced first wife, whose chicanery had robbed her and Philippa of his estates when he died.

Andra had been merely her business partner in those days, someone in the background. She'd been alone, obsessed with taking revenge on the first Lady Dapifer, which eventually she had, oh, she *had*, and never regretted it.

She remembered, agonizingly now, how she had defined the matter for herself then: did she love her daughter enough to abandon the struggle and go back to America—possibly a better mother but undoubtedly a beaten woman? And the answer had been no, she didn't.

Now, again, she heard Philippa make her decision.

'I think I should like to go. Just for a visit.'

Don't go. Stay here. *'Are you sure?'*

'Yes.'

It had been punishing at that moment to experience what the child must have felt every time Makepeace had left *her*. How much greater the punishment now.

So she had let her go. She'd watched Susan and Betty, her best and only women friends, take Philippa's hands and lead her up the gangplank of the America-bound boat, all three of them alienated from the woman to whom they'd been devoted because she hadn't had time for them. And with them had gone another beloved child, Betty's son Josh.

At the last, Makepeace had reached for her daughter.

'I'll come and fetch you back, you know. If you like America, we might even stay there together.'

The small body resisted. It had been the worst moment then; it was the worst moment now. Philippa hadn't believed her.

The wave that had gathered speed and weight somewhere out in the Atlantic to come rushing at her crashed over Makepeace. She couldn't see; she was thrashing about in a roaring darkness.

Oliver tried to reach her. 'Don't, Missus, don't. We don't know yet. There's a thousand explanations . . .' She wasn't hearing him. He could only hold her close and wait for the initial agony to subside.

Unmarried and childless, Oliver could only guess at her pain but he suspected guilt was part of it. He'd once asked his father why Philippa had gone away. Andra had said: *'Weren't my choice, lad. We weren't wed then. I'd have kept the lass, we got on well, her and me, the time she lived at Raby before she went. I'd've loved her like my own.'*

And he would have done, Oliver knew; Andra Hedley's reverence for all living creatures was especially for children. Reluctant that his son should think less of Makepeace, he'd added: *'Weren't her fault, neither. The bairn's birth were a time o' despair for her. Husband just dead, filched of home and fortune that very day by as brazen a pair o' schemers as ever graced a gibbet. Beat dizzy, she was. Took years to get back and by then there'd opened a breach twixt her and little lass they could neither of 'em bridge. Philippa'd become closer to others than to her ma and when they upped sticks for America, she went an' all. Nobody's fault, lad, nobody's fault.'*

Oliver neither understood nor approved of those parents, the very rich and the very poor, who sent their children to be brought up in other households; he didn't come of either class. Neither, he thought, does the Missus. Her first marriage to the aristocrat, Sir

Philip Dapifer, had been only a temporary elevation; by birth and breeding she was as bourgeois as himself, the daughter of a Boston innkeeper.

Yet he considered that even now, secure and happily married once more, the Missus was not sufficiently attentive to the two daughters she'd had by Andra. Too often, in Oliver's opinion, she stayed overnight in Newcastle through press of work, rather than returning to Raby.

True, the little girls were happy and vigorous children, well looked after by his and their mutual Aunt Ginny, apparently not aware—as Philippa must have been—that they weren't receiving full value from their mother.

Scenting disapproval, his father had emphasized: *'Oliver, tha marries who tha marries. I wed a businesswoman and knew it afore I wed her. I'd not change her.'*

He'd not received full value himself, which is why the matter weighed on him; he'd been motherless with a father working long hours in the mines to keep them both—and, this was the rub, that same father often abstracted during their precious hours together. For if Andra had married a businesswoman, Makepeace had married an engineer, self taught but boiling with invention, his mind bent on lessening the dangers miners faced every day underground. But that was nature; Andra Hedley was a proper man. To be a proper woman, Makepeace Hedley had also to be a proper mother. And she was not. And now suffered because she was not.

Censorious he might be, but it was impossible for Oliver to watch, unmoved, the crucifixion of a woman who'd always been kind to him.

'I drowned my baby,' she kept saying, 'I drowned her and Susan.'

'We don't know,' he kept saying in return, 'we don't know, Missus. Let's find out afore we give way.'

In the end, he managed to reach her. His words began to penetrate the deluge of despair she was lost in and she grabbed at them as if he'd thrown her a rope.

'Might not be that, might it?' she begged. 'Might be something else. Could've been blown off course, couldn't they? Landed in the West Indies, maybe?'

'Certainly they could.'

'Who'd know?'

'The Admiralty,' he said, firmly. '*Lord Percy*'s a naval vessel, ain't she? The Admiralty'll know what's happened to her. I'll write this very day—'

'No,' she said. Somehow she'd got herself in hand, even if that hand was trembling, and Oliver saw not just the acumen but the courage that had made his stepmother the woman she was. 'No more damn letters. We'll go to the Admiralty and we'll go today. I'll get some answers out of their damn lordships or I'll know the reason why. When's the next coach to London?'

Chapter Three

THE Commission for Sick and Hurt Seamen and the Exchange of Prisoners of War, more generally known as the Sick and Hurt Office, was under the direction of the Lords of the Admiralty in London and, as such, reflected their lordships' demand for spit and polish.

The sailor who stamped along its immaculate corridors beside Diana wore dress uniform so stiff with starch and wax she decided he'd been lifted into it by traction. The waiting room he ushered her into had Caroline elegance; even the restrained sun of a muggy day coming through the windows was reflected in an oak floor lethal with over-buffing and the scent of unexpected roses, standing to attention in a centrepiece on the great walnut table, was overpowered by a smell of beeswax and turpentine.

She was asked to wait. 'Mr Commissioner Powell has been delayed a minute, ma'am.'

She frowned; she was not used to being kept waiting by underlings. However, she was on an adventure and she had nothing more important to do. 'Very well.'

There were two other occupants of the room, a woman of about her own age and a young man, sitting silently on adjoining chairs at the table. The Dowager lowered her head as she passed them on her way to look out of the window. The young man acknowledged her politely, rising for a slight bow; the woman ignored her.

In one look, Diana had automatically assessed to what social order they belonged. Decent enough young man, neat, well dressed but not quite the *ton*: a professional person from the provinces. The woman was less easy to place. Good clothes, really *very* good, nice silk, but worn without care, distressing red hair escaping from a hat that didn't match the gloves. In misery, from the look of her. A wife of the mercantile class in some distress.

Below the window, in Horse Guards, a Grenadier company was parading in full battle gear to the accompaniment of drummers and fifers. From the Dowager's high viewpoint they looked like pretty squares of tin soldiers. Having attended reviews of the Earl of Stacpoole's Own Grenadiers, she could guess that under their fur mitres and carrying a weight of sixty pounds in knapsack, blanket, water flask, ammunition and weapons, they were not feeling pretty. As she watched, one of the toy soldiers fell flat, fainting, as if flicked over by an invisible child. The roar of the drill sergeant's disapproval coincided with the entry of Mr Commissioner Powell behind her.

'My goodness, so sorry to keep you waiting, your ladyship. Dear, yes, I hope they made you comfortable.'

She'd expected a naval officer but Mr Commissioner Powell was a lawyer and his neat subfusc looked dowdy and civilian amidst such shiny naval order. He was flurried by her importance—in her note she hadn't scrupled to emphasize her title, the late Earl's eminence and her son's position at Court.

'There's sorry I am for your bereavement, your ladyship. A loss to us all, indeed. Such a great man. Please come this way, your ladyship. My office . . .' He bowed her towards the door.

'We were here first.'

The Dowager looked round. The woman at the table had raised her head. Mr Powell stopped, amazed. 'I beg your pardon?'

'I *said*,' the woman said, 'we were here first. We been waiting and I want for you to deal with us now.' The voice was toneless but the American accent was strong.

Colonial mercantile, thought the Dowager.

Mr Powell wasn't impressed either. 'But, madam, you can understand . . .' His hand indicated not only the Dowager's position but her widow's weeds.

'Sorry for your loss, ma'am.' The woman didn't look at Diana; her eyes were on Powell. 'But, see, my daughter's missing and that man there knows where she is.'

It had been a terrible day, a terrible week for Makepeace and Oliver Hedley. After a breakneck journey from Newcastle to London, it had transpired that Andrew Ffoulkes, the rising young luminary of the diplomatic corps on whose help Makepeace had counted, was absent, sent abroad on a secret mission. At the house of the Marquis of Rockingham, another influential friend, they'd learned that the master was in Yorkshire.

Though they'd scattered money like rose petals around the Admiralty, its clerks had been too harassed by the developing situation at sea to search for the information needed by an increasingly distraught woman. When, finally, they'd managed to trace the fate of the *Lord Percy*, the news had been awful.

Nor had it been final; that was the thing. Apart from the fact that they had been involved in dreadful events, whether Philippa and Susan were alive or not was still uncertain; they had been supercargo, civilian passengers, and, as such, no department had been willing to assume responsibility for them.

At last, one clerk had been helpful. 'You want the Sick and Hurt Office, ma'am. They got them sort of records.'

'*I* know where she is?' Mr Powell asked now.

'That's what they told me.' Makepeace was keeping her voice steady, but when she tried to get up from her chair she sagged. She hadn't eaten and had barely slept for seventy-two hours.

Oliver began to fan her with his hat. Idly, the Dowager handed him her fan. 'Use that, young man.' She recognized desperation when she saw it and was touched. She turned to the commissioner. 'Perhaps you had better deal with this person, Mr Powell. Now, I think, and here.'

'Oah, but all records are in my office.'

'They can be fetched,' the Dowager told him with finality. The woman was obviously exhausted. In any case, she found herself intrigued and had no intention of missing the story about to unfold. 'I am prepared to wait.'

'Very well, if your ladyship is sure.'

She was sure. She took a chair at the back of the room out of everyone's eyeline. 'Please proceed.'

Obediently but somewhat put out, Mr Powell seated himself at the head of the table opposite Makepeace and Oliver. 'Name?'

'This is Mrs Hedley. I am Oliver Hedley, her stepson.' Oliver took up the running. He produced a notebook. Having won her point and the necessary attention, Makepeace had slumped.

'March the sixth this year,' Oliver said, 'a Royal Navy dispatch carrier, the *Lord Percy*, left New York bound for London. My stepsister and a friend, Miss Susan Brewer, were onboard. Halfway across the Atlantic, the *Percy* was engaged by the American navy corvette *Pilgrim*. *Percy*'s captain was killed.' Without looking up from his notes, Oliver put a hand on Makepeace's shoulder for a moment; she'd been fond of Captain Strang. '*Lord Percy* was forced to strike her colours and the remaining crew and passengers were taken aboard *Pilgrim*. That is what the Admiralty told us.'

Mr Powell rose from his chair. Makepeace looked up, quickly. 'Are you listening?'

'I'm sending for the records, madam,' Mr Powell told her. He went out into the corridor to speak to someone and came back to Oliver. 'Yes, yes, continue. Your sister and friend, now aboard the *Pilgrim*. American vessel.'

'They *were*. But on May the fourth *Pilgrim* encountered a British man-of-war, the *Riposte* and'—again Oliver's hand reached for Makepeace's shoulder—'the *Riposte* sank the *Pilgrim*.'

There was silence. The Dowager averted her eyes and stared instead at a portrait of Commissioner Samuel Pepys.

Mr Commissioner Powell said, quite gently: 'So the American vessel went down . . .'

Oliver nodded. 'So the American went down but . . . but some of her people were picked up. The Admiralty says the *Riposte* took on survivors and headed for England. Home port Plymouth. She arrived there in June, we've learned that much. The Admiralty told us American prisoners were onboard and they were put in gaol. They don't know how many or their names or where they are . . .'

'Excuse me again.' Once again, the commissioner went to the door and gave more orders.

Makepeace said, her voice rising: 'So where is she? Where's my Philippa? Where's Susan Brewer? If they're in gaol . . . if you've put them in gaol . . .'

Mr Powell tutted. 'No, no,' he said, 'we don't put females in prison. Boys under twelve and females are set at liberty, see, but I'm not sure we keep the names.'

The starched and waxed sailor who'd accompanied the Dowager to the room came into it with a pile of ledgers.

'Now then.' Mr Powell peered at the books. 'Plymouth, Plymouth . . .' He selected one and licked his fingers. 'June, June. Busy month, June and, o' course, Plymouth is a busy port. But yes, yere we are, HMS *Riposte*. Docked June the seventh to unload prisoners. Look at this now, there's near a hundred of 'em, French as well—she must have sunk a Frenchy on her way home. Prize money there then, I expect. Name again? Hedley, is it?'

'Dapifer,' said Makepeace, her voice suddenly strong, like a tolling bell. 'Her name is Philippa Dapifer.' It began to break as she added: 'She's eleven years old. Twelve in September. Travelling with her godmother, Miss Susan Brewer.'

'Sir Philip Dapifer was my stepsister's father,' Oliver added, knowing it would help.

It did. Mr Commissioner Powell looked up. 'Not Sir *Philip* Dapifer? There now. Sir Philip. A good friend to the Admiralty, Sir Philip. Not that I knew him well, mind, but . . .'

'Just get on,' Makepeace said, wearily.

Encouraged that he was not dealing with hoi polloi anymore, Mr Powell got on, his spectacles glinting in the turn from side to side as his eyes searched the page of a closely written list.

At the back of the room, the Dowager's interest increased. Sir

Philip Dapifer, well, well. She had met him rarely and only then by chance—being a liberal Whig and an influential supporter of the Marquis of Rockingham, he had been anathema to Aymer who'd refused to meet him socially—but she had liked what she'd seen of him. Charm and *excellent* breeding.

The same could not be said of Sir Philip's first wife. Well born and exquisitely pretty but a voracious trollop. Aymer had not been so particular about *her*, the Dowager recalled. There had been a rumour that they'd had an affair, one in a long line of various affairs for them both; the woman had been shameless. Hadn't there been something about her and Dapifer's best friend?

Yes, there *had* been, and Dapifer had gone to America to divorce her quietly, trying to protect her name and his. And returned . . . yes, it was all coming back now . . . and returned with a totally unsuitable new wife, an American, a serving girl from a Boston inn—something like that. So that poor female there had been the second Lady Dapifer, had she?

But Dapifer had died, suddenly and much too young. The Dowager remembered the surprisingly sharp pang with which she'd heard the news, as if something valuable had been taken out of the world . . .

Mr Powell was muttering to himself. 'Dapifer and Brewer we're looking for. I've got a D'Argent here, no, no, that's a Frenchman . . .'

He's not going to find them, Makepeace thought. They're not there. It's coming and I won't be able to bear it. This is like it was when Philip died. It was a return to affliction, an old terror come again so that she felt she did not belong where she sat but should be somewhere else.

Behind her, the Dowager continued to squeeze her memory. Yes. The first wife had claimed the Dapifer estates back after Sir Philip died on the grounds that the divorce had not been legal. The scandal sheets were full of it at the time. And then she and her lover had frittered the lands away and somehow—the details were hazy—

this second wife had got them back. Now, poor thing, she'd lost her daughter.

The commissioner's finger was approaching the end of the list.

'No, no,' he said, 'I'm sorry . . .' He turned a page. 'Wait now, here's something. Supercargo.'

Yes, Makepeace thought, please. *Please*.

Mr Commissioner Powell tilted his book to see the page better. ' "Supercargo, American. Two . . ." ' he read, ' "one female, one ship's boy. Released June the seventh." ' He looked up, smiling as if he had not just turned the screw to the rack's limit. 'There we are then.'

The Dowager took a hand. 'Names?' she suggested. 'Ages? Location? Are such people let go to wander as they may when they arrive on these shores? A child? In this case, possibly two children?'

'Well.' Mr Powell blew out his lips; some people refused to be satisfied. 'It just says "supercargo" yere. I agree with your ladyship, the names should be on the list but when a captain's engaged with the enemy . . . and by rights, supercargo's not our concern, there's charities to deal with them, we got enough with prisoners. I'm sorry I can't tell you more, Mrs Hedley. Perhaps there's some record in Plymouth.'

She felt helpless before the world's oppression, but while there was a crack of hope in it, she had to go on. 'Plymouth then, Oliver,' she said.

He nodded and took her arm.

As Mr Powell opened the door for them, the Dowager was moved to say: 'Have you a conveyance, Mrs Hedley . . . ?' It was kindly meant; the Dowager was a kind woman and, had the answer been no, would have gone on to offer the coach in which she had travelled from Chantries. However, her accustomed languid tone fell on Makepeace's ears as condescension.

For the first time Makepeace became fully aware of the woman who'd been sitting behind her, listening to her misery. She was tall, elegant and, from what could be distinguished beneath the veil, beautiful. But she also looked disdainful and belonged to a class that, with one or two exceptions, had always treated her, Makepeace, like a squaw wandered into its midst with a tomahawk. She represented a female set which, during her first marriage, had patronized her, belittled her and, when she'd been brought low after Philip's death, had not lifted one of its beringed fingers to help her.

She stiffened. She said: 'I got my own coach, thank you.' There was no gratitude in her voice. She went out.

Yes, well.

The Dowager crossed to the table, sat down and picked up the fan that Oliver had left on the table, also without thanks. What else could one expect of the low-born?

Mr Powell tutted in sympathy. 'Now then, your ladyship, we can attend to your request. A Lieutenant Gale, was it? One of our prisoners?'

'Grayle.'

'Grayle, of course. American. May I ask your interest in this person, your ladyship?'

The Dowager appeared to consider. 'I don't think so, no.'

'Oah.' Some pink appeared in Commissioner Powell's cheeks but the rebuff merely emphasized the blueness of her ladyship's blood and, therefore, her right to administer it. 'Well there, I found *him* at least. The *Sam Adams*, you said in your note. And here she is.' Mr Powell inserted a finger behind a bookmark and opened one of the ledgers. 'American sloop, three hundred and eighty-five tons, eighteen guns, taken at Cap La Hague, December the third last year, surviving crew forty-one.' Mr Powell ran his finger down a list. 'And here *he* is, Forrest Grayle, Lieutenant.' He looked up, a terrier dropping a bone in her ladyship's lap.

'Where?'

'What? Oh.' Mr Powell found more bookmarks. 'Where's that report of the action, now? Yere 'tis . . . nyum, "Exchange of fire . . ." nyum, nyum, "several hours . . ." Oh, a real battle, this one. "Badly holed but seaworthy . . . taken under tow." Ah yes.' Again Mr Powell was triumphant. 'Plymouth. There's a coincidence, isn't it? Plymouth all over the place today. Yes, she was taken to Plymouth and the crew incarcerated in Millbay Prison. There's lucky for them.'

'Really.'

'Indeed.' He leaned forward. 'It would be the hulks else and I won't hide from your ladyship, whilst we do our best for these souls, what with French and Americans, let alone the occasional Spaniard, every prison in the country at our disposal is crowded out and hulks have to take the overflow. Believe you me, Millbay is better. It's on dry land for a start.'

He's probably quite a nice little man, Diana thought, if undoubtedly Welsh.

She said: 'Obviously you have your problems, sir, and I am here to relieve you of one of them. I wish to arrange for Lieutenant Grayle to be exchanged.' She added lazily: 'One would be happy to pay for such an arrangement.' For a while, she could still draw upon the Stacpoole bank account.

'Oah.' Mr Powell sat up with surprise. 'Exchange, is it? No, no. There can be no question of an exchange for American prisoners. Absolutely not. Nothing I can do for your ladyship in that quarter, do you see.'

'I do not see, I'm afraid,' she drawled. 'One was led to believe you gentlemen incorporated the exchange of prisoners of war in'— she waved a hand—'whatever it is you do.'

'Prisoners of war, yes, prisoners of *war*, that's right enough. But Americans aren't prisoners of war, your ladyship, not like the French. We'll be able to send French prisoners back in return for some of ours but strictly *speak*ing Americans are rebels against their lawful king. Captured in British waters *attack*ing English shipping, they are. Traitors, in fact. Felons, pirates.'

'Why not hang them, then, and be done?' She was nettled by disappointment. It would have been nice to send Martha back her son.

'Oah, we can't hang 'em.' Mr Powell smiled. 'No, no. Legally we could, mind, but I doubt there's gallows enough in the country to take them all. Coming in by shiploads, they are. Might set a bit of a precedent, do you see? We wouldn't want our brave lads captured by the Americans *in* America strung up in response, now would we?'

The Dowager sighed. 'Mr Commissioner, one is not concerned with causing an international incident, merely the fate of one miserable young man.'

'There's sorry I am to disoblige, your ladyship, very, very sorry. I'm not saying we commissioners wouldn't be happy, *happy*, to exchange the Americans—indeed, more than once we've lobbied their lordships to that effect. Difficult . . . dear, dear, you wouldn't believe how difficult they are. More trouble with them, there is, than all the rest put together: riot, demands, attempts to escape, oh dear, dear . . . but my hands are tied, do you see?' Mr Commissioner Powell closed his books. 'My advice is to send the lieutenant a nice parcel of comforts, I'm sure the governor . . .'

The Dowager left the Sick and Hurt Office dissatisfied on her own account and oddly saddened on little Philippa Dapifer's. There lay the trouble with chance encounters; one remained ignorant of an outcome. Her interest had been aroused, and with it her sympathy—less for the awful mother than for Sir Philip's child, if it *was* the child, who had been set adrift in a city like Plymouth, full of sailors, to meet the fate of all lost young girls.

Would the Hedley woman find her? And, if so, in what condition?

Qualified as she was to know the damage done to mind as well as body by sexual violence, the fact that it might be being inflicted on a child even younger than she had been when it was inflicted on her was disturbing—she was surprised how *much* it disturbed her. It happened on the streets every day, possibly to thousands. Yet this was a case she knew about, it had been given a name, she had overheard its history. If the girl had survived that terrible voyage across the Atlantic, she'd already suffered enough.

'Be not curious in unnecessary matters,' Ecclesiasticus said. The Dowager reminded herself that it was not her concern. She had her own problem; she could report only failure to Martha Grayle—

always supposing it would be possible to report at all. *Your son is in a Plymouth prison, Martha. It is better than the hulks.*

Yes, well.

She stood for a while on the Admiralty steps, looking for her coach in the heavy Whitehall traffic. Tobias must have had trouble finding a place for it in which to wait for her.

In view of her insistence, both Robert and Alice had eventually reconciled themselves to her departure on what Alice called 'Mama's visiting spree'. They had given her Tobias and Joan to take with her and allowed her the third best coach but no coachman, so Tobias had been transformed into a driver—a job he performed excellently, as he did everything.

It had amused the Dowager that her son and daughter-in-law had stipulated—without actually using the word—that she return to Chantries for Christmas and settle down. It made her feel like Cinderella commanded to leave the ball by midnight or else . . . to quiet them, she had agreed to spend the Twelve Nights with them. As for settling down, well, she would see.

Expecting London to be comparatively quiet with Society having retired to the country for the summer, she found it actually busier than ever, full of soldiers and baggage trains on their way to the ports for embarkation.

A column of footguards marched past her, sending up dust, their Brown Bess flintlocks gleaming. A useless weapon, Aymer had called it, unreliable in bad weather and at anything over eighty yards' range. Women and children ran beside them, some cheering, others weeping.

She was suddenly oppressed by dull heat, crowds, dust and the doom to which all these men were going. The war was undoubtedly necessary—colonies could not be allowed to secede as and when they pleased or they would not be colonies—but how many of these soldiers would return from it? How many young men on both sides, how many children, would be parted forever from their mothers?

I will not think of it. There is nothing I can do for any of them.

After twenty-two years, I am allowed some liberty of my own, a little healing.

The sea, she thought. I need to be near the sea and breathe clean, free air.

She would go to Devon, the county of her ancestors which, unaccountably, her family had deserted for London and its environs. Not Torbay—there was no suitable house there and, in any case, she did not want to face the memory of the young Martha now that there was only failure to report to the mother Martha had become. T'Gallants, that was the place. Home of the founding Pomeroy. She had never seen it, but it was on the sea. It had been tenanted for years but its lease was falling due—she had looked it up in the Chantries property book before she came away.

Diana smiled to herself; had she unconsciously intended to go there from the first? Yes, there were friends in the area. The Edgcumbes would put her up while she investigated. Devon would serve very well for her escape from the dowagerhood Alice and Robert wanted to inflict on her.

The fact that both the Edgcumbe home and T'Gallants were only a few miles from Plymouth had nothing to do with the matter.

Chapter Four

By the time she set off for Plymouth, Makepeace had clutched at the straw of hope that the young girl landed with the American prisoners at Plymouth was her daughter, and was managing to keep herself afloat on it.

Of *course* the child was Philippa. The fact that, if it was indeed her daughter, she had therefore been on English soil without word for two months . . . well, that could be due to anything, loss of memory, kidnapping, *anything*. As for Susan Brewer, perhaps she had been landed somewhere else, had also suffered loss of memory, been kidnapped . . .

So Makepeace forced herself to recover some equilibrium and thereby lost her temper, as she always did when she was fighting fear.

She cursed the friends she had expected to turn to for help and who had proved absent, her brother, her doctor, all of them having deserted London for the summer with the rest of Society. She cursed, with tears, her husband for choosing such a time to go to France. And she cursed Oliver for wanting to accompany her to Plymouth.

'Who's going to run the damn business if you're traipsing all over the country with me? You get back to my girls and see nobody kidnaps *them*.'

'Missus, you are not going alone.'

'No, I'm not. I'm taking Beasley. You get back to Newcastle and try to get word to your father—that's if nobody's kidnapped *him*.

Call on Rockingham in Yorkshire on the way home and see what he can do.'

Oliver conceded. There was undoubtedly a need to have other irons in the fire, like the Marquis of Rockingham, and he could heat them better if he were not employed in combing the streets of Plymouth. Also, it would profit nobody if the business went to the wall in the Missus's absence. John Beasley might be a peculiar choice as a travelling companion but, in this case, his particular peculiarity might prove useful.

Oliver, however, used as he was to his stepmother's eccentricity, was still concerned that she would be travelling with a man to whom she was not related and without female accompaniment. 'Won't you take a maid with you?'

'No.' Her regular lady's maid was out of commission and there were few other women for whom Makepeace had any use. 'I ain't listening to feminine chatter all the way to Devon, drive me lunatic.'

'It will look improper, that's all.'

'Improper?' Makepeace stared at him as if he was deranged. 'Philippa's missing and you think I care about looking improper?'

She never has, Oliver thought, even when Philippa wasn't missing. He sighed. 'All right, Missus.'

So Makepeace, Peter Sanders, who was her favourite coachman, and John Beasley set off on the Great West Road for Devon in her favourite coach. With Sanders up on the driver's box, there was only Beasley on whom her all-pervading spleen could be vented for the next two hundred miles.

'Damn you, I didn't ask you to come.'

'Yes you did,' John Beasley said.

'You didn't *have* to.'

'I said I was sick. Coaches make me puke. I didn't say I didn't want to come, I just said travel was a bugger. And the Plymouth press gangs might get me.'

'They wouldn't want you,' she said. 'Job's blasted comforter, you are.'

It was unreasonable, she knew. She would have been sent mad

by reassurance when there was so little reassurance to be had. But anybody was her kicking boy at that point so she berated Beasley for providing no comfort at all. He was morose—he was *always* morose—and refused to pretend to be sanguine about the journey's outcome. He slouched in his corner, allowing his body to flop with every bounce of the coach, looking ill—he *always* looked ill—and watched her fidget.

'You'll ruin that satin,' he said.

She kept rubbing her hands over her thighs and knees, up, down, up, down, stretching the delicate material and leaving a mark on it from the sweat of her palms. 'It's silk.'

'Why di'n't you bring your maid?'

'Hildy's mother's dying. I couldn't bring her.' She scored her hands over her knees again and added nastily: 'You're all there was.'

She couldn't rile him—his own manners were too surly to mind surliness in others—and she was forced to give up. The moment she stopped talking, she heard Philippa calling for her. Desperately she started again: 'What you done with all your money, anyway?'

As with all the friends who'd supported her through distress and penury after Philip Dapifer's death, she'd subsequently tried to make him rich by giving him shares in the mine, but money flew away from him: some into the hands of needy acquaintances; some down the drain that was his publishing business. Last night, to free him for this journey, she'd had to pay off the bailiffs occupying his rooms in Grub Street.

He shrugged. 'Government keeps smashing my presses.'

She said, 'I don't blame it,' not because that's what she thought but because it was there to be said. Nevertheless, that the government's antipathy to John Beasley ran as deep as his to the Tories was no surprise. He was against government on principle; he was against any authority.

Even Makepeace, a natural rebel herself, became impatient at the number and diversity of evils he attacked in his various publications: the King, Parliament—he'd written an article calling it 'the most listless, loitering, lounging, corrupt assembly in Europe'—the

Church, judges, rotten boroughs, pocket boroughs, enclosures, high prices, press gangs, crimp houses, public executions and whippings, the oppression of the Irish and all Roman Catholics (though he loathed popery), the Excise, sweat-shops and workhouses.

On the American war, he had spread himself, calling for Lord North to recall his 'butchers' from their 'slaughterhouse', publicizing the fact that the British army didn't scruple to let its Red Indians scalp the colonists and that 'Americans have all rights to independence from the dunghill its oppressors have made of their own country'.

But, despite his calls for revolution, it was impossible, he said, to goad an England that had no revolutionaries of its own into revolution. Despite widespread poverty, despite the fact that the war was not going well, the English refused to rise to his call to overthrow their government. Its middle class infuriated him by indifference and its deprived masses seemed, he said, lulled by the opiate of the Poor Law that kept them alive. Occasionally they might riot but they would not rise.

His publications were constantly being suppressed and their printing presses destroyed. He'd been in prison four times for debt—she'd had to rescue him—twice for libel and once for sedition.

He was at liberty now only because John Wilkes, that equally libertarian but outrageously effective hornet, had stung the authorities so effectively on behalf of gadflies like Beasley that they were chary of losing even more popularity by swatting them.

He even insisted that Makepeace was exploiting her miners. She'd pointed to the village she and Hedley had built for them at Raby, a model of its kind. It didn't satisfy him. 'You bloody rich only keep poor people alive so they can fight your wars or make you richer.'

Yet she stuck to him; indeed could talk to him as she could to nobody else, and not just because he'd proved a rock in her time of necessity; there was something about him. Andra thought very well of him and, for all his monosyllabic loutishness, he was highly regarded in the coffeehouses where he could count men like Dr Johnson and Joshua Reynolds among his friends.

Best of all, in their present situation, he was in touch with an entire network of those who didn't fit into respectable society, people who lived metaphorically underground and emerged, pale and seedy as Beasley himself, to strike at authority before submerging again. If Philippa had fallen among thieves or into the hands of a sect or rebels or the Irish or any other thorns in the side of the establishment, then Beasley was the man to find her.

But, knowing this, Makepeace's discontent chose to twist it against him. 'Why don't you mix with *important* people? I need influence.'

His mouth twisted, the nearest approach he could make to a smile. 'Fell the wrong side o' the bloody hedge this time, then, didn't you?'

Oh God, he can't understand. He doesn't know; he doesn't have children. He thinks this is ordinary horror—he thinks I'm feeling what he would if he was being dragged to gaol or hung over a cliff.

The childless, she thought enviously, had a limited experience of suffering, they saw it merely in terms of torture or famine or illness; they couldn't take the leap outside that circle of Hell to the wasteland stretching beyond it for bereft parents. She was sharing this coach, this arctic, with the emotional equivalent of a Hottentot.

She wanted her mother, she wanted Betty, who'd been better than a mother, that black and mighty fulcrum she'd taken for granted, as she'd taken Susan Brewer and Philippa for granted, until Betty and her son Josh too had joined them on the boat for America.

Impossible to whip up resentment at Betty's desertion because the desertion had been her own and, anyway, Betty was dead. 'A sudden death,' Susan had written three years ago. 'She clutched her bosom and fell. We buried her like the Christian she was and surely the trumpets sounded for her on the other side as they did for Mr. Standfast.'

I didn't stand fast by her, I didn't stand fast by any of them . . . young Josh with his talent as a painter . . . and this is my punishment.

'I'm going to puke,' Beasley said.

'Do it out the window,' she said, grimly. 'We ain't stopping.'

Arriving in Plymouth, they had trouble finding accommodation. Owing to the war, the town was stuffed with navy personnel: every house for rent was taken, and so was every room in its inns. In any case, a woman travelling without a female companion and with a man not her husband wasn't a guest welcomed by any respectable hostelry.

It wasn't until Makepeace slammed a purse full of guineas on the table of the Prince George on the corner of Stillman Street and Vauxhall Street that its landlord remembered the naval lieutenant in a back room who hadn't paid his rent for three weeks. The lieutenant was evicted, Makepeace installed, John Beasley was put in an attic with Sanders, while the coach and horses went into the George's stables which were big enough to accommodate them as well as the diligence that made a weekly trip back and forth to Exeter.

Under other circumstances, Makepeace would have liked Plymouth very much. More than any port in Britain, it most closely resembled America's Boston in the quality of light bouncing off its encircling, glittering water onto limestone houses, large windows, slate roofs and the leaves of its elm-lined streets. There was a similar sense of unlimited fresh, salt air, the same smell of sea, fish, tar and sawn wood, even a flavour of Boston's bloody-minded independence—despite a desperate siege, Plymouth had held resolutely for Parliament during the Civil War.

It was from Plymouth that Makepeace's ancestors had set out in the *Mayflower* to the New World and the shuttle of trade between the two had never been lost. Plymouth's merchantmen knew the coast of America from Newfoundland to New York better than she did, their owners sadly regretting that it was now enemy territory.

Many of Plymouth's common people were regretting it too. This was a sailors' town and, while Plymouth-launched ships were inflicting heavy damage on America's fleet, the losses were not one-sided. Mourning bands and veiling were everywhere.

But since it must fight, Plymouth had rolled up its sleeves. By no means the biggest port in England—Liverpool and Bristol were larger, owing to their slave trade, while London outranked them all—it was Plymouth that directly faced the enemy when war broke out with France, Spain or America, and it geared itself up accordingly, as it had when the Armada came billowing up the Channel.

The streets were almost impassable for baggage trains bringing supplies to be shipped across the Atlantic to the army. Wounded ships limped into the Sound to be mended and sent out again; new ones were being built on the great slipways. Marines and militia paraded to the roll of drums on the gusty grass of the Hoe, just as they had in the days when Drake played bowls on it.

But to Makepeace it became a jungle where the shrill chatter of posturing apes echoed back from the darkness that hid her child. She watched the mouths of Admiralty clerks, corporation officials and harbourmasters as they made words, and could only gather that they were saying no.

Beasley had to interpret for her as to a bewildered child.

'He says *Riposte* anchored in the Hamoaze in June. Her prisoners were put ashore and the militia marched them off to prison. He doesn't know which prison, he says he doesn't handle that end of it.'

At the local Sick and Hurt Office: 'He's got a record of two supercargo, one of them female, like they told you in London. He thinks they were separated from the other prisoners and told to wait on the quay until they could be dealt with but either they ran off or nobody bothered with them. Jesus *Christ*'—this to the clerk—'no wonder you ain't winning this bloody war.'

It was Sanders who, on Beasley's secret instructions, made enquiries at the local coroner's office. He came back, equally quietly, to say that while there had been several inquests in the last six weeks, two of them on drowned women, none of them had concerned the body of a girl of Philippa's age.

'Either of 'em Susan Brewer?' Beasley asked quietly.

'Could've been. They wasn't named. Don't think so, though.'

They asked at the churches, at watchmen's stands, they questioned parish beadles and people in the street. They tried the Society for Distressed Foreigners, which turned out to be an attic in a private house containing a lone Lascar hiding from the press gangs.

To facilitate the search, they decided to divide: Beasley to contact publishers and book-sellers, who kept their fingers on the pulse of the town, as well as less respectable Plymouth inhabitants; Makepeace to visit the institutions.

Accompanied by Sanders, Makepeace knocked on the forbidding door of the local Orphanage for Girls in Stonehouse and was received by an equally forbidding-looking clergyman.

'Yes,' Reverend Hambledon told her, 'we took in two girls in June, mother dead and their father lost when the *Buckfast* went down. However, they are younger than the one you describe.'

'She's young for her age,' Makepeace said, desperately.

She was shown into the dining hall—it was breakfast-time—where forty-two children in identical grey calico uniforms sat on the benches of a long table eating porridge from identical bowls with identical spoons. High windows let in bars of light that shone on heads whose hair was hidden beneath all-covering identical grey calico caps.

The room was undecorated except for some embroidered Bible texts on the bare walls. It smelled of whale-oil soap.

Reverend Hambledon ushered Makepeace in and forty-two spoons clattered down as forty-two girls stood to attention. She was led along the rows. 'This is Jane, who came to us in June. And this is Joan. Say good morning to Mrs Hedley, girls.'

Two mites chorused: 'Good morning, Mrs Hedley.'

Reverend Hambledon's voice did not alter pitch as he added: 'Sometimes they come in with unsuitable names and we rechristen them. Most had not been christened at all.'

Holding back tears, Makepeace smiled at the little girls and shook her head.

When she got outside, Sanders said: 'Bad, was it, Missus?'

'I'd like to adopt the lot of 'em,' she said.

There'd been no evidence of unkindness there, but none of kindness either. The porridge they'd been eating did not smell unappetizing but nor did it attack the nose with pleasure. The children did not look unhappy yet they weren't happy.

What had stabbed her was that, as she'd entered the dining room, every head had turned to her before expectation died in the eyes, as it died in her own. Well, there was little she could do about that but she would send money to Reverend Hambledon on the understanding that it was spent on dolls and pretty dresses.

She found herself longing for the two little girls she'd left behind in Northumberland. God spare them from the unloving wilderness in which the children she'd just left had to exist.

'I tell you this much, Peter,' she said, 'I'm going to let Andra and Oliver run the business from now on. When we get home I'm going to *stay* home.'

Sanders nodded without conviction; he knew her.

But she meant it. She was being punished for neglecting her eldest child. Philip Dapifer's accusations haunted her dreams. She would not do the same by Sally and Jenny. And she would take in some of those poor scraps she'd just seen, dress them in colours, let them run free over the Northumberland hills. Oh yes, when she got home . . .

It occurred to her sharply that, if she did not find Philippa and Susan, she could never go home. How could she abandon the place holding the vague promise that they might turn up one day? She would have to stay, like a dog waiting forever by the grave of its lost master . . .

She balled her fists and knocked them together so that the knuckles hurt. Cross that bridge when you get to it, Makepeace Hedley. You may not have to.

She returned to the search.

She scanned rows of uniformed children in another orphanage, shaven-headed children in the hospital and dispensaries, children spinning yarn in the Home for Foundlings, children knitting stockings in the workhouse, picking oakum in the prison, young women chanting their catechism in the Asylum for Deserted Girls, dumb and staring wrecks in the local bedlam.

'Dear God, Peter,' she said, crying, 'where d'they all come from?'

'It's a sailors' town, Missus. Wages of sin.'

She began to break down and at nights Sanders had to assist her, almost too tired to walk, back to the inn.

Beasley had no success either.

They sat in facing settles across a table in a dark corner of the George's large, low-beamed taproom. The windows were open, allowing in the scent of grass and the calls of men on the inn's skittle ground. Further away, someone was playing a fiddle.

'I reckon we're looking in the wrong place,' Beasley said, when they'd ordered food. 'The *Riposte* anchored in the Hamoaze, which is over that way.' He jerked his head to the west. 'So that's where the prisoners were put ashore. Not in Plymouth at all.'

'Oh God,' said Makepeace, 'there's another town?'

'It's called Dock.' He shrugged. 'Because it was a dock at one time, I suppose. But it's grown so it's . . . yes, it's another town.'

'Then that's where we'll go tomorrow.' Makepeace closed her eyes for a moment. 'I think I'll get to bed. I don't want anything to eat.'

The two men watched her go.

'She can't stand much more,' Sanders said.

'She'll have to,' said Beasley. 'We're never going to find that girl. Or Susan Brewer. They went down with the bloody boat—if they were ever on it in the first place.'

'I don't think that's right, Mr Beasley,' Sanders said. 'There was a young girl landed here, we know that. Well, how many children *would* be on a warship, eh? It's got to be Miss Philippa. About Miss Susan I don't know.'

'Yere you are, my dearrs. Mrs Hedley not eatin' tonight?' The landlord, John Bignall, had brought their food. An enormously fat man—he was known for his ability to bounce troublemakers out of the door by using his stomach as a battering ram—he ran a good inn and had warmed to these, his newest guests, in the days since they'd been with him.

Makepeace he'd decided was respectable but strange—for one thing, she allowed her coachman to eat at the same table and at the same time as herself. Curious about those whose provenance mystified him, he'd learned something of Makepeace's by plying Sanders with after-hours ale. Immediately, his sympathy had been engaged. 'Poor little maid being chased by they American pirates across the ocean,' he said. 'Enough to make any soul lose its wits.'

'I can see from your sad faces as you an't had no more luck finding that little maid than yesterday,' he said now.

'No,' Beasley told him. 'We're going to try Dock tomorrow.'

'Iss fay, I was thinking of Dock, plenty of places in Dock,' Bignall said.

'What sort of places?'

The landlord tapped his nose. 'Ah, that's why I been slow to mention 'un to Mrs Hedley. If so be the maid's in Dock,'tis mebbe better she an't found at all.'

'She knows,' Beasley said. 'She still wants her found.'

'Fine woman, that. No side to her.' The innkeeper finished putting dishes on the table. 'Good luck to ee then, an' mind the press gangs. My brother-in-law from Bovey Tracey, he was a tailor. Three year ago he took a dress coat to Dock as a cap'n had ordered. Us bain't seen 'un since.'

'Jesus,' Beasley said, watching him go. 'Missus doesn't realize. I've been looking over my bloody shoulder for a week.'

'Me and all,' Sanders said.

Acting on behalf of a seriously undermanned navy, the wartime Impressment Service was ubiquitous throughout the country but its greatest activity was in the ports, its gangs waiting behind corners like lurking octopuses to haul in unwary passers-by into His Majesty's service.

Both Beasley and Sanders, neither of whom possessed the

exemption certificates carried by men in protected trades, had been at risk merely walking along a Plymouth street, and knew it. Dock was likely to be even more dangerous.

'I got better things to do with my life than get beaten and buggered for the rest of it,' Beasley said.

'Beggin' your pardon, Mr Beasley, but I don't intend to. There's a lot I'd do for Missus but I got a wife and childer. I ain't going with her to Dock. I'll go round some more places here.'

'I suppose I could dress up as a woman,' Beasley said gloomily.

Sanders's gravity flickered. 'Can't say you got the bubbies for it.' Then his face returned to its usual impassivity. 'Cheer up, sir. We'll find 'em.'

Beasley just sighed.

Chapter Five

WHEN the Dowager remarked, and meant it, that Mount Edgcumbe's prospect was as fine as any she had seen, Admiral Lord Edgcumbe said: 'Thank you, ma'am. The Duke of Medina Sidonia is supposed to have been good enough to say the same when he sailed past at the head of the Armada. He mentioned that he was resolved to have it for his own when he won England.' There was a well-rehearsed pause. 'He was disappointed.'

A legend worth repeating, and Lord Edgcumbe obviously repeated it often, but Diana believed it; the Spanish fleet had indeed swept past the slope of the wooded deer park in which she stood looking out to sea, while the house commanding it was enviably beautiful.

She turned to her left and shaded her eyes to stare across the river that separated her from Plymouth. 'So that is Devon and we are in Cornwall.'

'No, ma'am. This *used* to be Cornwall, the Hamoaze markin' the division, but it is now Devon. A fifteenth-century ancestor of mine married an heiress from across the way who brought with her the property of the ferry. It would have been inconvenient to have a county boundary splittin' the estate so . . .'

'So he moved it,' she said, smiling. Again, it wasn't bombast. She'd asked, he'd answered; the Edgcumbes had no need to embroider history in which their name was already sewn large. Hardly a land or sea battle in which an Edgcumbe hadn't fought like a tiger—

to be suitably rewarded. Yet her host's father had been the first to recognize Joshua Reynolds's genius, while the Mozart this battle-scarred sailor had played for her last night had been as pretty a performance as any she'd heard from an amateur.

Never having penetrated so far into the South-West, she had expected, in her cosmopolitan way, to find its nobility embarrassingly provincial. Yet it appeared she had stepped back to the Renaissance and the venturing days of Elizabeth, when men of action were also dilettantes and vice versa.

Lady Edgcumbe too was, as ever, a relief, hospitable without being overwhelming, and with a confidence in her pedigree that showed in her choice of dress, which was eccentric but comfortable.

The Dowager would have forgiven an admiral overseeing the naval movements of one of the busiest ports in the country for being too occupied to pay attention to his guest but, like Aymer, like most aristocratic holders of office that she knew, Lord Edgcumbe saw no reason to curtail in war too many of the activities he had enjoyed in peacetime. His otter- and foxhounds were being kept in readiness for the hunting season, and he entertained.

Both he and his wife had greeted her as if it were perfectly normal for a widow to go visiting so soon after her husband's funeral. Admiral Edgcumbe was a distant cousin of the Stacpooles, though his and the Earl's acquaintance had been based on their professional meetings—Edgcumbe's as a high-ranking admiral, the Earl's as a Secretary of State. Their friendship was for his Countess, formed during the times they had stayed at Chantries.

The visits had not been reciprocated. Despite numerous requests for the Earl and Countess to come to Devon, Aymer had refused them all. *'Damned if I'm venturing into here-be-dragons country to stay among a lot of canvas-climbers. Ruins the complexion, all that salt. Look at Edgcumbe's—leathery as a tinker's arse.'*

Though nothing was said outright, Diana suspected that they had seen enough of her marriage to commiserate politely with her on the Earl's death but not as if she were expected to be inconsolable. 'Of *course* you need a change of air after all you've been through,' Lucy Edgcumbe had said, with what Diana construed as double meaning. 'We are so very pleased that your first sight of Devon is with us.'

She was grateful to them, and pleased with this part of Devon, with the marriage of land and sea and the dark moorland that brooded behind it.

For the first time in years she breathed in the air of outgoingness, of infinite possibility. There was something for her here. Not on Mount Edgcumbe itself, perhaps, but somewhere about . . . This was where she belonged, where she came from.

'Over there's the Eddystone, and that's the cape Richard Hawkins sailed past on his way to the South Seas, there's where James Cook set off on his circumnavigation and that's where the blasted captains who deserted Benbow were shot . . .'

Ships were packed so thickly abreast in the Hamoaze that the miniature ferry she could see scuttling between them was almost redundant—you could cross by stepping from deck to deck. She wondered which were the prison hulks.

The birdsong around her was answered by the tinny sound of officers being piped on and off their ships. From the height of the Citadel opposite came a bugle call and the tramp of marching boots. She had the impression that everyone in Plymouth could see her where she stood, outlined against a Grecian white folly; certainly she felt that she could see everyone in Plymouth. Was Philippa Dapifer one of those ants?

'And that's Millbay. See the Long Room? Centre of Plymouth social life, the Long Room. There's to be a civic reception on Saturday. Be an honour for the Mayor if you'd come but no need if you prefer to be quiet. I shall attend, of course. Keeps up the town's spirits, that sort of thing.'

If it was a matter of encouraging civic morale, she could do no less, despite her mourning, than to accept.

He was pleased and turned back to the view. 'Funny place to put

the Long Room, same shore as the prison. However, no accountin'
for what the blasted corporation gets up to . . . See those blocks?
Crammed to the gunwales with Frenchies and Yankees.'

She saw them. Row upon row of rectangles, like a child's building bricks scattered in the dust.

He looked down at her as if she'd flinched, which she hadn't.
'Perfectly safe, y'know. We keep 'em well locked up.'

'My goodness,' she said, lazily.

No need at this stage to mention Lieutenant Grayle. Caution
had been driven deep into the bone by her marriage; for the female
to show enthusiasm was to court mockery and disappointment
from the male. She might raise the question of a prison visit later, as
if it did not matter to her one way or the other.

Which, she told herself, it did not.

She took the Admiral's arm and they walked back to the house.

From the look of it, Plymouth's Long Room had been an attempt to
recreate the Assembly Rooms at Bath. It had a ballroom, card
rooms, a tepid bath but, Cotswold stone being unavailable, it had
been built of red brick which, in the Dowager's opinion, meant it
fell short of elegance.

It had a lawn sloping down to the water of Millbay, consequently
presenting a distant glimpse of the prison on one side of the bay and
a barracks on the other. At work or play, Plymouth society liked to
be on the tide's edge and, with the view it gave them straight ahead
of a low sun warming and gilding both sea and grass, the Dowager
tended to agree with them. She wondered if Lieutenant Grayle
could see it from the window of his cell.

Supper was very good, the music so-so.

The various dignitaries and wives introduced to her were what
her experience of corporate entertainments had led her to expect:
hugely pleased with themselves, overlarge, overdressed, accepting
of why she was there—after a bereavement she would naturally
wish to be heartened by a visit to fair Devon—and, as far as she

could judge, unread except for stock market prices or the *Lady's Magazine*.

Following the neglect of the navy during the uneasy peace after the Seven Years' War, hostilities with America had stirred things up again and the town was prospering as never before. The building of new barracks, batteries and blockhouses as well as the necessary enlargement of docks for the influx of shipping was putting money in the corporation's pocket.

A new dock had begun to be built big enough to take American and French prizes and it was rumoured that the King would be coming to Plymouth to see it under construction.

Several of the guests were in the later stages of mourning for young men lost in battle but the Dowager was credited with being as brave as they were in showing those damn Yankees that Plymouth could hold up its head under fire.

She was complimented on it. 'Good of ee to come,' the Mayor said. 'It do encourage us all to see a Pomeroy back in Deb'n.'

'Will you be thinking of settling down yere, your ladyship?' said the Mayor's wife, a lady who made up for shortness of stature by a towering wig.

'Possibly.'

'Where? T'Gallants? I heard the lease was up but they reckoned as it was to be sold.'

'Really?'

'So I heard. Course,'tis your family home, I know . . .'

They were not put off by her unwillingness to be pinned down; property was interesting. 'Ah reckon as ee'd be better off in something modern—my brother-in-law do know of a place in Newton Ferrers, very nice that is. Hear that, chaps? Her ladyship's a-thinkin' of taking over T'Gallants at Babbs Cove. Fallin' down I reckon it is by now. I've said to her as my brother-in-law . . .'

'We shall see,' she said and turned away.

The music began again and, as her semi-mourning excused her at least from dancing, she was able to retire to an empty table at the far end of the room. It was the first time in many months that she had attended a social event and now she was wishing she had not; she found burdensome the noise, the heat from bouncing bodies, the requirement of constant conversation.

She had intended to slip quietly into this countryside for relief from the last twenty-two years in quiet and solitude. It had been unexpected and somewhat distressing to discover that the arrival of a Pomeroy would cause such interest.

'Countess? Lady Stacpoole? Oh, let me sit with you, Ah'm overcome that you'm gracing our poor liddle Long Room.' It was a woman with a headdress of feathers and a large bosom, all quivering.

Without warmth, the Dowager indicated a chair and the woman fell onto it. 'You don't know who I am, do ee?' she said, roguishly. 'I'm Mrs Nicholls, Fanny Nicholls.' She paused, as if waiting for the surprise to sink in.

'How do you do.' A minor official's wife. To be discouraged as soon as possible. Feathers and bosom displayed on public occasions. The lace on the purple dress slightly careworn and with a suspicion of grubbiness. She had the most peculiar eyes, very still, their gaze attaching onto one's own like grappling irons. Above a constantly moving mouth, the effect was disturbing.

'We'm related, you know,' Mrs Nicholls said. 'My maiden name was Pomeroy.'

'Indeed.'

'Oh ye-es. Your ladyship's great-grandaddy and mine were brothers. Jerome Pomeroy was my great-grandaddy.'

'Indeed.' The Dowager appeared unmoved but she was caught. *Great-great-uncle Pomeroy*, well, well. One of those unfortunate scandals occurring in even the best-regulated families.

'Your great-grandad's elder brother, he was. You've heard of him, surely.'

Diana was spared a reply because Mrs Nicholls, in manic chatter, expanded on the story at length while the Dowager dwelt on a more edited version among her own mental archives.

Jerome Pomeroy. The only one of her ancestors for whom

Aymer had shown any admiration, one of the rakes whose debauchery had flourished with the encouragement of Charles II, libertine and poet, a member of the Earl of Rochester's set until, like Rochester's—*and* Aymer, come to think of it—venereal disease had sent him frantic for his soul's salvation, to which end he had joined a sect of self-professed monks in East Anglia and died, raving.

At that point a certain Polly James, actress, had entered the scene, claiming the Pomeroy barony for her infant son on the grounds that Jerome had married her three years before. The hearing in the Court of Arches had proved that, if there had indeed been a marriage, it was of the jump-over-broomstick type of ceremony and, in any case, could not be proved.

Polly and her son were subsequently provided for, sent into oblivion and the title had passed to Jerome's younger brother, Diana's great-grandfather.

'. . . there,'tis wunnerful strange, your ladyship. You and me sitting here so friendly. Both of us Pomeroys. Just think, now, if it had gone the other way, I'd be the ladyship, wouldn't I? And my son over there, he'd be Baron Pomeroy.' She waved a waggish finger. 'I do hope as we're not going to fall out over it.'

'I doubt it.'

The woman's account of their kinship might or might not be true—it very well could be. In either case, it hardly mattered now; since she herself had been an only child, the title had passed to a distant cousin in Surrey and a claim to it could not be resurrected at this late stage.

'Very interesting, Mrs Nicholls. Now, if you will excuse me . . .' She rose to get away from the eyes that were so at odds with the woman's over-jovial manner.

'Oh, but you got to meet my son.' Mrs Nicholls gestured frantically at a man over the other side of the room, watching the dancing.

Diana had already noticed him. Amidst all the gaudiness and glitter, the plainness of his uniform stood out, though it was undoubtedly a uniform—like a naval officer's dress coat but lacking its ornamentation. Without the epaulettes, braiding and the silver binding to the buttonholes, its dark blue cloth seemed to take in light and give none back.

So did the man, which was why the Dowager had noticed him. He was thirtyish, regular-featured, not unhandsome, yet there was an extraordinary non-reflectiveness to him, as if the chatter of the people around him and the music were being sucked into a well. He was alone, even in a crowd.

At his mother's signal, he came towards them without changing his expression.

'Yere, ma dear,' Mrs Nicholls said. 'This is the Countess of Stacpoole—you know who *she* is, don't ee? Your ladyship, this yere's my son, Captain Walter Nicholls. We gave 'un Walter in memory of Sir Walter Pomeroy, him bein' a descendant.'

Captain Nicholls's response to knowledge of who she was puzzled the Dowager. It might have been that of a hunter who had waited all his life for the sight of one particular quarry—yet there was no excitement in it, merely an added, almost relaxing, quietness. Had he been a master of hounds, his so-ho would have been uttered in a whisper, but both dogs and fox would have known it was doomed.

Most disturbing. Did he resent her? No, it wasn't resentment, it was . . . she didn't know what it was and would spend no further time on it.

'Your ladyship.'

'Captain Nicholls.'

The mother prattled on regardless. 'And a fine son, tew, your ladyship, though it's me as says it as shouldn't. Educated and on his way up, aren't ee, Walter? Board of Customs Comptroller for this area, goin' to root out all the dirty smugglers along the coast. And if he dew, the Lord Lieutenant's promised as King George'll give him a knighthood, idden that right, Walter? So us'll soon be back to greatness, won't us, Walter?'

'Mother,' Captain Nicholls said, flatly.

Mrs Nicholls clapped her hands over her mouth, but over them her eyes remained fixed on Diana's. 'An' you'll never guess, Walter, but what her ladyship's thinkin' of returning to T'Gallants, our mootual ancestor's home. Ah,'twill be like Sir Walter Pomeroy come back, like Good Queen Bess's olden times.'

Yes, well. The Dowager bowed and made another move to leave but now it was Captain Nicholls who barred her path.

'T'Gallants?' he asked abruptly. 'You're going to live at Babbs Cove?'

The Inquisition would have had better manners. 'I don't know, Captain Nicholls. Whether I do or not is a matter of concern only to myself.'

'No, it isn't.' He darted his sentences, each as unornamented as his dress, and stared after them into her face, as if to make sure they arrived at their destination before he began another. Somewhere along the line he had discarded the Devonshire accent but his eyes were his mother's. 'I must have your permission to search the house before you take possession.'

'Indeed?' He was mad; they were both mad.

'Yes. I've tried before. The caretaker refuses to let my men in.'

Was this lunacy or total lack of social grace? Either would hamper his rise in his profession, yet, if his mother were telling the truth, the title of comptroller suggested fairly high authority. She suspected obsessive efficiency.

Then she thought: Caretaker?

He jerked out the next sentence. 'And the local magistrate refuses me a warrant.'

There was something childlike in his confession to being thwarted; in anyone else it might have been endearing but nobody, ever, would find this man endearing.

She did not like him; she did not like his mother. Most certainly, she did not want him rootling in her house, whether she occupied it or not. 'If a magistrate refuses his warrant, I fear I must withhold mine,' she said and moved away.

Again he blocked her, presumably to argue, but she was rescued by Admiral Edgcumbe. 'What's this? What's this? We leave business at the door, Nicholls, along with our swords.'

'That gentleman appears to want to search my house,' she said as they walked off.

'He would. Recently been made comptroller for the area. New broom sweepin' clean. Typical blasted Customs. Hard worker, though, always looking for hidden contraband.'

'Really ? Does he think there is some at T'Gallants?'

'There probably is,' the Admiral told her.

'Really?' She was shocked.

'Oh yes,' the Admiral said, without concern. 'Smuggling's the local industry round here. Fishing and smuggling, the two are synonymous.' He patted her hand. 'No need to worry, Diana, your Devonshire smuggler's a rogue but not a dangerous rogue. And he'll be facing a hard time now that Nicholls has been appointed to catch him. A regular ferret, our Nicholls. And out for glory. If he can sweep the coast of smuggling, he'll be well rewarded.'

He sounded regretful. Diana thought he showed extraordinary laxity to a trade she knew by hearsay to be ugly; the Fortescues in Kent, with whom she'd stayed occasionally, gave blood-chilling accounts of smuggling gangs torturing and killing Revenue men sent to round them up. Not, she remembered, that such murders had prevented Lady Fortescue serving tea on which no duty had been paid.

'That's *Kent*,' Admiral Edgcumbe said dismissively when she mentioned it. 'East of England villains. Ugly. Different again from your Devonian or even your Cornish lads. Your West of England smuggler's a fine seaman, d'ye see? Has to sail further to fetch his goods from France.'

The Dowager failed to see how good seamanship necessarily denoted good character, nor how an admiral presently engaged in a war with France could tolerate with such apparent charity fellow-countrymen who traded with the enemy. But Lord Edgcumbe appeared to regard the supply of cheap brandy, Hollands and tobacco as necessary to the country's morale.

That used to be Aymer's attitude, the Dowager remembered—

until he'd became a minister in His Majesty's Government and discovered by how much the Treasury was being welched.

His Majesty's Exchequer had estimated that duty, standing at four shillings per pound, was collected annually on 650,000 pounds of tea. Less happily, it also estimated that the nation's annual consumption of tea was at least 1,500,000 pounds and therefore it was losing nearly three million pounds in uncollected revenue. As for brandy, smugglers could provide it at five shillings a gallon (and make a handsome profit for themselves while doing so) which left honest wine merchants and publicans with the choice of staying honest and paying for legal brandy at eight shillings a gallon or going out of business.

From then on Aymer had advocated drawing and quartering for offenders against the Revenue.

At supper—the second of the night; *how* these people ate—she found herself surrounded by a blue and gold coronal of naval officers who, spurred by the story of Nicholls's attempt to search her house, were a-brim with tales of smugglers and smuggling.

She looked covertly towards their wives, who had formed a separate nosegay of their own, to see if they minded. She must be careful; if she was to settle in this area, she must not outrage its female society. Already she had refused all invitations to dance and was emitting no signals saying she wished to flirt, which she did not. Aymer had knocked such playfulness out of her very early on.

Admiral Edgcumbe, she knew, was merely paying her the attention due to an esteemed guest by a kindly host. The others? Well, she was new on stage and, despite her listlessness and the grey dreariness of her dress, still not totally repulsive.

Her main concern was Captain Luscombe who'd proved most eager to bring her an ice from the supper table, which, since he had been introduced to her as the officer in charge of Millbay Prison, she had graciously allowed him to do. But as the good captain was a fat fiftyish bachelor, susceptible, as she'd learned from Lady Edgcumbe, to anything in petticoats, she didn't think the ladies of Plymouth would begrudge her this minor conquest.

The glance reassured her; the women were serene, they saw her as no threat. Perhaps jealousy was an emotion naval wives could not afford, or was reserved for the unknown women their husbands encountered in other ports. The Admiral and his cronies were being allowed to entertain a newcomer with tales the ladies had heard many times before, while Lady Edgcumbe and *her* cronies indulged in more interesting local gossip. Satisfied, the Dowager inclined her ear to stories related with affectionate shakes of the head more usually awarded to naughty children.

It was a relief that Babbs Cove was not the centre of them.

Babbs Cove? Probably did its share but no more than any other village nearby—*that* privilege was reserved for Cawsand along the coast in Cornwall, *what* a smugglin' nest, its fishermen more familiar with brandy and lace than fish, bold, cunnin' ruffians that they were. Courageous, though; bitter work to sail to and fro from Roscoff and Cherbourg in winter, got to hand it to 'em. And its women just as audacious . . .

'Remember old Granny Gymmer? Crossed the sands regularly carrying bottles of Hollands wrapped in a child's shawl and when the Revenue complimented her on such a nice quiet baby, had the nerve to say: "Ah, but I reckon her do have plenty of spirit in her."'

Amused, Diana asked: 'Why then does Captain Nicholls not devote all his searches to Cawsand if it is so notorious, rather than Babbs Cove?'

'Well, you know these fellows who come from the wrong side of some noble blanket . . .'

Mrs Nicholls, it appeared, had made public property of her son's connection to the Pomeroy name.

'. . . probably thinks the house would have been his had his great-granny been given her rights. Jealous, like all bastards.'

Obviously, Captain Nicholls was not liked. Her informants' antipathy was compounded by his profession. Diana was surprised by their animosity towards an upholder of the law that they had not displayed to the breakers of it. His Majesty's Royal Navy, it seemed, loathed His Majesty's Board of Customs. Excisemen could get prize money and bonuses for a successful capture without leaving the comparative safety of home waters. They were the night-soil collectors of maritime society—necessary but not to be fraternized with. There were other sins . . .

'Limpin' home in *Lancaster* after Quiberon Bay, we were,' the Admiral said, spraying vol-au-vent and resentment, 'just about to enter harbour when up sails a blasted Revenue cutter, flyin' the pennant if you please, and you know and I know that's not allowed 'less they're in pursuit. "Comin' aboard to search for contraband," the 'ciseman says. "You're damn well not," I said. I admit we had a few ankers of brandy in the mess, some trinkets for the ladies and God knows what the crew had stowed away, but fightin' for our country we damn well deserved it. Wasn't going to let some ribbon-flutterin' shore-hugger take it for nothin'. "You sheer off," I told him, "or I'll turn my guns on ye. An' haul that damn pennant down."'

The anecdote and the applause that greeted it provoked a certain sympathy in the Dowager for that particular exciseman and, had he been more likeable, even for Captain Nicholls himself. Both were pursuing their rightful office, after all. Nevertheless, when she looked around to see if the man had overheard, she was unaccountably relieved to find that he and his mother had gone.

It took some doing on her part, but at long last she was able to steer the conversation so that someone, not her, mentioned the prisoners of war. As she'd hoped, the Admiral's memory was pricked.

'By the by, Luscombe, I hear that Howard fella's inspectin' prisons in the area. You lettin' him have a look at Millbay?'

'Thought I might, thought I might,' Captain Luscombe said. 'Fearfully overcrowded at the moment, of course, but their lordships seem keen on it; show the fella how the navy runs things, eh?'

The Dowager was relieved. The name of John Howard had previously been unknown to her, the fame attached to it having sprung up during her incarceration in her husband's sickroom. Only since being with the Edgcumbes had she learned of the man's marvels in uncovering the filth, disease and corruption of common prisons and exposing them to the light of publicity. 'Summoned to the bar of the

House, my dear,' Lady Edgcumbe had told her. 'Thanked for his contribution to humanity, written a book and I don't know what-all.'

She'd been amused to see that the Edgcumbes and their set were no less susceptible to Howard's celebrity and the general excitement that he was in the area than anyone else. Let the incarcerators of thieves, murderers and debtors tremble at his name; the Admiralty was assured he'd find nothing wrong with its treatment of prisoners of war.

'Rather be in Millbay than Newgate any day,' said Lord Edgcumbe, voicing the general opinion. 'Practically wake 'em up with breakfast in bed, don't ee, Luscombe?'

Captain Luscombe was not prepared to go as far as that. 'Haven't the funds I'd like, my lord, and the overcrowding's—'

Lord Edgcumbe overrode him: 'By the by, Lady Edgcumbe was wonderin' if she should bring in some goodies for the prisoners when Howard comes, like she did last year. Show the fella we ain't heartless. Only this mornin' Lady Stacpoole expressed a wish to accompany her, didn't you, your ladyship? Thinks the son of one of her old servants is among the Yankees.'

It had taken considerable and subtle manoeuvring to allow both Lord and Lady Edgcumbe to adopt the idea of a prison visit as their own. At no stage had Diana actually said Martha Grayle was once a servant, she'd merely allowed the Admiral to infer it; her set understood *noblesse oblige* better than some more intimate interest. She rebuked herself; she *was* acting from *noblesse oblige*.

'Servant emigrated to America,' the Admiral went on. 'Wrote to her ladyship—was her boy bein' treated properly by the naughty British? I said you'd produce the lad for her ladyship's inspection. That's all right, ain't it?'

The Dowager shrugged deprecatingly; such a lot of trouble, but if Captain Luscombe would not mind . . .

'Dear lady, of *course*.' Luscombe was delighted; she should see the prison along with the fella Howard and they'd produce the young man for her. What was the name? Grayle, as in Holy, yes, he'd remember that.

There was a little teasing: nice for Luscombe to have someone wanting to get into his prison rather than get out. The ladies joined in with mild anxiety on her behalf—was she strong enough? Very well, then soak her handkerchief in vinegar against infection like Lady Edgcumbe had only last Christmas when she'd delivered warm clothing to Millbay's inmates.

It was done, accepted without amazement. So easy. There had hardly been need for guile. Diana felt warmly for the normality of these people, their openness, and at the same time regret that the years of her marriage had warped her own character away from the straightforward.

I have lived too long with duplicity, she thought.

Then, once more, she thought: *Caretaker?*

Chapter Six

JOHN Beasley appeared at the head of the Prince George's stairs. He'd found a wooden leg and a crutch from somewhere; the first was strapped to his bent left knee inside his breeches, the second tucked under his left armpit. He was defiant. 'Either of you going to help me down these bloody stairs?'

It was Makepeace who guided him down—Sanders was helpless, holding on to the newel post, almost sobbing.

'What you do?' she asked, grimly. 'Trip up a Chelsea Pensioner?'

'I ain't being pressed for you or anybody. The landlord got 'em for me.'

'Fat lot of help you'll be,' she said. But she was touched; she hadn't realized how frightened of impressment he'd been, probably rightly. He was a good friend. Ridiculous, but a good friend. And his grunts as he hopped across the Halfpenny Bridge to Dock—the man on the tollgate was most concerned—made her laugh for the first time in two weeks.

Dock, however, was not amusing. It was vast. Since the first spades dug the first foundations of William III's Royal Dockyard, it had sprouted wet docks, dry docks and slipways around which had sprung up warehouses for rigging, sails and stores, rope-walks and mast-yards, all in turn giving rise to houses for men to run them. It was now bigger than Plymouth, as if a monstrous oedema had outgrown the body on which it was an accretion.

Their landlord had warned them. 'Over two hundred inns, they do say, if so be you can name 'em such.'

From the vantage of the bridge they could see spacious, tree-lined streets but tucked in alleys behind them, like stuffing coming through the back of an otherwise elegant chaise-longue, were lath and plaster tenements spreading in a mazed conglomeration as far as the eye could see.

'Bugger,' Beasley said, looking at it.

It was a landscape Makepeace knew. Her dockside tavern in Boston had been a clean, hospitable model of respectability but it had stood, a Canute-like island, against an encroaching sea of gambling hells, gin parlours, brothels, the tideline of filth that marked every port in the world.

She was well acquainted with Dock without setting foot in it. And she knew something else; her daughter was dead.

Whatever the circumstances, Philippa would have escaped from the wasteland of flesh and spirit that was here. However naive, the girl was intelligent; even penniless she'd have found some official, some charity, to send word to her mother on her behalf.

It was something Makepeace had known from the first but it had taken recognition of this view, this seagulled, mast-prickled, rowdy, ragged-roofed agglomeration of chaos and order, vitality and disease, this other Boston, to drive it into her solar plexus with the force of a mallet.

She kept walking forward, but as an automaton in which the clockwork had yet to run down.

There was a quayside with bollards. Beasley sank onto one, complaining of his knee rubbing raw. Makepeace walked stiffly on, past a pleasant, open-windowed inn and into the mouth of an alley behind it.

Yes, here it was. Her old enemy. Unraked muck, runnels of sewage. A door swung open to spill out an unsteady woman smelling of gin. Further along, some girls in an upper window were shrilly encouraging a man who headed for the door below them, already unbuttoning his fly.

Suppose, argued Makepeace's Puritan upbringing desperately, suppose she's too ashamed, too ruined, to come home?

Howay to that, answered the older Makepeace, she knows I love her regardless . . .

Does she know that? What does she know of me these last years except from the letters I've sent her? What do I know of her, except from the dutiful replies?

She felt a tug on her skirt. A waif, sitting in the gutter, its sex indistinguishable by its rags, reached out a filthy, fine-boned small hand. 'Penny for bub and grub, lady, penny for bub and grub.'

It gave a funny little cough, much like Philippa had always done when she was nervous, so that Makepeace cupped its face in her hands and turned it towards her. Perhaps, perhaps . . .

But, of course, it wasn't Philippa; she'd known it wasn't—the child was far too young. She began to say: 'Have you seen . . . ?' but the sentence she'd repeated and repeated these last days died in her mouth, as this child would die, as Philippa had already died. Her knees folded suddenly and for a moment she crouched in the alley, the fingers of one hand on its cobbles to steady herself.

Andra, I need you now. Take me home, let me hold my little girls and keep them safe forever and ever. I've lost her, Andra. I've lost Philip's child that I never understood because I never understood her. I can't bear the pain on my own. Where are you?

The small beggar watched incuriously as Makepeace dragged herself upright and, fumbling for her handkerchief to wipe off the dirt, found some coins, dropped them into the waiting claw and went back the way she had come.

John Beasley was twisting frantically round on his bollard. Catching sight of her he raised the crutch, pointing with it to an old man sitting on a neighbouring bollard. 'He's seen her. He saw her.'

For a moment she didn't believe him. *Don't let me hope again.* Then she ran forward.

'Tell her,' Beasley said. 'He saw the *Riposte* come in, didn't you? Tell her.'

'That I did,' the old man said.

Boston had these, too: palsied old mariners, more sea water than blood in their veins and nothing to do but watch, with the superciliousness of experts, the comings and goings of other sailors, other ships.

'Saw the prisoners brought ashore, didn't you? June it was. Stood on this very quay, they did. Tell her.' Beasley looked round the stone setts as if Christ's sandalled foot had touched them. 'Same bloody quay.'

'Very same quay,' the old man agreed.

'A girl round about ten or eleven, he says. And a boy.'

'Powder monkey, I reckon. Always tell a powder monkey. Black hands.'

Beasley couldn't wait. He'd heard it already, in slow Devonian. 'They were put to one side while the militia came for the prisoners. An officer told them to wait where they were 'til he'd finished seeing to the men. Nobody paid them attention, did they? And the boy slipped off.'

The old man nodded. 'Diddun want no more o' the navy, I reckon.'

'But what did the girl do? Tell her what the girl did.' In an aside to Makepeace, he said: 'His name's Packer. Able Seaman Packer.'

The old man snickered. 'Like I said, she were wunnerful fond of one of the prisoners. Blackie, he was. Black as the Earl of Hell's weskit. Kept hollerin' to 'un she did and he were hollerin' back.'

'But what did she *do?*' insisted Beasley. 'Tell her what she did.'

'Prisoners was lined up,' Able Seaman Packer said, slowly. 'Job lot, Yankees mostly. Hunnerd or more. Militia got 'em into longboats and made 'em pull down the Narrows, round Stonehouse towards Millbay. And the liddle maid, she ran along the bank after they, far as she could 'til she come to the watter, so then she makes for the bridge, still hollerin' to the nigger, tryin' to follow him, like.'

'But she came back, didn't she?'

A nod. 'She come back. Liddle while later, that was. Girnin' fit to bust.'

'Crying,' translated Beasley. 'She was crying.'

'Wouldn't let her over the bridge, see. Hadn't got a ha'penny, see.' Satisfaction bared teeth like lichened tombstones. 'Right and proper, too. Comin' over here, usin' our bridges for free when a honest man as served his country has to pay.'

'She couldn't pay the halfpenny toll,' Beasley said. 'She was trapped in Dock. She couldn't get in to Plymouth proper. She's here somewhere, don't you see?'

She *was* seeing it. Philippa. No Susan, just Philippa. Who was the black man? Someone who'd been kind to her, perhaps, now being taken away from her. She was running along this very quay, desperate not to lose, among terrifying officialdom, one person who'd shown her humanity.

'What did she do then? Where did she go? Have you seen her since?' begged Makepeace.

Faded little crocodile eyes looked at her briefly but the answer was made to Beasley. 'Didn't see her after that day.'

She fell on her knees to the old man. 'Where would you look? If you were me, where'd you look for her?'

'Been near two month,' he said. Again it was Beasley whom Packer addressed. Makepeace realized that he thought he was talking to a fellow war veteran. If it had been her sitting on the bollard, she'd still be in ignorance. 'If so be she were a maid then, she bain't now.'

She wanted to kill him. *Mind your own business, you old devil*. But if he minded his business, she wouldn't find Philippa. She got out her purse and extracted a guinea from it, waving it like a titbit to a dog.

He took off his cap and laid it casually across his knees. She dropped the guinea into it. 'Please.'

'You come back yere four bells this evening,' he told Beasley, 'you might . . .' He paused, searching for the phrase, and found it triumphantly. '. . . might see something as is to your advantage.'

'If you know something, tell us,' Makepeace pleaded. 'I'll pay whatever you want.'

'Pay us at four bells.' Further than that, he refused to budge. Here was drama to enliven his old age, better than gold; they were to return, the second act must be played out.

Beasley reverted to his accustomed gloom, as if ashamed that he'd shown excitement. Hopping back over the bridge, he said: 'Four bells?'

'Six o'clock,' Makepeace said. 'Second dog watch.' She hadn't run an inn on the edge of the Atlantic for nothing.

Back at the inn, Makepeace forced herself to eat—a matter of fuelling for whatever lay ahead. Beasley urged her to get some sleep and she tried that, too, but kept getting up. She ordered a basket of food in case Philippa should be hungry when they found her.

She knew they wouldn't find her, the old man was playing games with them for the excitement. Then she added a cloak to the basket because Philippa's own clothes would be rags by now.

She buried her child again—what possible advantage could the old bugger on the bollard promise her? Then she put her medicine case into the basket . . . She was worn out by the time they crossed the Halfpenny Bridge again.

The clang for four bells sounding on the anchored ships skipped across the Hamoaze like uncoordinated bouncing pebbles, none quite simultaneous with the others, summoning new watches and releasing the old. The flurry on the river increased as off-duty officers were rowed ashore, hailing their replacements in passing.

It was nearly as hot as it had been at noon; the setts of the quay threw back the heat they had absorbed all day. John Beasley, lowering himself gratefully onto his bollard, rose again sharply as its iron threatened to scorch his backside.

Able Seaman Packer was still on his. Fused to it, Makepeace thought feverishly, like a desiccated mushroom. 'Well?' she demanded.

'Missed 'em,' he said. 'Should've been here earlier.'

'Missed who?'

'The whores.' He nodded to a flotilla of rowing boats with wakes that were diverging outwards as they approached the fleet anchored in the middle of the river. At this distance, they seemed full of gaudy flowers.

'Don't hit him!' John Beasley caught Makepeace's arm before it connected with the old man's head in a haymaker that would have toppled him onto the quay. Balancing awkwardly, he pushed her behind him. 'Tell us, will you, or I'll let her at you. Is our girl on one of those boats?'

'Ain't sayin' now.' Packer's lower lip protruded in a sulk that lasted until Makepeace, still wanting to punch him, was forced to move away.

She watched Beasley pour more of her money into Packer's cap and the old man's need to stay the centre of attention gradually reassert itself.

Beasley hopped over to her. 'She's not in those boats. He says her friend is.'

'What friend?'

'A woman who talked to her the day she landed.'

'He didn't tell us that. He said he hadn't seen her since.'

'No more I haven't,' the old man called; Makepeace's wail had carried.

'He's eking out what he knows, he don't get much of interest,' Beasley said. 'He's lonely. His daughter doesn't let him back in her house until night.'

'I wouldn't let him back in at all.'

'Apologize to him, for Christ's sake, or we won't get anything either.'

Makepeace took a few steps forward and grated out: 'I'm sorry.'

'Should be an' all. I fought for my country.'

'Very noble. Who's this friend?'

'Whore.' The word gave him satisfaction.' Whaw-wer. That's what her's a-doin' out there along o' the others, whorin'. Spreadin' her legs for sailors.'

'And where's my daughter?'

Packer shrugged his shoulders. 'Dunno, do I? *She* knows . . .' A nod towards the ships, a huge and vicious grin. 'Have to wait here for 'un to come back, won't ee?' A pause. 'That's if I decides to tell ee which one she be.'

She couldn't stay near him; it was like being in the power of a beetle, a petty, insignificant thing that, ordinarily, she could have stamped on with all the force of her wealth. And I will, you old bastard, you wait and see. She strode up and down the quay, letting Beasley try to tease out of the man what information was left in him.

It was the time of evening for gathering in taverns before going on to entertainment elsewhere. The inn that faced the quay was full; young officers and midshipmen overflowed its doors, drinking and talking, occasionally commenting on the red-haired woman who passed and repassed them without coquetry. 'A drink, madam?' one of them asked.

She didn't hear.

Beasley pantomimed a request for ale and two tankards were brought out to him and Packer.

Eventually, he hopped over to her. 'There was just this woman. She saw Philippa crying, they talked and went off together. He ain't seen Philippa since but the woman's one of them that goes out to the ships every night. Comes back in the early hours, he says.'

'How'll we know which one?'

'He says we'll know her when we see her.' He added abruptly, because he didn't want to say it: 'He calls her Pocky.'

'The pox,' Makepeace said, dully. 'She's got the pox.'

Beasley shrugged and went off to see if they could hire a room overlooking the quay in which to wait. There wasn't one; Dock was as crowded as Plymouth. 'But he's got a settle on the landing upstairs,' he said, coming back. 'We can wait there for a couple of shillings.'

She put out her hand. 'What'd I do without you?'

He became surly. 'It's my bloody knee I'm thinking about. Rubbed raw.'

A window on the inn's first floor faced south-west and threw light onto a breakneck stair down to the taproom and a corridor with doors leading to bedrooms. It had a wide sill and, below it, a settle that Beasley threw himself onto with a groan.

Makepeace climbed onto the sill, shading her eyes against the lowering sun. Below was the quay, the old man on his bollard, and a view across the Hamoaze to the green hill that was Mount Edgcumbe. The tide was turning and three of the warships were getting ready to make for the open sea; with no wind penetrating the protection afforded by the river's bend, they were having sweeps attached to pull them out.

Usually ships and their manoeuvres were beautiful to her; this evening she saw them as the lethal artefacts they were, off to blow into pieces other ships and men. French? Americans she'd grown up with?

England had been good to her; it had allowed her that magical man, Philip Dapifer, before taking him away again. At the last it had given her happiness with Andra and wealth and employment she loved. Yet it had done so with reluctance; if she hadn't had astounding luck and the ability to fight like a tiger she, too, could have been reduced to somewhere like Dock, struggling not to drown in its filth.

And who would have cared? God knew, this was an uncaring country. With Philip she'd sat at tables loaded with plate worth a king's ransom and listened to conversations in which the poor were derided for being poor, where landowners had boasted of the poachers they'd hung, where magistrates lobbied to have more capital offences added to statute books that already carried over one hundred.

It hadn't occurred to them that they were the culprits, that what they called criminals were ordinary people made desperate by enclosure of what had been common land, by their fences being thrown over, by costly turnpikes on roads they had once used for free.

She had supped with those who made their own grand theft into law and she had walked in the dust thrown up by their carriage wheels with those they used that law against.

Oh no, there'd be no cheers from her as England's ships sailed off to impose the same inequality on her native country. America deserved its freedom, had to have it, would eventually gain it.

She knew that, in the two years since the war began, she had puzzled Andra and Oliver, both of them supporters of the American cause, by her refusal to pin her flag to the mast of her native country.

Yet what freedom had America allowed her, an insignificant tavern-keeper, for rescuing Philip Dapifer from Bostonian patriots trying to kill him merely for being English? For that act of humanity, they'd tarred and feathered her brother and burned her home. Even now she could only hope that it did not cherry-pick which of its citizens were to be free. Would it include Indians, like her old friend, Tantaquidgeon? Negroes like Betty and her son? Are *you* fighting somewhere across that ocean, Josh, my dear, dear boy? For which side?

It wasn't only business that had stopped her from visiting Philippa in America or fetching her back. It was reluctance to return to a country that talked of liberty but had punished her for not falling into line. Oh God, to have patriotism again, certainty of country, right or wrong, like that old bugger on his bollard.

The sun lowered, lighting the underside of sea-going gulls and seeming for a moment to preserve the Hamoaze in amber. The noise in the taproom started on a crescendo to the slam of doors in the corridor as guests departed to their various night activities.

Riding lights began to make reflective twinkles in the water.

Further along the quay, out of her sight, there was a sudden commotion, scuffling, male shouts, female screams. A longboat emerged into view, heading for the fleet; it was difficult to make out in the twilight but it looked as if a sack in the thwarts was putting up a fight.

'What's that?' Beasley asked.

'Press gang, I think,' she told him. 'Your disguise ain't in vain.'

He grunted. After a while he said: 'See, Missus, they don't let most of the crews come ashore. Afraid they'll abscond.'

'I know,' she said.

'Giving 'em women stops 'em getting restive.'

'I know.'

She heard him struggling with straps to ease his cramped knee. 'Think anybody'd notice if I swopped peg-legs?'

Beasley, she knew, was telling her to be sorry for whores, perhaps preparing her for Philippa being one of them. To him they were victims of a vicious society. She had never seen them like that; her Boston Puritanism had left her with a loathing for the trade; she could pity all those forced into criminality by poverty, except those who sold their bodies. Over there, below those sweating decks, women were allowing themselves to be used as sewers, disposing of effluent so that His Majesty's Navy could function more efficiently. If Philippa . . .

Her thoughts veered away and fractured into illogical fury at the husbands who'd deserted her, the one by dying, the other by travelling.

I was always in second place for you, Andra Hedley, wasn't I? The lives of miners were your priority, not me. Finding out about fire-damp, why it blows miners up. I don't *care* why it blows the buggers up, I want you *here*, I want Philippa . . .

Heavy boots on the stairs jerked her to attention. Revellers were coming back from wherever they'd been, talking, breathing alcohol, one or two uttering a tipsy good-night to her as they went to their rooms. It seemed only a moment since they'd been leaving them . . .

She looked out at the view and saw that Packer's bollard was empty, the old man had gone; she'd been asleep.

She trampled Beasley as she scrambled from the window-seat, screaming: 'I fell asleep, we've missed 'em!'

He joined her out on the quay where she was running up and down, hopelessly trying to distinguish the shape of rowing boats against the loom of ships' sides which were casting a shadow from the low, westerly moon.

To keep her sanity there was nothing to do but assume that the prostitutes were still prostituting. She refused to leave the quay in case she fell asleep again and paced up and down, the click of her heels the only sound apart from ripping snores coming from an open window at the inn and the occasional soft cloop of water against the quay wall.

The sky, which at no point had turned totally black, began to take on a velvety blueness.

'I think they're coming,' Beasley said.

A light like a glow-worm had sprung up and was heading for the quay, showing itself, as it came, to be a lantern on a pole in a rowing boat which led a small flotilla of others. It swayed, sometimes reflecting on water, sometimes on the mushrooms that were the hatted heads of women clustered above the thwarts.

'Missus, you're not to pounce on this female,' Beasley said. 'We got to keep her sweet.'

'I don't pounce.'

'Yeah, you do. You're too much for people sometimes, especial other women. You bully 'em. You're an overwhelmer.'

What was he *talking* about? Granted, she had to be forceful or she'd have remained the poverty-pinched wreck left by Dapifer's death. You try coping politely with Newcastle coalers. And other women managed their lives so badly . . .

'You do the talking then,' she snapped.

The leading boat held back, allowing its link-boy to light the quay steps for the others. The sailors who'd done the rowing leaned on their oars, letting their passengers transfer themselves from the rocking boats to the steps.

Beasley positioned himself at the top, holding out his hand to help the women up to the quay. Some took it, some didn't. As they came the link lit their faces from below, distorting their features into those of weary gargoyles.

Makepeace moved back under the eaves of the inn—and not just to allow Beasley free rein but because the harlots repelled her. How can he touch them? Yet why wasn't he questioning them? Which one was he waiting for? The old man had said they'd know which she was, but how?

She teetered in the shadows, wanting to interfere, not wanting to interfere, watching one or two of the women limp off into the alleys. Others waited for their sisters, dully, not speaking, presumably needing light to guide them to the deeper rat-holes.

The last boat was debouching its passengers and still Beasley was merely hauling them up. She could see the tip of the link-pole as it lit the last few up the steps.

That's her. Oh God, that's her.

The link-boy had joined the women on the quay and was guiding them away into the alleys but, as he left, his lantern had illumined one of the faces before it turned away as if light was anathema to it, or it was anathema to light.

Makepeace had seen the damage done by smallpox before but never with the ferocity it had wreaked here. The woman's features might have been formed from cement spattered by fierce rain while still soft. In that brief glimpse, it appeared to be not so much a face as a sponge.

Pocky.

Having helped her onto the quay, Beasley was holding on to the woman's hand. Makepeace heard her say, tiredly: 'Not tonight, my manny. I ain't got a fuck left,' then pause as he shook his head and put his question, politely for him, giving his explanation in a mumble.

The woman's reply carried. 'I never knew she had a mother.' Her voice was surprisingly tuneful, with a lilt to it Makepeace couldn't place.

Mumble, mumble?

'I might do. Or I might not.'

It's going to be money, Makepeace thought. Let her have it, let her have anything, only get me my child back.

It wasn't so simple; Beasley was obviously making offers, the woman temporizing.

The link-boy emerged from wherever he had taken the others, disturbed that he'd left this one behind. He coughed and called: 'Are you coming, Dell?'

At that instant Makepeace's legs urged her to kneel on the stones in gratitude for the moment when God opens his Hand and allows His grace to shower on poor petitioners. Instead they carried her forward, stumbling, so that she could snatch the link-boy to her and rock him back and forth.

After a moment, Philippa's arms went round her mother's neck and she wept. 'I knew you'd come,' she said. 'Oh Ma, I knew you'd find me.'

Beasley looked round the door of Makepeace's bedroom. 'Is she all right?'

'She's asleep.' She had Philippa's grubby little hand in her own. Not once had she let go of it as they'd all hurried away from Dock to the privacy and shelter of the Prince George.

She answered Beasley's unspoken enquiry. 'And she *is* all right.' She might not be able to understand her daughter as other women understood theirs but she was not mistaken on this; Philippa had suffered greatly but her eyes on meeting her mother's, her whole demeanour, declared that her virginity was still intact. 'I reckon we got a lot to thank that woman for.' It occurred to her that she hadn't done it. 'Where is she?'

'Ordering breakfast. Everything on the menu.'

'Give her champagne.'

'She's already ordered it.'

'Good.' Makepeace balled her free hand into a fist. 'John.'

'Yes?'

'Susan's dead.'

It was the one question that had been asked and answered before Philippa's eyes had glazed with exhaustion and remembered terror, at which point Makepeace had tucked her child into bed and soothed her to sleep.

There was a long silence before Beasley said: 'How?'

'Killed when the *Riposte* fired on the *Pilgrim*. It's all I know—it cost her to say that much. We'll find out when she wakes up.'

Beasley nodded and went out.

In the days when Makepeace had shared a house with Susan Brewer in London, she'd wondered if there was . . . well, a something between her two friends. But if there had been, it had come to nothing; Susan was the marrying kind, Beasley was not. Yet Susan had remained unmarried, instead pouring her affection onto her godchild, Philippa.

And Philippa had loved Susan, which was why she'd been allowed to go to America with her.

Everybody loved Susan. Since they'd met on the *Lord Percy* bringing them both to England nearly thirteen years before, she and Makepeace had been fast, if unlikely, friends—Susan so feminine, earning her living in the world of fashion and caring about clothes, everything Makepeace knew she herself was not.

The Lord giveth and the Lord taketh away. You can have Philippa back but I am taking Susan.

And Makepeace wept for the friend who would have been content with the choice.

She lifted the little hand she held in hers to put it against her cheek. Dirty, yes, but the nails were short and perfect. Philippa had always been a neat child and Susan had taught her well.

The male disguise had been effective because of the girl's thinness; she'd grown a little, not much; the pale, plain face was still the image of her father's with its almost clownish melancholy, but where Philip's had been amusing, Philippa's suggested obstinacy. And suffering.

It irked her that she could not read her child. She did not understand Philippa, never had; her teachers said the girl was gifted in mathematics and the businesswoman in Makepeace had been gratified—until Susan had explained that it wasn't shopkeeper mathematics Philippa was gifted in but pure numbers, whatever they were. Nor could Makepeace, who believed in airing her problems, often noisily, be of one mind with someone who would not openly admit to a difficulty until she'd solved it, and sometimes not even then.

Gently, she laid her daughter's hand back on the counterpane. 'We got to do better, you and I.'

The movement disturbed her daughter's sleep. She woke up and Makepeace busied herself fetching breakfast and popping morsels of bread charged with butter and honey into her daughter's mouth, as if she were a baby bird. 'I can feed myself, you know,' Philippa said, but she allowed her mother to keep on doing it. They were preparing themselves.

At last . . .'Now then,' Makepeace said.

There'd been two sea battles. In mid-Atlantic *Lord Percy*, with Philippa and Susan aboard, had encountered the American corvette, *Pilgrim*.

'That wasn't a very big battle,' Philippa said, 'but Captain Strang was killed by the first broadside and *Percy* was holed below the waterline, so she surrendered quickly.'

An Admiralty report from the lips of an eleven-year-old, thought Makepeace.

'And I was glad.'

'Glad?'

'I wasn't glad that Captain Strang was dead, he was a nice man. But the *Pilgrim* was going to take us back to America and I *wanted* to go back. It was Aunt Susan who said we had to get away from the war. I didn't want to, I wanted to stay and fight for freedom.' She darted a look at her mother. 'England's a tyrant.'

Makepeace opened her mouth, then shut it again. 'Go on.'

'And Josh was onboard *Pilgrim*.' Philippa took in her mother's reaction. 'Didn't you know?'

'Josh? In the American navy?'

'Didn't you know?'

'No,' Makepeace said clearly, 'I didn't. How could I? I didn't even know you and Susan had set out for England 'til two weeks ago. The mail's interrupted. Small matter of a war, I guess.'

'Is that why you didn't come for me sooner?'

'Of *course* it was. Did you think I . . .' Makepeace bit her lip, this was no way to resume their relationship. 'So Josh was a sailor on the *Pilgrim*.'

'Able seaman, bless him. He joined to fight England's tyranny.'

'Go on.'

And then, Philippa said—she was trembling—a British ship of the line, the massive *Riposte*, caught up with *Pilgrim* and opened fire with broadsides of fifty-one guns.

Makepeace held the child's hands tight while she relived it, saw the mouth twist to try and find words to express the inexpressible—'noise', 'explosions'—and find them inadequate for the horror of being bombarded, of panic's indignity.

'You can't get away, Mama. We'd been put below deck but . . . we stuffed our cloaks in our ears . . . I was scuttling. Like a rat.' She looked at her mother with her teeth bared. 'Like a rat. Screaming and piddling . . .'

Thank God she's telling me, Makepeace thought, and said: 'Anybody would.'

Philippa shook her head. Anybody hadn't—she had. 'And then, things were breaking. Aunt Susan flung herself on top of me. Everything went dark. Then there were flames and I saw Aunt Susan . . .'

The broken sentences flickered like gunfire on a broken ship, a broken body. Susan staked, like a witch at a crossroads, by a giant splinter through her spine. Susan of the pretty fingernails, Susan . . .'*Green curdles my complexion and I shun it like the plague.*'

Makepeace let go of her daughter's hands and covered her face with her own. What had Susan to do with their filthy war? How could men look at her body, at the child beside it, and not see the obscenity of what they did?

Her voice going high as she tried to control it, Philippa went on. 'Josh found me and got me into a boat. He swam beside it until a crew from the *Riposte* picked us up. They took Josh away then and locked him up with the rest of *Pilgrim*'s survivors. They put me in the care of the ship's doctor.'

Makepeace dried her eyes. 'Were they kind to you?'

'I suppose so. I hated them. They lined the ship's rail and cheered as *Pilgrim* went down and Aunt Susan with her.'

Makepeace said: 'I never had a friend of my own age. When I

met her coming over, she was . . . well bred, not well off but well bred. I was a tavern-keeper, I'd lost everything, or thought I had. Susan dressed me in her own clothes, taught me to walk so your father would notice me. God rest her soul, she was the most generous person I ever knew.'

'She was.'

The noise from the taproom came up through the floorboards into the quiet of the room in waves of increasingly enjoyed hospitality and Makepeace realized that, though she and Philippa had been eating breakfast, it was approaching evening.

She tensed herself for the next round. 'What happened when you landed?'

Philippa, too, gritted her teeth. 'They lined Josh and the other men up on the quay. There was me and a little boy from the *Riposte*, a ship's boy. He didn't like it in the navy. Mr Varney, he was one of *Riposte*'s lieutenants, he told us to stay where we were, somebody would come to dispose of us. I was afraid they'd put me in an orphanage or some terrible place. Jimmy, that's the boy, he didn't like it either. As soon as Mr Varney's back was turned, he ran away, I don't know where.'

For the first time, Philippa started to cry. 'Then . . . then they put Josh and the others in a boat to take them to prison. He'd been shouting, telling me to go to a church and tell them who I was so they'd send for you. He was frightened for me. And I was so frightened for him. The British treat prisoners of war like vermin. They shut them up in prison ships so they die of hunger and smallpox. Everybody in New York knows about the prison ships. I tried to follow him but I didn't have any money and it was . . . horrible. I didn't know what to do, Ma. I just stood and cried.'

Makepeace kissed her. 'I wouldn't have known what to do either.'

'Wouldn't you?' Philippa dried her eyes. 'And then Dell came up and said that once upon a time she'd stood on a quay and cried and nobody had helped her but she wanted to help me. She took me home.'

'What sort of home?' Makepeace asked sharply.

'It's a room above a pawn shop in Splice Alley. She doesn't keep it very clean . . .' Philippa's voice became prim. 'I had to clean it.' She became aware of her mother's tension. 'You needn't look like that, Mama. I know what she does.'

'What?'

'She sells her body to men. She says when you've got nothing else to sell, that's what you have to do.'

'Does she.'

'She didn't bring any men to the room, if that's what you're worrying about. She works the ships.'

Makepeace looked around the inn's bedroom with its lumpy walls and furniture. I am hearing these things from my daughter's lips, she thought. We are having this conversation.

Yet, at least, her diagnosis was being confirmed; her daughter had been kept at one remove from the wretched woman's occupation or she wouldn't be talking about it with this judicial remoteness.

'She's a kind person,' Philippa said, wagging her head at her mother's expression. 'She protected me. She wanted to because I was in danger. I was her good deed. She said I was the brand she plucked from the burning. "Sure, I'll be brandishing you to St Peter at the Gates, and maybe he'll unlock them and let me into Heaven, after all." '

The imitation was startling not just for its exact Irishness nor the affection with which it was done but because gaiety was inherent in the mimicker as well as in the mimicry. Makepeace hadn't, she realized, heard such lightheartedness from her daughter since a brief period at Raby when she and Andra, still only business partners, had been getting ready to dig for coal and Philippa had played with the miners' children.

She was happy then, before I took her away. I thought she deserved better as Sir Philip's daughter. *Better* . . . Dear God, look what better brought her.

'Dell's a child, really,' eleven-year-old Philippa said.

Makepeace couldn't resist saying: 'She's a child who left you waiting all night in a boat while she cavorted with sailors.'

'That was only for the last few nights,' Philippa said, calmly. 'She had to take me with her. Her pimp had just been released from prison and she was afraid to leave me behind in case he put me on the game.'

Makepeace lowered her head into her hands.

'I was gainfully employed most of the time, Mama, truly. I worked for Mrs Pratt in the pawn shop downstairs, calculating the interest charges. She ran a small gaming room at the back as well, and I'd work out odds for her.'

A gambling hell. Was the girl doing this deliberately? Makepeace searched her daughter's face for some sign of provocation but saw only a small, intent camel looking back at her.

'So you earned money,' she said.

'A little. Not much. Mrs Pratt isn't very generous.'

Makepeace gathered herself. Now they came to it. 'Then why didn't you send for me?'

She might as well have taken an axe and cut the bridge between them. The girl's face became dull and sullen.

Makepeace said: 'You were landed here on the seventh of June. I found that out from the Admiralty. *I had to find it out.*' She tried to get her voice back to level pitch. 'That was seven weeks ago. Why didn't you send me a message?'

There was a mumble.

'What?'

'I knew you'd find me eventually.'

'That was luck, not judgement. If it hadn't been for John Beasley I wouldn't have found you at all. Do you know what I went through?'

Tears trickled down Philippa's cheeks but she remained silent— and Makepeace, not usually percipient about her daughter, was vouchsafed a revelation. 'It was a test,' she said, wonderingly. 'You were testing me. Making sure I'd come.'

'You didn't come over to Boston when Betty died.' It was an accusation.

No, she hadn't. The removal of that old woman, the only constant in Philippa's disrupted life, just as she'd been the only constant in Makepeace's, had left a chasm which she should have acknowledged by her presence.

But suddenly she was tired of flagellating herself. 'I was eight months pregnant,' she said. And if it was the wrong thing to say, it was the truth and Philippa could put that in her pipe and smoke it. '*What?*'

Still mumbling, her daughter said: 'And you might have taken me away.'

'*Of course I'd have taken you away!*' Makepeace shrieked. 'I'm picky. I don't like my daughter consorting in back alleys with trollops, kind as they may be.'

'You're forgetting Josh,' the girl shouted back. 'I'm not leaving him.'

Oh, dear Lord. She hadn't forgotten Josh but this talk with her daughter had been like a stoning—rocks thrown at her from all directions; she'd had to dodge them. There'd been so many.

'I smuggle money to him,' Philippa went on. 'In the prison. We go there on Sundays, Dell and I, and we see him sometimes. We're going to help him escape. You can escape from Millbay. Some men have done it.'

'You think I'd leave that boy in prison?' She'd got up now and was walking the room. 'Leave Joshua to rot? Betty'd turn in her grave. Lord, Philippa, what do you . . . ?' She stopped in front of her daughter and leaned down to peer into her eyes. 'Damn me,' she said slowly. 'You think I'm one of the tyrants.'

It came rushing out. 'You're American but you've never been back or sent any money to help the cause of freedom or said anything or, or *anything*.'

'No.' Such a gulf of experience between them, bigger than the Atlantic. 'No, I gave up the cause of freedom when they tarred and feathered your Uncle Aaron. I don't like causes, they hurt people.' She sighed. 'Don't worry about Josh. We'll stay 'til I get him exchanged, or buy him out or something. That's easy. I can cope with that.'

And now it was Philippa grabbing for *her* hand. 'I know you can.' It was an accolade of sorts.

Makepeace left her then and went to find Beasley. He was in his attic, sitting hunched, staring out of the window.

After she'd told him what needed to be told, she said: 'And young Joshua is a prisoner of war in one of the gaols here. We got to get him out.'

Chapter Seven

SINCE the Earl of Stacpoole's philanthropy towards inmates of gaols had been restricted to the dictum 'the bastards should've stayed out', his Countess's only acquaintance with imprisonment had been marriage itself. She was therefore unprepared for the contradictions of Millbay.

As the Edgcumbe carriage, followed by Tobias and a footman in a cart piled high with hampers, approached the prison, her nose was offended. 'How many men does the place hold?'

'Over seven hundred, I believe,' Lady Edgcumbe said, 'and more arriving every day.'

It was a hot, blazingly sunny day and following the prison's high perimeter wall was like encircling a noisome planet. She had an image of being led into labyrinthine tunnels dripping with sewage and wondered why she had gone to such trouble to enter them. Lady Edgcumbe, whose charity had been distributed in darker areas than her own, seemed sanguine enough, however.

Heading for Captain Luscombe's house, they drove into the prison's main gates which were open and along a track that took them once more out of the prison grounds to a lane on the other side. On the way, they passed a compound where boards and stands were being set up as stalls.

'The Sunday market,' Lady Edgcumbe said.

'There's a market? Here?'

'Oh yes. The prisoners make all manner of artefacts in their spare time. It's very popular with the townspeople. One can pick up quite surprising bargains. Why do you smile?'

'My husband would not have approved. I'm not sure I do.'

'But why should they not earn some money?'

'They're given an allowance, I'm told. Why should they make a profit?' Decent treatment need not include indulgence; these men were the enemy after all.

The captain's house was a pleasant Queen Anne building on the other side of a lane from the prison's back entrance. The ladies' carriage had to wait to draw up to the gate because a hackney coach was already blocking the approach and a dispute was in progress between its passenger, a man with a high, carrying voice, and its driver whose deeper grumbling contained words the ladies, being ladies, affected not to hear. Another man, standing back and carrying a large satchel, had the dress and demeanour of a servant who'd witnessed such scenes before.

'I am prepared to pay the fare, my good man,' the passenger was saying. 'But you drove too fast despite my repeated requests for you to go slower. Therefore you deserve no extra emolument. However'—the thin, precise sentences cut like squirted lemon across the driver's complaint—'to show you that it is not being withheld through parsimony, I shall give the present you *would* have had to the next poor person we see. Kindly wait until . . .'

The driver didn't wait. Still grumbling, he whipped up his horses, throwing up a disapproving trail of dust as his coach rocked away down the lane and setting the ladies in the carriage to flapping their fans in an attempt to disperse it.

The passenger was unperturbed and stood where he was, his eyes on the lane's few pedestrians. Spying an elderly woman leading a goat, he went up to her and pressed some coins in her hand, tipped his hat, said, 'God bless you, ma'am,' and turned in to the house, followed by his servant.

'That oddity, I presume,' said Lady Edgcumbe, blinking, 'is our great philanthropist Mr John Howard.'

The Dowager, too, was disappointed. She had expected this supposed Herculean cleaner of Britain's Augean prison stables to be somehow *large*, in attitude if not in body, but John Howard was meagre in both: a thin, spindle-shanked man in the plain coat of a Puritan.

His nod to Lady Edgcumbe and herself was perfunctory and he refused Captain Luscombe's offer of cake and Madeira with an impatient: 'No, I thank you. I prefer to be about God's work at once.' He seemed to be conferring a favour on Millbay by being there at all. When he was told that the two ladies wished to join his tour of inspection, he weighed the matter before nodding. The Dowager wondered, perhaps unworthily, whether if they hadn't been titled they would have been refused.

Behind his back, Lady Edgcumbe caught Lady Stacpoole's eye. 'Trade,' she mouthed. Diana nodded; the man was bourgeois. Furthermore—a phrase of her maid's entered her head—he thought no small beans of himself.

Captain Luscombe was not to accompany them. He explained the arrangement of the prison's day-to-day running which, though he was the overall governor, was in the hands of the army, while guard duty alternated every day between soldiers of the 13th Regular regiment and the local militia. Today was a Regulars' day and they were to be conducted on the inspection by a Sergeant Basham.

After following Luscombe across the lane and through a guarded wicket into the grounds of the prison, the party was handed over to a beefy, blank-faced soldier whose eyes appeared to have been skewered to look permanently to the front.

'Mr Howard's to be shown anything he wishes, Sergeant,' Luscombe said.

'Yes, sir.'

'But perhaps the ladies shouldn't be introduced to the French quarters.'

'No, sir.'

'Are the French so amorous?' asked Lady Edgcumbe, amused.

'Naked, ma'am,' said Sergeant Basham over her head.

'Naked?'

'They gamble,' said Luscombe. 'They wager anything, even their clothes. I'll say this for the Americans, they keep themselves better ordered.'

'All that can be said for them, sir.'

'Sergeant Basham doesn't like the Americans,' explained Luscombe. 'They make his job harder. Very difficult prisoners, Americans. Always riotin' or protestin' or tryin' to escape. Off you go then, Sergeant.'

'Yes, sir.'

It was not at all what she'd expected. The Dowager's first impression was of bleached neatness. Packed earth had turned grey under the heat of the sun, to match surrounding palings and walls. No litter, no trees, not a blade of grass. The prison buildings were grey blocks. She wondered why a scene of such sterility should smell so badly—the place appeared to be empty. Where were the prisoners?

'The Meadow, ma'am,' Basham said. 'It's the exercise yard. We won't be going in.'

'I wish to see it, Sergeant,' Howard snapped.

One by one, the inspection party was allowed to climb the steps of one of the four wooden towers, one on each corner, from which armed guards kept watch over the scene below. When it was the Dowager's turn to view she realized that this was where the prison's stink came from: six or seven hundred men crowded, presumably for hours, in an area which had no sanitation, or none that she could see. 'The Meadow' was a misnomer; so was 'exercise yard'. There was no grass and no room for exercise.

The compound was large but black with bodies as if a swarm of flies had landed on a biscuit. Men pacing the perimeter faced the constant interruption of having to step over the squatting figures of their fellow-prisoners. No shade, no room for sport or games, just clusters of sitting men which, even in that congestion, managed a demarcation between what she supposed—and Sergeant Basham confirmed—were the different nationalities. 'Yankees don't mix with the Frogs, Frogs don't mix with the dagoes,' Basham said, with satisfaction, then pointed to a particularly black group on the far side. 'And nobody don't mix with the niggers, Frog or Yankee.'

It was surprisingly quiet. She hadn't expected to witness exuberance but the dull buzzing that arose from the yard had a menace to it. Not flies, she thought. Hornets ready to swarm. Sergeant Basham, of whom she had formed no high opinion, suddenly appeared as her outnumbered and beleaguered defender. She was glad of him, glad of the guards' muskets, gladder yet to reach the ground and walk away.

Howard's servant, Prole, had produced a slate and chalk from a satchel. The slate had 'Overcrowding' written on it.

The next stop was one of the American dormitories, a long, low building with huge barn doors at either end that today stood open, each guarded by an armed soldier. Sparrows flirted in the rafters and a row of small, high windows threw splashes of sunlight onto a swept earthen floor.

Except for a few men occupying beds that neatly lined each side, it was empty.

Good enough, the Dowager thought it; not unlike her son's old dormitory at Eton, although even at Eton the smell had been somewhat fresher than Millbay's.

She glanced down the row of beds. All the men in them were too old to be Lieutenant Grayle.

'How many sleep in here?' Howard asked.

'Varies, sir,' Basham said.

'I see hooks,' said Howard.

Now he mentioned it, so did the Dowager. Fitted into the wall and pillars, descending in straight lines of three. 'Hammock hooks.' Howard counted them. 'For three hundred and fifty hammocks.' He turned sharply to one of the occupied beds. 'How many men sleep in here, my son?'

The answer was slow in coming; the man in the bed looked at Howard as if the latter were laying on a puppet show for children, it amused him but he was too old for it. It was the same look, the Dowager thought, as Sergeant Basham's; different men, one skeletally thin, the other fat, who, for undoubtedly differing reasons, despised these questioning civilians.

'Like you said.'

Howard nodded. 'Overcrowding again, Prole.'

Prole bent to his slate.

Three hundred and fifty. Howard's question changed the Dowager's perspective; what had seemed a dormitory, quite good enough, became a box. The little high windows were all at once pigeon-holes. At night men slept here in three hammocked tiers, as if a ship cramming on sail were turned on its side. In the Dowager's mind's eye three hundred and fifty mouths gasped for air.

'Inevitable, sir.' Sergeant Basham was volunteering a statement, his eyes fixed on the doors at the far end. 'Prisoners taken daily from American privateers, one hundred to three hundred men a time, sir. Extra prisons being built, sir.'

'Meanwhile these men suffocate.' Howard turned back to the man in the bed. 'Do you receive your due allowance of rations, my son?'

The American's eyes slid towards Sergeant Basham. 'Pay no mind to him,' Howard said, sharply, without looking, 'I'm the one to attend to. Are you fed and clothed according to regulations?'

'What regulations might them be?' The American's hands were linked behind his head to form a pillow. Against the clean, undyed cotton ticking of the mattress, his skin showed dull yellow.

Howard tutted. 'Regulations and Victualling Rates to be displayed in the prisoners' quarters. Make a note, Prole. How else can the men know what they're due, Sergeant?'

Sergeant Basham remained silent, his expression suggesting what he thought the Americans were due.

'You are ill, my son.' Howard's voice lost some of its acidity when addressing the man in the bed. 'Why aren't you in the hospital?'

The American's mouth went into a rictus of a grin. 'You seen the hospital?'

After Howard had prayed over the man—'My God, my God,

give me the victory over all unkindness, through Jesus Christ, our Lord'—the party turned to go.

There was a yell from behind them. 'An' put on your slate it's the first clean bedding we seen in two years.' The American had struggled up on one elbow. With his other hand he was directing a gesture at Sergeant Basham that was new to the Dowager but one she interpreted as impolite and, in the circumstances, rather brave.

The kitchens, their next stop, were not in use: 'It being a Sunday,' Sergeant Basham said, 'and the rations already distributed.'

John Howard, however, rootled in store cupboards until he found a leftover loaf. 'Is this an example of the prisoners' bread? It is very brown.' He sniffed it. 'And the flour is musty.' Scales were produced from Prole's satchel, the loaf was weighed and found to be four ounces short.

'Wouldn't you just hate to be married to him?' Lady Edgcumbe whispered.

By the time they left the kitchens, Prole's slate was full and he'd brought out another.

'Now I will see the Black Hole,' Howard said.

'The what, sir?'

'The Black Hole. The *cachot*. The punishment cell. Don't haver with me, Sergeant, I know there's one here.'

There was. It turned out to be a stone cube fifteen feet square in a compound of its own. A vertical light in each side, like an arrow slit, gave it a medieval air though it was probably the newest building in the prison.

A soldier with musket a-slope stood on guard at its iron-braced door. In response to Sergeant Basham's nod, he leaned the gun carefully against the wall, sorted through the keys of a chatelaine hanging from his belt, unlocked the door and swung it open, quickly picking up his musket again.

Equally quickly, the ladies applied their vinegar handkerchiefs to their noses; heat and stink came roaring out at them like disembodied demons, as if the soldier had unloosed the cover to Hell. The cube held six men and a bucket. Sun from the slits lay across the panting bodies in stripes.

One man turned his head slowly towards the door, then turned it back.

'Water, where's their water?' Howard demanded.

Basham pointed to the bucket.

'Then what do they use for their evacuations?'

Basham shrugged. It appeared to be the floor.

'I insist fresh water be fetched for these men immediately. I shall not leave until it is.'

While it was brought, the two women moved away; to witness such suffering was obscene in itself. 'What have they done?' wailed Lady Edgcumbe.

'Tried to escape, ma'am. Need to be made an example of.'

'How long do they have to stay in there?'

'Forty days, ma'am.'

'And they come out alive?'

'Ain't lost one yet.' Sergeant Basham sounded regretful.

In order to get to its last port of call, the hospital, Howard's party had to cross the main compound where the Sunday market was now well under way. There was a festive feel to it which even the presence of armed guards lounging against the circumference fencing and others watching from turrets did not dispel.

Bunting hung over the entrance gate; some of the prison vendors shouted their wares like professional hucksters; crowds of chattering townspeople haggled over their purchases.

The stalls displayed beautifully carved boxes, horsehair rings, ships in bottles, corn dollies, clogs, drawings, picture frames. One man, presumably ungifted, had laid out what seemed to be his possessions on a groundsheet: a powder horn, a pair of worn shoes and a rather fine brocade waistcoat. A French prisoner was entertaining children by using his long fingers to make shadow pictures of animals on a wall. Another man, a hat at his feet, was playing a flute.

Vendors from outside the prison had been allowed in; there were apple and vegetable stalls, two cows were dispensing milk, a booth selling ale and cider was doing a brisk trade.

It might have been any normal market in any town square anywhere in England.

But Diana Stacpoole, now seeing through John Howard's eyes, was looking at its underbelly. There was desperation. She saw old heads on young shoulders, faces impassive with hopelessness—and a common denominator to these men who came in different heights and colours from different parts of the world: they were all thin. They wore gauntness like a uniform.

A visitor in the smock of a farmer heaved up a piece of earthenware piping lying in a corner with a view to buying it. In the blink of an eye, a nearby prisoner snatched at the crushed and yellowing nettles the pipe had been hiding and tucked them in his shirt.

A dog at that moment running around the compound and being watched by a dozen pairs of hungry eyes was, she felt, taking a risk.

She looked for her companions. Lady Edgcumbe was poring over a stall selling wooden puzzles. Howard was questioning the flute-player whose answers were being recorded on Prole's slate.

She waited until the interrogation was finished and he was walking away, then fell into step beside him.

'I had been led to believe that there were good conditions here,' she said. This was the place the Admiral and her companions at the civic reception had been complacent about. 'Yet these men are starving.'

He was composed. 'It's the contractors, of course, the usual venality—supplying short weight, made shorter by theft by the prison staff. The provision for the men that the government has laid down is generous enough; it is the avarice of subordinates by which such humanity is nullified.'

'What can be done about it?' she asked.

'What I *am* doing.' And, suddenly, he was angry—but at her. 'Lady Stacpoole, do you realize that Millbay has a lower rate of death than many a civilian prison? Despite some of its men being brought in wounded? Do you know that we allow more of our criminals to die of neglect and fever than are executed each year? Do you care? Do you know that even when they have served their sentences many are still kept in their filthy cells because they cannot pay some arbitrary fee to get out? I tell you, by their standards, Millbay is passable. Not good enough, but passable.'

He recovered himself, stopping his fussy little fingers from flickering by clutching them together. 'Yet you are right, there is considerable undernourishment here, and I am concerned about the hospital. The men appear to fear it, preferring to treat their own wounds and illnesses. They allege that the doctor is a drunkard. I am going there now but you may not wish to accompany me—it is likely to be unpleasant.'

Lady Edgcumbe caught them up. 'Where are we going now?'

'The hospital,' the Dowager told her.

Howard said: 'I should point out that my own continuing good health, despite exposure to gaol fever in the hundreds of prisons I have visited, is an immunity given to me by God.' Lesser mortals, they inferred, might not be similarly blessed. 'Temperance and cleanliness are my preservatives.'

'Then let us hope they will be ours as well,' Lady Edgcumbe said, brightly.

But suddenly there was activity; whistles were being blown and guards were marching into the market place, driving the prisoners away from their stalls and back to their barracks. Visitors were being bustled to the exit.

'What is happening, Sergeant?'

'Sounds like a new consignment of prisoners coming in, sir. Afraid that's the end of the inspection.'

'Why?'

'New prisoners being brought in, sir.' Basham was patient.

'So you said. Your orders, however, were to show me what I wished to see. I wish to see the hospital. Until you have other instructions to the contrary, I insist on seeing it.'

Not a man of initiative, Sergeant Basham glanced around for

orders which nobody had the time to give him. They had a brief glimpse of Captain Luscombe pulling on his coat as he hurried down the track that led to the prison gates, brushing away civilians and military who tried to delay him with questions. 'Won't be nice for the ladies, sir.'

'What applies to Mr Howard applies to us, Sergeant,' Lucy Edgcumbe told him.

They followed him as he led the way to a dilapidated cottage on the edge of the prison grounds.

Behind them, the market place was now empty, the last civilian stragglers being ushered out of the gates as a long column of ragged, weary men limped through them, accompanied by marines with muskets, heading them towards the barracks. The Dowager thought of the shelved hammocks in the Americans' quarters and Lady Edgcumbe whispered: 'Where on earth can they go? There is no room.'

Presumably to make it more difficult to transport wounded men to it, the hospital was on the cottage's upper floor, though the downstairs appeared unoccupied and free of furniture.

An upstairs dividing wall had been knocked down to make a ward large enough for a dozen beds. Some of the rubble from the alteration still lay on the floor, and the resultant dust was on everything.

There were only three patients, two of them groaning. The third was manifestly dead. Nobody else was in the room.

Even Sergeant Basham felt this called for an explanation. 'Men only brought in yesterday, sir. Wounded during the capture of their vessel. Attendants must have just left to make the disposal arrangements, sir.'

'Sergeant,' said Howard, quietly, 'go and fetch some people to take this poor fellow away.'

When he'd gone, they waited, unable to help the living men because the dead one transfixed them as if demanding an attention he'd not received in life.

He'd died screaming, head thrown back, jaws open at their widest, legs drawn up. He'd emptied his bowels in dying and flies were clustered on the ordure and on the bandage round the top of his head where the blood showed black. Rigor mortis had set in.

Two warders arrived with the sergeant. As they carried the sheeted, ungainly bundle past the other beds, one of the men struggled to sit up. 'Is he daid, is ol' Billy daid? He'd stopped yellin', I s'posed he was better.' He was a young man. A bandage was wound round the length of one of his legs but left its shattered toes exposed.

Howard went to him. 'Your friend has gone to a better place. Let us pray together, my son.'

The other patient, whose torso was bare, had a large and pus-stained piece of lint on his stomach. Apart from some dirty swabs that lay on the floor to which flies had attached themselves, there was no sign of dressings or medicaments. The open door of the room's only cupboard revealed that it was empty.

Prole's chalk squeaked frantically over his slate.

Again, the suffering men were striped with sunlight, this time coming from a hole in the lath and plaster ceiling. To the end of her days, the Dowager was never to be rid of the memory of light as a form of corporal punishment.

She thought: Did they allow us to see this charnel house because they thought it was *all right?*

Howard finished his prayers and turned to the other bed. Gently, he lifted an edge of the lint on the stomach injury. 'This wound has maggots.'

'Maggots eat the gangrene, sir,' said Sergeant Basham. 'Best thing for it, doctor says.'

'And where is the doctor?'

'Sunday, sir. Don't come in Sundays.'

I don't know what to do, the Dowager thought. We are all standing here like an audience. I am standing here watching this.

'Sergeant,' said Howard quietly, 'I want both these men to be taken to the Royal Hospital in town immediately. I shall go at once to Captain Luscombe to arrange the necessary order but in the meantime you are to fetch two litters and have a cart—with *shade*—standing by.'

'Captain's busy at the moment, sir . . .'

There was a call from below. 'You up there, Joe?'

'Showin' visitors round,' Basham called back with irony.

'Come down here and help with this lot. And Captain Luscombe says the visitors to go back to his house immediate.'

Basham breathed with relief then his tone sharpened: 'Out you go then, ladies and gents. No more to see today.'

'You know who my husband is, Sergeant?' Lady Edgcumbe had stepped forward, very small against Basham's bulk, very deadly.

'Yes, ma'am.'

'Then get some help for these men.'

'Yes'm. Moment we can, ma'am. Now outside, *if* you please.' He swept her and Howard and Prole towards the stairs.

Diana ignored them; she had to do *something*.

The man with the wound in his stomach was delirious and calling for his mother. She wiped his face with her handkerchief and did the same for the other, then, helplessly, she stood between the two beds, waving the air over the man on her left with her fan, the other with her hat.

The boy with the shattered leg managed to grit his teeth against pain long enough to thank her. 'I wish my mammy was here too,' he said.

'Where is she?'

'Maryland, ma'am, Frederick County.' His hands were at his sides, griping the dirty palliasse on which he lay. He was being brave. 'I hurt awful bad, ma'am.'

'They'll have you better soon.'

'Be good.' His round, countryman's face crumpled suddenly. 'I don't want to die. I'm skeered, I don't want to die.'

She leaned over him so he could see her face. 'Then don't. Fight. Your mother would want you to fight.'

The boy stared at her. Perfect white teeth showed in a panting grin. 'She would, wou'n't she?'

A heavy hand landed on her shoulder. 'Out, ma'am, or you'll have to be carried. There's more arrivin'.' Basham had come back for her.

She glanced up at him. 'Get some help . . . *help* them.'

'Out, ma'am.'

He had her arm. She was forced to the top of the stairs and then had to stand back as a litter was carried up and past her, then a smoke-blackened, injured man came by, helped by another, then more, another litter.

'Hold up down there,' Basham called. 'Make way for her ladyship.'

She stepped in blood as she went down.

Outside the cottage, carts had come in, filled with wounded. Guards were heaving those who couldn't walk off the tailboards like sacks of wheat, one to each end, and about as gently.

How will they find room in the cottage for so many?

'Go easy, there, blast you.' Followed by an orderly, a Royal Navy surgeon was going along lines of men who already lay on the ground, stooping over some and muttering. 'These are men, not meat. And someone fetch blankets. And some water.'

'Where's this lot from, sir?' one of the guards asked him, conversationally.

'The *Canaan*. We captured her off Dartmouth this morning. We can cover this one, Peters.'

Evening sun shone on the rows of men with a soft rose light that failed to give any colour to the pallor of their faces. Diana had never imagined such wounds; some had been mercifully bandaged but others . . . there were collops of bloodied skin hanging loose, bits of bone poking through flesh, one man's brains were on show, another's intestines.

One man who seemed uninjured died as she looked at him; she saw the muscles of his face smooth into relaxation, the sun into which he'd been staring reflecting gold in his open eyes. Close his eyes, she thought, somebody close his eyes. As she moved forward to do it, a man lying next to the corpse put up a hand and tugged at her skirt hem. 'Water, ma'am. Please, I need water.'

It might have been a signal, all over the grass men began begging for water. The naval surgeon became angry. 'Get them water, for the love of God. Where are the damn orderlies? Where's the doctor?'

'Don't come in Sundays,' Basham told him.

'Don't come . . . ? Fetch him. I can't manage all this on my own.'

'He'll be drunk,' Basham said indignantly, as if the doctor's insobriety was an urgent appointment.

'Then get another one from the damn town.'

Basham nodded at a guard who went off grumbling: 'I'd give 'em water. I'd've let the buggers drown.'

Water. I must get water. The Dowager looked around; at that moment she'd have sold her soul to see a pump. 'Where is there water?' she called to Basham.

He became aware of her and came up. 'Get me shot, you will. Come along now, there's a good lady.' He tucked her arm firmly under his and led her off towards Captain Luscombe's house.

All the way she begged him to let her take water to the men. It was like walking away from Golgotha; it was against every tenet. *I was thirsty and ye gave me drink.*

They won't let me, God, they won't let me.

'Don't take on now, ma'am,' Basham said. 'We'll see to them.'

'Then in the name of Jesus do it,' she said.

As he left her at the gate of the house, he said: 'They was in *our* waters,'scuse me for saying so, ma'am. Could've been our men wounded.'

Later she was to realize that the point was well made. But she hadn't seen British wounded nor, for that matter, American wounded; she had just seen suffering men being allowed to go on suffering.

In any case—this was when she could think logically—there was an excellent hospital for Royal Navy men in Plymouth; it had been built on Edgcumbe land, and had one of the lowest mortality rates among service hospitals in the country.

But I have seen Millbay's and I am ashamed.

To the Dowager, England's honour and her own were indistinguishable. Her family and Aymer's were the aristocracy and therefore the representatives of their country. Now it was as if the uncaring inhumanity of Millbay had been laid at her door. And she could not bear it.

A footman informed her that Mr Howard and his servant had already gone, Captain Luscombe was overseeing the disposal of the new prisoners and would be back when he could. He showed her into the parlour where Lady Edgcumbe was drinking Luscombe's sherry like medicine. He poured a schooner for Diana and left.

The two women sat and sipped in silence. Lucy got up and poured them more sherry.

The Dowager was remembering the times when Aymer had beaten her, debasing them both. It's the same, she thought. She was being bruised and debased by her own country. It was allowing Plymouth merchants to enrich themselves by cheating the most miserable of beings of their food, while those meant to look after them were complicit in the theft. Injured men were left in the care of absent drunkards unfit to tend pigs.

'We could get up a public subscription,' Lucy Edgcumbe said, after a while. 'Build a decent hospital. Whether people would subscribe for war prisoners, I don't know.'

'They would if they saw what we've just seen.'

'That's it. They don't.'

The smell of honeysuckle came through the parlour's open window, bewildering in its sweetness. Somewhere in a garden hedge a nightingale began its crescendo.

'Mr Howard will surely rouse the public,' Lucy said. 'He was very cross when he left.'

'Good.'

'A giant in his way, I think.'

'Yes,' said the Dowager, and realized it was true. Great Hercules in the guise of an irritating, persistent, pedantic little man. 'Yes, he is.'

And she was ashamed again that Hercules of the Augean stables was a commoner who did not have the same responsibility for cleaning them as the leaders of the nation. Those men she'd seen, those *children*, might be the enemy but her country had made a promise to treat them with decency, if for no better reason than, tit-for-tat, British prisoners of war should receive the same courtesy.

The bargain was not being kept. Her nation, which should be as fastidious in honour as herself, had broken faith.

'Excuse me, your ladyships.' It was the footman. 'But her ladyship expressed a wish to interview one of the prisoners and he's under guard in the garden room, waiting.'

Lieutenant Grayle. Captain Luscombe's order that the boy be produced for her was being obeyed though the sky fell in. She had forgotten—they had all become Martha's sons to her. 'Very well, I shall come.'

This, after all, had been the object of the exercise.

She was led to the back of the house where a small, white-wood room gave on to the garden.

Lieutenant Grayle took up most of it, an enormous figure with his back to the setting sun so that his outline was that of his uncle as she had last seen Martha's brother, like the etching of a Viking outlined in gold. He dwarfed the two guards standing on either side of him.

'You are Lieutenant Forrest Grayle? Of Virginia?' But she knew he was; she had been taken back twenty-seven years.

'Yes, ma'am.' He stared fixedly over her head; he might have been taking lessons from Sergeant Basham.

'I am Lady Stacpoole,' she said, gently, 'I knew your mother a long time ago. She has written to me asking after your welfare. Would you like me to write back to her on your behalf?'

'No, I thank you, ma'am.'

Probably he didn't understand. 'You don't want me to write? I believe I have sources through which a letter could reach her.'

'No, I thank you, ma'am. I don't want you should write to my mother.'

This was hopeless. The sun, which was sending its last rays into her eyes, was hiding his from her. 'May you not sit down?' She indicated a chair.

One of the guards prodded the boy with his musket's butt. 'Sit when the lady asks you.'

As he moved to the chair, she saw that Grayle's arms were at an unnatural angle behind him and she said: 'Are you pinioned?' To the guards: 'Untie him, please.'

'Ain't wise, your ladyship,' one of them said. 'Despite all, he can still make a run for it. Knocked down Sergeant Lewis once and run for the gates.'

'I doubt he will try to escape at the moment.' She turned to Grayle. 'Will you?'

'Not tonight, ma'am.'

'So untie his hands, please.'

There was a guffaw from both guards. 'Can't do that 'zackly, your ladyship,' one of them said while the other fumbled at Grayle's back, releasing his arms from the rope that had imprisoned them. 'Show her your hands, son.'

For a moment, the Dowager thought the boy was going to knock the three of them down; she could almost feel the violence surging up in him. But after a moment his eyes went back to the point above her head and he allowed himself to be pushed round to face the light, the overlong cuffs of his dirty coat turned back by the guards to display what they had hidden. Which was nothing.

Lieutenant Grayle had no hands.

Chapter Eight

ON the first Sunday after the finding of Philippa, she and her mother, Beasley and Dell walked along the Hoe towards Millbay. It was a beautiful, very hot day. Sunday or not, the streets were too crowded with military supplies on their way to the docks to warrant using the coach, whereas the Hoe was a pleasant way to take, arm-in-arm among the strollers, listening to the band.

Both the band and the atmosphere of holiday were having to compete with loud booms coming from two ships of the Western Squadron which were testing their guns on a target out in the sparkling Sound.

Beasley and Makepeace were arguing.

'They won't *do* it,' Beasley said for the third time.

'Of course they will,' Makepeace said. 'If the commander of the prison won't, I'll go higher. I'll get Rockingham to approach the Admiralty and tell them I'll outfit a frigate or something . . .'

That was the extraordinary thing about the Missus, Beasley thought, she doesn't recognize the impossible. 'You can outfit the bloody fleet,' he said, irritably. 'Missus, listen to me—they won't *do* it. They can't. He's not a prisoner of war, he's a rebel, he's been convicted of high treason. It's the law, it's policy. Admit Americans are prisoners of war and you admit America's a sovereign nation, like France. That's the point, it's why England's fighting the goddam war in the first place, to prove it isn't.'

'Oh, hush.'

He'd raised his voice and a clergyman on his way to church turned a scandalized head, tutting. Beasley glared back at him but continued more quietly. 'You'll just draw attention to yourself, which'll give them a nice clue as to who's helping him if and when he manages to escape. They'll pick him up in no time.' He added with gloom: 'And us.'

'*Escape!*' Makepeace said. 'That's typical of you, you can't think of anything less'n it's breaking the law.'

'It was Philippa's idea,' Beasley said sulkily.

'She's a child. It's a child's idea.'

Makepeace felt uplifted, her spirits gliding with the seagulls Philippa had been returned to her—a sign, she felt, that God was relenting and would soon send Andra back too. As for Josh, she would buy him out. She was a wealthy woman and over these past years had become used to procuring what she wanted through money. Money, enough of it, never let you down.

Soon she would be shepherding both her lambs northwards. She imagined the scene as Ginny came running out with the two little girls to greet Josh and their long-lost sister. Oh, and Dell.

She turned her head to where Philippa was walking behind her with the one cloud on her blue horizon.

Dell.

Left to herself, Makepeace would have loaded the prostitute with gold and said good-bye, but Philippa refused to be parted from her. 'I owe her a great deal, Mama, and she wants a new life.'

She ain't having yours, Makepeace thought. She had the sense not to say so; Philippa's attachment to Dell was strong, as was Dell's to Philippa, and there was no doubt she had done a kindness for which she could never properly be repaid. But Makepeace couldn't stand the woman. Not because of her past trade, nor her disfigurement, nor even the admirable, matter-of-fact stoicism with which she bore it. It was her cockiness. In the novels Makepeace had read, a woman shamed acted like a shamed woman; Dell was cheerful.

The outing to Plymouth's shops to buy her and Philippa some decent clothes had been of teeth-clenching embarrassment. With her disfigured face and in a dress that shouted harlotry, Dell attracted attention. Given a choice, she would have dressed herself at Makepeace's expense in exactly the same style. 'I need a low-cut bosom, d'ye see,' she said artlessly, 'it shows I've got *some* decent flesh on me bones.' It was true that her body skin was very fine. 'And a hat now, it must be big to shade me poor face from the sun. Will you look at that one with the roses, isn't it *gorgeous?*'

She was given no choice. In a light blue linen dress over a white flowered petticoat and with a fichu around its neck and hatted by a simple, wide-brimmed leghorn, she looked, to Makepeace's eyes, considerably less alarming. Lovely, Philippa said: 'And isn't she brave?'

Makepeace added a light veil, which Dell accepted graciously because, she said, her pimp would then not notice her if they met in the street.

And her lies. When she'd contracted the illness, where, who had nursed her through it, how she had fallen so low: these events were uncertain because she gave different accounts of them to different people.

It was the same with her history. One day she was descended from the great O'Neill of Ulster, the next from the pirate queen of Connaught, Grace O'Malley. She'd been an actress in Dublin before smallpox ruined her career. No, she'd been a friend to Emily, Duchess of Leinster. She'd been forced to leave Ireland because the Duke had designs on her virtue. No, a scion of the Ascendancy had secretly married her and brought her to England, only to abandon her at the insistence of his family, horrified at his entanglement with a Catholic.

She backed up these claims by acting out her idea of a well-born lady so that the sight of a mouse sent her into hysterics and a pretended faint, a baby into a frenzy of diddumsing. She passed beggars with her nose exaggeratedly in the air and was even capable, if they hadn't noticed, of going back to pass them again.

There was one, and only one, consistency in all the stories. At some point she had stood on an English quayside, penniless and weeping, and, for lack of Christian help, been pulled into a life of sin.

To Philippa, to Beasley, her tales were endearing embroideries on an existence too stark to go unadorned. To Makepeace, who couldn't dissemble to save her life, they were plain lies. She laboured to recompense Dell for keeping Philippa safe, but did it clumsily. When, on the shopping outing, Dell had asked her for some white lead to disguise the damaged face, she'd exclaimed: 'Heavens, no, that'd make it even worse.' She spent extravagantly on safer powders and paints for the woman but in Philippa's eyes they did little to ameliorate the 'even worse'.

She knew she was confirming herself as a tyrant, the political role in which her daughter cast her because she would not take the side of the war that Philippa wanted her to, but the knowledge only meant that, more and more, she conformed to it.

The prison walls, when they reached them, were decorated by wanted posters giving the names and descriptions of escaped prisoners in alarming print.

Whereas these **American Pirates** *of the name of James Bland, Harry Fullerton and Phineas Smith have this month* **unlawfully Absconded** *from Millbay Prison and are* **loose upon the Publick** *to its* **great Danger** *. . .*

Whereas this **American Pirate** *John Hathaway . . .*

'Lord, how many are there?'

' "Ten guineas' reward for information leading to recapture",' read Philippa. 'I wonder where they all are. It shows how easy escape is.'

'I say good luck to 'em,' Beasley said.

'And me,' said Dell. 'Let the poor lads have their freedom, I say.'

Makepeace raised her eyes to heaven. Undoubtedly, the posters suggested that Millbay Prison was as holed as a colander and—she could not help a flush of pride—her countrymen were taking advantage of it, but she held to her plan of procuring Josh's liberty by legal means, if you could call bribery legal. Despite the many times when she had fallen foul of and fought authority, Makepeace was not a natural rebel. Beasley's first choice was to flout the law; hers was not.

At the prison gates, entrance to the Sunday market was being delayed by a team of soldiers which was searching those wishing to go in.

'Shall I send in my card to the commandant?' Makepeace wondered. 'Or see Josh first?' How nice to greet the dear boy with the news that he was to be freed.

'See Josh first.' Beasley was definite, so was Philippa.

They joined the line of people waiting to be searched, and were shoved aside by a heavy-handed guard in order to allow a carriage through. It was driven by a liveried black man and carried two women holding sunshades. It awakened a democratic resentment in those swallowing the dust from its wheels as it went by.

'Haughty, haughty,' somebody said, and an old woman asked querulously of the soldiers: 'Why'n't ee searching them Lady Muck 'n' Mucks along of we?'

'Because they're Lady Muck 'n' Mucks,' a militiaman said. 'Come on, Gammer, let's see what's in that basket.'

When it was Makepeace's turn to be searched, the contents of her basket—intended for Josh—a cut of ham, a cake and a bottle of cider, were confiscated. 'You feeding the prisoners?'

'We was going to sell 'em,' Beasley said, quickly.

'Not here you ain't,' the guard said. 'Need a licence. An' we got to sample 'em, ain't we, Charlie?' He winked. 'Case you're trying to smuggle a file in for one of the Frenchies to saw through his bars. Very susceptible to the Frenchies, the ladies.'

Makepeace glared at Philippa—only fierce argument had stopped her daughter putting a file in the cake.

The market was bigger than she'd expected, and more popular. Already it was becoming crowded. The smell of fruit, fish and meat from the licensed stalls mingled with a stink that seemed to have settled on the prison like a fog. The discordance of flute-players vying with fiddlers and singers afflicted even Makepeace's unmusical ear.

Philippa looked round anxiously. 'He isn't always here. He says they draw lots for which of them can be allowed to sell whatever they've got to sell. If they don't win, they spend the day crammed into a compound.'

Makepeace had tried to learn from her daughter what conditions were like in the prison but Philippa had been unable to tell her anything much. 'Josh says they're "middlin'"' but I think he's being brave. I think they're awful.' However, Makepeace thought her daughter was prejudiced by the accounts of how the British army in America treated its prisoners which, if the half was true, was appallingly. Philippa had heard of huge mortality rates among men kept in prison hulks, of smallpox, hunger, overcrowding, even bayonetings. Whether these were tales merely to increase hatred for the British among American patriots, it was difficult for Makepeace to know. Philippa believed them.

On this evidence, Makepeace thought, Americans and now presumably the French were being more kindly treated in this country—that there was a market at all must surely prove it. Bunting, the calls of hucksters, the music . . . this was a surprisingly festive place. Nor did there seem any animosity towards the enemy from the townspeople who were bartering and buying and enjoying the entertainments as they would at any fairground.

Standing on tiptoe to look around she saw a good sprinkling of black faces among the stall-holders—none of them Josh's—as there were among their customers, presumably the servants of big houses. Navies, American or British, never minded a man's colour as long as he could haul on a rope and press gangs were democratic; they trawled all nationalities so that, as Makepeace knew from her tavern days in Boston, there were some ships of His Majesty's Navy where the only common language on the lower decks was pidgin.

In fact, pressed or volunteered, black men, especially former slaves, usually turned out to be good sailors who could be trusted not to abscond, mainly because shipboard life, hard as it might be, was egalitarian and therefore preferable to the one they'd led on shore.

'I can't see him,' she said, despairingly.

They split up, Beasley and Dell going one way, Makepeace and Philippa another, having to struggle through an increasing crowd.

Then, for Makepeace, it all fell away: the sounds, the people. Josh was there, behind a stall near the wall; she could pick him out of thousands.

She began to move forward quickly but Philippa held her back. 'Don't draw attention to yourself, Ma. You're not supposed to know him. He's just another prisoner.'

Not to me. Never to me. He'd seen her and, oh God, had begun to cry. Josh, who never cried, was weeping. She'd loved him always but never, until that moment, had she known what she meant to him; each incorporated memories of his mother for the other.

She had to walk away so that she didn't run to hold him and tell him it was all right, she was here now. She put her hands over her face and Philippa led her to the shelter of a booth.

'I taught him to read,' Makepeace said, breaking down, 'but he drew like an angel at the age of three.'

'I know, Mama, I know,' Philippa said—and then to a concerned enquirer: 'No, I thank you, she's quite well. A touch of the heat.'

Furiously, Makepeace rubbed at her cheeks. 'Now's a fine time to water the morning glories,' she said, sniffing. 'Let's go and see to my poor boy. Philippa, he's so *thin*.'

'They starve them,' Philippa said.

They pushed their way through the crowd, trying to look insouciant.

Josh's stall was next to that of a woman selling cider from a barrel and doing a brisk trade among the thirsty. She appeared to be on intimate terms with the off-duty militia, two of which were leaning against the wall watching the activity and teasing the woman as they drank. As Makepeace came up, she called out: 'Best cider, ladies. Three ha'pence a cup.'

'Guaranteed apple-free,' one of the militiamen said. 'Rot your socks.' The cider woman gave him a playful push.

Makepeace ignored them. Not looking at Josh, she examined what he was selling: a selection of bric-a-brac and objets d'art made by different hands, some of them dire, some astonishingly clever. She picked up a ship in a bottle. 'How much for this, young man?'

'Shillin', ma'am.' The tears still gleaming on his face could have passed for sweat except that there was not enough fat on his bones to produce any. There was a cut high up on his cheek. She was appalled at how he'd aged; the twenty-year-old skin was unlined, the eyes were those of an old man. But one of them winked at her. 'Good to see a mother and daughter out together, ma'am.'

'Yes,' she said. 'We're staying in the neighbourhood. We're waiting for a young friend to join us.' Under cover of a burst of laughter at the next stall, she whispered: '*You hurt, lamb?*' and nodded at his face.

He shook his head. '*It's nothin'.*' He swallowed. '*Thank God, Missus. Oh, Missus, thank God. I been a-worrying for that girl.*' He raised his voice: 'There's other pieces might interest you, ma'am.' He bent down to pick up something from under the stall and handed it to her.

'What is it? *I'm getting you out. I'm going to the chief man in this place right now.*'

'*They won't . . . You'll make trouble . . .*' In his distress, he attracted the attention of the men at the cider booth. 'No, ma'am, I cain't sell at that price. Ain't worth it.'

One of the militiamen strolled across to them. 'What you selling, Quashee?'

Makepeace looked at the thing in her hand. It was an oval that had been cut from a piece of wood, then planed and treated to hold an ink drawing. It was her old inn, the Roaring Meg, come to life again in monochrome, every detail remembered: the rackety jetty and Tantaquidgeon standing on it, arms folded; a downstairs shutter hanging askew as it always had; a seagull perched on the starboard chimney; Betty flapping a duster from an upstairs window.

'Grew up there,' Josh said, looking at Makepeace. 'Happy times.'

She couldn't speak. She dug the wooden edges of the frame into her hands. Philippa took over. 'It's quite pretty,' she said, primly. 'How much is it?'

Makepeace smelled a sudden whiff of apple, alcohol and bad

teeth as the militiaman peered over her shoulder. 'Who done that?'
he asked. 'Not you, Quashee, I'll warrant. I'll have it.' He called
across to the cider woman: 'It's a picture of some tumbledown ol'
pile, reminds me of my missus.' The cider woman laughed.

'I'm buying it,' said Makepeace.

'Yeah, but I'm havin' it,' the militiaman said.

Josh reached over, took the piece from Makepeace and handed it
to the militiaman. 'Don't matter,' he said, quickly. 'They take the
earnings off us anyways.'

'You shut your mouth,' the militiaman shouted, 'or your black
carcass'll be in the Black Hole.' He was pleased with that, repeating
it as he rejoined the cider-seller with his spoils. 'Black carcass in the
Black Hole.'

Josh shook his head in a warning to Makepeace. He knew her. So
instead of getting a hat pin from her hat and killing the man with it,
she asked him, quietly enough: 'What's your name?'

'What's it to you?'

'I'm going to remember it.'

He was getting angry. 'What's yours?'

Philippa pulled her away. 'Come along, Mama.'

She was led off. 'I can't bear it for him, Pippy.'

'He's bearing it. We've got to.'

They found Beasley at the other end of the market.

'I've been talking to an American captain. I bought his boots.'
He swung the tired-looking bundle he was holding by a piece of
string. 'I was right. There ain't a possibility of exchange. He says
there's a young prisoner here lost both his hands in action and they
won't even exchange him. This captain, I asked him if money would
do it and he said his family had tried—and they're rich as Croesus.
They used diplomatic channels and got hold of Tom Hutchinson
but even he can't and he's—'

'I know who he is.' As Lieutenant-Governor of New England,
Hutchinson had been the most distinguished of the men ruling it
for the Crown and, when hostility to Britain broke out, the most
hated. He was exiled in London now, a friend of royalty. Though

she'd had no use for him when she'd been a patriotic Bostonian, she'd been holding him in mind for using his influence with the King on Josh's behalf.

But if Hutchinson couldn't even get a rich, white American captain released from Millbay, there was no hope for Josh.

'That boy is not staying here,' she said, quietly. 'They're beating him. I saw his face.'

Beasley shrugged. 'Only one way then.'

'Yes.' She sighed at the inevitable but had to face it. 'If they don't want their damn laws broken, they shouldn't make 'em.'

They spent most of the day moving inconspicuously through the crowd, keeping an eye on the cider stall and waiting for the militiamen to leave it. They didn't; they became increasingly drunk to the point where Makepeace decided they could barely see and chanced a foray to Josh's stall on her own. He'd sold very little.

'How much for that ship in the bottle? *Can you escape?*'

He nodded. 'Sixpence. *Me and a friend got a plan.*'

'What is it?'

A hand caught hold of her shoulder. 'Got to go now, lady.' A soldier had a musket pointed at Josh. For one hideous moment she thought they were going to shoot him. *They heard us.* But the man was merely urging him to get in line with other prisoners, ready to be marched to their quarters.

The two drunks at the cider stall were sobering quickly. All over the market place there was commotion as townspeople were herded towards the gates, some of them protesting.

She turned to the soldier who'd told her to leave. 'What's happening?'

'Closing up. We got more prisoners coming in.' He turned away to order the cider woman to shut up shop.

Makepeace made as if to join the crowd edging towards the gates and then dodged back to where Josh was trudging towards the line of other prisoners.

'I'll be back.' Her voice was covered by shouted commands and the banging as trestles were collapsed.

Josh kept walking. 'Don't worry 'bout me. Take Pip home.' He paused. 'Any vittles?'

'They took 'em off us.' She could have cried; he was *hungry*.

The last thing she saw of him before being carried away by the crowd was a guard pushing him with the butt of a musket to make him hurry up.

At the gates they had to stand by as a detachment of marines brought in the new prisoners. They had been marched straight from the docks, their capture so recent that many of the faces were still black from gunsmoke. Only a few had shoes.

There were boos and catcalls from the onlookers as they trudged by, their eyes fixed sullenly ahead. 'Teach you to blow up our lads,' somebody called out. But when the carts carrying the wounded started to come by there was no more booing; the misery contained in them was too great. A man stepped out of the crowd with a handkerchief and gave it to a sailor, one of the few sitting up, who was holding a bloodstained rag to his cheek.

'Have this, son.'

A woman took a punnet of strawberries out of her basket and, for lack of anyone fit enough to take it, placed it on the tailboard between a pair of naked feet. Dell had taken off her fichu and was trying to tie it round a bloodied hand that trailed over the edge of the cart. One of the marines pushed her back into the crowd.

Whether the men were American or French, Makepeace couldn't make out; she didn't know uniforms and few of them had any. Philippa did; she'd had reason to. 'They're American,' she said.

It shouldn't matter, Makepeace thought. They're somebody's sons.

But it mattered, if they were American, that they had lost their liberty in fighting for their country's. I'm proud of them.

She knew her allegiance now.

The business premises of Spettigue and Son, Law Merchants and Land Agents, were old and on a corner of the Barbican, one of a row of Elizabethan houses whose top storeys inclined in Tudor confidentiality to those on the opposite side of the street in front but with windows also facing the harbour on the side.

A bell jangled above the heads of Makepeace and Beasley as they stepped through the door, to which the clerks, sitting and writing at high desks, appeared too busy to pay attention. Instead, an aged footman in a floured wig took their cards and carried them on a tray to a room at the back.

A plump young man appeared in its doorway. 'Delighted, don't ee know.'

Beasley coughed. 'It's about some perishable goods we—'

'Ah,' the young man said, no less delighted. 'Show these good people upstairs, Godsafe.' He smiled at Makepeace. 'Join you in a dash,'f you'll be so good as to wait.'

They followed Godsafe upstairs. 'We wanted to see Mr Spettigue,' Makepeace said.

'That *is* Mr Spettigue, madam.'

'Are you sure?'

'Yes, madam.' The old man was not put out by her incredulity; had probably met it before. 'Old Mr Spettigue as was is no more. This is his son.'

The linenfold panelling of the room into which they were ushered glowed with two hundred years of polish so that in the light coming from its leaded casement they seemed to be encased in the midst of a dark jewel.

They were offered sherry and biscuits on another salver and left alone.

Makepeace glared at Beasley over her glass.

He shrugged. 'Well, that's what I was told. A good man, they said.'

'Huh.'

Once she had reconciled herself to the fact that the only course was to procure Josh's escape, she had turned to Beasley who'd advocated it all along, despite suspecting his motives for doing so.

He was fond of Josh, as she knew; it had been Beasley, recognizing Josh's gift for painting, who'd persuaded Joshua Reynolds to take the boy as a servant-cum-apprentice. It had come to nothing, though that hadn't been Beasley's fault—it was the great man's refusal to allow his many pupils to do more than hack work that had eroded Josh's patience to the point where he'd left him, joining his mother, Susan and Philippa on the boat to America. But sometimes Makepeace wondered whether Beasley was animated by more than just personal concern for the boy. 'You want to spit in the government's eye,' she'd accused him.

'And why not?' He saw no other purpose to government than having its eye spat into.

Still, the escape had to be made. Makepeace's idea was that, somehow, Josh should scale a wall or two, that she'd pick him up in the coach at a prearranged spot and gallop off with him. Beasley had pointed out that this was too naive, not to say dangerous. 'There are guards, woman, patrols. They've got guns. We need expert help.'

Only he could make contact with the sort of people who had it; he was privy to an underworld of which she knew little and wished to know less. It was not so much criminal, though criminals could be found in it, consisting more of the disaffected, dissenters, the dispossessed, anarchists like Beasley himself, liberals for whom the Liberal Party was too Tory, the overtaxed, the underpaid, Catholics, Protestants who fought for Catholic emancipation, anti-slavery campaigners for whom the campaign was too slow, offenders against sexual mores, publishers of sedition and the unpalatable, cartoonists who went too far.

What always amazed Makepeace was that these square pegs for whom the English establishment provided no square holes could recognize each other's discontent, as if they were an order, like the Masons, who identified themselves not with a secret handshake but a sort of occult snarl.

In the search for Philippa, Beasley had looked up the Plymouth chapter of snarlers and, through them, had met English men and women who not only sympathized with the American cause but were prepared to put themselves in jeopardy by advancing it.

Such a one, he'd been secretly advised, was Mr Spettigue of Spettigue and Son, law merchant and land agent.

Yet, having glimpsed the man, Makepeace found difficulty in believing it. 'If that molly's a spy,' she said now, 'I'm a hippopotamus.'

'He's not a spy,' hissed Beasley, as nervous as she was, 'he's a sup-porter of freedom.'

'Not in those breeches, he ain't,' Makepeace said.

And indeed, when the door opened and Mr Spettigue came in— 'Mrs Hedley? Mr Beasley? Wonderful sorry to keep ee waitin''—his walk, which was splay-legged, like a child with knock knees, sug-gested either extreme modishness or restrictive trousering, and probably both. A strong whiff of camellias came in with him.

He was plump and dressed in pink and white, very tight as to sleeves and breeches, very long on lace. He had a lorgnette attached by a ribbon to a buttonhole. His wig was raised so high over its pads at the front that it gave the impression of a large egg balanced on a small egg-cup. He looked like a baby's rattle.

'Wonderful fine day, what?' he said.

He approached a chair opposite theirs and perched himself cau-tiously on its arm—the tightness imposed by the macaroni style required a mainly vertical stance—smiling foolishly and blinking.

Abruptly Beasley got down to business. 'Perishable goods.' It was the password. 'Pastor Thomas told me you could export some for us.'

'Fine man, Pastor Thomas. Said you might be callin'. Perishable goods, eh? Dare say, dare say. One has, ye know. Prob'ly could again. When, if you don't mind one askin'?'

A velvet beauty spot adorned one cheek and he brayed rather than talked, in the exaggerated vowels of an Old Etonian.

'As soon as possible.'

'Taken delivery yet, have you?'

'No.'

'Multiple goods? Or a single item?'

'Look,' Makepeace said, impatiently, 'we want to get an Ameri-can prisoner out of Millbay. Can you help us or not?' She caught

Beasley's look. 'Well, I don't want him reckoning it's turnips we're talking about. It's an escape and either we're going to trust each other or we ain't.'

Beasley apologized. 'Mrs Hedley likes to get things clear.'

'Don't she, though.' Mr Spettigue, who'd rocked a little, regained his equilibrium and look of idiocy. He addressed Makepeace. 'Well, ma'am, not to beat about the old bush, 'fraid we have to leave the prison end of things to the gentlemen concerned. Leapin' over walls, tunnellin', that's up to the inmates, can't help there. Any case, your countrymen seem to do wonderful well without assistance, what?'

So he'd caught her American inflexion when she'd snapped at him. Clever. In Plymouth it passed as a Devonshire accent, which it resembled.

Mr Spettigue, she began to think, was not the fool he looked.

'Where one comes in,' he continued, 'is usually at the next stage, findin' 'em boats for France, puttin' 'em in safe refuges while they wait. That's the difficult bit of the proceedin's. Not easy, if I may say so, what?'

'I've got my own boats up in Newcastle,' Makepeace said, 'and I've got my own coach here.'

'Mmm. Thinkin' of gallopin' the goods up the length of the country, eh?' Mr Spettigue blew out his cheeks like a goldfish. 'Not sayin' it can't be done but . . . well, we've lost a fair few consignments on coaches. All the stoppages, d'ye see. Militia checkpoints, inns, turnpikes. Dangerous. Long way to Newcastle. Get him to France, my advice. Nearer, safer.'

'I'll buy a boat down here then. Put my boy in it and shove him off.'

Mr Spettigue hummed again, 'Mmm. Few flaws, though. Need a crew for one thing. An' somewhere to stay a while if the wind don't suit.' He shook his ridiculous head sadly. 'Which it invariably don't.'

'What then?' She was beginning to score her hands up and down over her knees.

Mr Spettigue looked in pain at the stretching muslin of her skirt.

'Don't distress yourself, dear lady. Got more up our sleeves than our elbows, what? Now then, refuge, refuge. What do we have? Not easy, this.'

He got up and tottered to the window, opening it to look out, as if the view was a ledger containing details of escapers' hiding places. Immediately, the beautiful room was filled with noise from the harbour's fish market below and, further away, the gunfire of practising cannon. Midway between the two sounds, one high, one deep, came the tolling of a bell.

'If that ain't a coincidence,' Mr Spettigue said. 'Hear that?'

'What is it?'

'That, dear lady, is Millbay Prison's alarm bell signallin' another escape.' He wagged his head. 'Tut, tut, this goes on the place'll be empty.'

'You mean somebody's just escaped?' Beasley asked.

'Just *discovered* somebody's escaped. Roll call, d'ye see. Poor Captain Luscombe—that's the prison commander. Not efficient. Nice man.' He turned back. 'An' poor me, if I may say so. More perishable goods to be dealt with, I expect, what?'

'How do they hear about you?' Makepeace asked.

Mr Spettigue waved his scented, plump hands vaguely. 'Word gets around, don't ye know. And, of course, one ain't the only perishable goods merchant in the county, though I have to say most of one's refuges have already got some American or another champin' to get home.'

He looked back out at his panoramic ledger. 'There is a place,' he said. 'Owner recently died and one's expectin' the new owner to want to sell.' He glanced back at them, slyly. 'One's been usin' it for other business purposes. Big house. On the sea. Bracing and all that.'

He came back to the arm of his chair, beaming and blinking and looking for all the world, Makepeace thought, like a toddler expecting praise for having used a chamber pot. 'Does one gather that cost ain't a stumblin' block, Mrs Hedley?'

'No, it isn't.'

'There y'are then. Suggest you put in an offer to buy. Always sell again. Might buy it myself then, would have done already if Mrs Spettigue and the children weren't so settled out at Plympton. Bit further along the coast than one would like but ideal in other respects.'

Makepeace was still trying to envisage Mr Spettigue as a family man. 'I've got a house,' she said. In fact, she had three. 'I don't want another. We're staying at the Prince George, I want this business done with.'

'Dare say you do, ma'am, dare say. But while our American friends might appear to be poppin' out of Millbay like rabbits, one's informed it takes plannin'. Guards ain't too amenable an' every escape puts 'em on their mettle. Might be some time before they're lax enough to allow another.' He shook a finger at her. 'My advice: keep a room at the inn but buy the house. Remote, I grant you, but that's all to the good, and the crossin' to France is guaranteed.'

She was deeply disappointed; she had expected some *deus ex machina* who would spirit Josh out of Millbay immediately so that she could take him home.

Mr Spettigue, encouraging her, said: 'Bein' a house-owner gives one validity for loiterin' around, d'ye see. Avoids suspicion if one has to be here any length of time.'

She nodded, reluctantly. Makepeace was a realist; all the gains in her life had involved time and difficulty. Here was another. But she was coming round to Mr Spettigue; if he regarded a journey to Newcastle as too dangerous then it probably was—there was no point in consulting an expert on something as vital as this if one refused his advice.

'This crossing to France,' she said. 'Who does that?'

'House commands a fishing village,' Mr Spettigue said.

'Smugglers?'

Mr Spettigue fluttered his fingers deprecatingly. 'Shall we say that certain of the fishermen co-operate with one in the export an' import trade.'

Andra, she thought, I could get Andra back.

'Can they bring people back from France as well as take them?'

'Depends, ma'am. We ain't in the business of importin' French spies.'

She said, gently: 'This man ain't a spy. He's my husband. He's been trapped over there by the war.'

'Dare say, then. Dare say.'

Mr Spettigue's scheme was becoming more attractive by the minute. She considered it while the men watched her.

They could not stay at the Prince George much longer; its landlord was already beginning to wonder why, now that Philippa had been found, they were staying on at all. The idea of moving from inn to inn was not pleasing and, in any case, would attract comment—with Sanders they made an odd quintet, and publicans chattered to other publicans, she knew; she'd been one. Last of all, if she had to live in close confinement with Dell much longer, she would go mad.

She made up her mind. 'Make the offer, Mr Spettigue.'

Before they left, she asked him: 'Have you ever been to America?' He intrigued her; she couldn't place him. By the lights of English society he was aiding the enemy. He wasn't doing it for financial reasons; apart from the commission he might or might not receive from the sale of the house—if it came to a sale—he was taking no money.

'No, ma'am. Like to one day, but no.'

She wondered what sober Boston would make of pink pantaloons. She had to ask him straight out. 'Why are you doing this, Mr Spettigue?'

'Oh, well, d'ye see.' Vaguely, he waved the lorgnette. 'Liberty and all that . . . wonderful idea, what?'

Chapter Nine

THE public subscription for the Millbay hospital was posted with the names of the Dowager Countess of Stacpoole and John Howard, though without that of Lady Edgcumbe whose suggestion it had been.

She was embarrassed and apologetic. 'But the Admiral feels it might carry a political nuance, and in his position . . .'

'I understand,' Diana said, relieved that as a widow she was a free agent. 'Aymer would turn in his grave, I fear. He didn't even approve of prison for Americans but would have hanged them all.'

'Yes.' Lucy was still uneasy. 'How do you think dear Robert will feel? His position with the King . . .'

'I am doing this for the King,' the Dowager said, firmly, and she truly believed that in part she was. England's, and therefore the Crown's, honour should not be besmirched by inhumanity—the sights inside and outside the Millbay cottage still haunted her dreams. If Parliament could not afford to build a decent hospital for wounded prisoners, then somebody must.

She framed the preface to the subscription accordingly and with a nod to the Admiralty's difficulties: 'Whereas allotment of monies is of necessity used up in the prosecution of the war, we appeal to the public . . .'

It was lodged in banks in Plymouth and Exeter and sent by mail coach to the Dowager's own bank, Coutts and Co., in London.

The response was immediate, both good and bad. Money

flowed in from those whose compassion extended beyond England's shores and criticism from those whose did not. A great deal of the latter came from Aymer's friends, as well as some of her own; she was bombarded with letters expressing disappointment, even shock, at what was regarded as her lack of patriotism. All their opprobrium was heaped on the head of the Dowager and not that of her co-signatory: John Howard was of a class that the aristocracy expected to be a nuisance whereas Lady Stacpoole, one of their own, should know better.

'Lady Aylesbury deprecates my willingness to side with the enemy,' she told Lucy, 'and is sad to inform me that the Attorney-General has called me a traitor. How am I a traitor?'

'I shouldn't worry about that. Loughborough still defends burning women murderers at the stake,' Lucy said.

Other letters told Diana that if she wished to do good there were better causes to which her energy should be applied at home: foundlings, slavery, child chimney-sweeps—an endless list.

But I have been presented with this one, she thought. Those charities already had organized support; the wounded war prisoners had none.

The letter that most disturbed her came from Robert.

Judge my horror but yesterday when His Majesty addressed me in harsh terms. 'See to your mother, Stacpoole, she begs money for pirates.' This, from the lips of the King! I was loth to believe my humiliation caused at the hand of a parent and fear you have fallen among ill-advisers and told His Majesty so. He was so good as to advise me to part you from them. Thereto, as head of the family, I must ask for your return to Chantries that we can see your allowance better spent than in succouring rebels.

The last sentence made her angry. The fifty pounds with which she had headed the subscription—feeling it could be no less—had been from the sale of a very fine emerald necklace and earrings left to her by the Torbay aunt. All her other jewellery must eventually pass to Alice but the emeralds she had regarded as her own.

Robert had not only limited her income but was telling her how to spend it.

Then she read the letter again and recognized panic. Poor Robert, who had always marched in step to the King's tune, to find his mother breaking ranks . . . it was a shock for him.

Perhaps I should have warned him, but a letter in much the same vein would only have arrived for her sooner. Nor would she have obeyed it; she had no intention of obeying this one. Royalty was above criticism but there were times when it had to be stood up to for its own good.

There was no turning back. It had been unbearable to discover that the boy from Frederick County who'd wanted his mother had died three days later, still lying on a dirty mattress in the cottage's upstairs room and still, as far as she could discover, with his wounds untreated. And what of young Lieutenant Grayle, both his hands cut off in battle yet incarcerated, to England's eternal disgrace?

She wrote to Robert giving these reasons for the subscription, asking him to explain them to King George, and made no mention of returning to Chantries. She had put her hand to the plough and would not stop until she saw some yield from her efforts.

What worried her was the implied suggestion in Robert's letter that both he and the King blamed the Edgcumbes for leading her astray.

Again, she was angry. Did they think she had no will of her own? But she was also concerned; it would harm the Admiral's career to offend the King; no wonder he had forbidden his wife to be a signatory to the subscription. If she was to be a source of offence, she must remove herself from under the Edgcumbes' hospitable roof before she offended further.

It was a peculiar sensation for her to find herself at odds with the very society to which she had always conformed, whose mores and beliefs had been her own. She could have wished the revelation to have been vouchsafed to someone else. But it hadn't. When she had been forced to walk away from men pleading for water, she had heard the voice of her Saviour begging for help. She would not have described herself as a particularly devout woman but she knew that if she continued to ignore such a summons she would be doing violence to her immortal soul.

If she was frightened—and she was—she was also invigorated, like an explorer on a peak looking out on the unknown. After twenty-two years as the Countess of Stacpoole, years of being curbed, of self-abnegation and compliance to one man's will, she would be free of any rein.

It was time to see what stuff Diana Pomeroy was made of. Time to move on. Time to set up house by herself and on her own ancestral territory.

Time for T'Gallants.

The upper room of the offices of Spettigue and Son was respectable, old and well kept, exactly what the Dowager Countess of Stacpoole had expected from a firm of land agents who had managed the Pomeroys' Devon property to advantage for four generations.

Young Mr Spettigue was not. He favoured an imbecilic simper and a tight coat of lime-green and white—unwisely, the Dowager felt, in view of his figure.

'Wonderful happy to meet y'ladyship at long last, don't ee know, an' had ye told me of your intention earlier, I should, of course, have given notice to the tenants but as it is I doubt it will be possible for you to move in until the lease is—'

She fixed him with a look from under her lashes. 'The lease is up, Mr Spettigue. One studied the accounts before one came to Devon.'

'Ah, well . . .'

'And to which tenants do you refer, Mr Spettigue?'

Mr Spettigue wandered across the room to consult a ledger. 'Mr and Mrs Davis, don't ye know.'

'I think you will find they are no longer in occupation at T'Gallants House.' The Dowager had also been making enquiries locally.

'Really?' Mr Spettigue assumed surprise. 'Mr Davis did not inform me he was leavin'.'

'Probably because he was dead,' the Dowager said. 'His widow lives in Exmouth and has done these five years.'

'Ye don't say?' Mr Spettigue's face took on a look of complete vacuity. 'Wonderful odd, that.' He waddled back to the arm of the chair and perched himself back on it carefully.

'The wonderful oddness, Mr Spettigue, arises from the fact that the Stacpoole estate has been receiving rent for T'Gallants House all this time—without tenants to pay it.'

'Ah.'

'However, there seems to be a caretaker.'

'Ah.' Mr Spettigue attached his lorgnette to his nose and returned to his ledger.

She allowed him some rope and then said: 'Do sit down, Mr Spettigue. You fatigue me.'

With the utmost concentration, he lowered himself into the chair and gave a neighing noise which she took to be a laugh. 'No harm done, don't ye know. Blame's ours but so's the loss. Inefficient of us, very.' He wobbled his head amiably. 'Tell the truth, not a house your ladyship wants to bother with. Rent apart, that is.'

The Dowager yawned, tapping her fan gently against her mouth. 'I intend to look over the property today, if you will be so good as to fetch me the keys.'

'*Today?* Want to live there, d'ye mean?'

She raised an eyebrow. 'Is there any reason that I should not?'

Mr Spettigue's cheeks blew in and out. 'But . . . well, got the distinct impression from his lordship it was to be sold when the lease came up.'

'His lordship is dead, Mr Spettigue.' How typical of Aymer to decide that her family home, which she had brought with her into the marriage, should be sold without consulting her.

'Hardly fit . . . awful place . . . exposed to the elements and all that . . .'

'I shall judge for myself, Mr Spettigue.'

He burbled on. 'Damp, d'ye see, an' nobody worth knowin' for miles, an'—'

'The *keys*, Mr Spettigue.'

He was a long time fetching them.

The Dowager allowed her gaze to wander while she considered. From the carved chair in which she sat, she could just see the sails of Plymouth's fishing fleet, brown and yellow and dark red, giving a Venetian look to the sunlit quay of the Barbican.

No land agent, not even this inane young man, could possibly have overlooked the fact that his firm was paying rent for a property to its owner on behalf of tenants who were not there—and hadn't been there for five years. *Ergo*, Mr Spettigue was making a profit out of T'Gallants by some other means. And the means which suggested itself—Diana looked out again at the fishing boats—was smuggling.

She sighed. The unpleasant Captain Nicholls was correct.

By rights, she should allow him his search. She was reluctant to do so; she had not taken to Captain Nicholls, while the ridiculous Mr Spettigue, for all his deception, was of good class and not unlikeable. And he had not actually bilked her; the rent for T'Gallants had been a good one and paid regularly.

She decided to wait and see what transpired this afternoon when she visited the place. After all, there might be some other explanation. And she would be in no danger; she would have the navy with her—the Admiral was allowing her the use of his barge.

Mr Spettigue returned, flustered and teetering on his heels like an unsteady blancmange. 'Been lookin' for the spares, y'ladyship. Original keys, well, fact is, only yesterday gave 'em to a lady who wanted to view, possible purchaser, d'ye see?'

Now she was cross. 'Mr Spettigue, do I understand that you have put T'Gallants up for sale? And have now sent some personage to view it?'

'Misunderstandin', I'm afraid. One gathered from his lordship . . . when the lease was up—'

'His lordship is *dead*, Mr Spettigue.' The Dowager rose. 'If there is any more difficulty over this house, you may wish that you had joined him. Good-day.'

Once he'd handed the Dowager into her carriage, Mr Spettigue summoned his footman. 'Need to send a message to Mrs Hedley at the George, stop her goin' to Babbs Cove.'

'I think she's gone, sir,' Godsafe told him. 'She was in a coach. She called in earlier to ask for instructions how to get there.'

'Ah,' said Mr Spettigue, weakly. 'Should be an interestin' encounter. Ever seen Greek meet Greek, Godsafe?'

'No, sir.'

'Don't, my advice. Get caught in the crossfire.'

'The barge will be at the water steps in an hour,' Lady Edgcumbe said. 'I don't know why they call them barges when they have sail. The Admiral wishes you bon voyage and says there's a nice offshore breeze that should take you there and back at speed.' She made a face. 'I know these offshore breezes, they mean *tilt*. I would come with you but I am invariably ill, I hope your stomach is stronger. Poor Joan, I imagine you will take her with you.'

'Joan is a hardened sailor, like all Devonians. Whether the same can be said of Tobias, I don't know, but I shall take him too. He will have to act as my steward if we move in and I trust his judgement. This is most kind of the Admiral—I gather that to go by road takes considerably longer.'

'An age. There's the coast path, of course, but . . . Oh, my dear, I forgot—Captain Nicholls has called on you. With his mother.' Lady Edgcumbe rolled her eyes. 'Where did you put them, Hill?'

'In the *second* drawing room, your ladyship.' Hill placed visitors by his assessment of their status.

It wasn't the Grand Salon or the Gallery or *the* Drawing Room, but nevertheless Hill's allotment to the Nicholls was beautiful, like all the Mount Edgcumbe rooms. Against its eggshell-blue and white simplicity, the stark uniform of Captain Nicholls showed up to advantage, his mother's flowered sack dress of mauve and red somewhat less so. Today Mrs Nicholls had opted for the pastoral effect and, to that end, had added an apron—ill-advisedly in the Dowager's opinion. Not so much a milkmaid as a washerwoman, she thought, and then chided herself for lack of charity.

'Oh, Countess, your dearr ladyship, I wonder . . . may I? . . . What do ee think, Walter? Dare I address her ladyship as "cousin"?'

'No.'

The Dowager was grateful to him; he'd precluded her from the same reply. Cousin, indeed.

Mrs Nicholls was not put out. 'We'm here on two errands, in't we, Walter? Foremost to say how we do admire your ladyship on being so brave about the hospital and those poor men. There's not many as care about prisoners, but I be one of those that feels for all wounded creatures. Yere, my dearr, and God bless ee.'

Some coins in a piece of paper were pressed into the Dowager's hand.

'Only a few shillin' 'tis,' Mrs Nicholls said, her blank eyes engaging Diana's, 'but our Lord do account the widow's mite same as the rich man's gold. Now then, Walter, tell her ladyship what you be about.'

His brusqueness was a relief, though apparently he was making an effort towards sociability. 'My mother tells me I was rude the other night, ma'am for which I apologize. My work places a strain on my temper.'

'Wunnerful work 'tis, though. He'll be knighted for 'un, won't ee, Walter?'

'There is no need for an apology, Captain Nicholls. I quite understand, and now if you will excuse me—'

'A moment.' It was a command and stopped the Dowager in her edge towards the door. 'I have not yet stated my business. I understand that T'Gallants is for sale, in which case I should like to buy it.'

Mrs Nicholls broke in with the ornamentation: 'He can meet a fair price, can't ee, Walter? Earnin' good money now. And wouldn't us all rejoice if the Pomeroy strain was back where it do belong.'

'Captain Nicholls, Mrs Nicholls,' the Dowager said, 'I am at a loss to know how the rumour got about that T'Gallants is for sale. I can only assure you that it is false.'

'You goin' to live there, then?' It was Mrs Nicholls who asked, but the disappointment of them both was alarming and Diana was aware that its intensity in the son was greater than the mother's.

'You must excuse me,' she said and left the room, beckoning for Hill to show them out.

Lucy Edgcumbe accompanied her to the water steps. 'Goodness gracious. I suppose he feels that to live in T'Gallants would be to regain the status of which bastardy robbed him. How peculiar these people are.'

'Yes. One thinks it's the mother but he's the moving force. It matters to him.'

'Hmm, I should not like to matter to our Captain Nicholls—look how he hounds the poor smugglers. Do you know that he *shot* a Cawsand man the other night? Killed him dead, poor fellow, and for a few bolts of lace. One supposes it's his duty but there's something horrid in the zeal with which he pursues it. My dear, don't look alarmed, he can't pursue *you*.'

'No.'

But looking back at Mount Edgcumbe as the Admiral's barge took her away from it, she saw two figures standing on the edge of the deer park, watching her go—and wished that she had not.

Chapter Ten

'WHERE is this village?'

'Only a few miles along the coast, Spettigue said.'

'We've gone more than a few miles.' Makepeace put her head out of the coach window. 'Hold up, Peter.'

The coach bumped to a halt and Makepeace got out into a blessed, bird-filled, sun-warmed quiet. She scrambled up beside the coachman to get a view over the lane's high hedges. 'Where are we?'

'Somewhere in the South Hams of Devon, Missus, danged if I know where.'

They were high up on one hill among many that had been left to sheep. In the distance to their left was the even higher sweep of moorland. The air was scented with yarrow and fern. Bees crawled into toadflax flowers along the roadside with a lazy repleteness. There was not a human being in sight, not a cottage, not a church spire. No sea, either.

'We're supposed to be on the coast.'

'You tell that to this danged sheep-track, Missus.'

It must be that tiny lanes left the seashore and then wound for miles to reach the road they were on, like tributaries flowing upwards into a river. Spettigue had said the coastal villages were connected more directly to each other by a path along the cliffs, but for the uninitiated the only route to them was by this meandering detour.

Sanders said: 'We'll see a signpost to this Babbs Cove sooner or later, maybe, but danged if I know when.'

'Should've gone by boat,' Makepeace grumbled.

'Quicker,' Sanders agreed.

But as she got back into the coach Makepeace thought that as a place to hide an escaped prisoner, Babbs Cove, if they ever found it, would be ideal. True, the journey to it would be risky, but they might be able to smuggle Josh along the coast path. There was such a general shortage of men, so many having gone to the war, and others being employed in the harvest, that few could be spared for catching runaway prisoners. Even going by road, as they were now, they had encountered no checks—despite the fact that during the previous night Millbay's great alarm bell had woken her up, tolling for another escape.

There hadn't even been a turnpike. Not that the way couldn't have done with being improved by profit from a turnpike, for its surface was dreadful. But travelling along it had proved one thing: they were in deep and largely uninhabited countryside with a thousand hiding places.

She was still not entirely convinced that she needed to buy a house here; surely Josh could be spirited away more quickly than Spettigue had suggested? She would try to talk to him at the next Sunday market and plan something. However, if she did need to, a property in this countryside, empty as it was, even more deserted as it must be by night, would be the one to buy.

Oliver's letter in return for hers telling him that Philippa was safe had been reassuring but made her homesick at the same time. The business was doing well—she read between the lines that he was enjoying his autonomy over it. He had arranged for her Newcastle bank to send an order to one in Plymouth so that she could draw money on it, so she wasn't going to be short of cash. But his account of her daughters, while it assured her they were flourishing and not missing her too badly, had made her anguished to see them. Jenny, the serious one, was learning her letters and showing every sign of becoming a scholar; Sally was enchanting her Aunt Ginny and running her skeletal at the same time . . .

I'm missing their growing-up, like I missed Philippa's. I can't.

Yet what could she do?

The thought that these fishermen, whoever they were, might retrieve Andra from his exile made her feel weak with hope. Andra would manage things, he would know what to do. Andra made everything safe.

And Josh. She could leave him, of course, trust him to Mr Spettigue and hope that he got away. But Spettigue had made it clear that he was only able to provide hiding places for prisoners once they *had* got away, the actual escape was up to them, as it had to be.

Makepeace, busybody that she was, could only think that such an escape would be bungled unless she had a hand in it; in her mind Josh was still the child she'd taught to read; he'd need her to be outside the prison, waiting for him. Besides, none of the wanted posters on the walls of Millbay Prison had been for a negro; being black gave Josh an extra disadvantage as a runaway.

That picture he'd drawn for her which she'd seen only for a second before it was dragged away—her Roaring Meg, her beloved Boston tavern, where she'd taken Philip Dapifer after dragging him from the harbour—the longing for the childhood Josh had spent in it was in every line, right down to the last splinter. They'd shared so much, she and Josh, how could she leave him to face Hell and slow starvation alone?

'Ain't this damn war ever going to end?' she shouted, making her travelling companions jump.

'The French don't seem to be making much difference,' Beasley said, gloomy as ever. 'And according to the Tory press, Washington's having trouble finding money enough to pay his troops. But somehow he's holding on.'

'And will hold on.' Makepeace knew her countrymen.

'Don't you worry now, Missus,' Dell said, 'Ireland's sure to rise, like America, and then we'll see an end to it.'

Makepeace glared at her. Ireland could stay out of it.

And there, opposite, was another cause of her discontents: Dell the prostitute. She'd wanted to leave the damn woman behind but no, Philippa had insisted on her accompanying them. 'She must come, Mama. She's family now.'

'Not mine she ain't.' Immediately, she'd regretted it; Philippa's face had resumed the obstinacy it wore so often nowadays. But, oh, the female was a trial. Everything she said and did irritated Makepeace almost beyond bearing, not least because her own response to it was driving a wedge between herself and her daughter. There the trollop sat, with her spongy face, serene as a duchess. Have a bit of humility, woman.

Like a duchess, she had actually waved graciously at such staring harvesters as they'd passed until Makepeace had told her abruptly to stop drawing attention to herself and the coach. 'We're *trying* to remain inconspicuous.'

What's more she had declared that her true name was Dervorgilla. 'I'd be glad to be known by it in future,' she'd said. 'I only changed it because the English have trouble gettin' their tongue round it.' So did Makepeace but Philippa was insisting that the former harlot should be so addressed. 'New life, new name.'

They heard Sanders call out: 'Signpost.' Immediately the coach began going down a steep incline, though the ubiquitously high Devon hedges prevented them from seeing whether or not the sea was yet in sight.

As they rounded a bend, there was a scrape on the brake and the coach stopped. In the silence they heard Sanders swearing.

'What is it, Sanders?'

'Harvest wain, Missus. Coming up the hill. Oxen.'

'Tell it to go back.'

'I have.' The coach fitted the lane so exactly that it was impossible to descend without tearing one's clothes on hazel branches, some of which were coming through the windows. It was equally impossible to reverse without unharnessing the team and pushing the coach up a gradient of one in five.

Makepeace began scrabbling for the pistol she always carried under the coach seat; it was unloaded but highwaymen didn't know that.

There was a heavy rustling, the crack of twigs and a vast red male face appeared at the window, bringing with it a strong whiff of sweat and grain. 'A'ternoon,' it said.

Fear, always present on the open road, was dispelled. The man was unarmed. He wore a round hat, a smock and an expression of such amiability that, in any place but this back of beyond, Makepeace felt, would qualify him for Bedlam.

She spoke slowly and clearly. 'Would you be so good as to move your wagon? We wish to proceed.'

'Ar,' said the man. He thought about it. 'So do I.'

He removed his hat, displaying yellow curls and a white band across his forehead where the sun hadn't reached, wiped the inside of his hat with his choker and put it on again. 'Where do ee be going?'

'Babbs Cove,' said Beasley.

'Oh-ar.' The information was allowed to sink in while the man's blue eyes studied each of them in turn. They blinked a little as they took in Dell but returned to Beasley. 'And what do ee want wi' Babbs Cove, my 'andsome?'

Makepeace took in a breath but Beasley said quickly: 'We're looking at property. Mr Spettigue sent us.'

'And we'd like to do it before the moon turns blue,' Makepeace added.

'Spettigue, oh-ar,' the man said. 'Nice day for it.' He looked them over again, suddenly winked at Makepeace and disappeared. They heard him call: 'All right, my boodies, back 'em up.'

As the coach proceeded, it passed a gateway into a cornfield where men and women were harvesting. The man on the ox cart waved at them.

'Inquisitive damn hayseeds,' Makepeace said.

'I don't think that was curiosity,' Beasley said, slowly. 'We're going into smuggling territory, don't forget. That was an inspection. We were tried but not found wanting.'

'Me heart was in me mouth,' fluttered Dell. 'Suppose if he thought I was a customs man in disguise?'

'Oh,' said Makepeace, 'was *that* it?' They had passed through a Babbs Cove sentry point. It was disturbing to discover a countryside in league with its law-breakers, and yet, if one were about to break the law oneself, also somewhat comforting; it suggested efficiency. 'I wonder what Farmer Hayseed would've done if he thought we *were* spies for the Excise.'

'At best, his wain would have stayed where it was.'

'And at worst?'

There was a reflective silence. They had strayed into an immense and primitive landscape almost impossible to police. The law doesn't run here, she thought. It might crawl, but it doesn't run. We're at risk. Anything can happen.

At the same time, she felt her wits honing themselves; there was something bracing about going beyond the pale. 'Smugglers, eh?' she said. 'Be like old times.' Virtually the entire clientele of the Roaring Meg had lived by smuggling in a Boston where avoiding British excise duty was a patriotic duty. If Devon smugglers were anything like her old customers, she was on home ground.

The deep anticipatory breath she took in was of sea air. The coach had stopped.

They got out, stiffly. As the crow flew, Babbs Cove was less than ten miles from Plymouth; as the road went it had taken them nearly three hours.

'Oh,' said Makepeace and Philippa, softly.

'Will you look at that now?' Dell said.

Some giant had cut into the coastline as if taking himself a wedge of cheese. At the thin end, little stone houses balanced themselves on higgledy-piggledy shelves of rock above a slipway running down to sand that widened into a fan before disappearing under the water of a small bay. A couple of small fishing smacks, upended on the slipway and obviously in need of repair, argued that the rest of Babbs Cove's fishing fleet was out at sea.

The wedge's sides were red, fissured, protective headlands, the one on the right dominated by a large and weatherbeaten house, its closed shutters making it sightless to one of the loveliest views in Devon.

'T'Gallants, do you think?' said Beasley.

'Must be.'

'Shall we go up?'

'Let's explore first.' Makepeace believed in reconnaissance.

There was no one about, though from a clifftop came a series of high-pitched whistles issued by human lips. 'I think we're being announced,' Beasley said.

They walked along a stony track past houses, the gardens festooned with fishing nets and lobster-pots, where doors stood open to show nobody inside them.

Rock pools at the edges of the cliffs winked in the sun and, with the sparkling stone of the cottages, it was as if they had stumbled across some shiny curled-up creature that was asleep.

The eastward headland sloped steeply backwards in a sheepspotted glide of grass and gorse until it joined the track as a mere hump, dividing the first cove from another, this one smaller and with a groyne at its entrance. And this one had a large boat on its beach, suspended in a wheeled cradle. And people.

They'd been expected. Women and children, with old men among them, had been busy careening the boat and were now still, staring in their direction. Makepeace's instinct was to put her hands up and shout, 'We're friends,' but suspected it would be superfluous. If whoever had whistled their arrival to these people hadn't thought them harmless they wouldn't have got this far. Nevertheless, suspicion came at them over the beach like a wave.

She and the others followed Beasley across the sand towards a man walking to greet them.

'A'ternoon.' He could have been the brother of the farmer who'd stopped their coach on the hill: the same barn-door breadth of shoulder, the same apparently simple round red face. But this was Neptune's version: his massive legs were trousered and ended in bare, horny feet; somebody had managed to find enough wool to knit him a tunic, now salt-stained; and there were dank ribbons on his straw hat. Instead of grain and sweat, he smelled of barnacles and sweat.

'We've come from Mr Spettigue,' John Beasley told him.

'Oh-ar.' He might never have heard the name.

'We're looking for Jan Gurney.'

'And what do ee want with he, my 'andsome?'

'We want him to export some goods for us,' Beasley said, sticking carefully to Spettigue's script. 'Perishable goods.'

'Oh-ar.'

'*Perishable* goods,' Makepeace repeated with emphasis. It was the password, their bona fides; it should have led to a relaxation of the tension that was beginning to weight the air.

It didn't. The giant went on being simple and there was lazy movement as the people round the boat began to drift towards them, slowly, as if they had nothing better to do, but gradually forming an enclosure around her and the others. They were mainly women, but the careening scrapers in their hands were nastily suggestive.

'Brought the Excise with ee, have ee?' the man said suddenly. He lifted his voice into a shout: 'How far off now, Jack?'

A cry came back, thin but audible. 'Thirty minute, I reckon. 'Tis the Admiral's barge, Jan. Still on our headin'.'

Dear Lord, their presence had coincided with a sighting of a naval boat. No wonder they hadn't been welcomed; to people as suspicious as these the two events had seemed connected. The ring tightened around them, like a stockade.

'Nothing to do with us,' Makepeace told them, gabbling. 'We came by road. I wouldn't bring the Revenue on anybody, I was a smuggler myself once.'

Gurney rocked back on his heels in exaggerated horror. 'Chaps, the lady's callin' us smugglers. That's right hurtful, that is. Why's she a-doing that, I wonder?'

Makepeace could have given him several reasons. She pointed to the cradled vessel. 'That bowsprit for a start,' she said. 'That's a smugglers' bowsprit. And she's got a tubrail inboard. We used tubs. And lobster-pots.'

He squinted down at her. 'Where was that then?'

'Boston. In America. I used to get my sugar from a cutter just like that one.'

'Americy?' said Jan Gurney. 'Deary, deary me, chaps. We got ourselves an American.'

An old man in the crowd said: 'Small wonder we'm at war with the buggers.'

There was a general snuffle of amusement and Makepeace knew it would be all right.

'What do ee want with us, then?' Gurney said.

'I want to get a friend of mine over to France. Mr Spettigue said as you might take him. For a price, of course.'

'Did he now? An' oo *is* this friend, if I might be so bold?'

'Another American. Will you take him or not?' They were demanding a great deal of trust from her and giving precious little in return.

'Escaper?'

She nodded reluctantly.

'Have to think about that then, won't us? We ain't in the exportin' business.'

She was getting cross and desperate. 'Well, while you're thinking about it, we're going to look at that house back there. It's for sale and I'm considering buying it.' He could put *that* in his pipe.

'Spettigue say you could buy it?'

'He did,' Beasley said. 'Temporary measure. For storing perishable goods.'

The giant seemed to make up his mind and again blasted their ears with a shout: 'How far now, Jack?'

The faint reply from the headland said: 'Twenty, twenty-five minutes, I reckon.'

'Keep working, chaps, get her done fast.' The cordon around the coach party returned to the boat to resume the work on its bottom.

'And cover that bloody bowsprit,' Gurney called after them before turning to Makepeace. 'Got the keys?'

'Yes.'

He set off across the sand and they followed him.

Makepeace discovered that sweat was trickling down between her breasts, and not just because it was a hot day. The encounter could have gone either way. If it had gone the wrong way . . . the crowd of still-faced women coming closer and closer wasn't an event she'd like to relive.

Beasley trudged along at her side, taking off his hat and wiping his forehead with a shaking hand. 'Phew!'

She nodded.

His eyes on Gurney's back, he muttered: 'What about the bloody bowsprit?'

'The length,' she said. 'Almost as long as the hull and that's illegal—leastways it was in Boston and I reckon it's the same here. You can cram enough sail on a jib like that to show the Revenue a clean pair of heels.'

'No wonder they're worried about the navy heading this way.'

Makepeace wasn't so sure. Unless the crew of the approaching craft intended to search the village—and the lookout on the headland had said it was a naval vessel, not Revenue—it might not see the cutter at all.

She looked back; this bay was considerably smaller and more hidden than the one around which the village clustered and from which its smacks went back and forth on the legal business of fishing. It was as if Babbs Cove proper had a drawing room in which it could innocently receive visitors, while the back room, the cove they were leaving, was kept for more nefarious activity. Certainly it could only be used by those who knew its waters well; its entrance between the groyne and the opposite cliff was narrow. As good as a postern, she thought. Rocks poked up round black heads, like unmoving seals in the swirls of an ebbing tide. Nobody, unless they'd been born to it, could get a vessel through there. Whatever else the men of Babbs Cove were, they were fine seamen.

She quickened her step to catch up with Gurney to test her theory. 'Leaving yourself open with that cutter on the beach, ain't you? If there's customs men coming, they'll take her as a prize.'

He just said: 'The *Lark* needed 'er backside seeing to.' He strode on, adding over his shoulder: 'Like all females from time to time.'

They went through the village, past an inn with surprisingly large stabling on their right where Sanders was watering the coach horses at a trough. The door of the inn itself was shut, as were its windows.

Just after the inn the track divided, one branch becoming the lane down which they had approached the village, the other turning westward to become a bridge leading towards the clifftop and the house above. Beneath the bridge a stream emerged from a reed bed and plunged energetically over rock to the beach.

Plenty of good water, Makepeace thought. Even in this driest of summers the whole village was beset by rivulets. If the house suits, I might keep it. Bring the girls in the summer.

Now a lane again, the way became cobbled as it led steeply upwards. They passed under an arch and into a courtyard. And stopped.

There was silence apart from the call of seagulls.

'Holy Hokey,' Makepeace said at last. 'That's not a house, it's a tomb.'

'It's horrible,' Philippa said, used to the modernity of America.

'I t'ink it's grand,' Dervorgilla said.

Beasley said nothing.

Here was bleakness and, worse, medieval bleakness looming above them as if the place was still expecting to repel attack by roving marauders from the Wars of the Roses. It repelled Makepeace immediately.

A flight of steps led up to an arched and heavy front door. What in any other house would be the ground floor remained an undercroft—with barred arrow slits instead of windows.

T'Gallants was not just unwelcoming, it was hostile.

'Let's hope it's going cheap,' Makepeace said. 'Who'd want to live here?'

'Thought Spettigue were,' Gurney told her. 'Said he didn't want strangers in. Give us the keys.'

He led the way across the weedy, cobbled courtyard, past a mounting block and an elaborate water trough, climbed the steps and inserted a key in the escutcheoned lock. As he opened the door he called out: ' 'Tis all right, Mrs Green. 'Tis only me, with some people Mr Spettigue sent.' To Beasley, he said: 'Caretaker. She don't like visitors, don't Ma Green.'

'Does she get any?'

Gurney handed the keys back to Makepeace and they passed into a screen passage, very dark. Dell squeaked as a figure slid round behind them, shut the front door through which they'd come and locked it, making everything darker, before disappearing again.

'This way.' They could just see Gurney's pale straw hat and followed it. He opened another door, one of two vast leaves, and at once they were in light. Space and light. A vast room of white stone, beautiful in its way with its elaborately fan-vaulted ceiling and two great windows, but too big, too cold, too grim, like the rest of the house. The only furniture was an enormous black-oak chair, like a throne, standing against the wall to the left of a fireplace that could have stabled a pony.

'Will you look at the view now,' said Dell, brightly. She stood by a long oriel window, on the opposite side to the fireplace, which commanded the courtyard and an outlook across the bridge to the village.

'Look at this 'un,' Gurney said from the front of the room where sun came in through the four lights of a vast window, sending coloured shafts onto the stone-flagged floor from a strip of coats of arms in stained glass. 'This 'un's the wreckers' window.'

They crossed the room to join him. Below them was a sheer drop of some hundred feet onto rocks. The view was glorious, almost gaudy, taking in the bright sapphire of the cove, its yellow sand, the even more yellow gorse running down the opposing headland which so completely hid the further bay where the smuggling cutter was that it might not have existed.

'What's wreckers?' asked Philippa.

'You don't want to know that, ma innocent,' Gurney said, promptly telling her. 'Naasty people, wreckers. Put a light in this window, along comes a big ship headin' for it, thinkin' she's found harbour, an' crashes onto they rocks down there.'

He lowered his voice to sepulchral doom. 'An' down go the wreckers, killin' and clubbin' the survivors, a-strippin' the rings off poor dead fingers and the jewels off the poor ladies' necks . . . oh, terrible. They do reckon that's how the Pomeroys made their fortune, wreckin'.'

'The Pomeroys?'

'Family as owns this place. Rich as nabobs, and all from wreckin'. Moved away from the house generations ago and went respeckable—guilt, they reckon. An' o' course, the place is marked on the charts nowadays so nobody don't wash up on they rocks 'cept by storm. But they do say'—his voice dropped another octave—'they do say as how on wild nights the ghosts o' dead souls come knockin' on this window a-callin' for revenge.'

Dell was squeaking with superstitious terror. Philippa grinned up at him. 'No good, Mr Gurney. I've been in a sea battle. Ghosts don't frighten me anymore.'

Makepeace was proud of her. She took her daughter's arm and led her away to investigate the rest of the house.

There was a dining room, nearly as big as the Great Hall but of nastier proportions, and an upstairs that defeated them, being tunnelled with corridors so dark that they could not investigate without a candle which they did not have, the spectral caretaker having vanished. 'Probably back into her coffin,' Makepeace said.

The kitchen was the crowning horror. They surveyed it in silence.

'Useful if you've got a hundred men-at-arms staying over,' Makepeace said, 'and a hundred cooks. We can't live here—not even for Josh.'

'Ma, it wouldn't be for long. Nobody'd find him here, we could make him well again and then get him to France. I know Mr Gurney would help us. He's a nice man, I think, he smiled when I said I wasn't afraid.'

The only other outside door in the entire place, as far as they could judge, was the one at the far end of the kitchen; that, too, had high steps to it that led down to an overgrown vegetable garden, and was heavily bolted.

When they got back to the Great Hall, Gurney was still by the wreckers' window. 'Yere they come,' he said. 'Admiral's barge but no admiral. What they a-wantin', I wonder?'

Beasley, nervously peering, said: 'Press gang?'

'Maybe,' Gurney said. 'Dressed up pretty, if so. And there's women with 'em.'

Makepeace joined him. Two jolly boats were approaching the beach rowed by smartly dressed sailors with ribbons in their hats. A woman holding a parasol over her head sat in one with an officer, the passengers in the other were another woman and a black man.

She watched the first boat ground on the sand and the woman lifted out by a sailor, carried through the shallows and set down, having maintained an elegant pose throughout—no mean feat. Once the others had landed, both parties set off up the beach.

Makepeace's eyes stayed fixed on the woman with the parasol, nudged by a memory of some painful experience which, she eventually concluded, must be associated with the married years when she'd moved in Society and beautifully groomed women like the one now stepping with grace across the sand had made clear that she was an unwelcome, low-born intruder.

'Comin' to the house,' Gurney said. 'Ma Green won't let 'un in, that's for sure.'

'Good.' Beasley was looking around for a place to hide.

Gurney nodded. 'If so be it is the press, 'tis best if they don't see no men.' He looked at Makepeace. 'You talk to 'un, p'raps. Open that window, see what 'un wants.'

There was a light in the oriel, like a wicket gate, which resisted movement so that by the time she'd got it open the party from the boat stood in the courtyard. The woman with the parasol was accompanied by an older woman and a negro in livery. A young lieutenant and two sailors brought up the rear.

'Afternoon,' Makepeace sang out. 'What's your business?'

The woman lowered her sunshade, displaying a modish hat that matched her dress, which was grey, so that against the greyer stone of the courtyard she could have been a statue possessing, as she did, the same stillness and poise.

Shouting up at a window was obviously beneath her; she spoke softly to the black servant who called: 'Open up, pleathe. Thith ith Lady Thtacpoole.'

Makepeace looked at Gurney who was keeping well back. 'Lady Thtackpoole?'

He shrugged his ignorance. 'Don't read the Society papers.'

She returned to the window. There was something about the woman . . . of more recent memory than she'd thought, but just as unpleasant. 'What does she want?'

'She wisheth to thee the houthe.'

The black man had raised his voice and, with it, his head, and the sun glinted on the collar he wore round his neck. It was a slave collar, gold and thinner than most, but still the unmistakable mark of ownership padlocked onto all human cattle sold in markets from Liverpool to South Carolina.

A *slave*. Betty had been a runaway slave, aided in her escape by Makepeace's parents, and Makepeace had absorbed hatred of the trade and the need for its abolition along with her milk.

'Well she can't,' she said, 'I'm buying this house.' She'd decided she wasn't, but the desire to thwart the slave-owning bitch in the courtyard was strong in her.

'Thith ith Lady Thtacpoole'th houthe,' the black man said. He was becoming agitated. She probably beats him, Makepeace thought.

Behind her, Gurney muttered, as if with a new and awful suspicion: 'Ask him what's her maiden name.'

'You,' Makepeace called as rudely as she could, 'what's your maiden name?'

She had the satisfaction of seeing the woman's mouth tighten but the slave answered for her: 'Pomeroy.'

'Dear, oh dear, we got the bloody Pomeroys back,' Gurney said, resignedly. 'Better let her in.'

'Not yet.' Makepeace was enjoying herself. She addressed the woman again. 'If this is your house, why ain't you got the keys?'

The slave waved a piece of paper. 'The houthe ith not for thale. Thith ith authorithation that her ladythip ith the rightful owner.'

'When did you get that?'

'Thith morning, from Mr Thpettigue, the agent.'

Lady Stacpoole was becoming restive; she turned to the lieutenant behind her and said something.

Makepeace admitted defeat. In a minute sailors would be battering their way in. She turned round to go and unlock the door.

Gurney and John Beasley had disappeared. 'Gone out through the kitchen,' Philippa said, 'just in case.'

Makepeace Hedley and the Dowager Countess of Stacpoole passed in the courtyard, ignoring each other.

With Philippa beside her, Makepeace tossed the keys to the poor slave. 'Wreckers' house,' she said clearly. 'Wouldn't live in it if you paid me.'

As they walked away she heard the woman say: 'You must be Philippa, my dear. I heard you were lost. How nice that you and your mother have been reunited.'

Makepeace turned round sharply. The woman was smiling gently and deliberately—at Dell.

When they'd crossed the bridge, Philippa had to sit her mother on a bench in the inn's courtyard to cool her off. 'How did she know about us?'

'She was in the Sick and Hurt Office in London when I was enquiring for you.' Makepeace pounded the bench's arm. 'What's she doing here? I *knew* I'd seen the high-nosed baggage somewhere, God rot her.'

'I think it was an honest mistake, Mama.'

'Of *course* it wasn't. That . . . that Dell, my daughter? She was having the last laugh. I'll give her daughters.'

They would have to remain where they were for some time. Both Gurney and Beasley had taken cover somewhere: a sensible precaution. The young lieutenant had joined his crew on the beach while he waited for his passengers and the sight of two able-bodied men who could be pressed into the service of the navy might be too tempting for him to resist. Sanders had also made himself scarce.

The enforced delay stretched Makepeace's temper. The fact that Dell had wandered down onto the beach and was talking to some of the sailors didn't improve it either.

One or two women came up from the far cove and knocked on the door of the inn to be admitted.

Now that she'd calmed down a little, Makepeace could hear the sound of raucous breathing coming from an upstairs window and the mutter of prayers.

'I think there's illness in the house, Mama. Let's move away.'

They walked down to the sand. Waders, who'd been scared away by the arrival of the boats, had returned and sedate oyster-catchers were feeding at the water's edge. An elderly man and woman had also come round from the far cove and settled them-selves on upturned buckets by the slipway. Surrounded by withies, they were weaving, to the exact, timeless shape, the wicker baskets in which Makepeace had once caught the lobsters of Massachusetts for consumption in her tavern.

In fact, she was so reminded of those days that anger began to be replaced by regret. She liked this place, she'd liked Jan Gurney; it was sad and irritating that she should be being chased away from it by the damned owner of T'Gallants.

Now Spettigue would have to find another boat and another smuggling crew somewhere else to take Josh to France and bring Andra back. And here would have done so well. Damn the Stacpoole female or Pomeroy or whatever her damn name was.

Typical English aristocracy, thought they owned the world. Well, America was showing them they didn't, bless it. Fight 'em, boys.

She turned to look back at the inn and felt the same nostalgic pull that had tugged at her when she saw the lobster-pots. It was the only building in the village made of wood. Clapper-boarded, weath-erstained, it was her Roaring Meg blown across the Atlantic to land on this other coast.

There were differences, of course. A tattered Union Jack flew from a flagpole on the roof and a very English inn-sign, too worm-eaten to be read, hung on a pole outside it; nor had the Roaring Meg possessed a coach-house and stables. But the inn, like her old tavern, faced the sea full-on and two twisted chimneys at either end of the roof suggested a long room such as the one from which she had dis-pensed ale and flip and broiled buttered lobster to men not unlike Jan Gurney.

She saw again the burned spars that had been her last view of the Roaring Meg, saw them through tears.

Dell joined them. 'The officer says they'll be off soon because of the tide. The grand lady's only come to look over the place before she settles in it. She's a widow with a husband just dead. It was her family's place and she's to retire here for the seclusion, he says, and live in it by herself. Poor soul, she'll be wanting to nurse her sorrow.'

'I'll give her sorrow,' Makepeace said. Still, it sounded as if Babbs Cove's activities were not going to be curtailed by the presence of a great family and its guests—for which it would be grateful.

When the party from T'Gallants returned to their boats, Make-peace was talking to the couple making lobster-pots and ignored its departure.

Once the Admiral's barge was well out to sea, Gurney and Beasley emerged from behind the big house and joined the three women. John Beasley was wiping his neck in relief.

'Pity,' Jan said to Makepeace.

She nodded. 'Would you have taken my perishable goods?'

'Reckon we might've. Course, I'd have had to talk to the others when they're back from fishin'—generally us don't cross the Channel till the winter. Revenue don't harass poor free traders so hard when 'tis stormy. But, yes, reckon we might've—for a price. *Oh my Lord.*'

He was looking towards the inn. The flag on its roof was being lowered to half-mast.

One of the women who'd gone inside the inn while Makepeace and Philippa sat outside it was hurrying towards them. 'He's gone, Jan.'

Gurney took off his hat. 'God rest his soul.'

Obviously, it was time to go. Sanders was turning the coach and team so that they faced the road leading out of the village.

Quietly, Makepeace said: 'I'm sorry for your loss. We'll be away now. Perhaps we'll meet again.'

He nodded.

She said: 'Good man, was he?'

Gurney sighed. 'He were a mean-spirited old bugger, but I reckon as how the Lord'll be happy to see 'un.'

Once they were in the coach, Philippa said: 'I wonder who it was who died.'

'Landlord,' Makepeace told her. 'Those old lobster-potters told me. They say it's a freehold inn.' She took off her hat and fanned herself with it—the sun was beginning to go down but was, if anything, hotter than ever. She added casually: 'And they reckon his daughter'll want to sell it now he's gone.'

Chapter Eleven

CAPTAIN Luscombe was pleased with the first fruits of the public subscription as displayed on the banker's draft the Dowager Countess, of Stacpoole handed to him. 'Three hundred and fifty guineas, splendid, splendid.'

'There should be more to come,' she told him. 'Mr Coutts has written to say that the response in London has been quite good, even better than locally.'

'More sophisticated, Londoners.'

The Dowager suspected that it was not so much to do with sophistication than with the fact that London was less plagued by escaping Americans than were Plymouth and Exeter. She forbore to say so. A good man, Captain Luscombe, and with none of the prejudice with which her appeal had been met by what she was beginning to think of as 'Aymer's set'. He was genuinely concerned for the prisoners in his care, ashamed that the Admiralty kept him too short of funds to house and feed them properly and had been stung by John Howard's damning report on conditions at the hospital.

'Splendid,' he said again. 'Thank you, your ladyship, and be assured that the money will be well spent.'

She smiled at him. If Luscombe thought that was the end of her interest in the matter, he was mistaken. A good man, but not a good administrator.

The money was indeed going to be spent well—she would see to it. Overwhelmed by his responsibilities as he was, Luscombe would of necessity have to leave the improvements to subordinates who had already proved themselves not only lazy but corrupt. There must be changes—the doctor would have to be dismissed for a start—or wounded men would continue to die unattended and in filth.

However, she would have to go carefully; female interference was never welcome.

She said prettily: 'Now that my interest has been aroused, Captain, I do hope that I may not be excluded from helping in other ways. Mr Howard writes to me of his insistence that a new hospital should be built.' She raised her hand to show that she understood the good captain's instant alarm. 'Yes, I know, he has no conception of the disruption and cost such a project would entail. But that old warehouse to the north of the prison—one glimpsed it the other day. Might that not be much more cheaply and effectively brought into use? Does it belong to the Admiralty?'

She didn't add that she knew it did. She'd already inspected the place.

Luscombe was doubtful. 'I agree the warehouse would be healthier, dear lady,' he said, 'and it certainly belongs to the Admiralty. But it's outside the perimeter fence. Couldn't be guarded.'

The solution was staring him in the face though the Dowager refrained from rubbing his nose in it; one mustn't irritate men by appearing clever. She said: 'Of course, how foolish of me,' but kept the conversation going on the subject, waiting, issuing hints so light that they landed on him like feathers, until he said thoughtfully:

'I suppose we could move the fence.'

She greeted the idea like the discovery of gravity. 'What a splendid thought, Captain. You gentlemen are so inventive. Would you wish me to engage some of Admiral Edgcumbe's own workmen on the project? He is enthusiastic for it and you know how slow official channels would be otherwise.'

She overwhelmed him with powerful and noble connections. 'The beds . . . perhaps you would wish me to employ the people who supplied the furniture for our servants' quarters at Chantries. The Earl found their work both cheap and of good quality . . . I know that Lady Edgcumbe is eager to see to the provision of linen . . .'

By the time she'd finished with him, she was virtually the unofficial site engineer in charge of contractors, responsible only to him.

'My dear Lady Stacpoole, I hope you will not overtire yourself on these matters. You have your own concerns—I hear you are moving to Babbs Cove. Will the journeying not be too much for you?'

She waved away such triviality. 'Yes, I am moving tomorrow—the Admiral is lending me his barge again—but it is not too far, one can come back and forth fairly easily.'

'Then I should be grateful for your assistance.' He wiped his face with a large handkerchief. 'I will not hide from you that this continuing influx of prisoners proves a great trial, a great trial. The French—well, they are the French and always recalcitrant but the Americans . . . rioting only yesterday over the state of their food, escape attempts . . .'

'You are beset, Captain. In the circumstances, I think you manage wonderfully. I have written to Lord North to say so.'

'Did you?' He was pitifully grateful.

'Indeed.' While carefully stressing Luscombe's industry to the Prime Minister, she had not scrupled to expound the prison's evils. She didn't tell him this, either.

'I have had Grayle brought to the garden room,' Luscombe said.

'Thank you. I hope to have the contraptions fitted on him today. Have you received any reply from the Admiralty?' Of the many scarifying horrors at Millbay, it seemed to her that the retention in prison of a handless man was the most shameful. She had included it in her letter of protest to the Prime Minister.

'I fear that they are obdurate. There can be no exchange.' To do him credit, Luscombe was humiliated personally by having to keep Grayle captive. 'The young man does not help himself, having twice attempted to escape—a marvel in itself, I suppose. He had help, of course, but if he does it again I fear he may face the Black Hole. I have made an exception in his case so far.' Luscombe sighed. 'I hope the fitting goes well, though I fear it is no sight for a lady.'

'Captain, my husband's final illness was prolonged and distressing. Having attended on him throughout, I can make some claim to being a nurse.'

He laughed politely, as she had intended him to, as if she'd said she made a good fist at sweeping chimneys. Yet she found herself wondering why female professional nurses should attract such opprobrium or, for that matter, why they were the sort of women to whom opprobrium was attached.

The sexual element, she supposed; decent women being expected to have no familiarity with the male body other than their husband's. Were men so intrinsically vile that, even when ill, they might be expected to ravish their carers? Or women so abandoned that the sight of male anatomy, however frail, sent them into a fury of lust? Or sensitive to the point that they must faint at the sight of a boil? She recalled Aymer's body as it had been towards the end. What a strange conception it was that men had of women.

She left the problem and, calling for Joan, proceeded to Captain Luscombe's garden room and Lieutenant Forrest Grayle.

The guards were used to the arrangement now and left him unbound in her presence; today they had even gone outside into the garden to smoke their pipes. Good, perhaps she could persuade the boy to talk to her.

'Well, they are finished, Lieutenant,' she said. 'Mr Rutley has worked to the casts as best he can and now we must see if the result fits.'

She had hired the artificer who produced wooden legs for amputees at the naval hospital in Plymouth to carve artificial hands, working from casts she'd had made by the Millbay cook from plaster applied to Grayle's stumps.

Artificer Rutley had been intrigued, having made single hands a-plenty for various wounded but never two. 'Careless of him,' he'd said, 'losing both.'

'I gather he was trying to raise a sail that had come down during the battle for his ship. A piece of cannonball sliced through the rope and his hands with it.'

The information had been vouchsafed to her by Captain Luscombe who'd had it from the master of Grayle's ship. Grayle himself said nothing of it. Since the evening when he'd refused her offer to write to Martha, he'd said nothing at all.

Today he sat in a chair, leaning forwards and staring at the carpet, his capless, Viking head hanging down with indifference to everything about him.

'Stand up, Lieutenant.' The Dowager had learned not to show sympathy. 'Go ahead, Joan.'

'Let's take our jacket off. There. Us'll leave the shirt for now. Now our sleeves up, there's a good boy.' Joan insisted on treating her charge like a baby which, in many ways, Diana considered him to be.

The stumps were exposed; they'd been instantly plunged into a caulking barrel by a crew member who'd been hauling on the rope with him, cauterizing them in the smoking pitch and preserving the young man's life, but the result was unpretty.

The Dowager reached into her holdall and brought out the hands Tobias had fetched that morning from the naval hospital. A harness attached to the wrist section, which ran nearly to the elbow, was for buckling around the shoulder. With considerable skill, Rutley had articulated the wooden fingers by inserting steel spirals at the point where there should be joints. By using his right hand to shape the fingers of the left, and vice versa, Lieutenant Grayle would be able to pick things up, even to grip.

Unresisting, the boy allowed Joan to insert his stumps into the arm section, standing like an ox while she buckled on each harness.

'There, now we'm vitty.' Joan's Devon accent, the Dowager noticed, had gained force since her return to her home county. 'In't we splendid, your ladyship?'

'Indeed we are.' *Perhaps we should have painted them flesh-coloured,* she thought. Artificer Rutley had gone for serviceability rather than aesthetic effect; the raw wooden fingers with their steel insets suggested the claws of a raptor. However . . . 'Don't you think they're splendid, Lieutenant . . . Oh, my dear boy.'

Tears were coursing down Grayle's cheeks. 'Take 'em off.'

'Try them,' the Dowager pleaded.

'Take 'em off, take 'em *off*.' He was shaking his arms so that the hands wobbled on their harness like floppy gloves. He sank back into his chair. 'I don't want 'em, I don't want anything.'

She sat down beside him. 'Of course you do. You want freedom, you keep trying to escape.'

'So I may find a cliff and throw myself off it.' The boy's voice went into a wail. 'They don't let you kill yourself in here. I know, I've tried.'

In the shocked silence, the Dowager's eyes sought her maid's. *What's to be done?* Joan raised her hands helplessly.

Diana had tried to imagine what it was like for the boy, his captivity doubled, tripled, by the extra imprisonment of handlessness, unable to dress or feed himself, open a door, write a letter, turn the leaves of a book . . . in her mind, she had listed the thousand things he could not do.

Viciously, he yelled one more: 'I can't even wipe my own arse.'

She hadn't thought of that one.

What to do, what to do? She had been so pleased with the artificial hands, sure that they would provide him with some capability—which, given a little adjustment and practice, she was still certain that they would.

He'd gone into the pit of despair that only youth could dig for itself; having been beautiful, healthy, rich, the object of an adoring mother, he could not tolerate to be less than he had been. *When you are my age, young man, you will know that life is to be valued under almost any circumstances and be less careless with it.*

Should she refuse to remove the hands and say that he must learn to use them, thus compounding the very helplessness and dependence that was maddening him?

She said: 'Very well. We will take them off. They need adjustment. In time they will be of greater use than you think. I want you to look ahead, think of the estate in Virginia you will inherit, the servants who can make up for any deficiencies . . .'

'I ain't going back. I ain't never going back. D'you think I'd let Miss Henrietta see this freak? She'd run a mile.'

Of course. There would be a Henrietta, very young, very pretty.

'Not if she loves you. You can still walk, talk, make her happy.' She thought to herself he still had the other pieces of his anatomy which Henrietta might appreciate if she truly loved him, but one did not talk of such things. 'And think of your poor mother and her great joy when you return to her alive after the war.'

'I ain't never going back.'

'*Lieutenant.*' The rap of her voice snapped his head up so that he looked at her for the first time. 'I am sending you safely back to Martha Grayle one of these days if I have to use parcel post.'

He said wearily: 'It don't matter. Why are you concernin' yourself with me?'

'Let us say I consider myself *in loco parentis*. You *will* go back. And if your attitude to adversity is anything like your countrymen's, it will be sooner rather than later since America will have abjectly surrendered. In the meantime I shall see that those arm pieces are padded, which should help the fit. Next week you will start to use them. I have not gone to trouble and expense in order for them to go to waste.'

As Joan unbuckled the harness, the boy said, looking at her: 'America won't surrender, ma'am. Not nohow.'

She surprised herself by saying: 'Good. Then neither must you.'

But I *want* America to surrender, she thought. Why am I encouraging the enemy? Because he wasn't the enemy to her; he was a beaten child, as all the maimed and sick of Millbay were beaten children. She had lifted the flap on a dark cellar of misery and had been allowed a glimpse that had thereby made her responsible for it. *In loco parentis*. Who would lighten it if she did not? To let the flap fall and walk away would be desertion of a call even higher than that of country.

*   *   *

It was rather jolly, billowing along a coast of such amazing diversity. Cliffs changed colour from the slaty blue-grey of gneiss to red sandstone, flecked by sudden white beaches and splintered by mysterious caves.

Tobias had gone to Babbs Cove by road, driving the coach and taking linen and china and other necessities she had purchased in Plymouth from her alarmingly dwindling resources. The barge was carrying the beds and such pieces as Lucy Edgcumbe had insisted on giving her for her new home: an easy chair, a charming writing bureau, a looking-glass.

For the rest she would have to rely on supply from T'Gallants's undercroft which, on her initial inspection, she had discovered to be full of furniture, all of it heavy and not to her taste but . . . well, beggars couldn't be choosers.

'What of servants?' Lucy had said. 'You cannot live in a house like that with fewer than ten servants at the least.'

'I have Tobias and Joan and I expect the village will provide others. Babbs Cove must have a laundress.' She would not shame Robert by admitting that her pension was too small for adequate staff.

'Joan seems unwilling to go.'

It was true; Joan had disliked T'Gallants on sight. 'Castle Grim', she'd called it.

'She will settle to it, I'm sure.'

But Lucy, dubious, had insisted on providing a cook and a scullery maid, putting them into Tobias's coach like a mother stuffing a last-minute cake into her son's tuck box before sending him off to school. 'You can send them back when you are settled.'

So the only cloud on the horizon was the one that blew along behind her. It had a black hull, tan sails and flew the long red pennant of the Board of Customs—a liberty that infuriated the sailors on Admiral Edgcumbe's barge as if they were bulls being teased by a red rag.

Young Lieutenant Damerell, who was in command, was much put out. 'Damn fella's followin' us—beggin' your pardon, ma'am.'

'Is it Captain Nicholls?' the Dowager asked, shading her eyes.

'The *Wasp* all right. Nobody else'd be so damn bold—beggin' your pardon, Lady Stacpoole. If we didn't have ladies onboard, I'd turn and ram the hell hound, beggin' your pardon, ma'am, but damned if I wouldn't.'

'He's probably got Mummy with him,' Diana said, wearily.

Mrs Nicholls was everywhere. The woman had called again at Mount Edgcumbe where, the Dowager being absent, she had not been admitted. The next day she'd been outside the gates of Millbay, waiting, she said: '. . . to get a glimpse of they poor lads I gave money for,' and sent off with a flea in her ear which had not stopped her appearing, apparently accidentally, as the Dowager emerged from the office of Spettigue and Son. 'In't this a happy meeting, your ladyship? Arrangements for T'Gallants, was it? Don't ee forget now, if you find it should'n suit, my Walter wants first refusal.'

Appalling woman.

In fact, the Dowager had been delivering another well-bred flea into the ringed ear of young Mr Spettigue.

'I was forced to stand like a petitioner at the door of my own house, Mr Spettigue.'

'Devastated, ladyship. Wonderful embarrassin'. Mrs Hedley offered to buy, d'ye see? And I understood . . .'

'You understood T'Gallants was for sale. Unless you are now finally disabused of that idea, one will have to find oneself another land agent.'

The humiliation to which the Hedley female had subjected her still stung. In the race for the cup to be held by the female the Dowager Countess of Stacpoole would most like to see roasted on a griddle, Makepeace Hedley was beating Mrs Nicholls by a short head.

Lieutenant Damerell had to beg her pardon for swearing many times more. The Revenue cutter stayed exactly one mile astern with an unpleasant doggedness.

Was this pursuit part of Nicholls's Revenue duties? If so, why was it so reminiscent of a creature stalking its prey? Did he hope to harry her out of T'Gallants that he might be restored to what he fancied was his ancestral home?

When pigs fly, Captain Nicholls, when pigs fly.

'Babbs Cove coming up to port, your ladyship.'

The place twinkled in the sun, as it had done when she'd first seen it, though to her it was not as if a giant had cut a piece out of the coastline as it had been to Makepeace, but as something a giant had tucked into it, an artefact precious to him, to be returned for later.

Yes, she thought.

Just as it had on her first visit, T'Gallants tricked her eye at first glimpse into thinking it just another part of the cliffside.

In a way, Joan was right: it was hardly a castle, but it was certainly grim. Even with its angular roofs set against a sky so perfectly and uniformly blue that it might have been plastered into place, T'Gallants House could not be flattered. The granite of which it was built seemed to have shot upwards from some ancient seismic eruption and solidified before it could fall back, leaving a freakish, vertical piece of the rock itself. There was no ornament, no architectural softening, just a harsh perpendicularity. The original builder had sited it so that it refused protection from any lash of the sea, any blow of wind, but instead met them head on.

And something dark in the Dowager's nature, something she was almost ashamed to discover, exulted at it. Here was her reply to twenty-two years of servitude.

Dear, dear, she chided herself. He is dead; I am free of him. But she was not, and now knew she was not; almost every action she had taken in the last weeks was in response to the spirit that had overpowered hers for over twenty years—and still did in calling forth defiance to it. As she had organized the public subscription for the prison hospital, she had heard Aymer writhe. He who had so loathed all charity, what would he say to charity for rebels?

I can conform to my own nature now, she'd told that unquiet spirit, you shall suppress it no longer. I wish to do this and I will do it.

And T'Gallants is also my rebellion. It is mine. I am the master of something as harsh and unyielding as you were. The Pomeroy answer to Stacpoole domination. Did you expect me to retire, defeated, to the Dower House and lick the wounds you inflicted? Then look here.

She heard one of the crew mutter something.

'What did that sailor say?'

'Nothing, your ladyship.' Lieutenant Damerell was uncomfortable.

'Yes, he did. He said "wreckers".'

'An old tale, a myth. Attaches to every house on the coast. Nothing to worry about, ma'am.' Lieutenant Damerell became busy.

It was the second time she had heard the word in connection with T'Gallants. The Hedley harridan had flung it, like mud, as she'd left the house.

She looked to where the sea was gently soothing the rocks at the cliff's foot and tried to imagine human beings, flapping like injured birds in the water as they were clubbed to death. No. Damerell was right; it was the house's position that gave rise to such a calumny. The early Pomeroys might have been rascals, like all Tudor adventurers, but there'd been no suggestion they killed anything other than Spaniards.

It took time to transfer herself and Joan and the furniture to the beach and by the time they had been, a new rowing boat full of men was being drawn up on the sand to debouch Captain Nicholls of the Revenue.

He marched across to her, a matt, neat figure with the peculiar quality she'd remarked on before of taking in light and giving none back. He approached until he was too close, standing with his face only eighteen inches from her own, staring at her with an intensity that suggested there was no one else on the beach.

'Lady Stacpoole, again I must ask you to let my men search your house before you enter it.'

She moved back two paces, her hand instinctively covering the chatelaine of keys dangling at her waist under her cloak. 'Have you a warrant this time, Captain?'

'I am asking as a matter of courtesy. It will be better for you.'

She looked towards the village, where she could see her coach—two coaches—tucked within the coach-house of the inn. Tobias was talking to somebody outside it. In other doorways, women, children and old men were watching her arrival.

Smugglers they might be, but they were also her tenantry; she did not wish to start off on bad terms. Apart from the fact that the thought of Nicholls searching her house was odious, here was the opportunity to show one's people that, though one was not necessarily running with the hare, neither was one hunting with the hounds.

'I shall decide what is best, Captain Nicholls.'

He leaned forward. 'You must know I am not without influence, ma'am. I am pressing the Lord Chancellor to have Mr Chauncey replaced.'

She was becoming bewildered. 'Mr Chauncey'?'

'The local magistrate. He favours these rogues, as do local juries.'

Oh, she was tired of it. This was to be her private place. 'Lieutenant Damerell,' she called, 'perhaps your sailors would be good enough to carry my pieces to the house. My man Tobias will help them.'

Expressionless as ever, Captain Nicholls turned away.

'Lead on, your ladyship,' Damerell said, coming up.

Over the bridge and up the cobbled way to the gatehouse. As they went through, she noticed what she had not during her first visit—her family coat of arms, a coronated apple, carved in stone above the archway.

Of course the courtyard was dilapidated and the view of the house's west wing nearly as chilly as its frontage, but its saving grace was a beautiful bow oriel standing on a base of branching stone, a gracefully feminine thing in a plane of dour masculinity.

Behind her a sailor carrying her clothes chest puffed: 'Move on, there's a good lady. This here's heavy.'

By the time such furniture as she'd brought with her was in place and the beds made and Mrs Clarke, the cook, with the scullery maid Polly, had investigated (and deprecated) the kitchen, the crew of the barge had to leave or miss the tide.

The place was clean; the caretaker had done his job—where was the caretaker? To the Dowager's relief, there had been no sign of smuggled goods, though there had not been time to investigate all the rooms on the upper floors.

In brief glimpses from the windows during all the activity, she had seen that Nicholls and his men were searching the village. Air from the open casements carried the sound of crashing furniture and the shouted remonstrances of its owners. She was sorry for it but there was nothing she could do; if the villagers were smuggling, they must expect it.

Now, standing at the front window of the Great Hall, she watched with relief as the *Wasp* followed the barge towards Plymouth and found exultation in her command of the view. Here, at last, was freedom.

It had to be admitted that it was not luxury.

T'Gallants possessed nothing so feminine as a parlour—presumably when Pomeroy gentlemen had roistered, Pomeroy ladies retired to their bedrooms—so she'd had to annex the Great Hall as her sitting room. In any case, she was unwilling to relinquish such a view. But her few tables and chairs looked pitiful in its vastness and it was still dominated by the dragon's gape of the fireplace and the oak throne on the west wall which had proved too heavy to budge. And by the front window: the most wonderful thing in the room, with its hundreds of latticed panes so mellowed by time that, when the sun had shone through their amber and greenish glass, the effect was that of a vast honeycomb thrown on the floor.

But now the sun was going down, its rays full on the houses of the village but missing the hall's window and putting the hall into an early dusk.

Joan had sunk onto a packing case, tired and obviously depressed.

'Candles,' said the Dowager, 'and supper. You'll feel better with something inside you. Shall we see how Mrs Clarke is getting on?'

They walked along a passage that had become very dark to an ancient arched door. Kitchens were not in the Dowager's line, she had rarely visited one, having chosen Chantries's menus from the decency of her sewing room, but she had recognized on her first visit that T'Gallants's was a pig.

Some centuries-dead Pomeroy had visited France and recreated the kitchen of Fontevrault on a Devon clifftop. A giant pepperpot of a building, the middle of its ceiling was so high as to be lost in darkness. Four enormous fireplaces, each with its own flue, stood ready for an invisible army of cooks to roast invisible oxen. Between them, whitewash fallen off the stone left leprous, grey patches on the walls. Spiked hooks hung down from the roof. Bread ovens were gaping holes, reminiscent of wall graves. A well-head with bucket attached stood in one corner. Only a gleaming collection of pans and skillets suggested that the place had been used since the Black Death.

For which, thought Diana, it could have been responsible.

Mrs Clarke and Polly stood at its vast central table, chopping onions brought with them from the Edgcumbe kitchen garden and radiating resentment. Tobias was up a ladder washing one of the tiny, high windows in an attempt to increase the miserable lighting.

'I wath thaying it'th nithe and cool in here, your ladyship,' he called in the artificially bright tone of encouragement. 'Better than motht kitchenth on a hot day.'

He was right. Even with one of the ovens lit, it was downright cold. In winter it would be icy.

'And *I* was saying, your ladyship,' declared Mrs Clarke, 'that I never worked in a kitchen where I had to wind up water in a bucket. There's no pump!'

'One supposes it was useful in a siege,' Diana said.

'Well, all I hope is we don't have no sieges and not too many guests neither.'

'No, Mrs Clarke, I shall not be entertaining.'

'There ain't even anywhere to sit down and my poor legs . . .'

'An' 'tis spoookish,' Polly said, dragging out the word and shivering. 'I do swear I saw a spectrish figure flittin' along that passage there.'

'It would be the caretaker, he hasn't presented himself yet.'

'Didn't look like no living man to me, all flowy it was.'

'An' my poor legs . . .'

She'd always had people to stand between her and the earthier side of domestic management before; she must learn to cope with this. 'Follow me, Mrs Clarke, and you shall choose a chair to your liking from the undercroft. Tobias, you'd better come too to carry it. Bring a candle.'

Halfway down the circular stair that led to the undercroft, Diana decided she'd made a mistake to bring Mrs Clarke with her. Polly had followed, declaring herself too frightened to stay in the kitchen on her own, and drew in hissing breaths at the shadows cast on the walls by Tobias's candle.

The undercroft was low-vaulted and, as far as it was possible to see, ran round the foundations of the house itself. Carved pillars held up the roof. One wall was piled with furniture, bric-a-brac, portraits—a painted face peered from a frame, the candlelight lending it a leering squint. A tattered tapestry of a hunting scene, complete with eviscerated stags, covered another section of wall between two pillars. Such light as there was coming through the barred windows fell on a massive table that dominated the place and on which a mound was covered by a carpet. Tobias moved towards it and reached out his hand to twitch the carpet off.

Immediately, Diana wanted to stop him. The atmosphere of the place was tomblike and affected even her. There could be nothing good under there. It resembled a catafalque.

The carpet slid away and she was horribly right. It was a coffin.

With a corpse in it.

Tobias and the Dowager led a screaming Mrs Clarke and a near-fainting Polly back to the kitchen where Joan, attracted by the noise, revived them with cooks' brandy before escorting them to the bedroom they insisted on sharing together, being too scared to sleep separately.

'Tobias,' the Dowager said, 'I want you to go to the village and enquire for the head man, captain, parish councillor, beadle, whatever he calls himself. Tell him I require him here and I require him now.'

'Yeth, your ladyship.'

Joan was unpacking the hamper good Lady Edgcumbe had provided for dinner and which they had been too busy to broach. It was all the food they would get now.

'They'll go,' she said.

The Dowager sighed. 'I know.'

'Me too.'

'*Joan!*'

'Oh, I'll wait 'til you got somebody in my place, but I knew I was too old for this afore I came. Got soft, I reckon. An' with Torbay being so close . . . well, reckon it's time I went home. My sister's there. Remember Rosie? Second parlour maid to your aunt, she was.'

Stricken, Diana caught the old woman's hand and held it to her cheek. 'I can't do without you.'

Joan stroked her forehead. 'I were never a proper lady's maid, not like all the fancy French pieces served other ladies. Always had to get in M. Alphonse to do your hair, di'n't you?'

'You were better than a lady's maid, you were a friend.'

'That's why I stayed,' Joan said, 'I saw how you was treated . . . There, I won't go on'—the Dowager had stiffened—'but many's the time I wanted to take a knife to 'un. That's over now, thanks be to God, and you've got life back in your eyes, same as you had when we used to go down the beach when you was a girl.'

'I'll always thank you for that.'

'And I've got that annuity he left me in his will and I reckon that's a-due to you, for surely he wouldn't have given me tuppence on his own.'

Diana remained silent. But it was true; it had taken everything she knew to keep Joan as her attendant and have her suitably rewarded. *'Buck-toothed old hag. Why can't you have a maid like Sophie Buckingham's? Pretty little thing with a bit of go in her.'*

That was why.

She clung harder. 'Don't go.'

'Won't be far away, will I? No, your ladyship's passed through the Slough o' Despond now and you've a-come to your Delectable Mountain'—here Joan looked around her—'though 'twouldn't be my choice o' perch, I must say.' She kissed Diana's hair. 'Time I went home, my dear, I'm tired.'

She looked at the man standing before her with disfavour. Massive as he was, the shadow he cast on the wall of the Great Hall in the candlelight was almost frightening. 'Mr Gurney?'

'Jan Gurney, your ladyship. Welcome to T'Gallants and Babbs Cove. 'Tis good to have a Pomeroy back.'

'Is it? One feels, Mr Gurney, that the welcome would have been slightly warmer without the corpse.'

'Ah, well.' He shuffled his big feet. 'You'm owed an apology there, but we wasn't expectin' you to move in so soon and what with it bein' hot weather and havin' to send to Newton Ferrers for a parson for the funeral an' Henry Hobbs not gettin' any prettier, we reckoned as how—'

'One's undercroft is not a mortuary, Mr Gurney.'

' 'Tis cool, though.'

He puzzled her. She was at her loftiest, a stance which usually reduced peasants to slithering subservience. She'd encountered this man's assumption of equality once or twice from the *nouveau riche*; men of the manufacturing class, waving their democracy in her face in an attempt to show that Jack was as good as his master. But where they had merely been brash this enormous tatterde-malion was assured.

The two of them studied each other while Diana mentally examined her family's records. Gurney, Gurney. We hanged one of them for poaching in the 1590s. And there'd been a female Gurney in 1666 to whom Sir Peter Pomeroy left a suspiciously large amount in his will. In its way, this man's lineage was as long as her own . . .

'How did you get in?' she asked.

'Always had a key. Village uses the place for storin' goods, like—nobody 'abn't minded before.'

He was being surprisingly honest. She said: 'Do I gather these goods have not been subjected to duty—?'

'Free trade, we call 'un,' he interrupted.

'—and are therefore the reason why Captain Nicholls has been so insistent in wanting to search my house?'

'Stood up to 'un for us, didn't ee?'

Oh Lord, they thought she had done it for them; that she had some sort of knowledge of their activity and had believed there to be contraband in her house. 'Are there any goods here at the moment?'

'No. You forgot, seemingly. 'Tis summer. 'Tis fishin' with us in summer. I'd'a been at sea along o' the others if *Lark* hadn't needed her old bottom scraped. Winter's the time for free tradin'.' He added disgustedly: 'I'd'a thought Nicholls would've known tha-at.' He smiled at her. 'Only spirit in this house be Henry Hobbs's.'

She refused to be charmed. 'Very well. But I must make it clear to you that henceforth T'Gallants will store nothing. No bodies and especially no contraband. Is that clear?'

'Pity,' he said. Obviously, in his view she was making a mistake on her own account.

'Is that *clear*, Mr Gurney?'

'It is.'

'Then you may sit down.'

He dragged up a chair and dwarfed it.

'Mr Gurney,' she said. 'Twice now I have heard the evil of wrecking attributed to T'Gallants and the Pomeroy name . . .' She was going to go on and say she wanted the suggestion stamped on, her family was an honourable one, but she was stopped by the look in his eye, which was alarmingly regretful.

'Wicked old days, they was,' he said.

'You are not suggesting it was true?'

'So they say. Them forebears of ours ain't much to be proud of.'

Again the sense of shared experience; they were complicit in long-dead wickedness.

'I refuse to believe it,' she said. Birthright delineated her honour. The role the Pomeroys had played in England's pageant had given her integration with its history, the right to be proud, the recognition of the justice by which her family and fellow-nobility ruled its acres and directed its government. If it was not God-given, if her ancestors and this man's ancestors had waded through blood-stained water, feasting like sharks on the helpless, she was less than she had thought herself to be.

Gurney shrugged and pointed behind her, to where the sound of the sea's gentle shushing came with moonlight through an open casement. 'That's been called wreckers' window so long as I can remember.' He leaned forward as if to pat her knee, then thought better of it. 'Reckon we've all lived more decent since then,' he said. 'Washed the guilt away, like, though I do still send up a prayer for forgiveness when I think of ut.'

How odd, she thought. This man too, this common smuggler, feels the weight of his ancestry. He is giving us both absolution.

'Ye-es,' he said, reminiscing, 'they turned to free tradin' after that. My great-great-great-grandaddy sailed back and forth to Roscoff free tradin' for Sir Peter—proper Pomeroy, he was—oh, many and many a time. Course,'twas easier in them days. Revenue weren't so sharp.'

'Sir Peter Pomeroy died fighting the Dutch off North Foreland,' she said, sharply.

'And Great-great-great-grandaddy Gurney died with 'un.' He got up, rearing over her like a freak wave. 'Better be gettin' back, your ladyship. I'll see to the corpse come mornin'. I'll be a-mendin' 'til then—them whoreson Revenue went through my cottage abreakin' everything, even the baby's cradle, dang 'un.' He grinned at her, winking. 'Us won't forget you stood up to 'un, though. Proper Pomeroy, you are. Welcome home.'

Home, she thought, when he'd gone. I have come home. To what? To some sort of criminal democracy?

Yet she was warmed by his assumption that she had returned to where she belonged. The odd thing was that, despite everything, she felt that she had.

Joan had gone to bed. The Dowager took her supper alone in the Great Hall; the dining room still lacked chairs and, anyway, had a deadening atmosphere which the hall, for all its severity, lacked. Although the food was from a hamper and she was prepared to make allowances tonight, Tobias's sense of what was proper demanded she eat in style.

She watched him as he laid a little table by her chair at the oriel window, seeing how his black face disappeared when he turned away from the candelabra so that he was a headless body with white gloves.

'I fear Joan is leaving us, Tobias.' It was only now, in losing her, that what existed between her and the woman who had shared the last twenty-odd years with her she knew to be love, something she had not imagined between mistress and servant. Affection, yes, but not love. Joan, she realized, had been more of a mother to her than the beautiful, unapproachable, generally absent woman who had given her birth.

'We'll mith her, your ladyship.'

'Yes.' Very much, *very* much.

'I fear the cook and the girl may be going ath well, your ladyship.'

'How will we manage, Tobias?'

He was undisturbed. 'I can athk in the village, I dare thay.'

'In the morning.' She could imagine his effect on some fisherman's wife as she opened the door to him at this time of night. 'When you've finished here, go to bed. It has been a long day.'

'Yeth, your ladyship. And I can turn my hand to motht thingth, your ladyship.'

So he could. It struck her that if he left her she would be virtually helpless, yet she had uprooted him from Chantries as casually as breaking off a leaf to transplant it somewhere else. He was a comfort. Although it was a given that negroes were eye-rollingly superstitious and afraid of the dark, like children, when he'd uncovered the dead man he'd merely blinked.

'Will you be happy here, Tobias?'

'Oh yeth. I like the thea, your ladyship. I wath born near it.'

Was he? How little one knew about people one was surrounded by.

A white cloth was put across his arm as he carved some chicken and poured her wine.

'And there's the caretaker,' she said. 'He seems to have kept things clean at least. Have you found him yet?'

'No, your ladyship. I've heard thomeone murmuring.'

'So have I. I thought it was the sea.' With the advent of night, the house had developed echoes that had not been apparent by day. Tobias's lisping voice domesticated a space around her that was becoming alien.

A napkin was laid across her lap and she could keep him no longer.

'Good night, Tobias.'

'Good night, your ladyship.'

In her room, a decent enough chamber at the back of the house, the Dowager found it ridiculously difficult to retire. She had a struggle to get out of her clothes and trouble finding her nightgown in the chest Joan had been too tired to unpack. She cleaned her teeth and washed her face. Brushing her own hair was an unusual experience but she persisted. Really, preparing for bed was exhausting.

Sleep, however, eluded her. The events of the day seemed to have altered her. The conversation with Gurney had reduced her yet introduced a new factor into her outlook on things.

Then, Joan. She thought of Joan as she had first seen her, the plain, friendly servant in Great-aunt Pomeroy's house in Torbay who, even then, must have seemed so important to her that she had begged her mother to take her as a maid. Memories of Joan led to memories of Martha and to an image of her as she would be, grieving, waiting . . .

I must get word to her. I need not tell her of her boy's affliction, merely that he is alive. I shall write to Fred North. Surely there is some diplomatic contact with the Americans.

Then it was the hospital, all her plans . . .

Eventually she got up, threw on a shawl and went downstairs.

The house seemed more alive now than in daytime, full of rustling and unexplained movement. Bats and owls, she told herself, but the faraway murmur she and Tobias noticed earlier persisted, as if somewhere in its depths the house was talking to itself.

In the Great Hall, she went to the wreckers' window. I will not call it that; we Pomeroys could not have had our start in such a way. There is no evidence for it.

The cove was silvered by moonlight and for a moment she thought it deserted. No, it wasn't. A ship rode on the water. *Nicholls.* God damn the man, would he never leave her alone?

Then she saw that it wasn't the Revenue cutter. She knew little about boats, but the one out there was surely larger than the *Wasp* and its hull and masts were totally black so that her eyes had been momentarily fooled into thinking the inlet empty. Floating in the moonlight, apparently deserted, the thing looked sinister. A skeleton ship.

The Dowager chided herself. It was most likely part of Babbs Cove's fishing fleet which had returned; the night-time atmosphere of the house was turning her fanciful.

She crossed the room to the oriel and opened one of its lights, letting in warm night air. The sea was out of sight from here, the sound of it just audible as it drew out and brushed in sand with a regular sigh very different from the murmuring she had heard.

She need not be concerned. A stream echoing in a cave far below, perhaps. But she was suddenly reluctant to face the passages back to her room and settled herself on the oriel seat because the view took in the moonlit village where families were, where outhouses held chickens and where waking babies were suckled back to sleep.

How comforting the ordinary was, she thought. There was a light at the inn. Tomorrow she must go and give her condolences to the relatives of Henry Hobbs; these were her people, after all.

Something was being dragged along on the other side of the room. There was nothing there, the moonlight coming through the wreckers' window showed empty stone, yet something invisible was slithering across it. In fear that it would be attracted in her direction, she blew out her candle.

The slither became a rumble, she felt the window-seat beneath her thighs vibrate, the merest frisson, before returning to solidity.

The house was moving; it was going to fall on her.

Her lips tried to form the prayer of deliverance from terror by night but they were rigid against her teeth.

Then the singing began. A deep sound, the words inextinguishable except for one.

> *'Margot, ooodooodoooodo,*
> *Margot, odoooodoooododo . . .'*

There was scrabbling behind the great black chair. The piece of carpet in front of it began to wrinkle. With a scraping sound the chair was moving slowly outwards of its own volition, swinging to one side. In the hole left behind it was a flame and a head. They rose upwards, ascending from Hell until the full demon was revealed.

It stepped forward, holding the flame aloft, stumbled over the wrinkled carpet and said, '*Merde.*'

She'd held a breath so long that she had to let it out. A whimper went with it.

The thing straightened. '*Mama Green? C'est toi?*'

She was outlined against the window. He came striding across the floor, flambeau held high so that he could peer at her face. After a moment he said: 'Definitely, you are not Mother Green. Who are you?'

He had a pistol in his belt; a scalp dangled from a ring next to it.

She said, in a high, unnatural voice: 'I am the owner of this house and in the name of Christ I bid you be gone.' Even in terror, she remembered what it was one said to demons.

There was a snort. 'Who else is here?'

'I have men all over the house,' she said.

He took the pistol from his belt and stood still, listening. After a while he grunted. 'Nice quiet men.' But the pistol stayed in his hand. He leaned forward so that his face and the flambeau were close to hers. She flinched. 'I am the Devil. Cry out, one move and I eat your head.'

She nodded.

He sidled away from her, heading for the wreckers' window but keeping her in view. 'One move.'

Another nod.

He looked around, found a sconce and lodged the flambeau in it. Then he opened one of the lights, put his fingers in his mouth and whistled three times.

There was a faint answering whistle from below.

She saw him pick up the flambeau and come back down the hall, heading for the door. On the way he shoved at the big chair with his foot and it swung back into place. The pistol was still aimed at her. 'Remember. I am not gone.'

If she'd wanted to, she couldn't have moved. Her muscles were in spasm.

A light flickered beyond the door. He was coming back. Jesus be with me in this hour, he's coming back.

He'd left the flambeau behind and now held a candle. The pistol was in his belt once more—next to the scalp. 'One man,' he said. 'There is only one man. Some old women.' He paused. 'And you.'

He had supernatural knowledge; there hadn't been time for him to look in all the rooms.

A thin, faint voice of sanity said: The caretaker told him.

He came over to her, hoisted himself onto the window seat and held the candle so that he could peer at her face, examining it inch by inch, like an aggressive doctor. There was a grunt and he leaned back, putting the candle in the space between them. He blew out his cheeks and said, aggrievedly: 'You frightened me, you know.'

She managed to say: 'Did I?' before she vomited onto the candle.

'Yach!' She heard him move quickly away. She went on being sick until she was merely retching.

A cold cloth was being applied to her face. He lifted her carefully off the sill and stood her in front of him while he wiped her down as if she were a grubby child, talking all the time. 'I hate a vomiting woman. It is not attractive.' He turned her round so that she faced the moonlight and made a last dab at her face. '*Voilà*.' And hoisted her over his shoulder.

He knew his way through the unlit passages, taking long, confident steps that made her hanging head bob like a dead rabbit's. At one point he called out: 'Which is her room?'

A voice, a whisper, said: 'At the back. Over the garden.'

He'd felt her stiffen at the mention of bed and gently thwacked her bottom. 'Not tonight. I am too tired.' Further on, he said: 'And we have not been introduced.'

Light. They were in her room. He rolled her off his shoulder so that she flopped onto the bed. He stretched, painfully. 'You set off my back,' he accused her. 'I have trouble with my back, you know.'

It was then that some vestigial reasoning returned to her. The Devil didn't complain of back trouble and neither, she hoped very much, did rapists.

His appearance was not reassuring. He wasn't young, in his forties perhaps. The candle threw shadows upwards on his face, distorting it. His head was bare and the dark hair had been cropped so short that it bristled like a gooseberry. He could have been a convict ready to be transported except that his shirt, which was open at the powerful neck, was of good linen.

The scalp at his waist was his wig. He was large and ugly but he wasn't the Devil. He was French. Nearly as bad.

She said: 'I want you out of my house.'

He paid no attention, being busy unscrewing the cap of a hip flask. She pursed her lips and shook her head as he put it to her mouth but with his other hand he wangled a finger between her teeth and made her sip.

It was excellent brandy. She took another sip, then a gulp.

'*Bien*,' he said.

She clawed for some dignity and sat up, clutching the bedclothes to her chest. 'Leave at once.'

'I stay for the funeral,' he said. 'The man in your cellar. So sad, you know. A friend of mine until he turn to the good.' He settled himself, as if for a chat. 'You live here now, Madame Pomeroy? You like it?' He put his head on one side, looking at her reflectively. '*Pomme de roi*. Yes, but the apple is a bit green, uh? Maybe when your nose runs not so much and the eyes are not so red—'

'Get out.'

'Yes.' He gave an exaggerated sigh. 'I must go. *À nos moutons*.' He took up the candle and went to the door, shambling like a bear. 'I regret I frighten you,' he said, 'I think the house was empty. But you were brave. Not bad at all.'

The door closed behind him. The echoes of a great, untuneful voice dwindled down the passage.

> '*Margot, pour té que j'endure de maux,*
> *Margot, pour té que j'endure!*'

He was singing.

Then she turned over and cried. Cried and cried, rubbing her forehead against the pillow, seeing the carpet in the Great Hall wrinkle, the chair swing open like the door to Hell.

I want him dead. Nobody should be made so afraid. She had been unwomanned, the person she had built up so painfully to withstand her fear of her husband ripped apart and reduced to a lone shard of terror. A victim again.

And yet it had been a different fear. And he was a different man. God knew what he was, but Aymer's savagery was missing from him. She forced herself to stop crying and begin thinking, jerking occasionally with a dry sob. She was alive and unravished. He wasn't going to hurt anybody. How did she know that? She did.

But the caretaker, who was his accomplice, would have to go. Mama Green, indeed.

There was some contraption behind that chair. He used it often; he was familiar with the house. In league with the village and the caretaker. He brought in contraband and used a secret way into T'Gallants to stack it. He's a smuggler, she thought drunkenly, in league with rabble and caretakers. A nice taste in brandy. A common criminal; an uncommon, common criminal. French. Enemy . . . Nice taste in brandy . . .

She woke up to a sea change. Something had happened. For a moment she was hard put to it to remember what it was, except that it had been massive. When she did remember she discovered that the change was personal, as if the events of yesterday and the terror of its night had lodged something different within her. Good or bad, it was difficult to say, but birdsong, sun and the air of a lovely summer morning coming through her bedroom window carried a new expectancy.

Fresh clothes had been draped over the bed end and on the table were a basin and ewer which hadn't been there the night before.

As she dressed, she could see out to an overgrown garden where goldfinches fluttered to balance on seedheads.

The house still held a murmur, but now it gave the impression of being companionable and contributed to by different voices. It drew her to the kitchen.

Nobody noticed her. The large Frenchman was at the table stuffing down porridge and talking loudly at the same time. Tobias and Joan sat next to him, listening and relaxed, pecking at slices of bread and butter. Another woman, who had grey hair flowing down her back, stirred a pot hung over a fire in one of the hearths, muttering with dubious sanity.

'Tobias,' the Dowager commanded, and retired.

Buttoning his jacket, Tobias followed her into the Great Hall.

'Shall I therve breakfatht, your ladyship?' He seemed perfectly normal, in fact the apparent normality of everything was making her head feel loose on her shoulders, as if, like Gulliver, she had emerged onto a land where freakishness was the standard.

She went to the wreckers' window to peer down at the cove. The inlet was empty; the black ship had gone. 'Well?'

'Mithith Clarke and Polly have already left, your ladyship. They are at the inn and I promithed to drive them to Plymouth later, with your permission. The gentleman, that'th Guillaume de Vaubon—' Tobias had the pronunciation correct—'he'th jutht going. He'th the Frenchman who landed latht night.'

'We met,' the Dowager said, grimly.

'He told me. He giveth hith apologieth for the alarm. He thought the houthe unoccupied.' Tobias allowed his gravity to slip a little. 'They all theem to know him round here. No harm to him, your ladyship, for all he'th French. I hope I did right to give him breakfatht. A very entertaining gentleman.'

'Highly entertaining.' We have undoubtedly landed on the moon, she thought. Even Tobias accepts the arrival of an enemy with his ship as part of the everyday round. 'Has his boat left without him?'

'It'th round the headland, your ladyship, in the other cove, more out of the way. I think he'th a thmuggler, your ladyship, but, like I thay, no harm to him.'

'Go on.'

'The grey-haired lady, that'th the caretaker. They call her Mother Green. She talkth to herthelf a lot.'

'She must go.'

He looked worried. 'Perhapth your ladyship should not be hathty. I've been down to the inn to thee about hiring more thervants.'

'And?'

'Not until after the harvetht, your ladyship. Even then they are unlikely to live in. I shall try further afield, of courthe, but . . .'

'I see.' It would be a hard enough struggle to run the house as it was; without someone to do the cleaning it would be impossible. She shrugged. 'Very well. What is one more madwoman in this Bedlam? But I shall talk to her. You may serve breakfast now.' She was raveningly hungry. 'I'll take it in here.'

'Oh, and the French gentleman wanted me to hand you thith.'

It was a gilt-edged visiting card printed with the legend: '*Guillaume de Vaubon vous fait ses compliments.*' Underneath a bold hand had written: 'Also his apologies and pleads you will dine with him tonight.'

She threw it on the floor. 'There is no reply, Tobias.'

'Very well, your ladyship.' He bent to pick it up. 'He thaid he'll call for you at eight.'

When he'd gone, she made for the chair and tried to pull it outwards. It didn't budge. The back was flush with the wall, admitting no leverage.

She kicked away the piece of carpet. Ah-*ha*. So she hadn't dreamed that particular nightmare; the throne was made to move. The carpet concealed two arcs scraped into the stone floor where the feet had scratched it in swinging out from the wall.

She went down on her knees. *There we are.* In front of the chair's back legs, painted black to escape attention, were two stout, knobbed pieces of iron like door-bolts, but vertical, let into the floor. She manoeuvred them sideways and up and felt the chair shift slightly as it was released.

'Morning, your ladyship.'

She hit her head springing up. 'Mr Gurney, does nobody around here use the damn door-knocker?'

'Sorry, your ladyship. Mother Green let me in earlier, when us come to take the corpse away.'

'I shall miss it,' she said, coldly. 'It raised the tone. And the other foreign body?'

'Gil? Well, us weren't sure he were comin' neither. He just turns up, like.'

'Bringing contraband with him, I assume—you being too busy fishing.'

He sighed. 'See, us've got customers to supply even in the summer.'

'Though we're at war with France?'

'Oh, tha-at,' he said. 'Us can't take notice o' wars, not us free traders can't. Country's always at war with some bugger.'

She supposed it was philosophy of a sort. She asked, really wanting to know: 'Have you no patriotism?'

He was indignant. 'Course we have. Us do risk our lives to bring in England's fish.' He pointed towards the wreckers' window. 'That's a battlefield out there, every day, not just wartime. Bloody sea don't need cannonballs to kill us, does it by its danged self. And bugger all we'm paid for ut.'

He leaned forward, stooping to look her in the eye. 'Don't suppose your ladyship do bother yourself with the price of cod, do ee? Miserable, 'tis. Don't pay for our widows and orphans and we got plenty o' they. 'Twasn't for free trade, they'd starve.'

She hadn't thought of it; in stepping out of Chantries she had entered a world of which she'd known nothing, as if she'd been living behind a convent wall.

She said: 'Help me with this chair.'

'What chair's that?'

'Oh, for goodness' sake.'

He helped her pull. Essentially, the thing was a door concealing an aperture about five foot high. Gurney put out a hand to stop her as she approached it. 'You mind. 'Tis a long drop.'

Cautiously, holding onto the jamb, she peered in. It wasn't a cupboard or a room: it was a shaft set in the thickness of the wall. Just beyond her feet was a dark drop. A smell of fresh seawater came up to her. 'Where does it go?'

There was a cave at the bottom. A natural fissure of rock running from it up to the clifftop, too steep for stairs but wide enough for a shaft, had been exploited for the purpose of transferring goods between the two.

'Been there long as anyone can remember,' Gurney told her. 'Useful when 'tis necessary to bring in stuff secret like. In the bad old days, I reckon it weren't just free-trade goods, neither.'

She met his eyes. They were telling her of ancient screams that had echoed in this shaft before being silenced, of wealth hauled up it from battered ships and torn bodies. We've sprung from wreckers, you and I, his gaze said, our ancestors were equal in evil. That's why I trust you; we share an old, old guilt.

She turned back to the shaft. Ropes as thick as hawsers ran between hoops on either side of it. 'Platform works on pulleys and ratchets, see,' Gurney said, breaking the silence. 'Haul on one rope down there and up her comes, easy as milkin'. Pull on the other and her ratchets lets her down just as easy. But us keeps them ropes in good condition, I can tell ee. Don't want to drop a hundred and fifty feet too fast.'

'I see.' So that was how the Frenchman had risen like the Devil from Hell. 'It must not be used again, Mr Gurney. I shall have it blocked up.'

He was philosophical. 'Reckoned you might. Pity, though.'

She said: 'Did you have a purpose in coming to see me?'

He slapped his forehead. 'Nigh forgot, didn' us? We was hoping as you might like to attend Henry Hobbs's funeral. We know he'd be pleased, and his family. You being a Pomeroy and lord of the manor, like.'

She stared at him. They used her house without permission, coming and going willy-nilly, filling it with contraband, madwomen and Frenchmen, treating her as if she were of no account, yet would she please honour one of their number by attending his funeral?

And, of course, she would have to. *Noblesse oblige.*

'Very well.'

Chapter Twelve

MAKEPEACE had not yet decided whether she should buy the Pomeroy Arms. Its excellence as a venue for sending Josh to France was undoubted, as was Jan Gurney's ability and probable willingness to get him there, but she wasn't so nostalgic for her days as an innkeeper as to want to be one again.

However, Mr Spettigue was eager that she should. 'Buy it one-self,' he said, 'but the Revenue looks at public-house licences an' it might seem somewhat rum. Don't want to attract attention. Better to stay a sleepin' partner.'

'A sleeping smuggler,' Makepeace accused him on the way to Henry Hobbs's funeral. 'Babbs Cove is a smuggling village, I found that out.'

'All are, dear lady. Fire cannon at any inlet on this coast and hit a free trader. Not saying one's not involved in the trade—don't know anyone who ain't—but this other matter, been keepin' Babbs Cove up one's sleeve.'

'This other matter being escapers?'

'Exactly.' He dabbed carefully at his cheeks with a heavily scented handkerchief. It was hot in her coach and his rouge was beginning to streak.

He was in funeral black, as she was, but where hers was staid, he was sporting a very short, very tight-fitting frock coat that would have pursued its intended slim line with more success had it been on a slimmer body. His silk breeches were of black and white stripes, black stockings curved luxuriously over his calves and ended in flat dancing pumps with black flowered buckles. The tiny hat balanced precariously on top of his wig looked as if someone had skimmed a small plate at his head and it had stuck.

In the fashionable parts of London, he might have gone unnoticed. In Plymouth, merely mincing across the street to get into her coach he occasioned ribaldry from small boys. Yet, deliberate or not, she thought, his foppery was an excellent disguise. In so outrageously attracting the eye, he was immediately counted as a fool and guilty of nothing other than vanity. But there was a great deal more to young Mr Spettigue than that; clothing his body as he pleased was an outward extension of a belief in the freedom of the individual that went to the bone.

Makepeace had already taxed him with the mistake he'd made over T'Gallants but he'd protested that, in principle, he'd been right. 'Nobody'd told me T'Gallants ain't on the market. Think we'll still keep your offer on the table.'

'I wouldn't live there if it was lined with diamonds.'

'Wouldn't have to for long. Matter of keepin' it in safe hands.'

'You buy it then.'

He shook his head. 'Told you, ma'am. Too dangerous to flaunt me connection. Need to have a new name on the deed but one that's on our side.'

He wouldn't be moved and made no apology for using her. If he was going to smuggle out Josh and future American escapers from Babbs Cove, she must help him by providing a refuge from which to do it.

She had considered Beasley and all the other Englishmen who were publishing their support for America's liberty to be brave enough; this ridiculous, plump young man and his friends were going considerably further than that. She, who was American, could do no less.

Which was why, on this hot Sunday, she and Mr Spettigue were on their way to the funeral of a man she had never met.

Being Sunday, it distressed her that she was not at the Millbay market, but on the last occasion she'd had an encounter with the same militiaman with whom she'd quarrelled over Josh's painting. He had spotted her trying to pass Josh some food that she'd smuggled in under her apron.

'What's this? What's this?'

'It's a cheese,' she'd said.

'Why you giving it to this black bugger, 'stead of a handsome chap like me? By rights, I should report you. Precious fond of this nigger, ain't you, lady? After a bit of black pork, are we?'

She'd wanted to kill. Instead she'd said, as composedly as she could: 'It's called charity, officer. These men look famished.'

'Don't stop the bastards ecapin'. I'll overlook it this time an' I'll just confiscate the cheese but I see you in this market again you'll be up afore the commandant.'

Even so, she would have risked a return but Beasley had pointed that she was merely bringing attention to herself and Josh, a dangerous combination if an escape were to be successful. Instead, he and Philippa would go. 'She and I keep out of trouble,' he'd said, pointedly.

Thus, when calling on Mr Spettigue to berate him for exposing her to humiliation from 'a high-nosed bitch calling herself Lady Stacroy or something' at T'Gallants, Makepeace had been free to accept his suggestion that she should ingratiate herself to the people of Babbs Cove by attending the obsequies of the late Mr Henry Hobbs—and cast her eye over the inn while she was about it.

She looked out of the coach window. They were descending a familiar hill. 'Last time I came this way, the farmer stopped us. John Beasley said he was a sort of sentry.'

'Be Ralph Gurney,' Spettigue said. 'Three Gurney cousins. Run the trade here. Ralph—farmer, supplies the ponies. Hard fellow, Ralph. Jan and Eddie—two free-trade boats. Jan, the *Lark* and Eddie, appropriately enough, the *Three Cousins*.'

'D'you think,' she said—and this was the other reason why she had agreed to come today, 'if they take Josh to France . . . do you think they would fetch my husband back?'

Oliver's latest letter had said there was still no word from Andra. Well, there wouldn't be, but she had hoped.

'Likely, ma'am. Likely. Have to ask 'em, of course. Whereabouts in France is he?'

'Paris, the last I heard.'

'Ah, Paris!' Mr Spettigue fluttered his handkerchief. 'Wonderful *parfum*, vile drains, viler monarchy.'

'*Would* they?'

'Don't think King Louis'd take kindly to English boats sailin' up the Seine in wartime, not even free traders. Have to get your husband up to the coast where he can be picked up.'

'How?'

'Send someone to fetch him. Mr Josh might oblige, when he gets there.'

'Yes.' Two birds with one stone. Some of the sense of oppression lifted slightly. She was a woman who needed to be doing something . . . well, she *was* doing something. If she had to buy this entire damn county, she'd get both her men to safety, one to France, one to England.

Cheered, she looked out of the window. 'Still harvesting, even on a Sunday?' she said.

'Vital, ma'am. No harvest, no food. Stop for the funeral, perhaps, but guaranteed back in the fields by evenin'. Bad harvest last year, year before. Starvation, high prices. Nasty.'

Indeed, when they got out of the coach onto the inn forecourt, the village appeared deserted. The fishing fleet had returned, boats with their sails furled had been anchored into the sand of the beach. But even their crews, apparently, had gone to help with the harvest. The only activity was in the Pomeroy Arms itself where a woman in its kitchen was trying to make pastry, both helped and hindered by a gaggle of children.

An old man, doing nothing at all, was sat on a stool.

On seeing Mr Spettigue, the woman burst into tears and wept on his shoulder, leaving flour on his jacket. ' 'Tis so good of ee to come, Mr Spettigue. Do ee want to see Dad? We've had to put 'un in the coach-house because he's aginning to smell, but we ab'n put the lid down on 'un yet. He's covered with gauze agin the flies.'

To his credit, Mr Spettigue allowed tears and flour to be pressed on his coat for a full minute before he dried the woman's eyes with his beautiful handkerchief and made the introductions. 'Mrs Hedley, Mrs Hallewell, late landlord's daughter. Splendid daughter in his illness, weren't ee, Mrs Hallewell?'

'He had a hard going of it, Mr Spettigue. I were up with 'un all hours.'

The old man was introduced as Mrs Hallewell's Uncle Zack.

Mrs Hallewell, so tired out from nursing her father that she looked ready to join him, bobbed a curtsey to Makepeace and began crying again. 'Mortal sorry I can't attend on ee, Mrs Hedley, but I don't know how I'm a-goin' to get all ready for arter the service. They'll be in from the harvest and needin' a pasty at the least and how that's to be done . . . An' look what the Revenue done to the place last night.'

The inn was a wreck. The door to a cupboard had been torn off, bayonets had prodded holes in the plaster of walls and ceiling, barrels had been tipped over or smashed open.

Makepeace took off her hat and rolled up her sleeves.

Babbs Cove chapel was small and plain with a barrel roof and a smell that mingled mouldy stone and fish, a result of its age and the fact that ships' nets waiting to be mended were stored in its tiny vestry.

It had no pews and no priest of its own; the minister responsible for its parishioners' souls was peripatetic and difficult to contact, which is why Henry Hobbs had waited so long for burial. He had longer to wait yet, for the chapel didn't have its own graveyard either. After the service, he'd be taken to his rest in the cemetery at Newton Ferrers by wagon.

Mrs Hallewell had been in agony over the funeral. As she'd told Makepeace when they were getting ready together, Dad had been a Methodist, and ought by rights to be buried as one. She didn't hold with it herself; Methodism wasn't a proper religion, seeing as how the Church of England wasn't reconciled to it.

In the end, she said, Jan Gurney had persuaded her towards a service in the established faith. 'Like Jan said, us'd be put to it to find a Method preacher and by the time us did, Dad'd be leaking out of his box. But whether his poor spirit'll be at rest, I don't know.'

Methodism was blamed for having run the inn down long before the advent of Captain Nicholls and his destruction.

'Only ale?' Makepeace said, unbelievingly.

Mrs Hallewell nodded and her Uncle Zack said: 'An' only that what he brewed hisself. Pisswater,'twas.'

An ale house, and one selling only pisswater if the old man was to be believed, at a time when ale houses even in towns were disappearing—hardly a good business proposition. According to Mrs Hallewell any spirit drinkers in Babbs Cove had been forced to imbibe them in their own homes or, if they sought conviviality, make the long walk to The Sloop in the next village along the coast.

'Weren't always so,' Mrs Hallewell said, apologetically. 'Dad ran a good inn once.'

'All the fault o' that John Wesley,' Zack said.

Mrs Hallewell nodded. 'So 'twas.'

'Went to Totnes to hear 'un preach, Henry did,' continued Zack. 'Sets off as good a landlord as you'd find in a month o' Sundays. Comes back a man ravin' agin the evils of drink. Abstain, he said. Wine is a mocker, strong drink is ragin', he said. Look not on the wine when it is red, he said. We bloody couldn't neither; old bugger wouldn't stock it.'

'Nor brandy nor geneva,' Mrs Hallewell said, sadly.

'That were the worst,' Zack said, shaking his head at an horrific memory. 'Watchin' the ponies go by of a night carryin' ankers o' best French and Hollands . . .'

'Zack,' warned Mrs Hallewell.

'. . . and not a bloody drop for the inn they was passin',' Zack continued, undeterred. 'She'm all right, Maggie. She'm a free trader. Told Jan Gurney so.'

So now Mrs Hallewell knelt in the front row with her children, weeping from grief, exhaustion and guilt.

At the back of the church, Sanders knelt next to Makepeace on one side and Mr Spettigue on the other, his handkerchief in use on his own eyes. Apparently he always cried at funerals.

Makepeace, too, cried quietly, though not for Mr Hobbs.

Here, in a simplicity reminiscent of her old Boston meeting house, to the call of seagulls outside and the pruk, pruk of a raven pecking insects in the open doorway, with the sun transmuted by the stone trefoil windows into bright pennies scattered harmlessly onto the shoulders of the congregation, here at last was a proper place and time to thank God for giving Philippa back to her. She asked that He do the same for Andra and keep Jenny and Sally safe for them both to come home to. She begged Him to deliver Josh from prison. She prayed for the soul of Susan Brewer to be received into Heaven with the honour it deserved.

Then she stood up to rest her knees and slake her curiosity. In Boston she had been in congregations that had held people coloured red, black and white but she had never expected in England to see such diversity as was present in Babbs Cove chapel this Sunday. There was Mr Spettigue to start with, a gleaming magpie among the duller black of the villagers, many of whom hadn't had time to do more than switch a black cloak around their harvest clothes.

And there was the Countess of Stacpoole, still and elegant at the front of the church in a chair the sexton had rushed to provide for her, having arrived only at the last minute with the unflurried nod that said *now* the service might begin.

How did they do that? Makepeace was punctual to a fault and her sojourn among aristocrats had left her amazed at their lack of concern for other people's time and their resultant magnificent, but late, entrances.

From the first, Makepeace had been suspicious that the woman was here at all. Having discovered this remote hidey-hole for Josh, it had been unnerving to find a member of the establishment just settled in it. It was like fleeing from a crime to far Cathay and encountering one's local magistrate. Had the female followed her from London after their meeting in the Sick and Hurt Office and, if so, why?

'What's she doing here?' she'd asked Mrs Hallewell.

'Come back to live in her family's old home, seemingly.'

'Won't it cramp free trade, having her here? She might be spying for the Revenue.'

'Oh no. Jan says she's a proper Pomeroy.'

Whatever a proper Pomeroy was, Makepeace felt they were taking it on trust. But then Mrs Hallewell had added cautiously: ''Sides, we can land free-trade goods in Other Bay, where her won't see 'un.'

Then there was the Frenchman, his lovely boat—a smuggler if ever Makepeace had seen one—now floating like a black swan on the turquoise water of the cove, making no attempt to hide in the less public Other Bay next door.

He had burst into the inn with Jan Gurney just before the funeral and taken Mrs Hallewell in his arms. If anything had done the poor woman good, it had been his arrival. ''Tis a blessed, blessed day that you're yere, Gil. He'd be that pleased, he were powerful fond of you, for all he changed.'

'Maggie, Maggie, I do not know he was ill. I cross oceans for him if I know, but *le bon Dieu* bring me here today of all days, I think.'

'Who's that?' Makepeace had whispered to Jan Gurney.

'That's Gil.' As if everybody knew. 'French. Brings in goods in summer. We fetch 'em from his place in Normandy come winter. Doin' it for years.' Jan shook his head, lovingly. 'I know he'm an ugly bugger, but he's a good friend to Babbs Cove.'

Which showed, thought Makepeace, how unreliable was one man's judgement of another man's attraction. The Frenchman's nose was too large, his mouth too wide, his voice too loud, his clothing too careless for beauty; there was altogether too much of him. But, oh my . . .

She felt herself become prettier when he turned to her. 'The

American! Jan tells me of you.' She was picked up so that her feet dangled and kissed on both cheeks. 'We are allies, you and I.'

And she knew they were.

There he was, holding Mrs Hallewell's hand. Lucky Mrs Halle-well. His crew had come with him, their red stocking caps scattered among the congregation's astonishing variety of headgear, two black men among them, which pleased her. They were, used to negroes here then. La Stacpoole's poor slave had caused no com-ment when he'd come in behind her and her maid, carrying her tiny ivory prayer book for her in case its weight dragged her down. Josh would not be regarded as singular.

The wide-shouldered trio obstructing her view of the table altar would be the Gurney cousins, Ralph, Jan and Eddie, the first two with hair like corn, the last's as black as a Spaniard's.

She looked back to the Frenchman. The amazing virility radiat-ing from him had emphasized the chastity she'd endured since Andra went away. Suddenly she was lusting for her husband with a physical intensity that was indecent in these surroundings.

It was *hot* in here. The press of bodies, some still sweating from the harvest fields, the smell of wormwood in which Sunday best was laid away, Spettigue's scent . . . if that priest didn't stop quoting from Job and let them all out into the fresh air, there'd be no need to bury poor old Mr Hobbs, they could just pour him away.

She began worrying about her patties, even now burning to a crisp in the inn's oven if the child they'd left in charge hadn't remembered to take them out.

A long time since she'd made patties. Then it had been in a tav-ern on one side of the Atlantic and now, here, in a tavern on the other. There was a symmetry to it.

The chapel fell silent for the dismissal, the pall-bearers took up the coffin and marched it out to the waiting cart where Henry Hobbs's eldest grandson and nephew would escort it on its journey to Newton Ferrers. Makepeace waited until Mrs Hallewell and her children had gone by, then dodged through the crowd like a ferret to get to the inn and its kitchen.

Even so, she was stopped for a moment by the view's assault of colour; she would never get used to it.

From behind her came the aristocratic drawl of the lady of the manor bestowing attention on her people.

'Please accept my condolences, my dear,' she was saying to Mrs Hallewell.

'Thank you, your ladyship. I do hope as your ladyship'll come back to the Pomeroy Arms for a glass.'

'Of course.' And to another villager: 'I suppose you have lived here all your life . . . ?'

Raising her eyes to heaven, Makepeace fled.

Despite all doors and windows being open, the inn was hot. The entire village crowded into it, munching and chattering with a gusto arising from the sense of a job well done. Children played on the stairs; babies crawled over people's boots.

Makepeace, helping to hand things round, was greeted by name. Though nobody referred to it, her purpose in coming to Babbs Cove was obviously known and accepted. If Mr Spettigue and Jan Gurney vouched for her, her credentials were good and that she was helping Mrs Hallewell approved of.

In fact, she felt (with pleasure) that she was being treated with a bonhomie not accorded the Dowager Countess of Stacpoole who, by right of ancestry, more properly belonged to the village. But then, she fitted a tavern; her hoity-toity ladyship did not.

She noticed that among all the crowding, the Dowager was given space, as if her class imposed an encirclement of isolation. People talked to her across it in their broad Devon accents, listened respectfully as the answers came back and kept a steady three feet away.

Both women ignored each other.

Guillaume de Vaubon shouldered his way to the top of the room, kicked a crate into place and placed one large sea-booted foot on it. In a long wig and leather jacket, he looked like a pirate. '*Mes amis*. Will you permit that a mere Frog pay tribute to 'Enry 'Obbs?'

There was a roar of permission. 'Go on, Gil.' 'You tell it, my son.'

It was a masterly valediction. The huge, authoritative voice drew a picture of the Pomeroy Arms's warmth and conviviality under Mr Hobbs in his pre-Methodist days that drew sighs of nostalgia from its audience.

'When he changed, for me, I was sad. A good inn is of God's own grace. Our Saviour's first miracle was to provide wine at the Cana wedding.' He paused. 'But it is wrong to blame. 'Enry, he thought of his own path to salvation as all must and which of us sinners will say he mistook the way?'

The taproom shook with cheers. Makepeace, admiring, watched the tension ease from Mrs Hallewell's worn face. She glanced towards the Dowager, curious to see how a lady of standing reacted to this volcanic intrusion from enemy shores.

The woman was regarding the Frenchman with impassivity but for a moment Makepeace experienced a reluctant and horrified pity. There was *something*. Another one, she thought, who's been without a man for a long, long time. Well, he'd liven her up. She'd be lucky to get him.

The Frenchman had not finished. He raised his hand and there was immediate silence.

'And now, dear friends, we say good-bye. I go home to prepare *La Petite Margot* for war. Louis is a bad king but this war I must fight. It will not be long perhaps but now, until peace comes, I leave to you the last run of goods.'

Mrs Hallewell began crying again and more than one of the mourners joined her. 'Bloody war,' one of the men said, wiping his eyes.

The Dowager bestowed a last condolence on her hostess and left with her elderly maid and her manservant, who still carried her prayer book, walking behind her.

Makepeace sought out Jan Gurney. 'If she's only just arrived in the village, how do you know she condones all this free trade?'

'She'm a Pomeroy, she won't give us away. Stood up to Nicholls like a soldier.'

'Nicholls?'

'Revenue man.'

'Oh, one of *them*.' The Revenue had been the bane of Make-peace's life in her tavern days, as it had of all right-thinking Bostonians. Well, that was one thing she and the high-nosed madam had in common.

The mourners went back to the harvest fields, leaving the inn to the crew of *La Petite Margot* and their hosts.

'Better get the goods ashore, Gil,' Jan Gurney said. 'And I should take *Margot* round to Other Bay after. Revenue's no respecter of Sundays nowadays.'

'You keep a lookout?'

'Course.'

'Then I outrun the bastard.' He looked round the devastated taproom. 'Do they find all the *cachettes*, Maggie?'

'Most of 'un. Second cellar. An' they kept pokin' the walls with their bagginets 'til they found the cupboard in the wall. Nothin' in 'un, o' course. Terrible it was, Gil. Didn' look in the well, though.'

'Then we put it there. It is sad you lose T'Gallants.'

'A blow, that,' Gurney agreed. 'But I got hopes her'll come round.'

'You goin' to work on her hiding places, Gil?' Zack said gleefully.

De Vaubon tut-tutted. 'I merely take the lady to dinner before I sail.'

Lucky lady, Makepeace thought. She said: 'Monsieur, I want to get a letter to my husband. He's been trapped in Paris by the war. Will you send it for me when you get back to France?'

'Of course, madame.'

'Makepeace.'

'Gil.'

They shook hands on it. 'It is important, this letter?' he asked.

'*He's* important. I want him home.'

'If you like,' he said, 'I send one of my men to Paris. We make sure the letter arrives, uh?'

She bit her lip in order not to cry with gratitude. 'Damn the war,' she said. 'You keep yourself safe now.'

'All war is damned,' he said, 'but America will win this one.'

While he and his men transferred contraband from *La Petite Margot* to the tunnel in the Pomeroy's well that ran upwards to an underground room, Makepeace, Sanders and Mrs Hallewell cleared up, watched by Zack and Mr Spettigue.

'What will you do now, Mrs Hallewell?' Spettigue asked her.

'I don't rightly know, sir. I want to get back to my little cottage with the children, I never liked inn life, not even as a girl. I'd sell 'un, but who'd buy ut like 'tis? Nobody in the village do want the work yet ut's got to stay in safe hands, as you well know.'

Spettigue glanced at Makepeace. 'I was going to suggest you keep the licence, ma'am, and take in paying guests.'

'Oh no, Mr Spettigue, I couldn't cope with 'un—'

'*Working* paying guests,' Makepeace said. 'Just for a while, to see how we all get on.'

'You, Mrs Hedley?'

'Me, Mrs Hallewell.'

Mrs Hallewell smiled for the first time that day. 'Reckon I could manage that,' she said.

The return journey from Babbs Cove to Plymouth was made through a countryside replete with golden evening sunshine and, on Makepeace's part, a feeling of achievement and therefore happiness. She had approved of and been approved by Babbs Cove. Arrangements were in place and a letter was on its way to Andra.

At his house, Mr Spettigue left her and she was driven on, more contented than she had been in weeks.

It was dark by the time the coach pulled up outside the Prince George; men were playing bowls outside it by the light of flares, watched by customers sitting on the benches under the trees.

Beasley had been waiting for her and when she glimpsed his face, she said: 'What is it?'

'Don't unhitch the horses, Peter,' he told Sanders. 'Let 'em drink and then come upstairs, we've got to go out again.'

'What is it?'

'Upstairs.'

Philippa was waiting for them in her bedroom, her face as pale as Beasley's.

'What *is* it?'

'Josh. He's going to escape tonight.'

'Josh,' she repeated. 'Tonight.'

'Yes. Jesus, I thought you'd never get back in time. We need the coach.'

Philippa thrust a piece of wood towards her mother. 'He gave us this. Well, John bought it. There was hardly a chance to talk to him. That militiaman, the horrible one, he was there and—'

Makepeace held up a hand. 'When is all this happening?'

'Tonight, I tell you. Half after eleven.'

'What's the time now?'

'Nearly ten.'

She took off her cloak and sat down on the bed, then made them sit down as well. 'Tell me.'

The two of them had attended the Sunday market as arranged. Josh was in his usual place next door to the cider stall and so had been Makepeace's *bête noire*, the militiaman. They had been extra careful because, they said, this time the militiaman had been more vigilant than usual.

'He was watching Josh all the time, wasn't he, John?'

Beasley nodded. 'Didn't take his eyes off him.'

'He may have been waiting for you to turn up, Mama, but he definitely suspected something.'

So they had wandered through the market for an hour before approaching Josh and even then Beasley had done so alone, in case the militiaman remembered seeing Philippa with her mother. 'And the moment I went up to him, Josh slipped that onto the stall.'

That was another wooden picture of an inn, this time only vaguely reminiscent of the Roaring Meg, the same background of sea but a different shape, a flatter roof with only one chimney, and the building outlined as if by a halo.

Beasley went on: 'Josh said: "Buy this, sir, and you can sit and look at it tonight." And he said "tonight" again and wanted to tell me something else but at that moment the militia bastard leaned over and took it out of my hand and insulted Josh, asking why he kept painting trash like that.'

'Did he actually say he was making a break for it?' Time, like Beasley, was running on and she'd still no idea from what part of Millbay's extensive perimeter Josh would make his escape. So far she'd heard nothing to convince her that he *would* make it.

Beasley expired. 'He couldn't, could he? That fellow was listening to every word.'

'So you bought the picture.'

'The bastard let me buy it in the end—and kept the money.'

'Did Josh say anything else?'

'He said I was to pay particular attention to the seagulls, he thought he'd drawn the path of their flight particularly well.'

Makepeace looked at the picture again. Two seagulls were depicted flying away from the chimney. They were nice seagulls, but she couldn't see anything special about them. She was having trouble throwing off her contentment at the day's achievements and was unreceptive to an excitement for which she could see little cause. Beasley and Philippa had lathered themselves into nervousness, Beasley particularly, through their imaginations.

'And that's all?' she asked.

'We came away then and—'

'But *I* was going to get Josh out.' She wasn't ready for it, preparations would have to be made, Spettigue alerted—Josh would have to wait for her.

Beasley was getting angry. 'How? How were you going to? We haven't access to the prison itself. That boy can't pick and choose his time, he's got to take an opportunity when it presents—and that's tonight.'

'How do you know?'

Philippa gave a push at the painting. 'Look, Mama. It's a map. Josh has drawn us a map. This outline is the road that runs round the prison, it's exact, we walked it afterwards, didn't we, John?'

'Don't ask me, ask your mother, she knows everything.' He

roused himself from a sulk. 'Listen, Missus, that house he's drawn is the same shape as Millbay Prison, it's even in proportion. The only difference is the chimney. The perimeter wall is rectangular and smooth, it doesn't have a protuberance anywhere. The chimney on the picture marks the point where Josh will make his exit over the wall or through it or under it or whatever he's going to do.'

He fell back on the bed, exhausted by explanation, then sat up. 'We've been studying the painting all afternoon and Philippa worked all this out; she's a clever girl, our Pippy.'

'We went to the place indicated by the chimney, Mama. It is ideally suited. There's a copse on the other side of the road from the prison and beyond the copse is a cart track that connects with the road further down. We can wait there with the coach.'

Oh no, we can't, Makepeace thought. Whatever happened tonight, Philippa was not going to be involved in it. Aloud, she asked: 'How do you know the time?'

'Look at the bloody picture, woman.'

She looked closer. The inn had a sign outside it showing a clock face, tiny letters at the bottom of the sign read: 'The Clock' as if that was the name of the inn. The hands of the clock stood at half past eleven.

A knock on the door announced the arrival of Sanders. Beasley and Philippa began their tale over again. Listening to it a second time, Makepeace began to give it credence.

She interrupted only once. '*Them?* Why do you say we will be waiting for *them?*'

'Two seagulls, Mama,' Philippa said, calmly. 'Josh never does anything without a reason. There'll be two of them making the escape.'

What an extraordinary child she is; she flounders me.

Makepeace took in a breath. 'You are not coming, Pippy.'

'I am.'

'You've been in more than enough danger this year, I am not taking you into more.' She saw the girl's resentment at being denied an adventure which, after all, she'd had the wit to decipher. I am being overbearing, she thought, but I can't help it—I will not risk her again. 'Where is Dell?'

'We told her to go to bed. Pip didn't want to involve her in this.'

One blessing.

She turned to Sanders, the only one among the four of them who could drive a coach. 'Peter, if anything goes wrong . . . I'll take responsibility, say you didn't know my intention, but it's right you should know it may be dangerous.'

'All right, Missus.' She had given him no option; he wasn't best pleased, she could see. But neither am I, she thought.

That left Beasley. 'I want you to stay with Philippa,' she said. 'If it does go wrong, there must be somebody who can call on lawyers, tell Oliver, whatever needs doing.'

He protested, blustering, but he was relieved, bless him; so brave in his principles, so afraid of physical risk.

She hated this; she liked matters planned, details worked out, not rushing unprepared into she-didn't-know-what. Food, Josh would need food. No time for any to be sent up. Clothes, he'd need clothes, maybe bandages . . .

Giving continual instructions, she began throwing things into her valise, then thought how suspicious it would look to be seen carrying it to the coach, then decided that it wouldn't if Sanders carried it, as if she were going to stay overnight somewhere.

In the end, she said: 'Oh, come on,' grabbed Sanders by the arm and rushed him out of the room, leaving Beasley and Philippa staring after them.

They had no trouble in finding Josh's 'chimney', a thick little wood of beeches and bramble opposite the north wall of the prison and divided from it by a wide road that ran east and west.

Entering the cart track that went behind the copse was another matter. At this time of night the road was busy with traffic heading for Dock as officers and men who'd been roistering in Plymouth went back to their vessels.

'We don't want to be seen going into the track,' Makepeace called to Sanders. As far as she could judge it led only to a farm and, in her inflamed state of mind, decided that a coach seen disappearing up it would attract suspicion.

Four times Sanders slowed his horses as they reached the track's entrance and four times she shouted at him to drive on because another coach, a carriage and, on the third occasion, a group of drunken sailors on foot, was either approaching or coming up behind them, an inconvenience that each time entailed Sanders having to drive nearly a quarter of a mile before finding a place with enough space to turn.

Eventually, Makepeace heard him say: 'Gor dang it,' and direct his team into the track in full view of a pair of passing horsemen who stared at them.

It was dark behind the wood. The coach rocked as it encountered ruts, its lamps bouncing light off an overgrown hedge to the left and pale, graceful tree trunks on the right. The smell from beyond the hedge suggested the site of a pig farm but, if there was a house, its occupants had gone to bed.

'Are we facing Plymouth?'

'Yes, Missus.'

'Can we get out to the road this way?'

They investigated, found that they could—the track formed an arc—and returned to the coach. 'You stay here then, Peter. I'll go into the trees and watch the wall.'

He glanced at the ghostly beeches. 'You don't want to be alone in there, Missus.'

'Don't be ridiculous. Stay here and get ready to leave in a hurry.'

'All right, Missus. Where'll we go?'

'Babbs Cove.'

'Horses are tired. They'll need a rest.'

'They're resting, aren't they? What's the time?'

He fumbled in his coat and brought out a timepiece, holding it to the lamps. 'Just after eleven.'

She set off into the copse and almost immediately had to come out again, ripping her skirts away from the brambles that made progress impossible. In any case, it was too dark in there to see her way. A vestige of moon enabled her to stumble along the track until she saw in front of her the dried mud of the road making a pale, wide ribbon with verges on either side. She stepped under a tree, peering through beech branches at the prison wall some twenty-five yards away.

The road was still busy and her view kept being blocked by traffic.

The wall was high; moonlight glinted on broken glass set into its top. Some way beyond it, she could just see the roofs of buildings like long boxes outlined by light that came from much further off, by the entrance gates. The boxes were in darkness. Did they shut the poor boys up without light?

The miasma of the prison's stink overpowered the freshness of earth and of the beech leaves among which she stood. Passing horses added a contribution to it, leaving a momentary and much more pleasant smell of their manure.

Two disembodied beams of light bobbed along the top of the wall, like marsh spirits, each coming from opposite directions. As they crossed, she heard an exchange of voices.

Guards. With lanterns. Guards were patrolling inside the perimeter. Did Josh know that? Shut up in his box, would he know that?

From the direction of Plymouth came the sound of church clocks striking the quarter past in counterpoint. She began to count. She'd reached three hundred when the lights appeared, bobbed and crossed again. Five minutes. The guards crossed that point every five minutes.

On this still night a breeze kept trembling the leaves she peered through. When she took her hand off the branch they stopped shaking.

The number of horsemen, coaches and carriages on the road began to decline; the good little Cinderellas of the Royal Navy had to be home by midnight. She watched a figure coming up the road from the Plymouth direction at stumbling run. Hurry up, you'll turn into a pumpkin. Then she saw it was John Beasley.

She called softly to him. He looked both ways and hurried towards her. He was out of breath. 'Decided. Ought to be. Here.'

She took his hand and held it against her cheek. 'What's the time?'

'Can't see.'

But just then the clocks of Plymouth told them it was half past eleven.

Makepeace kept turning her head to scan what length of the wall she could see. 'He'll come out somewhere along here? You're sure?'

'Philippa's sure. She's angry with you, not letting her come.'

'There's the patrol, look. It passes every five minutes. He'll have to be quick.' She began rubbing her hands up and down, thigh to knee, knee to thigh.

The clocks struck the quarter. They seemed more distant than before, as if they were losing interest. It's a wild goose chase. It was just a picture, I knew it, he never intended to come.

More bobbing lights along the top of the wall, then darkness.

Beasley nudged her and pointed. 'Something on the wall. There.'

Perhaps there was; the shards of glass that otherwise reflected the moonlight had developed a dark gap, as if somebody had flung a mat across.

She thought, afterwards, that she saw hands reaching up but her memory of the moment remained confused by the hell that broke out in it. The Plymouth clocks rang for midnight, the great bell of the prison began to toll, there was shouting, and from much nearer, so hideously near that the two watchers ducked, came the sound of musket fire.

Chapter Thirteen

'ONLY a little cheese and fruit tonight.' After the landlord's funeral, she had been required, for form's sake, to partake of a pasty or patty, or whatever they called the thing, and was not hungry.

Joan, who had drunk too freely, had gone to bed.

'Shall I therve it in the Great Hall, your ladyship?'

'Of course.' She always ate there; she hoped there was no meaning in his question. 'And send Mrs Green to me.'

When he'd gone, she crossed to the throne chair and made sure that its bolts were firmly in place. If the Frenchman disregarded her refusal to dine with him and came for her by way of the shaft he would find himself both mistaken and locked out. She must get the thing bricked up; she would not be prey to villains who thought to come and go as they pleased.

A rogue, she thought. A rogue and an actor. His speech at the inn praising the late Mr Hobbs had been a performance, a compelling one—which was why she'd been unable to drag her eyes away from him as he made it—but a performance nevertheless.

She looked out of the wreckers' window and saw *La Petite Margot* anchored in the bay, her riding light reflected in the water. On the beach, dark against the light sand, was a rowing boat, indicating that whoever had come ashore was still ashore.

He will be at the Pomeroy Arms, she thought, and went to sit in her favourite chair by the oriel window where scented night air came through its open lights with the sound of revelry from the inn.

She had been pleased by the encounter with her villagers, smugglers though they might be. Most courteous and respectful.

Why the Hedley woman had also been welcomed into their midst, she could not think, nor what she had wanted with Babbs Cove in the first place. Something to do with smuggling, perhaps; a woman like that would not scruple to make money from the trade. Well, she had gone away empty-handed as far as T'Gallants was concerned and it was to be hoped that this day would see the last of her.

Remembering how Mrs Hedley had seemed more at home among the people at the inn than she herself, the Dowager experienced . . . what was it? Wistfulness? Jealousy? But, of course, she was a common woman among commoners and spoke their language. Inevitably, she herself must remain isolated by her class from the people down there who talked and laughed together.

The loneliness of privilege, she thought, the privilege of loneliness.

It had been impossible not to contrast the funeral she had just attended with Aymer's, the emotion and camaraderie present in the impoverished little church with the lack of it in the over-decorated chapel at Chantries.

Past Pomeroys were recorded here and there on its walls, though their bones lay in the private chapels of other houses in other counties. There had been no memorial at all to Sir Walter.

Mainly, the wooden plaques on the walls of Babbs Cove's church bore witness to the price the sea demanded from its users. '. . . Drowned at sea in his seventeenth year.' '. . . Lost at sea, aged sixty.' Sons, husbands, fathers. On one plaque, fourteen names, ten from the same family, spoke of the loss involved when the *Jolly Harry* went down off Start Point in the gale of '89.

A certain Mrs Gurney—from the dates, the Dowager presumed she was Jan's mother—had lived to the age of fifty-seven, her death bewailed by the seven children given to her by a husband who'd drowned twenty-eight years before.

'Mithith Green, your ladyship.'

The Dowager turned to lecture the only living soul in Babbs

Cove who had not attended Henry Hobbs's funeral—and, seeing it face to face for the first time, was stopped by the woman's appearance. 'Are you ill, Mrs Green?' In the candlelight, the caretaker's skin showed livid over gaunt bones.

'Well enough.' The voice was hoarse, as if it were rarely used. 'Please sit down.'

The woman groped at the chair arms before lowering herself into it. Her eyes roamed the hall like someone seeing it for the first time, and every so often they darted back to some spot as if attracted by a sudden movement invisible to anyone else. This, with her hanging grey hair and the constant working of her mouth, would, the Dowager felt, have condemned her to the stake in the days of the Witchfinder General.

Her quarters were on the yet-unexplored upper floors of the west wing but some stimulus kept her on the move by night, using passageways that only she knew, filling the house with murmurs and restlessness as if she awoke its ghosts as she went.

After the funeral, the Dowager had asked one or two of the villagers about her but the response had been vague. 'Oh, she don't have much to do with us.' 'Keeps herself to herself, your ladyship.'

'Mrs Green, I wish to talk to you about the Frenchman who illegally entered this house last night . . . Do you have pain?' The woman had winced.

'I'm all right.'

'He calls himself Guillaume de Vaubon and I have reason to know you aided him in—'

The woman had smiled, showing broken teeth. 'Gil. He's the only one.'

'The only one of what?'

'Good to me. Kind, he is. Not like some.'

'Nevertheless, I am most displeased . . .' Again, she stopped; it was difficult to talk to a woman watching something over your shoulder that wasn't there. How could she dismiss a semi-deranged creature? What would become of her? 'Have you friends in the village? Relatives?'

'No. Nobody don't care for me.' The answer was almost casual, yet probably true. 'Cruel hard, men are. Only Gil—he be good to me.'

Diana began making mental excuses for her. Apart from her lapse in letting the Frenchman in—undoubtedly, it was she who had raised the bolts on the chair-door—the woman could not be accused of neglecting her position. T'Gallants was as clean as one person could keep it, and she had refused entry to Captain Nicholls and his Revenue men in a manner worthy of a Royalist retainer denying the master's castle to Cromwell's troops. To dismiss her because her appearance and manner were unfortunate would be uncharitable.

'Very well, Mrs Green. I shall overlook it this time, though not again.'

When she had gone, the Dowager sat on.

So the Frenchman was kind, was he? So rare in Mrs Green's experience. *So rare in mine.*

Oh, face it, woman. *You want him to come—as you have never wanted anything.*

Today, at the inn, watching him talk, she had been riven. An ugly, overlarge, common, criminal foreigner had set her body and soul agape. She could not understand it, certainly did not wish it. To be wrenched by desire like that, and for such a man, was inappropriate and undignified.

And it terrified her.

An invitation to dinner, inevitably to an *affaire* . . . did she flatter herself? No, the man was French, for him it would be *de rigueur*, a habit, an automatic seduction to which he undoubtedly subjected any woman catching his fancy. For her, it was unthinkable. She had position, honour, to uphold; she could not tumble into a smuggler's bed like some trollop he'd picked up in port.

No, she would not succumb.

Why not? Old age is ahead of you, my dear, and mere self-respect is a cold companion to it.

She knew why not. Because *physically* she could not; she had been Aymer's wife and their marital bed had been so terrible she was condemned to lie on it forever. The extraordinary liquidity of flesh she had felt on looking at the Frenchman today had dried up in the panic of what might be demanded of her tonight.

I am *frightened*.

Dear God, she would never be free of Aymer's chains; she was condemned to sexual timidity until she died. Daylight was too bright for eyes used to the dimness of a cell; safer, so very much safer not to venture out into it. Though the gaoler be dead, she thought, I am still his prisoner.

Therefore the bolts on the legs of the chair-door that led to the shaft were firmly planted in the stone of the floor. As a reminder to herself, she had dressed in black, though it was her best black and did contrast well with her complexion. She was waiting to hear knocking on the wall that would not be answered.

The knock, when it came, fell on the front door. It was a thing she'd not considered—that he would make a conventional entrance.

'M. Guillaume de Vaubon, your ladyship.'

Tonight he was dressed respectably enough in a quiet frock coat with silver buttons. A plain cocked hat was under his arm and an equally plain wig, tied behind with a bow, adorned his head. Except for his size and the sword, which looked unfashionably serviceable, he was unalarming.

Diana breathed a little easier; she could cope with him.

He even bowed. 'You look most charming, madame. However . . .' He turned to Tobias who was about to close the doors. 'The lady requires a cloak.'

'Yeth, sir.'

He went past her to the chair, tutted to find it wouldn't move and drew up the bolts. 'We go this way, I think. It is quicker.'

She said: 'I am not going down there. Alone? With you?'

'Most certainly not,' he said. 'Where is the maid?'

'Asleep.'

He swung the chair outwards. 'Then Tobias comes too. I must think of my reputation.'

It was like a reprieve. *'Tobias comes too.'* How could she not go?

There was a silver world outside and on this mad night she would allow herself a little madness. After all, she had been dying to see where the shaft went.

He stretched out a hand. 'Are you afraid?'

'Certainly not.' She took his hand and stepped through the doorway into blackness—and onto a platform. Tobias joined them carrying her best grey silk cloak and its huge, matching bonnet. While she tied the bonnet strings, the Frenchman put the cloak around her shoulders without emphasis.

He called, '*Faites descendre,*' and and the ropes on either side began to move, giving the impression that the walls around them were going upwards rather than that they were going down.

The three of them descended, terrifyingly, first into darkness and then into a glow.

Into a cavern.

Into where the mermaids went.

A shelf of rock ran round three sides of a tiny lagoon on which floated a small boat. Two men stood on either side of the shaft, easing the ropes so that the platform landed gently on the shelf. A lantern reflected its candle onto the water that in turn sent its flame onto the rock walls in wobbling patterns of light.

A hand like granite in sandpaper took the Dowager's and helped her off the shelf and into the boat. '*Attention, madame, ça glisse.*'

'Alphonse,' said his captain.

'Good evening, Alphonse.'

'Mathurin.'

'Good evening.'

'Madame.'

Once aboard, the Dowager looked around, seeing no exit. It was like being on a boat in a dark bottle but two powerful strokes took them to a part of the cavern wall that gave a little as the boat's prow touched it.

De Vaubon stood up and pulled a bit of the wall aside like a curtain, and she saw that it *was* a curtain, a long thin hanging of living gorse and grasses that had either matted naturally or been sewn together.

'Down.'

They crouched while he held it up, passing it from one hand to the other as they went through.

Then they were out in the cove and gentle night air. The light from her own house shone at the top of the cliff above her. She looked back and couldn't see the gap they had come through. She said so.

'The Revenue does not see it either, not yet,' de Vaubon said.

'Are we going to your ship?' she asked.

He was pained. '*Madame*, I beg you. *Margot* is not a ship. She is *un cotre*, a cutter.' He gathered his fingers into a bunch and blew a kiss with them towards the boat. 'Seventy foot. Square-rig and fore-and-aft on both masts. Crew, forty. Cannon, sixteen. The most speedy vessel on seven seas. Yes, she is mine. Yes, we dine aboard.'

Even in the moonlight, it was difficult to see the cutter from the angle of the rowing boat, just a slim black shape on black water. Which grew bigger.

Oh dear, scrambling nets.

But he had thought of everything. Tobias, Alphonse, Mathurin, even *La Petite Margot*'s captain had to scramble; the Dowager was winched aboard with a bosun's chair and dignity.

A table set for two and lit by silver candelabra stood on the quarterdeck.

She was introduced to Pierre, to Raoul, Laurent, Félix . . . some faces could have adorned a wanted poster, others a church choir. 'Bilo is our chef tonight. A bad cook, I fear, but a good gunner.'

'Good evening, Bilo.' Pink scars on a black skin, startlingly white teeth.

'*Madame*.'

'Take the lady's cloak and hat, Alphonse.' To Diana he said: 'But this is my *salle à manger*. It is a warm night, you do not wear a hat. I like your hair by moonlight.'

Her hat and cloak were taken below. Tobias went with them, to eat with the crew. Her chair was held for her by Mathurin, a white linen napkin flourished and set across her lap. Pale wine was poured into crystal glasses as fine as any she'd seen. 'From my own vineyard.' They might have been tête-à-tête in a dining room at Versailles, except that the ceiling was stars and the walls were cliffs and a twinkling village and infinite sea.

The first course was pickled beef in near-transparent slices with melon 'grown by the good Ralph Gurney'. He explained the process of the beef's pickling but had trouble translating some of the terms.

'You may speak French,' she told him. Her French was considerably better than his English, good though it was.

'You know French?'

'In my family one is considered uneducated if one does not.'

'Ah, the English aristocracy.'

'Yes.' And *because* she was an aristocrat, she said politely: 'Have you been a smuggler long?' Which made him laugh.

'No, I was a lawyer.' Which made *her* laugh. 'And my sons are lawyers.' He had three children, two sons and a daughter; Geneviève was in a convent, finishing her education.

'And does Madame de Vaubon approve of your present occupation?'

'My wife is dead,' he said. 'Thirteen years ago while I was in prison.' He shrugged at her expression. 'But it is an honour for a lawyer to be imprisoned by King Louis—the Fifteenth, of course, not our present gracious monarch. Not nice, but an honour; it showed I fought on the side of the angels. You see, I had the privilege to defend those who attacked the corruption and abuses of tax collectors and who urged that the administration be accountable and open to public scrutiny.'

'And you were put in prison for it?'

He shrugged. 'I was good at it. Unwise of me. I could even have put up an excellent defence at my own trial, except that there was no trial. Instead, a *lettre de cachet*.' He drew his forefinger across his throat. 'No trial, just imprisonment at the King's command.'

Their plates were taken away and a beautiful lidded salver put on the table. Another glass; this time the wine was golden.

'Bilo is giving us bass,' de Vaubon said, 'I asked him and he said he would. He is very temperamental.' He lifted the salver's lid and sniffed the steam. 'Not bad. He has left it simple. Caught today and just a hint of herb. Do you cook? You should. I am a superb cook. When I retire I shall do nothing else.'

She looked around, trying to trap some normality from the night—and found none. Strange enough to be on an enchanted boat on an enchanted sea, without sharing an enchanted meal with a kaleidoscope.

It was necessary for her to place him in a class she could recognize but he kept eluding her. The quality of everything around her argued taste. In that, at least, she thought, he is a gentleman. The 'de' of his name suggested a seigniory in his background, he had his own vineyard, yet he spoke with the thick accent of Normandy. He ate like a peasant, but most French nobility did. Since the middle classes of France had discovered table manners, its aristocracy had abandoned them as bourgeois.

Now a cook.

'How did you get out of prison?'

'My father, poor old man, he bought me out. He was very rich, my father.'

Ah.

'He was a butcher.'

Oh.

'He was a very good butcher. He began with a stall in a market, he bought some cattle with the profit, he bought some land for the cattle, more land, more cattle . . . he became very rich, a château or two, a house in Paris, horses.'

And all of it had gone in buying his son's release from the Bastille: 'Which was procured on condition that I stayed on my lands in Normandy for the rest of my life. But there were no lands—Papa had sold them for my sake. And Papa was dying and my wife was dead.'

He said it almost casually but the Dowager decided that, given the choice, Louis XV would have wisely chosen the smallpox that killed him rather than fall into the hands of Guillaume de Vaubon.

The vegetables were served separately, French fashion. 'Lightly cooked, you see. You English boil them until they surrender.'

'So then you became a smuggler.'

'Why not? I had my children to feed. And I am an excellent sailor.'

You appear to be an excellent everything, she thought. But, then, you probably are. He had . . . she found it difficult to pin down . . . a grown-upness—maturity was too smooth a quality for it—that was missing from Englishmen. He wasn't modest; he wasn't immodest. He wasn't trying to impress her, he was being factual. She could see the lawyer in him. It might be that the Bastille had stripped away any pretence or pretension, though she suspected he'd been born without either. She couldn't imagine him as a child.

'I was a happy small boy,' he told her when she asked, and spoke of sailing the dinghy his father had given him when he was six along the white, sand-hilled coast of the Cotentin where his father had his favourite estate of Gruchy.

'The château went in the sale to buy my release,' he said. 'I have bought it back since. It is very nice, you know.' He jerked his head towards the village. 'Jan and the lads will tell you. It is where they come to pick up the contraband.' He put an elbow on the table and cupped his chin in his hand. 'Shall we go there?'

She felt a stir of panic. 'No.'

'Why not?'

'We are at war. I would be betraying my King and country.'

'You cannot betray King and country,' he said. 'They are institutions. You can only betray people.'

'You are going to war for *your* King.'

'Good God, no,' he said, sitting back, 'I am not fighting Louis's war. I would not. I shall be fighting *with* him, not for him. Do you like the ragoût? *Viande-ragoût*, my own recipe.'

She hadn't noticed she was eating it. Stop it, she thought, stop feeling like this for a butcher's son who cooks. 'Who *are* you fighting for, then?'

'America.' He seemed surprised she should ask. 'America must win. When she has won her revolution and thrown off her King, the French revolution begins and we throw off ours.' He leaned back to address Heaven, displaying a magnificent throat. 'Thank you, thank you, the good God, for making Louis so magnificently, peerlessly stupid as to come in on America's side.' He allowed his chair to tip forward again and downed his wine. 'Ridding America of her King gives us carte blanche to get rid of him. He has signed his own death warrant.'

She said coolly: 'And that's a good thing, is it?'

'How not? You killed one of your kings and were better for it.'

'We replaced him with his son.'

He dismissed that. 'Yes, but the English are mad.' He leaned on his elbow again, bringing their faces closer. 'What are you doing here?'

'Here? You invited me.'

'There.' He jerked a thumb upwards. 'In that eagle's nest. Spettigue says you are recently widowed. Are you a hermit, in grief for your husband?'

'Of course. We were married over twenty years.'

His mouth went down in a caricature of disbelief and he rocked his head. 'Tell me who you are. I want every detail, from birth.'

Such a colourless story compared to his, she thought. Beautiful, unconcerned, absent parents, a life in the charge of servants and governesses. A father who'd no more think of selling his all to get her out of prison, as had de Vaubon's, than falling on his sword. Indeed, had sold her into one.

A monochrome life, its only warmth provided by two sunlit summers in Torbay. So she told him about those, which led on to Lieutenant Forrest Grayle and the Millbay hospital though, for the honour of her country, she did not tell him how awful it was. 'It's a political matter, I'm afraid,' she said, lightly. 'There can be no exchange for rebels.'

'You care for this boy?'

'He is touching.'

He was watching her closely. 'If you like,' he said, 'we can go now and fetch him. Sail in, direct my guns on the prison, sail out.'

She smiled—until she saw he meant it. 'Oh no,' she said, 'we couldn't do that.'

He wagged a finger at her. 'You care too much for patriotism, honour and such rubbish. You know why they breed it into you? To keep you bound, so that you will do what they say. Die for *La Patrie*, my good fellow. So off you go to die like a good fellow—but you find you are dead, not for country but for them. Shit to it. Fight for a good idea, fight for justice and equality, even fight for money, but not for them. Good, here are the kidneys. Gurney killed some sheep for me. Sometimes Bilo is mean with the wine for them but . . . no, not tonight. This one comes from the Languedoc.'

'I don't want them, thank you,' she said.

'Because I said patriotism was shit? Try them.'

He stuffed his mouth full and waved a fork at her. 'And women suffer the most, you know. Honour, sacrifice, duty, all of it to keep you down. Keep us fed, keep us clean, keep us warm in bed, have our babies but have no say in your governance, not one word against us. We can beat you without punishment . . .'

She could have sworn she hadn't even blinked.

'I am sorry,' he said, quietly.

'You are spraying gravy,' she told him in English.

Mathurin was at his elbow. '*Pardon, chef. La mer est étale.*'

He tapped at his mouth with his napkin. '*D'accord.*' He turned to Diana. 'I regret we do not wait for dessert. So sad. *Tarte aux pommes à la Normande*, the *pâte brisée* sugared and with egg yolks.'

'Your own recipe?'

'Of course.'

She had to thank the cook. Bilo came on deck with Tobias, both of them amiably breathing brandy fumes. She apologized for having no money on her with which to tip the crew but de Vaubon said: 'No matter, we steal some from the English navy.'

Before she got into the bosun's chair, he said: 'It is your last chance to come with me.'

She needed to carry something away from the night, so she found herself saying: 'Why do you want me to?'

'Because you are very brave. Because you are alabaster and still and sad, like Galatea before life was breathed into her.'

Serve her right for fishing. 'And you are Pygmalion, I suppose.'

He lifted her into the chair. 'I am a wonderful life-breather.'

She thought they would say good-bye then, but she had a little while longer with him. 'A gentleman always takes the lady to her door.'

They sat together in the stern of the rowing boat as Alphonse and Mathurin pulled for T'Gallants's cliff. All the way he told of what she was missing. 'My cooking. The revolution. We will give you the vote, you know. Women will be free as never before.'

The entrance slit to the shaft cavern was so well hidden that she didn't see it until he got up to lift it. Inside the cavern, he sent Tobias up first. While Alphonse and Mathurin were pulling the ropes, he said, quietly: 'Did your husband buy Tobias?'

'Yes.'

'Now he is dead, should you not both be free?'

She didn't know what he was talking about.

'The collar,' he said. 'The man wears the slave collar.'

She was so angry she could barely speak. 'Good night. I shall go up alone.'

But when the platform came down, he stepped onto it with her. 'You will be sorry, you know, if I am killed in this war.'

'No, I won't. You are unwarrantably rude.'

'Yes, you will. My bloodied body will be brought to you and you will unfasten your hair and spread it over my face as you weep.'

'Damned if I do,' she said.

The door to the Great Hall stood open. Tobias had made himself scarce.

He will kiss me, she thought.

And he did, a brief peck on both cheeks. 'If I kiss you properly, I shall miss the tide.' He sighed, as if it were a chore. 'I suppose I shall have to come back to do it.'

Then he shouted down the shaft to his men, and was lowered into the darkness.

She stood at the wreckers' window, watching the cove until *La Petite Margot*'s sails unfurled, like a black rose coming immediately into bloom. Square-rig and fore-and-aft on both masts, she thought. Crew, forty; cannon, sixteen. Which he will fire on my countrymen. He is the enemy, a butcher's son. If he continues to eat like he does, he will be fat. I'm well rid of him.

She waited until the sails were lost in the darkness, then took herself off to bed, kicking the chair-door back into place as she went—but leaving it unbolted. In case he came back.

Chapter Fourteen

'Mrs Hedley, your ladyship.'

The two women regarded each other across the length of the Great Hall. Both had changed a little since they'd last met but each disliked the other too much to notice.

'Sit down, Mrs Hedley. What may I do for you?'

They seated themselves on either side of the empty fireplace.

'Your ladyship . . .' Makepeace cleared her throat; this was gall and wormwood but she was desperate. 'Your ladyship, Mr Spettigue tells me you have some dealings with the hospital at Millbay Prison.' After calming her down in the early hours of yesterday morning when she and Beasley had roused him by hammering on his front door, it had been Spettigue's suggestion: *Try Lady Stacpoole. She has influence there, I'm told.*

'In fact, I am about to go to the hospital,' the Dowager said. 'Will this take long?' *She's nervous and so she should be; it is impertinent of her to come.*

Makepeace began rubbing her hands up and down her skirt. *Damn the woman, she ain't making this any easier.* 'There was an attempted escape there yesterday night.'

'Was there?'

'There was. The guards shot two American prisoners trying to climb over the wall.'

'Indeed.'

'One of them was killed.' Standing under the tree, she had known Josh was dead. *Known* it. The fusillade of shots had been too prolonged for him not to be. But Mr Spettigue's informant at the prison, whoever it was, had reported this morning: '*The blackie's alive. Don't know how much longer.*'

She took in a breath. 'You know I come from Boston . . . I'm an American?'

The Dowager inclined her head. 'How could you not be?'

Makepeace ignored it: 'Well, the other young man is . . . I think he's badly wounded and he's a friend of mine.' She took the bull by the horns. 'I want you to take me in to see him. If you will, please. *Please.*'

The Dowager watched the griping hands. 'What is his name?'

'Joshua Burke.' Betty had discarded the slave name given by her master as soon as she'd run away from him and adopted that of Makepeace's family who'd taken her in. 'He's a boy I helped bring up; he's . . . he's precious to me.'

An illegitimate son? The Dowager wondered what extraordinary circumstances had led Philip Dapifer to marry this redheaded, freckled and probably loose-living colonial. But, despite herself, she was touched; the agony of a mother for a child was here before her and could not be disregarded. How terrible that the guards had resorted to shooting. Inevitable, perhaps. The prisoners had been warned . . . But terrible nevertheless. So un-English.

None of this was apparent in her tone which, as ever, was dispassionate.

'Mrs Hedley, you should be aware that in endeavouring to improve conditions for the wounded and sick at Millbay, one is labouring under certain difficulties, not to say opposition. Furthermore, the work is only now under way and I fear I cannot consent to jeopardize it by introducing an unauthorized person into the prison at this stage. I shall most certainly enquire for this young man and do what can be done for him but that is as far as I can go.'

It was a statement of fact. In view of their previous encounter, the Dowager felt it was even generous.

It's because I was rude to her. She's taking it out on Josh for spite. Makepeace stood up: 'You won't let me see him?'

'I have explained. One cannot.'

'Then I hope one rots in Hell.'

'Possibly unwise?' suggested Mr Spettigue. He was in lemon today. 'Ladyship might have been worked on.'

'I know,' said Makepeace, miserably. She'd castigated herself all the way back from Babbs Cove. 'Can't you do anything?'

'Source in the prison is only prepared to give information. Frightened of doin' more. Too many escapes, you see. Discipline bein' tightened.'

'Discipline? They *shot* them.'

He fidgeted around her solicitously, tapping her back, waving a smelling-bottle under her nose. 'Strong young man . . . sure to recover . . . only wait . . .'

He'll die and no one to comfort him. *Andra, Andra, come home. I'm fouling everything I touch.*

She wiped her eyes. 'This won't get baby a new bonnet,' she said, wearily. 'We'll have to think of something else.'

'Will you return to the North?'

'And leave him?' She was incredulous. 'He's maybe dying. I'll get to him somehow, you see if I don't. If necessary I'll go back to Lady Tight-Boots and ram an apology down her neck, *make* her take me in.'

The thought of more anxiety-ridden days in Plymouth, at the overcrowded, ever noisy Prince George, was almost beyond bearing. 'I'll send Philippa home, though. She's looking peaked, she needs quiet and fresh air.'

'You'll be alone, time of trial, etc. Wouldn't the Pomeroy Arms suit? Quiet, sea breeze, friendly people.'

'Perhaps. I'll see.' Her instinct was to stay crouched outside Millbay Prison like a dog.

Mr Spettigue wiggled. 'Another matter come up . . . tenuously related, really, but wondered whether you'd think worth taking action . . .'

He told her what it was. In the state she was in, action of any sort seemed good to Makepeace—and this one had spice.

'Take it,' she said.

The warehouse had been raised in the fifteenth century but, for all that, would serve its new purpose very well. Once it had stood on Millbay's waterside but the sea had been pushed back by further quays furnished with more useful go-downs, leaving it stranded.

The great trussed-rafter roof was still a home for the occasional sparrow but the bays that ran along each side of an enormous aisle had been scoured and fitted with new truckle beds out of the public subscription fund. The high windows left it dim but mercifully cool.

Piles of fresh linen lay on each bed. At the far end, an open flight of steps led to a newly painted loft where shelves were stacked with medicine bottles, boxes of salves, rolled bandages, new chamber pots.

All it lacked was patients.

'Everything to your ladyship's specification.' Captain Luscombe was anxious. 'I hope it meets with your approval.'

'It is splendid, Captain, you have done marvels.'

'Yes, well, it was at a pace, but on your ladyship's urging . . .'

She praised him for a minute longer before adding: '. . . though one did hope that the men might have been moved in today.'

'Ah, well, yes, d'ye see, we've had something of an upset. Guards shot a couple of escapin' prisoners the other night. On the *qui vive*, for once. Had to sharpen them up—too many escapes lately. Two Americans tryin' to scramble over the wall. One of them's dead, I fear.'

'How shocking.'

'Sad, but shouldn't have done it. Funeral's later on this afternoon.'

'Does that prevent the orderlies transferring the patients this morning?'

'Ah, well, yes . . .' She was beginning to dread this prefix. 'Fact of the matter is, your ladyship, the orderlies take their cue from Dr Maltby and, well, not to beat about the bush, the good doctor ain't enthusiastic about the new hospital. Says it'll entail a good deal of walking.'

'I can see it would; there must be at least a yard and a half between the beds.'

'Fact is,' Captain Luscombe said, 'Dr Maltby don't take kindly to innovations, especially those suggested by someone else and especially if the someone else is, well, of the female gender. It might be your ladyship's charm could persuade . . .'

'Perhaps if, in the meantime, my maid could begin some bed-making?'

She left Joan to him and walked away towards the cottage.

The orderlies, all four of them, were sitting and smoking their pipes on the grass outside as she came up and wished them a bright good-day. She introduced herself and asked their names, which they gave with the willingness of men asked to deliver their savings. Payne, Davis, Watts and Farnham.

'It is lucky, gentlemen, we just have time to transfer the patients before the funeral this afternoon.'

Payne, leader and wit, shifted his pipe enough to say: 'Easier if we had litters. Only we ain't.' The others sniggered.

'Then we shall have to take the shutters off the cottage windows and use those, shall we not?'

He said: 'Dr Maltby didn't say nothing about it an' we take our orders from him.'

It was early to use the whip but if that was their attitude . . .

Her voice jerked the pipe from Payne's mouth. 'You take your orders from the Admiralty in whose employ you are. In this matter I am the Admiralty's representative and if you question it we can go straightaway to Lord Edgcumbe for the answer. Now take the shutters off those windows.'

Watching them shamble into action, she supposed that these were the dregs even press gangs rejected. Nursing was not regarded as a job for a decent sailor at the best of times, and when it came to nursing the enemy, it was left to the halfhearted, the half-dead and half-witted.

Downstairs in the cottage, it was difficult to see the men on its floor for the flies. The eyes, mouths, nostrils, open wounds of the insensible crawled with them. Those who had the strength batted them away so that the room was full of slow uncoordinated movement. Upstairs, where it was even hotter, the flies were thicker, as was the stench. Ten narrow beds had been crammed together in order to accommodate twenty-three men.

'Before these men are moved, they must be washed,' she said. To take them as they were would merely be transferring disease from one place to another.

The change of order brought resigned and meaningful nods from the orderlies. *Women.* Never know their own minds.

She wondered if she might wash some of the patients herself— cleaning so many bodies of their pus and sores would take a long time even for those with enthusiasm for it.

No, she dare not; the orderlies would delight in reporting the scandal. She had to go carefully. *I must have more help.*

'And I want their clothing taken off and burned. They are to be dressed in nightshirts.'

She left them to it and walked across the compound towards a gate leading to the area that now contained the warehouse/ hospital. A militiaman sentry pointed a musket at her. 'Password, ma'am.'

'But you have just seen me with Captain Luscombe.'

From the door of the warehouse, Joan shouted: 'It's Dandelion.'

'Dandelion.'

'Pass, friend.'

'New rule seemingly,' Joan said when Diana joined her. 'Last week a Frenchman tried to get out tricked up like a woman. I said to that booby out there, I said: "Do I look like a Froggy?" But he an't got the brains he was born with. If Cap'n Luscombe hadn't come up, I reckon he'd 'a shot me.'

'Very efficient.'

There were still beds unmade. With no one except Joan to see her, the Dowager felt able to indulge in making them. In his last days, Aymer could endure nobody's presence but hers and, as it had been necessary to change the sheets with frequency and he could not abide the merest wrinkle, she had learned to tuck in corners with geometric precision.

Their backs were aching at the finish. Definitely, she would need more help.

They went up to the loft/store cupboard and fetched the cotton nightshirts she had ordered from a Plymouth outfitters.

'Password, ladies.'

'Dandelion.'

For decency's sake the two women waited outside while the patients were put in their nightshirts. Immediately, a few looked better, as if cleanliness and attention had already set them on the mend.

The transfer took some time; the orderlies were slow and deliberately clumsy. Joan went to the warehouse to receive the patients and make sure they were put down gently. Diana stayed at the cottage, supervising their departure. 'Which one is Joshua Burke?' she asked Payne.

'Don't know their names.'

She called: 'Which of you is Joshua Burke?'

'He is.' One of the less seriously injured was pointing to the man next to him. She stepped across the bodies to look.

'No, this can't be Joshua Burke.'

'Surely is, ma'am. Heard his name when they dragged him in. Got shot trying to get over the wall. He's right poorly, ma'am.'

He's *black*.

She stared at the negroid head on its pallet, wondering at the life La Hedley had led that this young man was so precious to her, and not least at the fact that she hadn't mentioned his colour.

He was poorly indeed. There was a bullet wound in his neck

and, according to the man next to him, a mercifully clean bandage round his chest hid another. 'Think they got his lungs, ma'am. He's breathing terrible bad.'

'Payne, send for a doctor.' She touched the beaded forehead. He also had a fever. She wondered if he should be moved at all. No, he couldn't be left in this charnel house; if he was to die, he should do it in a decent bed.

'Ain't the doctor's day for comin' in.'

'Then send for one from town. I'll see he's paid.'

She was sharp with the orderlies when they lifted the boy. 'Take extra care, please.' She walked beside the litter on its journey to the warehouse to ensure that they did.

Halfway through the afternoon, she had to give the orderlies leave to attend the funeral of the prisoner who'd been shot. 'Got to pay our respects, your ladyship.' She felt that respect would be better lavished on the living but she did not want to push them too far. 'Very well.'

Captain Luscombe had wanted her to be there as well. 'Prisoners like to see their dead honoured. Only leads to riotin' if they ain't.' But she was reluctant to leave the hospital unattended so she and Joan watched the funeral of Lieutenant John Snodgrass, late of the American vessel *Pilgrim*, from the loft window, which had a view of the main compound.

'Was he a white man?' she'd asked.

'Yes, yes. Curious he tried to escape with a blackie, ain't it?'

In life, it appeared, Lieutenant Snodgrass had been popular with his fellow-Americans and his death now rendered him popular with the British, always generous to a fallen enemy once he'd fallen.

There was a prison band. Prisoners beat muffled drums.

There'd been a skirmish over what flag to lay upon the coffin, Luscombe had told her; the Americans threatening riot if it should be the Union flag, the British refusing to countenance the Stars and Stripes, which the rebel government had adopted the previous year and was now being flown by its shipping.

In the end Snodgrass went to his rest like a hero under the tattered, shot-holed spritsail of his captured ship.

It was evening before she and Joan felt able to leave the hospital and even then they had one more apppointment.

Lieutenant Grayle and his guards were waiting for them at Luscombe's house—as was a footman dressed in Stacpoole livery.

'Webb! What are you doing here?'

'Good evening, your ladyship. His lordship is in Plymouth and hopes you will join him at Government House. The carriage is outside.'

She was so tired that for a second it seemed to be Aymer who summoned her. Of course, she thought, Robert is his lordship now.

'How delightful.'

She sent Joan back with Tobias to the inn they were staying at for the night—the old woman was exhausted—and instead got one of the guards to buckle the artificial hands on Martha's son.

'They fit better now,' she told him. 'It is time to start using them.'

'I intend to, ma'am.' There was something new in his voice; his eyes were steady and looking forward.

She was suddenly immensely proud of him. '*Now* can I write to your mother?'

'Not yet, ma'am.' He even smiled a little. 'Wait a while.'

In the carriage, she tidied herself as well as she could, glad to be wearing black that hid some of the hospital's stains on her petticoat hem.

The Duke of Richmond, as Master-General of the Ordnance, had spared neither the public purse nor fraternal affection when ordering the building of the new Government House at Mount Wise, the current Governor of Plymouth being his brother.

As she followed Webb along a gallery, the Dowager realized that her time away from luxury had changed her; it was delightful to feel carpet beneath her feet, to be enfolded in silk-papered walls hung with good portraiture, but she was aware of the cost of these things as she had not been before. That sculpture of a nymph, for instance—a Bernini if she was not mistaken—would fetch a price that could purchase decent nursing and doctors for her hospital indefinitely.

The Earl of Stacpoole was in a room that gave on to a terrace. 'I am sorry to surprise you, Mama, but I could not come to Plymouth without seeing you.'

'Of course not.' She hugged him. 'My dear boy, I am overjoyed. I hope you will come to T'Gallants, I am still camping out but—'

'A flying visit only, I fear. Makin' arrangements for His Majesty's stay when he comes for the openin' of the marine barracks and the new dock. Goin' back day after tomorrow.'

'And Alice? Is she here?'

'Stayin' with the De Veres at Exeter. Asked me to convey her love.'

'How did you know I was at the hospital?'

He tapped his nose; there had been plenty of people to tell him. He was resplendent in full court dress. The Order of the Garter shone on a coat of blue silk embroidered with silver that curved away to display a long gold satin waistcoat which in turn curved over a stomach somewhat fuller than she remembered it.

She was relieved that mention of the hospital did not seem to displease him; he seemed almost apologetic for the fuss he'd made. 'Fact is, His Majesty's becomin' reconciled to the idea. Keeps being complimented on it by the liberal sort.'

She smiled. 'That must be a new experience for him.'

There was a small table, set for supper for one. 'I'd be happy to eat with you, Mama, but there's a banquet in town later and I'm representin' the King. Dreary but necessary.'

He sat with her while she ate; the pleasure that they were at ease with each other gave her an appetite.

'Robert, I wish to consult you on the matter of Tobias. Your father gave him to me, if you remember, so I hope you will not mind if I grant him his freedom.' She had every intention of doing so whether he minded or not but, since he was showing generosity, she wanted to compliment him back in displaying due respect for the head of the house.

'What a liberal you are become, Mama, you'll be wanting Parliamentary reform next. But I see nothing against it and he's your man now. I'd forgotten he was still enslaved.'

'So had I.' The collar had seemed a mark of the man's dignity, so much a part of him that she had been startled by the reminder that it denoted servitude.

All at once the penduled plaster ceiling above her was replaced by stars and the smell of beeswax candles washed away by the slightest of salt breezes. She rocked lightly on an anchored boat . . .

'I *said*, Mama, did you find the American woman's boy?'

She gave him her attention. 'I beg your pardon, Robert. Yes, I found him.' She was curiously reluctant to expose Grayle's wounds to her son. She wondered how he'd known about her search—oh, of course, Alice had read the letter from Martha, or the Edgcumbes might have told him.

'Then all's done. You can come home.'

'Home?'

'Mama, you have done all that could be expected for these fellows, it's time to leave it to those whose business it is to look after them.'

She thought of those whose business it was to look after them. Within days of her departure, the warehouse would be in no better state than the cottage had been. 'My dear, the work has hardly started; the nursing of these men is slapdash to the point of cruelty. It needs method, better orderlies, more proficient doctors. The country cannot hold up its head until it treats these unfortunates as well as it treats its own men.'

'Unfortunates? They came to these waters to sink our shipping.'

'That is not the point. I am sure we are doing our best to sink theirs in *their* waters . . .'

'They have no waters of their own. You appear to think America has right to its own sovereignty.' He was becoming testy and got up to move away from her.

She tried to placate him. 'Of course not. But if you saw them, Robert . . . Once a man is wounded, his politics are immaterial, he is merely a wounded man. Our Lord certainly thought so and gave us the parable of the Good Samaritan for our instruction.' Dear, dear, she sounded like a dissenter's tract.

Robert had been striding up and down the room. He stopped at the table, tapping it with his fingers. The light glinted on the star on his breast. 'I had not wished to mention this, Mama, since it shames us both, but I think you do not realize what joy you are giving to the opposition. Only three days ago, the Marquis of Selby spoke your name in the House of Lords.'

He leaned down to ensure she was sufficiently shocked. 'Your name, Mama. *Our* name. As usual, he was ranting about coming to terms with the rebels. I will tell you his exact words. "The government could pursue with profit the example held up to them by the Dowager Countess of Stacpoole, mother to His Majesty's own equerry, and her recognition that wounded American prisoners are but men prepared to sacrifice their lives in the resistance of tyranny and must therefore be accorded the dignity of humankind and not that of animals, as should their country." '

He took the chair opposite her. 'You are being used, Mama. However well intentioned, you are providing the Whigs with ammunition to fire at us. Until then, as I say, the King had become reconciled to your activities but now he sees what they can lead to, as I do.'

She was as shocked as he intended her to be, and angry. Good God, did men twist *everything* to their political advantage? 'Selby had no right to make capital of something which is innocent of politics.'

'Perhaps. But he made it. I am told Rockingham and his dogs roared him on. Now do you see why you must come away?'

She folded her hands in her lap and considered. Without his eyes leaving her face, Robert leaned over, took a fork and finished the chicken *à la crème* left on her plate.

'No,' she said at last. 'They may twist it how they please, but this work is done in His Majesty's honour and you must point that out when you next speak in the Lords.' She put out her hand to touch his. 'I know there are more sympathetic causes, my dear, but for some reason known only to God this has been put on my shoulders. I cannot abandon it.'

'God has nothing to do with it, it is some obstinacy of your own.' He jerked his hand away so fast that the fork fell to the floor. 'Very well, Mama. Since you refuse to accede to my wishes, you cannot expect to do so at my expense. I don't know how you will live if you persist in remaining in Devon, but it shall not be at T'Gallants. It is being sold.'

She remained calm. 'You cannot sell it. It is my property.'

'You have no property.'

True in its way, she thought. On the instant of her marriage she had become a femme covert, her existence covered by her husband's, her property his, the children his, with no rights to either. It had been her greatest fear that Aymer might cast her out, never allowing her to see her son again. He'd been entitled to do it; was freakish enough to do it; sometimes, when drunk, had threatened to do it. If he hadn't known *au fond* that no one would fulfil the role of countess so well, he *would* have done it.

It was a constant terror that had made her the woman she was: outwardly compliant but a secret manipulator, constantly shifting the pieces in the game of marital chess so that he might win yet keep her on the same board with the pawn that was her child.

She looked up at the man the child had become; he was looming over her against the candlelight so that she could not see his face. The figure was his father's—or soon would be.

Again she tried to conciliate him by mildness. 'Nevertheless,

T'Gallants was my dowry, along with much else; I brought it into the family. And, in justice, I am entitled to a messuage of my own,' she said.

'You have one, the Dower House.'

It was a bark, like Aymer's. The law laid down. And suddenly the table was tipped to the floor, the decanter spilling wine on a Persian rug and she was on her feet, ready to rend, a lioness snarling at a cub that annoyed too much. 'How dare you? How *dare* you?'

Instantly, he was reduced to a small boy. 'But it was always to be sold when the lease was up. Father intended it.' He was gaping at her, as if caught in a schoolground peccadillo: *Not me, not me, it was him.*

'He is dead. We are free of him. You award me a contemptible pension and I say nothing but I will give up neither the life nor the home I have chosen. Is that clear?'

The enslavement was over. He backed away from the harpy she'd become. In twenty-two years she had uttered no word against his father; he couldn't believe she was doing so now. 'It's too late, Mama. It's done. Spettigue came round with the papers this afternoon.' Still backing away, he added as if it would pacify her: 'We got a good price for it, more than it was worth.'

She screamed: 'How do you know what it was worth?' She went on screaming, astonished at herself but unable to stop the logjam of misery that had been piling up for twenty-two years sweeping out of her mouth, swirling and bumping her son around in a river of truths she had never wanted him to know—had never known herself until now.

'I will never come back, I hated Chantries, I hated your father. I will not live on his land. He was a tyrant. He is dead, thank God, and I will not tolerate a new tyranny set up in his place. If I have to beg my bread through the streets of Plymouth, I will be a free woman at last.'

She didn't stop shouting until she saw him reach for the bell pull and hang on to it, staring at her. 'You are gone mad,' he said. 'You are a madwoman.'

At which point, she left in case she proved his point by hitting him . . .

Chapter Fifteen

JOHN Beasley had made a friend of one of Plymouth's more radical publishers, a man prepared to ask questions of the Admiralty's local representatives and get answers. It was from him that they received news of Josh's condition.

'Bad, but they think he'll live,' Beasley told Makepeace. 'The Admiralty's vaunting the new prison hospital as a place of miracles, apparently. He'll survive, Missus. A stubborn young fellow, our Josh.'

Obviously, however, recovery would not be swift. 'Nothing we can do until he's better,' Beasley said. 'I think it's time you went home.' He became surly—his way when he was uncomfortable. 'Time I did, too.'

She was immediately contrite; he had spent weeks in her cause; of course he wanted to return to London. 'I don't know what I'd have done without you,' she said.

'What *will* you do?'

It was like being in a tugging triangle, Sally and Jenny at the apex, Josh and Andra in the other two angles. There seemed little she could do for Josh, yet to leave him, suffering, in prison was like abandoning a wounded comrade on the battlefield. Also, word was on its way to Andra that he had a passage to England if he could make the French coast. She had to be at Babbs Cove for that. On the other hand, she had been too long away from the little girls . . .

'Send for them then,' Beasley said. 'Get Ginny to bring them down for a holiday. They'd like Babbs Cove.'

It seemed a solution. In any case, to stay on at the Prince George without a male escort would expose her and Philippa to unwanted attention. Its landlord was protective and friendly enough, though he was now visibly and vocally curious about their extended stay. Nevertheless, they had to pass through the taproom on entering and leaving, which, if they were unattended, brought remarks and even solicitation from some of its more forward male customers—an embarrassment compounded by the presence of Dell whose hips had swayed suggestively too long for her to walk like a respectable woman. As the Irishwoman became easier with her position in Makepeace's entourage, she had become less insistent that she be addressed by her given, grander name of Dervorgilla. In any case Makepeace, not being able to pronounce it, didn't try. Even Philippa used her friend's diminutive, so Dell she remained.

Sanders, too, was due a reunion with his family. Once he had driven them and their luggage to Babbs Cove, he would take Beasley to London and then drive on up North for a vacation.

Makepeace's packing was interrupted by an excited serving girl. 'Real lady to see you, Missus. Countess of somewhere.'

'Show her up.'

'Real lady.' Well, she's not so real now.

Quickly, Makepeace tidied the room, kicking the half-packed valises under the bed.

The Dowager looked poorly, thin rather than slim, with dark smudges under her eyes. Her impassivity, however, remained impenetrable.

'We parted on bad terms, Mrs Hedley, yet I assumed you would be glad to know how your friend progresses. Mr Burke is by no means out of the woods, the doctor thinks a bullet may have nicked one of his lungs. Since he has survived so far, however, it is to be hoped he will improve. I hope you will take my assurance that everything is being done to ensure that he does.'

This was from the horse's mouth and carried a weight that Beasley's information had not. Makepeace sank down on her bed. 'Thank God, oh, thank God.'

'Indeed.' The Dowager was silent for a moment, then she said: 'There is another matter I should like to discuss with you.'

Here it comes. Makepeace prepared to enjoy herself. But it was not what she'd been expecting.

'I am dissatisfied with the standard of nursing at the hospital,' the Dowager said. 'To put it mildly, the orderlies are slipshod. One has petitioned the commander of the prison for better but the navy is short of men and improvement may take a little while. As a makeshift I have gained Captain Luscombe's permission to bring in women. I fear they will be regarded as menials, nevertheless one trusts the female capacity to keep an eye on things rather than the . . .' Diana's nose sniffed for the *mot juste* and couldn't find it. '. . . the gentlemen at present employed to do it.'

Makepeace saw a great light. 'Me? You'd let me work at the hospital?'

'You and others, if they may be found. Each only a day or two a week, to fetch and carry for the orderlies, empty the slops . . . not pleasant work. As I say, menial.'

'Ma'am,' said Makepeace, heartily, 'you wouldn't credit how menial I can be.'

The Dowager allowed herself a thin smile. 'I think I would.'

She made a joke. She actually made a joke. Makepeace leaned over and shook the woman's hand. 'Countess, you can rely on me.'

'I hope I can.' The Dowager disengaged her hand in order to hold it up as a warning. 'There must be the utmost discretion, Mrs Hedley. I do not know your politics nor do I wish to. I have come to you because, despite our differences, you seem intelligent. However, any woman working in the hospital will be on very thin ice. Very thin. The prison authorities must not be alarmed by impudence or quarrels or personal entanglements, and especially not by unweening sympathy for the American cause. Your Mr Burke has attempted one escape and paid for it—he must be dissuaded from another. Should the hospital become a place of disturbance it may well be reduced once more to the state in which I found it.'

'Bad was it?'

The Dowager nodded. 'Ghastly.'

'Count on me.'

'Very well.' She got up. 'Your main task and that of the other women we may employ is to be on hand should any of the patients relapse. The hospital doctor is unsuitable, mostly absent, and a practitioner from town must be fetched for cases that are *in extremis*. The one I called in for Mr Burke seemed very capable.'

'You called in another doctor for Josh?'

'Your friend was in a bad way, I could not allow him to die.' There was a pause. 'You did not tell me he was a black man.'

'What difference would it make?'

'In the event, none. Well, good-bye. We can make arrangements tomorrow perhaps.' She paused in reaching for her parasol. 'Is this a good residential inn?'

'Yes. Why? You thinking of staying here?'

'Perhaps. T'Gallants is sold.' She added, casually: 'It was always intended that it should be.'

Oh no, it wasn't. Not by you.

Spettigue had told Makepeace: 'The Earl's selling over his mother's head. Don't know why. Pompous fellow. No sense of style.'

She said: 'Do you know who's bought it?'

'No. I leave details like that to my son.'

She don't know, Makepeace thought; she truly don't. She didn't come here to plead or bribe. She wasn't good to Josh out of anything *but* goodness. Blow me down. The Dowager's manner and her ownership of a slave had accorded so completely with Makepeace's prejudice against aristocratic women that it had not occurred to her they might conceal a recognizable heart.

She said: 'But you're sorry to leave T'Gallants, ain't you?'

'One has certain regrets,' the Dowager said with indifference. 'It has been in one's family a long time. However, it is too large for one's needs.'

It had felt like a death blow; she would never get over its loss, nor that Robert had inflicted it. To sit at the wreckers' window, the freedom of the sea before her, watching for the return of the black ship, to share a history with that of the village . . . deprivation of these things was like the withdrawal of light.

'You can stay there on a lease if you want to,' Makepeace said. 'I wouldn't live in it for all the tea in China. I'm taking over the Pomeroy Arms.' She smiled. 'More fitting for a menial.'

Slowly, the Dowager returned to her chair. 'Do I gather that you are the owner of T'Gallants, Mrs Hedley?'

'I am. Signed the agreement yesterday. Pretty penny your boy wanted for it an' all.'

'Why? *Why* did you buy it?'

'Let's say it was an investment.'

'And you are prepared to lease it to me? Why?'

'You got in a doctor to save a black man's life.'

Mrs Hallewell and her children moved out of the Pomeroy Arms and back to her cottage in the village on the understanding that she would return each day to cook and clean.

It was an arrangement that suited both sides. There were eight bedrooms at the Pomeroy. Now its paying guests would have room a-plenty as well as privacy. In any case, none of them was of the sort that demanded to be attended day and night; if they needed a glass of water in the early hours, they would fetch it themselves.

Mrs Hallewell had scrubbed and polished the place for their arrival so that strong ceiling beams and good elm floorboards had emerged from under the coating of dirt which had accrued during her father's illness.

Makepeace had liked it on sight. The taproom's lath and plaster walls, bulging between oak stanchions, formed a long rectangle, almost identical in shape to that of the Roaring Meg's. The smell of a good inn, a mixture of wine and beer, tobacco and food, had not entirely deserted the Pomeroy Arms and a whiff of it reawakened old memories.

So Makepeace, Philippa and Dell—to whom Makepeace was becoming resigned as destined, like the poor, to be always with her—moved in.

Beasley and Sanders went off in the coach, taking the Dowager's Joan with them to be delivered to the Torbay flyer at Exeter.

Had Makepeace, however, been expecting the taproom to become a parlour where she and the others could sit quietly in the evenings, she was mistaken. The Pomeroy Arms was still an inn, Mrs Hallewell having taken over the licence. And now that the abstinence imposed by a Methodist landlord had been lifted from it, Babbs Cove expected it to *be* an inn.

This was not as wearing as it might have been. The men of the fishing fleet were frequently absent and the village women had other things to do with their time. In effect, there were only two regular evening customers: Mrs Hallewell's uncles Zack and Simeon, neither of whom talked to the other. What falling-out had caused the rift between the two brothers was too far in the past for anyone, including probably them, to remember, but at six o'clock sharp Zack would scuttle into the inn, sit himself in the corner settle like a spider returning to a favourite web, to be followed five minutes later by the slower-moving Simeon aiming for his bench by the window. Zack chattered almost constantly; Simeon said barely a word; both ignored the other.

Tobias, who was another evening regular when the Dowager could spare him, had to choose to converse with one or the other, but not both. Makepeace was amused to see that he was rigorously fair and would sit one night with Zack, the other with Simeon.

'No good you tryin' to get them two together,' Mrs Hallewell told Makepeace after an abortive attempt at conciliation. 'I gave that up years since.'

In fact, Makepeace rather liked the oddity. It was part of the warp and woof of any community and that the two old men exposed her to it threaded her into the village. Zack, particularly, made her welcome by acting towards her exactly as he did to everyone else. At first he'd reminded her unpleasantly of the elderly sailor who had tried her patience so hard on the night they'd found Philippa. But Zack, adviser, teller of tales, inquisitor, possessed a charm and goodwill that the other had not. Perhaps, unlike 'the old bastard on the bollard', as Makepeace still thought of him, Zack wasn't lonely. Babbs Cove looked after its own.

Had Makepeace and her entourage lit on a village in the interior of Devon or Cornwall, or in any of those places to be found in isolated areas of England that still believed foreigners had monkeys' tails, their absorption into it would have taken generations. But Babbs Cove had been 'free trading' with the outside world for a long time. In the past vessels from France, Flanders and Holland had anchored outside the cove to receive illegal consignments of much-prized English wool, just as Babbs Cove vessels had anchored off ports such as Roscoff, Cherbourg, Ostend and Antwerp to come away heavily laden with tobacco, tea, lace and liquor.

As a result the villagers were more open to strangers and new ideas than those in insular enclaves. Thanks to their friend, Guillaume de Vaubon, they knew more about Normandy than they did about neighbouring Somerset. There were illiterate men, and one or two women, in Babbs Cove who spoke French with a fluency that would have surprised their betters.

Spaniards, now, were a different matter. Memories were long in Babbs Cove and Spain hadn't yet been forgiven for sending the Armada. But America? Americans spoke Babbs Cove's language in more ways than one. Americans weren't trying to invade England—if they had they'd have been resisted to the last drop of blood; didn't hold with invasion, didn't Babbs Cove—they were merely fighting for the right not to be taxed by the bloody government, something the Babbs Cove population of 150 souls understood with warm fellow-feeling.

Minutes after she'd consulted Jan Gurney on the subject, nearly every villager had been aware that Makepeace Hedley wanted to smuggle an American out of England under the nose of the authorities, and would pay for the service. Well, authority's nose poked too often into decent people's business; ducking under it put her on their side of the law.

If Mrs Hallewell was busy elsewhere and Zack or Simeon or Tobias shouted for drink, it was Makepeace, answering a call that echoed in her blood, who poured it. Within a week, Philippa and Dell were helping while Makepeace had virtually usurped the position as landlady and begun grumbling—as she was expected to.

'You lot go on supping brandy you'll drink the well dry. When's free trading start again?'

Most of the contraband de Vaubon's men had stacked in the cellar that led out of the inn's well had already been loaded onto Ralph Gurney's ponies and started on its night-time journeying to its many customers. At the time, Mrs Hallewell had been too bothered and too poor to reserve much for an inn that she didn't want in the first place.

But it went against Makepeace's grain to see the Pomeroy purchase legal brandy at the duty-paid price of eight shillings per gallon when free-trade brandy could be bought for five.

'Have to wait, won't ee?' Zack told her. ' 'Twon't be yet. *Lark* and *Three Cousins* won't venture out 'til winter weather sets in. Blame that bugger Nicholls. We never had no trouble 'til he took over. Got a bellyful o' salamanders, I reckon, so hot he be to catch free traders. Trawls this patch o' coast like a bloody shark, he do. Can't be bribed, can't be frit, ye'd think it was personal with 'un, like us had insulted his bloody mother. Catched Cawsand's *Susan* last year. Fired on her 'til her had to strike her colours, then sold her crew to the navy, so he did. Be a long time 'til those poor lads see their famblies again— ifsoever they do.'

Makepeace nodded in sympathy. 'Blood money,' she said.

As in Boston, so here; the hatred of smugglers for the Customs was compounded by the reward paid to captains of Revenue cruisers for handing over captured men to the navy. Makepeace sometimes thought that it was the unremitting impressment of its men, more than taxes, which had scattered the seeds of hatred along the American coastline.

'Well, don't you let him come rummaging round while I'm at the hospital. I'm starting next week.'

'Me too.' Ready for a fight, Philippa looked round from the chair on which she was standing to clean the windows—evening sun showed up marks. Dell was chopping potatoes in the kitchen for Mrs Hallewell to put with lamb in the pasties that were Zack's and Simeon's supper.

Makepeace had been afraid of it. 'You can't come, Pippy. It's not decent for an unmarried girl to . . . to see hospital sights.'

'Dell isn't married and you said she could go next time.'

'Well, Dell's circumstances are exceptional.' She often wondered what the village made of Dell.

Philippa clambered down from the chair. 'Please come outside, Mama.'

Zack gave a whistle of anticipation.

They went into the forecourt. The setting sun washed beach, inn and houses with pink, emphasizing the loom of T'Gallants on its clifftop by a gold rim while leaving its landward side in darkness.

'She'll be lonely up there now her maid's gone,' Makepeace said.

Philippa ignored her. 'You are not going to stop me coming to the hospital, Mama. I will not be left behind this time. It isn't as if it's dangerous.'

'Philippa, it won't be decent.' Having never been inside one nor knowing anybody who had, Makepeace's idea of a hospital was guesswork. 'There'll be nakedness, screaming, sickness like you've never known. You'd have to empty pots for men with limbs blown off. You're too young.'

Quietly, Philippa said: 'I'm not too young to know about men's limbs being blown off. I saw it happen.'

I keep forgetting, Makepeace thought. The prim little person before her had witnessed more atrocity—and survived witnessing it—than she had.

'I'll discuss it with ladyship,' she said.

From the window, Zack said: 'You let the maid help out if her wants to. Reckon when your parts is blown off, it don't matter who sees ee.'

'Oh shut up,' Makepeace told him. But she knew she had lost.

On the day before they set off for the hospital, two men arrived on horseback and took the Dowager's coach and team away. It was Zack, looking after the horses during Sanders's absence, who alerted Makepeace.

'What you doing?' Makepeace shouted at them, emerging from the inn with Dell behind her and her unloaded pistol in her hand. Zack was already threatening the newcomers with a pitchfork.

'All's well, madam,' one of the men said, nervously, eyeing the pistol. 'We're sent by the Earl of Stacpoole.' They were identically and smartly dressed in cocked hats and caped coats.

'Don't care who you're sent by, that's her ladyship's property.' She thrust the pistol into Dell's hands. 'Make one move with them horses, she pulls the trigger and that man there'll toss your carcases on the dungheap.'

'Sure, it'll be a pleasure, Missus.' Dell was all at once an O'Neill who'd been hunted too far through the mountains of Connaught by English soldiery.

Up at T'Gallants, the Dowager was biting her lip but protesting that it was all right. 'Those are my son's coachmen and apparently he has a need for the equipage. They are to take it back to him.'

'Only got the one, has he?'

Diana tried to smile and couldn't. 'I will not hide from you that my son disapproves of my activities at the hospital and does not wish to aid me in them. It is understandable that he would prefer it if I returned to our estate in Bedfordshire.'

Makepeace didn't think it was understandable at all. 'I can send 'em away,' she offered.

The Dowager shook her head. 'He has the right, it is his coach.

However, we are in a difficulty now that yours, too, is away. How are we to get to Plymouth?'

'Easy. We'll hire a couple of ponies off Ralph Gurney, go along the cliff path. Zack tells me it's quicker, anyway.'

From the oriel window, the Dowager watched Makepeace stride back across the bridge, take the pistol off the other woman and gesture rudely with it.

One of the men was pleading for something—refreshment, probably; it was a long way to the next hostelry. Makepeace pointed at the horse trough and went inside.

Robert, don't reduce us both to this.

She had written to him, apologizing for losing her temper.

Thanks to the goodwill of the new owner, I am able to remain at T'Gallants and fulfil what I see as my duty. But do not cast me off, my dear boy. Repudiate me, explain to all and sundry that I am gone eccentric in my old age, but do not cast me off.

Her distress was for him and the man he had become. Underneath that increasing corpulence, that too-young middle age, was the desperation for an authority like his father's. If he could not control his mother, what hope was there of commanding the rest of his life or his position at Court, which he held by inheritance as his father's son and was, in fact, beyond his capacity? He might be revealed as the small boy beaten and terrified by a man he had nevertheless regarded as the acme of what a nobleman should be. He had seen obedience accorded to Aymer by vast estates, heard his father's opinions received respectfully by men of high standing, witnessed his father's behaviour overlooked and excused because of his wealth. He had taken Aymer's form and forced his own character into it like a hermit crab into a much bigger shell.

Robert, I beg you to understand I do not adopt another point of view from contrariness. I do not believe that I shall bring the government down by administering to wounded men, but will help to uphold it, for if we do not show principle and humanity when we fight rabble, we are no better than they and have lost our cause.

Over and over during his childhood, her heart had broken as if it mended itself only to break again. When she'd tried to protect him, the intervention had cost him a heavier beating than if she had not. She could still hear his agonized: 'No, no, Mama. Don't interfere, Father is right.'

If I broke my wedding promise to love your father, I hope I held true in honouring and obeying him. But your nature and mine are different from his and it would do violence to both if we continue to distort them into his image now that he has gone.

She sealed the letter. *I can't return to being the woman I was. I am not that woman anymore. Be free of him, my darling boy, as I am.*

They were shaggy Dartmoor ponies with an independent eye—and no side-saddle.

'How are we to ride them?'

'Astride.' Makepeace was wearing a large, faded, tammy overdress, borrowed from Mrs Hallewell, such as had been popular in the twenties. It was tied down the front and showed only a plain linen unrevealing bodice. Her hair was tucked into a voluminous mob cap. The ensemble had been agreed as a uniform for the hospital where the less attention women attracted the better.

In one movement, she reached between her legs, grabbed the back of her skirt, brought it through and began tucking it into the dress's ties.

The Dowager glanced anxiously at Tobias and saw him blink. 'People will see us.'

Makepeace glanced around. 'What people?'

A glorious summer was turning into a glorious autumn. On

their left the sea might have been lacquered blue and was scattered with bad-tempered, becalmed little fishing boats waiting for shoals to pass by. The path went along moss-coloured, russet-capped cliffs, sometimes descending to dunes where daisies grew among spiky grass before rising steeply back to views of the glittering Channel and short-springing turf starred with yellow cinque-foil and clicking with grasshoppers. Butterflies, disturbed by the beat of the ponies' hooves, flew up from the umbellifers and bounced around the riders in the clear air.

Down again to a white beach where Makepeace suddenly yelled 'whee' and cantered her pony along the water's edge, throwing up spray, and the Dowager, shouting the halloo, held on to her hat and followed her. Tobias kept to the sand, smiling.

There were people: the occasional women and children gathering molluscs on the white beaches, a shepherd, the chatty ferryman who took them over the estuary of the River Erme.

Awkwardly, the Dowager said: 'You will note that Tobias is free of his collar, are you not, Tobias? It was my oversight that he wore it so long. M. de Vaubon pointed it out.'

So did I, but I'll wager not so nicely. Poor thing, she has to mention his name.

As they approached the outskirts of Plymouth, the women let down their skirts, left the ponies at the nearest livery and hired a carriage to take them the rest of the way, Makepeace sitting in the front with Tobias.

'This is very expensive,' said Diana from the back.

'I'm a very rich woman,' Makepeace said. It hadn't sunk in until now that the Dowager was not, yet she remembered the Stacpooles being renowned for their wealth. *That damn son's keeping her short,* she thought.

At the gate into the hospital compound, the Dowager said: 'Primrose.' Captain Luscombe's passwords were unimaginative and had not been changed since the previous week anyway. 'And here we are,' she said.

So many. Makepeace's eye was pulled down a vista of suffering that seemed to her at that moment to have no end. 'We had an influx last week,' the Dowager said. 'The *Parrot*, forty-nine wounded, which brought us up to eighty-seven. God send we have no more for a while, there are only beds for ninety.'

A warehouse, thought Makepeace. It *is* a warehouse—for perishable goods.

She followed the Dowager up the aisle, wanting to see Josh but unable to stop looking at each face as she passed, finding a rainbow of men, mostly white but a heavy sprinkling of black, here and there a Lascar, one Chinese. Only a few looked back; once a man was well enough to take an interest in his surroundings, Diana had told her, Dr Maltby sent him back to the prison.

'This is Hedley,' the Dowager said. 'Hedley, meet Watts, Farnham, Payne and Davis. Hedley is here to take some of the domestic work off your hands, gentlemen.'

It was obvious from that moment that there would be no objection to women doing the menial work.

' 'Bout time,' said Payne. 'All very well your layin' down rules, your ladyship, but there's too many patients. Near a hundred on 'em, that's . . .' There was a pause as he worked it out. '. . . that's twenty-five each.'

Makepeace would have had more sympathy if, when she and Diana had come in, the orderlies hadn't been sitting round a table under the stairs to the loft, playing cards. Taking the work off those hands, she thought, wouldn't take much lifting.

'I hope to remedy that today,' the Dowager said. 'Have the patients had their morning drink?'

'Not yet.'

'Then get to it.' Even Makepeace jumped. This was a countess with a whip in her boot.

Watching them go, the Dowager said: 'You will find their initials instructive. W. F. P. and D. War, Famine, Plague and Death. I call them the Four Horsemen of the Apocalypse. Now then. Take that basket and pick up the soiled linen in the bucket by each bed and take it to the laundry. You will find your young man behind that curtaining where we put the more seriously ill. You may have two min-utes with him, no longer. There's work to be done.'

'Yes'm.'

Dragging a big washing basket, Makepeace lifted the canvas sail that separated five beds near the door from the rest of the ward. Josh was in the middle bed, gasping. His eyes were closed.

Makepeace fell on her knees beside him. 'Josh dear, Josh. It's Missus. I'm here to make you well.'

Either he didn't hear her or else he was concentrating too hard on the business of getting air in and out of his damaged lung. She stroked his hair and put her cheek against his. It was dry and hot.

'Hang on, Josh. You're going to get well. Missus is here.'

His upper torso was naked except for a bandage, which was white and clean, like the pillow under his head. She could have cried with gratitude for that at least. 'Hang on, lamb pie. Keep breathing.'

'Missus?' It was the tiniest whisper of precious air.

'Yes, Josh. Here now. Keep breathin', boy.'

'Missus,' he said comfortably, and turned his head so that it rested on her hand. She let it stay until she saw he was asleep and then, as she kissed him, she slid it away and went out.

There was work to be done.

Chapter Sixteen

THEY established a routine. Makepeace and Philippa attended the hospital on Mondays, Wednesdays and Fridays. Dell and Tobias took their place on Tuesdays, Thursdays and Saturdays. The Dowager went in every day, to see to correspondence, prevent the cooks and the quartermaster selling too many of the hospital's supplies for profit, do the ordering, try and find more nurses and ensure that the orderlies didn't slack. Tobias, her escort, also went every day and became part of the team—treated as a menial, like the women, and, like the women, working four times as hard as the other men.

Everybody went in on Sundays because, otherwise, the hospital would have been virtually deserted—that was when three out of the four orderlies took a day off.

The women were not allowed to outrage propriety by staying overnight so that during the hours of darkness, the patients were left in the care of one orderly and the guards.

It was a punishing regime. For all of them, even those who worked only four days out of seven, the eighty-minute ride home along the twilight clifftops was accomplished in the stupefied silence of exhaustion.

Their labour was made harder by Dr Maltby, a more frequent visitor since the advent of the Dowager had drawn attention to his absences. He regarded the presence of women in his ward as anathema and they were forced to disappear into the loft during his rounds and watch impatiently for him to be gone.

He brought terror with him, mixed with the reek of whisky. A vicious drunk, the sort Makepeace had met once or twice in her tavern-keeping career, able to speak without slurring but with a horrifying unpredictability. Why he hadn't been dismissed by the Sick and Hurt Office, she couldn't understand. The Dowager urged it but Captain Luscombe had admitted himself powerless: the man had friends in the Admiralty.

He'd been known to hit patients who displeased him. Twice he'd ordered an unnecessary amputation for a prisoner. Happily, most amputations had already been performed by the surgeon on whichever Royal Navy vessel had brought its enemy's survivors to Plymouth. Drunk as he was, he would have operated on gangrene patients in the ward but, again, the Dowager had forestalled him. Captain Luscombe, on her recommendation, had instituted a rule that men with gangrene be sent to the excellent Royal Navy hospital in town.

It didn't make Maltby's hatred of the Dowager Countess of Stacpoole any less, but it saved lives.

On Maltby days, the women kept their heads down, listening and wincing as the doctor sent patients who were manifestly unfit back to their barracks. 'What's he do?' Makepeace whispered to Philippa, 'get a bonus for every man he discharges?'

The doctor's voice roared out: 'And what's wrong with you, you damn malingerer? Look healthy enough to me. Get out.'

Latour, *marin simple* of the French navy, limped into their view on a crutch, his yet-unhealed broken leg trailing. '*Attendez* outside,' Makepeace hissed down at him. Later, she'd smuggle him back in; the only good thing about Maltby was that he didn't remember his patients from one visit to the next.

'And who in hell's this coaly bastard?'

Makepeace and Philippa looked at each other in despair. Josh.

But it wasn't Josh. Dr Maltby had glimpsed Tobias.

One of the orderlies muttered something.

'What the hell's the navy coming to? Well, just see he keeps his black hands off my bloody patients.' That from a man with the longest, dirtiest fingernails Makepeace had ever seen.

She heard Maltby move on to another bed and the voice of one of the new American patients, Captain Sugden, begin a complaint he hadn't stopped making since his arrival. Not now, she thought, not to him.

'. . . and I must inform you, sir, it is against all rules of warfare that officers be accommodated with enlisted men. I demand . . .'

This was Maltby's meat and drink. 'Fighting for the equality of Man, ain't you? We're giving you bloody equality. Orderly, get this man back to his barracks.'

When Makepeace helped Latour and Sugden back to their beds after Maltby had gone, Sugden was still complaining. 'French officers aren't treated in the prison like we are. They have their own quarters.'

'The French ain't rebels,' she told him.

In an odd reversal of sympathy, the Dowager thought it was awful that American officers were not segregated from their men as were the French. Makepeace did not; in this she agreed with Maltby. What were the new United States fighting for if not equality?

And it wasn't only officers wanting to be divided from their men—since the arrival of the crew of the *Santee* the possibility of a new and more ominous segregation was being bruited.

Santee's men were mostly young men from South Carolina whose captain had brought them from their river fishing and their rice and indigo fields to go privateering in the cold waters of the English Channel—with considerable success, until *Santee* had been holed beneath the waterline and sunk.

Of the two who'd been delivered to the hospital, one had a throat wound which prevented him talking, an omission more than made up for by his friend, Able Seaman Abell. And Able Seaman Abell also wanted segregation, not between officers and men, but between black and white.

The first indication of the trouble to come was a kerfuffle from his bay that brought Makepeace running. 'What's the *matter*?' Tobias was standing by the bed with a medicine bottle in his hands.

'Ma'am, I ain't takin' no physick from no nigger,' Abell said. He was dribbling blood: a broken rib had punctured one of his lungs.

'I read him the apothecary'th inthtructionth,' Tobias said, worriedly.

''Poth'cary instructions!' Abell panted with contempt. 'How's a nigger git book larnin'?'

Angrily, she snatched the bottle and rammed a dose of medicine into Abell's mouth. This was no time for confrontation—the boy was gasping and would rather die than receive succour from black hands.

Later she lectured him. 'You're lucky Tobias is a Christian and didn't smash that bottle on your scurvy head.'

Abell smiled at her ignorance. 'He cain't be Christ'n, ma'am. He's black. He's lucky he bin rescued from savagery by us civilized folk.'

For Abell, as for many of these volunteer sailors, there was no United States, only the backwoods territory of his home. The war had brought him for the first time in his life into contact with men who called themselves Americans but, in their belief that slavery was an evil, were as foreign to him as Indian Buddhists.

Without his bigotry, Makepeace could have liked Abell; he was a personable young man, and endured pain without complaint. Bewilderingly, when he and other survivors had been struggling in the water, he'd held up the *Santee*'s black cook, who couldn't swim, until they were rescued. But his conviction that negroes were only fit for slavery was a crusade with him; before long he had one or two of the other patients refusing Tobias's care, which put an extra burden on the women.

When she complained of him to one of her favourite patients, Sam Perkins, he said: 'The terror of the ignorant. Abell's illiterate, Tobias ain't. Abell's a white Gullah from the swamps, poorest of the poor. Negroes are all he's got to look down on. Take that away and he's nothing.'

Of all the Americans in Millbay, Sam Perkins, being a non-combatant, was the most likely to be exchanged. A little man, a middle-aged Massachusetts lawyer whose once-plump skin now hung on him, he'd been on his way to join Ben Franklin in Paris when, as he said, he'd been forced to make a detour—the sloop he was aboard had gone down to British fire off Finisterre. Makepeace liked him. The only fear of his life that she'd been able to discern was that of losing his spectacles. Thus far, miraculously, he'd been able to keep them intact.

Nevertheless, when she had time, Makepeace tried ramming inalienable truths into Able Seaman Abell. But his mind was a circular palisade. White folk had bestowed a blessing on black folk by taking them from the dark continent of Africa into the Christian light, yet that same light could not shine upon black folk because their skin showed the darkness of their origin.

There was no crack through which he would allow Makepeace's argument to enter. She made sure his bed was kept as far away as possible from those of Josh and the other black men.

Of all the patients, Andrew Abell was the only one she was almost sorry to see get better. On the morning when, with great sweetness, he thanked her for nursing him and was taken away to the prisoners' barracks, she felt as if she were loosing a fox into a hen coop. It made her wonder what sort of people would be populating the land of the free when it was won.

But she was learning. When they were well enough to do it, most of the men liked to show her the letters from home they'd received before they were captured and kept in their jackets. Illiterates wanted her to read their letters to them over and again. And through these worn, sometimes sodden, pieces of paper, Makepeace was given glimpses of the war her people on the other side of the Atlantic were fighting.

She was vouchsafed tableaux of starving men scratching at fleas and chiggers while they cooked firecakes—mixed flour and water—on an open fire, or roasted an old shoe to make a meal, or lay in wait to catch the Brigadier's pet dog and eat it.

Death from heat stroke in summer. Sleeping under snow in winter. Quiet farmyards turned into scenes from Hell as opposing armies descended on them. Men whose uniform was a hunting shirt with a knife in its belt fighting scrappy battles in fields of Indian corn against red-coated soldiers. Militiamen signing on for one campaign and then going home for the harvest, carrying typhoid with them. Boys of fourteen running away to join Washington's army and promoted to officers by the time they were sixteen.

Sometimes, in their letters, they swaggered. 'I had to snuff a little gunpowder for Liberty's sake.'

Sometimes they didn't. 'I confess to you, brother, I weren't thinking of Liberty when I fired, merely trying to stop the man opposite killing me.'

Some of the officers' letters reflected General Washington's irritation with the camp followers who slowed down the baggage trains, while in the next sentence described the women in them as washing or cooking or nursing or foraging for the men.

One letter said:

Mrs Landis with a husband in the artillery stayed with him all through the fighting at Monmouth. While she was reaching for a cartridge, a cannon shot passed between her legs without doing any damage except carrying away the lower part of her petticoat. She said it was lucky it had passed no higher or it would have carried away something more valuable, after which she continued her occupation.

But in their way, the letters from wives who stayed home were just as heroic. 'I ploud and hoed the corn, Tom, so's to raze bread for our childer. The chickens is doin well. Made chees, sat and spun 53 knots til dark then done the milkin by rushlight.'

This was not the glorious heroics lauded by its sympathizers, this was a common war fought, on the American side, mostly by the very young. Nor, again on the American side, was it homogeneous. There was as much mention of killing between patriot and loyalist,

red and white, black and white, red and black, as there was of battling against the British enemy.

Yet Makepeace found that a new word cropped up again and
again. Nationly. 'I felt nationly as I joined the sewing bee,' one
mother had written. A young wife who'd raised money for army
blankets congratulated herself on being 'nationly'. Men and women
signing the patriotic Covenant did it in a spirit of 'nationlyness'.

'But what sort of nation's it going to be when we win, Sam?' she
asked Lawyer Perkins. 'That's what I want to know. What sort of
nation?'

'Reckon it'll be one that asks questions, ma'am,' he said, polish-
ing his spectacles and smiling at her. 'They say a British officer gives
a command to his men, it's obeyed. An American officer gives a
command to his men, he has to tell 'em why.'

Makepeace wiped the sudden tears from her eyes. 'Oh, *that* sort
of nation.'

Josh began to get better slowly—and then very quickly. Makepeace tried to persuade him to feign weakness so that he could fat-
ten up on the food she smuggled in to him. He wouldn't. 'Can't do
that, Missus. Ain't fair to the other *Pilgrim* lads as are starving in the
barracks.'

'It helps if you starve along with 'em, does it?' she said.

She comforted herself with the thought that at least going back
would get him away from discrimination. The campaign for segregation that Abell had started before he was discharged was being
carried on by other Americans from the South and having its effect.
The Four Horsemen of the Apocalypse, she noticed, were beginning to allocate one section of beds, the favoured ones nearest the
loft stairs, to white men only.

'And escaping from in here ain't easy,' Josh added.

She was instantly terrified. 'Not again. Josh, don't try again.'

'Be all right this time,' he said and crooked his finger so that
she'd come closer. 'Word is there's to be a tunnel.'

Oh God.

She began to dread the next round by Maltby when, inevitably, Josh would be discharged.

The guards came first. 'Which is Joshua Burke?'

'That one,' Payne told him. 'Chimney-chops, second bay.'

The Dowager descended hurriedly from the loft. 'What do you want with him, gentlemen?'

'Punishment block, ma'am. He's got a stint in the Black Hole.'

Makepeace came running. The Dowager put out a hand and caught her tightly by the wrist. 'This man has been very ill,' she told the guards. 'He needs to recuperate. To put him in the Black Hole is out of the question.'

One of them shrugged. 'Orders, ma'am. He's an escaper. Ain't done his forty days.' He was a corporal of the 13th Regulars, neither liking nor disliking the job he was doing.

'He's been too sick, you meathead,' Makepeace shrieked at him. 'It'll kill him.'

At a sign from the Dowager, Tobias pulled her out of the ward.

'I shall protest to Captain Luscombe,' Diana said.

'Your privilege, ma'am,' the corporal said.

She went with them and Josh to the cubed blockhouse and inspected it before he was put inside. It had three inmates already. There was the same stink, the same stripes of sunlight falling on men who didn't move or look up as she went in. Covered buckets that she'd insisted be installed meant that there were fewer flies than the last time she'd seen the Hole.

She sent one of the soldiers for a pitcher of fresh water. 'I'm very sorry,' she told Josh.

He said: 'Look after the Missus for me,' then stooped and the heavy door was slammed and bolted behind him.

'And Captain Luscombe presents his compliments, ma'am, and will you call at his house,' the corporal said.

'It is regrettable,' Luscombe told her, 'but rules are rules, your ladyship, and I am being harried by Major Huntley to ensure they are kept.'

Major Huntley was his *bête noire*. The military presence, responsible for the prison's security, did not sit well with the navy in charge of the camp's day-to-day running.

'And I fear, dear lady, that you have been responsible for yet another escape. Did you hear the alarm bell last night?'

'No.' She was coldly offended. 'How am I responsible, Captain?' And then knew. 'Grayle.'

'Yes. He dug under the fence like a terrier, using those hands you gave him. Made a hole big enough to get out into the road and disappear down it.' Luscombe shook his head; he was becoming a very tired man.

An awful glee overtook her. *Run. Get away. Go home to Martha. Oh, run.*

'We caught him, of course. Fellow the size of a tree and artificial hands tends to be noticeable. But I thought . . . before he goes into the Black Hole . . . you might like to have a word with him.'

She looked at her own hand for a moment before she touched Luscombe's arm. 'I beg you, Captain. This is not civilized. The boy has suffered enough.'

'I'm sorry, your ladyship. But if he's able enough to escape, he's able to do his forty days.'

She pressed her lips together. 'One hopes he will be allowed the use of the hands in that time. You won't take them away from him?'

He smiled a little. 'No. I don't think even Lieutenant Grayle can dig through concrete.'

'Where is he?'

'Out in the garden.'

There were two guards with him again. His arms had been tied behind him once more and he was standing by an arbour that was covered in dog-roses, bending down towards the flowers as if putting the look and scent of their petals into a mental pocket for later. From the corner of his eyes he saw her coming and grinned shamefacedly. 'Mighty sorry, your ladyship.'

'Lieutenant, how could you?'

'Seemed like a good idea at the time, ma'am. The hands worked just dandy, dug like a gopher.' He sucked at his excellent teeth. 'Would've made it, too,'f I hadn't run into a patrol.'

'I hope you weren't looking for a cliff this time.'

'No, ma'am. You taught me that. This time I was going home to Mommy and Henrietta.' He smiled down at her. 'Guess you better delay that letter to my ma again.'

'Guess I had.' She broke off a trail of dog-roses and carefully threaded the broken end through a buttonhole of his jacket, so that the scent could reach him. 'I'm afraid they don't last long.' On impulse, she stood on tiptoe and kissed his cheek. 'Good luck, Lieutenant.'

'Good-bye, ma'am. See you in forty days.'

The Dowager had hoped to ease the burden on the women working in the hospital by hiring others, but recruitment was slow to the point of nonexistent. Plymouth's middle-class husbands would not countenance their wives donning a mob cap and emptying enemy chamber pots. And among the working people, with so many men employed in the war, women had their hands full managing their children, homes and vegetable plots as well as trying to keep their husband's shop, stall, livery stable, smallholding, or whatever it was, from going under while he was away.

'And there are so many ships coming and going that even the prostitutes are too busy,' Diana said, bitterly.

'One's enough,' Makepeace said.

Diana said, gently: 'If we had another like her, we would be fortunate.'

'I know.' Dell still had her airs and graces—she had become a fig-ure of fun to the orderlies—but she worked as hard as anybody.

'I notice that she won't touch the men,' said Diana, still gentle. 'She leaves washing and lifting to Tobias.'

'That's what I don't like about her,' Makepeace burst out. 'The way she treats Tobias. As if she's better than he is because he's black.'

'Perhaps she has to feel that she's better than somebody.'

'Well, she ain't.' She looked at the Dowager. 'You think I'm hard on her.'

'Philippa tells me she owes her a great deal. And she has obviously put her old life behind her.'

'Mmm. Maybe. Well, let's get on . . . What's to be done about the men coming in tomorrow?'

Thanks once more to the Dowager, Royal Navy ships bringing wounded enemy prisoners into Plymouth had been ordered to signal their number as they reached the Sound so that a message could be sent ahead to the hospital. Tomorrow there was to be an influx of eleven—for whom there were not enough beds.

'I suppose we could put the less serious cases in hammocks,' Diana said. She rubbed her forehead. 'I'll have to beg them from the quartermaster, obstructive man that he is. How very tiring.'

To Makepeace, who had never heard ladyship utter a personal complaint, this was a confession of exhaustion.

And no wonder, she thought, with what she's up against. Makepeace, who considered herself a champion at organizing, recognized that in the Dowager she had met her superior. Yet the woman faced obstruction everywhere. The male orderlies in particular resented her. 'We didn't have all this to-do before *she* come,' Payne had grumbled to Makepeace.

'I heard the patients kept dying.'

'Why not? Buggers came here to kill *us*.'

And Payne was typical of lower ranks who regarded the wounded, French and American, as hardly worth the saving.

The upper echelons, on the other hand, didn't mind saving them as long as it didn't cost much. But it did. The hospital was full because the Dowager fought tooth and nail to keep the patients in it until, in her opinion, they were able to survive the return to prison. And a full hospital meant extra men to guard it. The Dowager's demand for cleanliness and good food involved more work and expense for the laundry and kitchens.

And when winter came, there would be even greater demands in the way of blankets and firing.

The hospital's success was damning it.

Makepeace patted her hand. 'You stay here, I'll get the hammocks out of that bastard.'

Watching her go, Diana knew that she would. She saw a Frenchman put up his hand to touch Makepeace's shadow as it went by. Others tried to detain her to talk.

The common touch, Diana thought. She knew it was her loss not to have it; Makepeace Hedley made the patients feel better just by her presence, whereas her own daunted most of them. Where she gave quiet reprimands to the orderlies and was resented, Makepeace yelled at them in Anglo-Saxon and produced not only activity but a grin. After she'd told the prison's head cook that his soup was nothing but piss and pigswill, the hospital broth had begun to contain some nourishment.

Freckles, the Dowager decided. If one had as good a supply of them as Makepeace Hedley, people didn't take one amiss whatever one did. Freckles and courage and a high spirit and that mysterious common touch.

Three new women swelled the hospital nursing ranks. Having circulated every institution she could think of with a request for medical maids, the Dowager unearthed a pair of twenty-year-old female twins from the local asylum.

'Not prepossessing, I fear,' the asylum matron said. 'Tireless workers, though, and I shall be sorry to let them go, but they have been here since children and become very dull-witted. A change may brighten them. You'll make sure they are returned each night?'

'Yes.' They were big women and stood round-shouldered, blank-faced and unexpectant, like a matching pair of carthorses. She thought: the Missus will be cross with me for taking advantage of the half-witted.

'Tireless, you say?'

'Oh yes. They'll work 'til they drop.'

'I'll take them,' the Dowager said.

The third recruit was a volunteer.

'I wouldn't have sunk to it, your ladyship, not never, being who I am and having a regard for what people think, but when I heard you was in charge, I thought: Fanny, if her ladyship can lower herself, well then, being family, you can too.'

'It is exceedingly hard work, Mrs Nicholls, I don't think . . .'

Mrs Nicholls flexed large hands in lavender fishnet gloves. 'My goodness gracious, I can scrub and clean when I'm put to ut. Had to when I was puttin' my Walter through his educating through now, being who he is, we got a maid to do ut. I said to Walter: " 'Tis succourin' the enemy, Walter, do ee mind, you being who you are?" But he said: "Mother, if 'tis her ladyship, you go ahead because her can do no wrong in my eyes." '

Eyes, thought Diana. Why do her eyes always conflict with what she's saying? However, beggars could not be choosers . . .

'Then we shall be pleased to have you aboard, Mrs Nicholls,' she said.

So Captain Nicholls's mother joined the team and, indeed, proved nearly as tireless as the twins. Makepeace said: 'She may have spawned a blasted Revenue man, but she's a good worker. What've you got against her?'

There was a time when the Dowager would have turned the question aside as impertinent, a probe into personal matters. Now she said: 'I don't know what it is—I just feel I've been infiltrated.'

It was a week later that the Dowager returned to the hospital after leading the twins back to the asylum to find Makepeace waiting for her. 'Aren't you ready? What is the matter?' It was time to collect the ponies and go home.

'Ladyship . . .' For once, Makepeace was wordless.

They hurried together up the length of the ward to the curtained section where they put the dying. The sound of loud snoring came from behind it. 'We don't know what it is. The guard heard Josh hammering on the door inside the Black Hole and when they opened up, he was like this. I sent for the town doctor.'

Lieutenant Grayle was too large for the bed, his bare feet hung over the end. The snoring came from a mouth that had twisted on one side. 'We've done everything,' Makepeace said and added, awkwardly: 'We took the hands off. So's the harness wouldn't rub.'

She sent Tobias to fetch a chair so that the Dowager might sit beside the bed. Now she couldn't stop talking. 'Doctor'll be here soon. Big strong boy like that, he'll pull through. Would you like some tea? Oh, my dear woman, don't look like that.'

Neither the patient nor the woman sitting beside him heard her.

Such a nice-looking boy he must have been, Makepeace thought. Gawky. Should be sitting under a tree now, courting a girl, not dying, mutilated, in this sink-hole thousands of miles from home.

She went outside to swear.

Philippa said: 'I don't think she'll be able to bear it.'

'She'll have to. Bastards, didn't they do enough to that boy? I pray God to put them in a Black Hole to die, and make it soon.'

'She feels about him like we do about Josh. She knew his mother.'

'I know.'

'I've brewed some tea.'

Makepeace put her arm around her daughter. 'Shouldn't have brought you here, should I? But I tell you, Pippy, I don't know what I'd have done without you.'

They went and drank tea in the loft. After a while, Payne blustered up to them. 'Here, you can't stay all night. Time you was off.'

Makepeace looked at him and he went away.

The Dowager was thinking of Martha. Perhaps she's asleep and dreaming that her son has come home, she thought. The Admiralty will signal their navy and they will send the letter. 'We regret to inform you that your son, Lieutenant Forrest Grayle . . .' I must bear it for her until then. How can I? I must. I am *in loco parentis*.

The sprig of dog-roses she'd picked for the boy was still in his buttonhole, withered now. The hands she'd had made for him hung over the end of the bed on their harness, still with traces of dried earth on the wood and metal fingers he'd used to scrabble for freedom.

They brought her tea, which she didn't touch because she didn't notice it. When it got dark, somebody put a candle on the other side of the bed.

The town doctor came in, made a brief examination and went out again. 'It shouldn't be long,' he told Makepeace, 'not with breathing like that. Inflammation of the brain, I should say. One of those things that can happen to the healthiest.'

He looked around, unused to seeing so much attendance in a place where death was common. 'Is he somebody special?'

The breathing stopped in the early hours.

They put his hands back on so that they should be buried with him and the Dowager took the withered dog-roses from his coat to send to Martha.

The sun was rising as they rode along the cliff path. Just before they got to the ferry, Makepeace said: 'If it's the last thing I do, I'm going to see Josh escapes from that place. You object to that?'

'No.'

Chapter Seventeen

'Is it my fault?' the Dowager asked.

'Not at all,' Lucy Edgcumbe told her, determinedly cheerful, 'it has been presented to us as a promotion and I am sure that it is.'

'Ireland, though.'

'Ireland.'

The two women looked out on the sloping gardens of Mount Edgcumbe, considering the troubled land to which Admiral Lord Edgcumbe had just been appointed Vice-Treasurer.

'It's because of the hospital,' Diana said. 'The King is angry with him.'

'My dear, *something* had to be done about the place and the country should be grateful that you did it. The Admiral was happy to see you do so. In view of that, it seems unfair that the Admiralty is still tied to the whipping post as far as the Rockingham set is concerned. And of course their poodles in the press back them up so that Millbay is constantly before the public. Have you seen this?'

It was a newspaper calling itself *The Passenger*, a more lurid publication than both ladies were used to. The leading article, entitled 'Our Shame', went on to say:

The refusal by Lord North and his gang to exchange American prisoners of war is leading to increasing atrocity. We are informed of a young American lieutenant who lost both of his hands in battle and is now dead after receiving further punishment at Millbay Prison . . .

'I didn't know,' Diana said.

'Of course you did not. Nobody thinks you did. It is unfortunate that later on in the piece you are mentioned admiringly as protesting at the poor young man's incarceration. I'm afraid some of the more sober newspapers have picked it up, which will not please His Majesty.'

Nor Robert, the Dowager thought, wearily. It had been ominous that her son had not called on the Edgcumbes during his visit. As the virtual commander of naval Portsmouth, the Admiral was being blamed by the Court for the fuss her exertions had caused.

She said: 'I am ruining everything I touch.'

'Not so.' Lucy Edgcumbe hammered her little fist on the arm of her rattan chair. 'The death rate at Millbay has fallen wonderfully under your aegis. John Howard will be proud of you. I am proud of you. Humanity should be proud of you. Once we've beaten them, I expect the French will give you a medal.' She put her head on one side. 'I wonder what the Americans will give you. Something tasteless, I expect—such a vulgar country.'

Her eyes slid sideways, wondering whether it was too soon to deliver the next blow. 'More coffee?'

'No, I thank you.'

Lady Edgcumbe coughed and said casually: 'Captain Luscombe will be replaced, of course.'

The Dowager raised her head. 'Do you know that he will?'

'I'm afraid I do. Poor man, back to active service for him. Though he may find firing cannonballs at the Americans a good deal more restful than imprisoning them.'

'That's the end of me, then,' Diana said. 'A new commander is unlikely to put up with me.'

Lady Edgcumbe's silence was confirmation that he would not. The cooing of wood pigeons floated through the long open windows of her sitting room from somewhere in the deer park, where the trees had turned into their autumn colours against a turquoise sea.

'A good thing, too,' she said, suddenly impatient. 'You have tired yourself out. Had we not been packing for Ireland, I should have insisted you come here for a rest but I suppose you will return to that crow's nest of yours.'

'Eagle's nest,' said Diana, quietly. 'A Frenchman I knew called it an eagle's nest.'

'Did he? But there is one blessing. My good husband has sent for Bosun Tilley.'

'Who is Bosun Tilley?'

'My dear, he is the most wonderful man; the Admiral swears by him. They were together in the West Indies on the *Falcon*, no surgeon, nothing but flies and dysentery and the whole ship's company gone down with it including the Admiral—a lowly captain then, of course. Bosun Tilley was practically the only one on his feet and he not only ran the vessel, he physicked the crew so that merely two died, and they were cooks so it hardly mattered. A magician, my dear, better than a doctor, and the Admiral says that if the hospital must lose you it shall at least gain Bosun Tilley. Oh, *won't* he take a rope's end to those orderlies of yours and make them move!' Lucy Edgcumbe nodded with satisfaction. 'He should be here in a week or two.'

'Good.' A rope's end would undoubtedly profit the orderlies but could Bosun Tilley stand firm against the hospital's higher enemies?

They have beaten me, she thought, and I am almost too numb to care.

Lucy Edgcumbe accompanied the Dowager to the carriage that would take her back to the hospital and bade her good-bye, a recent conversation with her husband causing her much concern.

'The Whigs have done for her, Lucy. They've taken her up to make the King look a monster which, to do him justice, he ain't. And he's sensitive to criticism just now. They say he called her a madwoman out of Bedlam.'

'An unfortunate phrase from His Majesty at this moment. Diana isn't the one shaking hands with trees.'

'*Lucy!*'

*   *   *

At the hospital, the Dowager held out a copy of *The Passenger* to Makepeace, who read it and paled. 'Beasley.'

'A friend of yours?'

'Yes, I . . . well, yes, I wrote to him about what happened. I never intended he should publish it.'

'He has. And with great effect. Admiral Edgcumbe is being removed to Ireland, Captain Luscombe removed to sea and I . . . well, I am just being removed.'

Makepeace looked up into a face of marble. 'Diana, I'm awful sorry.'

'Worse than all that,' the Dowager continued, evenly, 'is that political rogues have felt free to use Lieutenant Grayle's death to chastise His Majesty and his government.'

Knowing there was no apology she could make, Makepeace began to bristle at the fact that one should be made at all. 'It's the truth, ain't it? That boy would be alive today if he'd been treated better.'

'You misunderstand me. This'—the Dowager tapped the newspaper with a fingertip—'will be meat and drink to the American press. The manner of his death will be bruited about to blacken England's name. Martha Grayle will learn what her son suffered before he died. One had hoped to spare her that.'

Makepeace was silenced.

'No, no, it isn't dismissal,' Captain Luscombe said, bravely. 'Happily, I am to be transferred to the active list—though rather lower down it than I could have wished.'

'And I am responsible for it,' Diana said. 'Captain, I am so very sorry.'

Luscombe didn't pretend. 'My fault,' he said, 'I was remiss. Luxuriating in having the burden of the hospital lifted off my shoulders, I forgot what was due to your ladyship's position.' He smiled. 'Yet so much has been achieved by your efforts that I cannot condemn myself too harshly, nor I think will God.'

'I know He will not.'

Luscombe nodded. 'You understand, of course, my successor has orders to refuse your ladyship access to the hospital.'

'I understand. Do the women remain?'

'For the time being.'

As the Dowager tidied her papers in the loft at the end of that day, only Makepeace, Philippa and Tobias knew it would be for the last time and waited for her to say good-bye to the men.

She didn't. For the orderlies her departure was a triumph and she would not give them the satisfaction of knowing it until she had gone.

To the patients, she knew, she was merely a presence that came and went on business that seemed to have little to do with alleviating their pain. Makepeace, little Philippa, Dell, Tobias, now the twins and Mrs Nicholls: these were the people who cared for them. She would not embarrass the men or herself with acknowledgement of a defeat of which they knew nothing.

At the door, she said her usual, 'Good night, gentlemen,' and waited outside while the nurses went down the aisle, doing what they could for the men before they left for the night.

She turned to look at the great shape of the warehouse in the evening sunlight and thought: I have achieved nothing. Within a week, unless Makepeace prevents it, men will be dying as they died before. And nobody will care. They are only the enemy.

Only two days ago, a woman outside the prison gates had screamed at her: 'Them cruel Yankees have got my man prisoner. What for are you comforting them in there?'

'In the hope that some Americans will comfort ours.' But the woman had continued to shout at her, as if the suffering of men she didn't know would ease her husband's.

The four of them rode in silence towards the eastward cliffs and the track back to Babbs Cove.

The weather was still duplicitous, pretending it was summer when, in fact, it was autumn. Blackthorn was covered with fat, blue-bloomed sloes that women were already picking to put in gin for Christmas.

'Evening, Mrs Letty. Not waiting for the first frost?'

'They'm ripe now, Mrs Hedley. Good evening, your ladyship, Miss Philippa. Never seen such a crop. 'Twill be a hard winter, look at the holly berries. Iss fay, a hard old winter be coming.'

As they rode on, Makepeace said: 'I hope the weather holds. My sister-in-law will be here tomorrow with Jenny and Sally. Sanders sent a note to the prison by the mail coach to say they'd reached Exeter.'

'You will be crowded at the inn,' the Dowager said. 'We had better change places.' T'Gallants is hers, after all, although so far she's charged no rent.

'We'll stay as we are.' That house is enough to frighten children into fits, don't know how she stands it.

As Mr Mattock, the ferryman, poled them and their ponies across the Erme, a cloud of sandpipers flew over their heads on their way south, giving reedy calls to one another. A deposit splashed onto the Dowager's shoulder.

'That's lucky, ladyship,' Mr Mattock said. 'Leave 'un to dry and that'll bring ee luck.'

She brushed it off, not hearing him.

I have done more harm than good. The Edgcumbes and Luscombe have paid the price of my attempts. Robert has been distressed. And what have I gained except laceration of the heart at the death of a young man I hardly knew?

It was getting dark by the time they rode up the hill to where the track made a wide half-circle around the rear of T'Gallants.

'I am sorry to prevail on you when you are tired, Mrs Hedley,' the Dowager said, 'but as you will have other concerns tomorrow, there are matters connected to the hospital which should be discussed tonight.'

Makepeace nodded to Philippa to go on down. The nights were becoming chilly and from up here the inn's lights gave it the look of a welcoming fireplace. T'Gallants was in darkness.

They'll have supper ready for me down there, she thought. What's this poor female got to come home to?

Tobias took the ponies and followed Philippa down to bed them in the Pomeroy stable. Makepeace stumbled through the unlit courtyard after the Dowager. 'Come and eat with us,' she said. 'Dell makes a good Irish stew, I'll say that for her.'

'Thank you, no. Mrs Green usually prepares a collation.'

She's still punishing me. Well, I'm ready for her now.

There was a single candle burning in a holder on a table in the screen passage. The Dowager took it up and led the way into the Great Hall where she used it to light a candelabrum. With the onset of the night's chill, the room's air was damp, its corners full of shadows. Chairs and a table were clustered around the huge empty grate but she noticed that the first thing the Dowager did was to cross to the front window and peer out of it, before returning and inviting Makepeace to sit down.

She looks for him every night. Same as I do for Andra.

The Dowager opened a drawer in the tiny occasional table and brought out a notebook on which was jotted a list.

'The food. I have stopped the cooks selling half the hospital's allotment of beef to the meat pie shop on the Parade but you must watch out for them. Weigh the loaves before they leave the bakery or they will give you short measure. The patients may ask for white bread but it is not good for them; however, rye is too harsh for their stomachs. Something in between.'

'Yes'm.'

'The cook's wife has the concession for cider and you should ensure she doesn't water it. The quartermaster . . . you have dealt with him, it seems, which is good. However, the laundry will revert to slackness if it is not bullied. See that the clothing of new arrivals is stripped off them and properly burned. The dispensary may refuse laudanum because it is too expensive and I pay them extra for it—I shall write you a letter for my bank; there is still some money from the subscription. Remember to keep fever patients away from those only wounded. One had hoped to have the cottage done up for them . . .'

The Dowager stopped. Her mouth was moving but her eyes had gone blank, one finger was paused over the list.

'Stay there,' Makepeace said. She took up the candle and made her way to the kitchen. Mrs Green, it appeared, had retired for the night. The place had the empty cleanliness to be seen in the houses of the respectable poor. A plate on the vast table contained a small wedge of cheese, the end of a loaf and some plums.

Of an evening, Tobias had taken to eating one of Mrs Hallewell's pasties with Zack and Simeon at the Pomeroy. And no wonder.

There was no fire on which to boil a kettle but Makepeace searched until she found some cooking brandy and a jug of milk kept fresh by standing in a bowl of water. '*Collation*,' she scoffed, gathering everything together and carrying it through to the hall.

The Dowager had slumped in her chair. Makepeace poured some of the milk into a beaker, added a good dose of brandy, curved the woman's hands round it and eased it towards her mouth. When it was empty, she poured some more. 'Open.' She popped a piece of cheese into the Dowager's mouth. 'Open again.'

The Dowager smiled; some colour had come back to her face. 'I can feed myself, thank you.'

'Looks like it. You're coming down the Pomeroy for supper every night from here on, you hear me?'

'Yes.'

'Open again.' She waited until the cheese was gone and then sat herself in the chair opposite the table. 'Now you listen to me. I'm sorry for young Grayle, God knows, and I'm even sorrier for his ma, but he ain't died in vain. What happened to him was a stain on this country of yours and it *can't* be kept private. Mustn't be. John Beasley was right, people should know and be shamed.'

She got up so that she could walk about; she was getting into full flow. 'Young Grayle ain't the only one. I'll wager there's hundreds suffering what he did. Do you know how many prisoners of war there are in Britain?'

'No.' The Dowager was watching her curiously.

'I don't neither,' Makepeace confessed, 'but I know it's thousands. Just because you saw what was needed at Millbay don't mean it ain't needed in the other camps. What I *do* know is there's one in Portsmouth and another at Norman Cross. And Liverpool. Dozens, and every one of 'em sink-holes as bad as Millbay if I'm a judge. Maybe worse.'

She turned again and put her hands on the table to lean on it. 'You know what Beasley wrote to me?'

Dumbly, the Dowager shook her head.

'He wrote there's a subscription been raised for the prisoners at Portsmouth. See what you've done? Pricked the public conscience, that's what you've done, you and John Howard. And my friend Beasley'll make sure it stays pricked. You got an objection to that?'

'No.'

'Good. Now get to bed or we'll look a dandy pair of hags by the time our men come sailing back to us.'

She went and the Dowager was alone in a hall that seemed to have been swept and garnished, its walls still reverberating with a New England accent.

What an extraordinary person.

She picked up the candelabrum and took it to the wreckers' window. She has stitched me together, she thought. The sutures are clumsy but they hold the wounds together.

Perhaps Martha Grayle would find some tiny comfort if her child's death proved of use to his countrymen. That was the letter she would write. 'If it helps, my dear, he did not die in vain.'

Public attention, though . . . she shrank from the thought of it. They will use my name over and again, for the newspapers love a title. Cartoons will portray me as the Dauntless Dowager or some such vulgarity. Robert will hate it. Yet she's right, the Missus is right. I had not thought of it, but there are other Millbays, other young men starving and dying excruciating deaths.

I shall begin to agitate for exchange, she thought. It is nonsense that there is none for Americans. The more we send back, the more of our poor soldiers and sailors can come home. That's what I shall do.

She looked out at the empty cove. And when will you come

back? I cannot live the rest of my life on the memory of one ship-board dinner.

Even knowledge that he was unlikely to did not hurt as badly as usual. Makepeace had done that for her, too; she did not regret any single action she had made in these last few months. Better a patched and painful heart than one of accreted stone, she thought.

Yes, that's what I shall do. I shall start a campaign for exchange.

'Where be her ladyship today?' Mrs Nicholls asked.

'Gone last Friday,' Makepeace said. 'It's up to us now.'

'Is ut,' said Mrs Nicholls, bitterly. 'That's where you're wrong then.' She took off her mob cap, fetched her hat and coat and marched out of the hospital.

'Damn you, Fairweather Fanny,' Makepeace said, angrily. 'I wanted to spend time with my daughters.' They were going to be desperately shorthanded; Philippa had already taken leave to make the acquaintance of the stepsisters she had never seen until now.

Luckily, there were only fifty-two patients in at the moment. Either the war at sea's running down, she thought, or the British are managing to capture vessels without hurting anybody. Neverthe-less, she and Tobias and Dell, who was coming in every day to cover for Philippa's absence, were attending to more than the menial work; the orderlies were allowing them to usurp theirs by changing dressings and administering physick.

She stalked up to their table under the loft where the orderlies, freed from the Dowager's cold eye, were gambling. She tipped it so that the dice fell on the floor. 'We're shorthanded,' she snapped. 'So you can get up off your fat arses for a change.'

She went back down the aisle and stopped at Lawyer Perkins's bed. 'How's the leg?' An ulcer on his calf that had begun to heal dur-ing his first stay in the hospital had grown so big after returning to prison quarters and an inadequate diet that he'd been sent back, unable to walk.

'Better by the day.' He never complained.

'Good.' She drew a page of *The Passenger* from her pocket. 'What's this?'

'A newspaper?'

'Very good. What is this on it?'

He adjusted his spectacles and took the paper. 'Ain't that grand? They've finally got round to printing the Declaration of Independence over here. You read it, Missus?'

'I did.'

'Gratified? It's a mighty pretty piece of work. "We hold these truths to be self-evident, that all men are created equal . . ." I tell you, missus, it still makes my hair stand on end.'

'Does it? Where does it condemn slavery then?'

'Ah.'

'Yes, ah.' She'd picked the latest edition up from the post office on her way in that morning; Beasley had sent it to her without comment. Everybody had paid for her anger since.

'My boy Josh is out in that stinking hole this minute for trying to get back into this war for equality. He's black. He going to be equal with all men when he goes home?'

Sam Perkins took off his spectacles and cleaned them on his shirt. 'You know, Missus, I was in that room in Philadelphia two years back. July the second, I'll never forget, and a darn hot day it was. We tried, the New England delegations near *bust* themselves tryin' to include abolition in that there Declaration. But South Carolina and Georgia, they objected, and they objected strong. Were we to jeopardize the birth of a United States of America for them two varmint peoples?' He looked up at her. 'Would you?'

'Yes. It's either freedom for everybody or it ain't freedom.'

He shook his head. 'We were not. For once, all the clocks were strikin' together. We were making a nation. "We hold these truths to be self-evident, that all men are created equal".' He put on his spectacles. '*All* men. It'll come, Missus.'

She sat down on the end of his bed and let her hands hang between her knees, suddenly tired. 'I hope so.'

'You be sure it will. Soon as the war's over and we get goin', it'll come.' He took a look around. 'Any news?'

She sighed and looked around for herself; imparting information about the progress of the war to the prisoners was strictly prohibited. The patients on either side were asleep. 'Told you about the League of Armed Neutrality, did I?'

She attempted to remember the things Beasley had told her in his latest letter. 'Catherine of Russia's trying to get all the powerful states in Europe, Prussia, the Dutch, Portugal, places like that, to join a pact of armed neutrality against the British, whatever armed neutrality is, and they say she'll likely succeed.'

Perkins clapped his hands like a child and she had to hush him. 'Holy Latin, ma'am! We can't lose, that's what it means. What are the French doing for the war?'

'Not much.' Newly arrived Americans tended to be scathing, not to say vitriolic, on the subject of the French intervention for which they'd had high hopes. 'Oh yes, they're sending a fleet under some admiral whose name I can't remember to the Caribbean to harry the British in the West Indies.'

'Grand.' Mr Perkins smiled at her. 'You ain't too interested in the war, are you, Missus?'

She looked up and down the rows of bed and the moaning, suffering men in them and she thought of young Lieutenant Grayle. 'It's dandy for blowing boys' arms and legs off,' she said.

'Ain't one of 'em wouldn't lose an arm or leg iffen he got Liberty in its place,' Perkins said.

'Liberty,' she said, hauling herself up. 'It better be worth it.'

She leaned forward until her eyelashes were nearly touching Lawyer Perkins's spectacles. '*You* got any news for *me*?'

'I heard they begun digging,' he said.

Having spent most of the afternoon paddling, Philippa and the Dowager sat on two lobster-pots and watched Makepeace's younger daughters build sandcastles. Their Aunt Ginny was asleep in her bed at the Pomeroy, still recovering from over a week's journey in a coach with two lively little girls.

'It is sad that your mother can't be spared from the hospital for long,' Diana said. 'I am sure Sally and Jenny were hoping to spend more time with her, as she was with them. But, as you and I know, the work is vital.'

'They'll get used to it,' Philippa said. 'It is always work with Mama and it is always vital. She is not a motherly person.' She said it without bitterness and smiled at the Dowager's shock. 'I used to mind. I think it was why I stayed away so long, to punish her, but I have come to see that she is a leopard and cannot change her spots.'

The weather was holding—just. Though the breeze was still warm, it was forcing energetic little waves nearly to the bare legs of the children and coating their red curls with sand.

'Should we interfere?' asked the Dowager, worriedly. Jenny had just jumped on Sally's sandcastle and was being made to pay for it. Diana was unused to little girls, especially such as these.

'I don't think so. Yesterday Mama let them fight it out. They are very like her.'

'Oh dear,' Diana said. 'In that case the country will need a new form of government.' She was pleased to hear Philippa laugh. 'And you, my dear, are you like your mother or your father? I met Sir Philip once, very briefly, but long enough to recognize a gentleman of great quality.'

She kept trying to place this ill-assorted family of Makepeace's but was lost for class pigeonholes. The grave, collected girl beside her was certainly more the father's daughter than the mother's, and yet the resilience and composure she had shown in the face of the hospital's horrors had been . . . unsuitable. A nicely reared young woman should not have known about such things, let alone coped with them.

Yet why not? The world is so much wider than I thought it was.

'I wish I'd known my father,' Philippa said. 'He died just before I was born so I don't know whether I'm like him or not. I don't think he was interested in mathematics.'

'Are *you?*'

'Yes. Aunt Susan used to say it was not an attractive trait in a female but she allowed me to study the subject. Mama seems to think that mathematics is bookkeeping and vice versa but Andra says he will find me a good tutor.'

'And what is *he* like? Your mother tells me he is a mine-owner.'

'He is a mine-owner now. He was a miner. I remember him before I went to America, rough looking but with a mind interested in everything and with a great will to make the mines less dangerous. A very kind person, too: he wrote to me every week while I was in America.'

'Did he?'

'Yes. He said there was no reason why a female should not be a mathematician or anything else that she pleases. He believes in the equality of women with men.'

'Goodness gracious.'

'And so do I,' Philippa said. 'I wish he would come home. You might not think it, but Mama is lost without him.'

The Dowager said: 'Jan Gurney will bring him back when smuggling starts again, I'm sure.' And shook her head at herself. 'Dear, dear, I make it sound like the beginning of the hunting season.'

Philippa smiled. 'Do you disapprove?'

The Dowager looked down at her bare toes and sighed. 'I am learning neither to approve nor disapprove of anything; I find myself confounded at every turn. There are more things in heaven and earth, Philippa Horatio, than have been dreamt of in my philosophy. And now I think we really must intervene.'

They went running to prevent Jenny Hedley's inhumation in the sand.

Josh came out of the Black Hole on the same day that Bosun Tilley took over as chief orderly at the hospital.

Like all the men who had served their forty days' punishment, Josh was too weak to be sent back to prison quarters immediately.

The area round his mouth showed the signs of scurvy. He was put by the door at the end of the ward now reserved for negroes.

Tilley looked at him impassively. 'Beef tea and fresh vegetables.'

'Why not champagne while you're about it?' Makepeace said, bitterly. With the departure of the Dowager, the kitchens had gone back to their bad ways.

'You,' Tilley commanded Payne. 'Go and fetch the head cook.'

The cook was fetched and shown the bag of bones held together by skin that was Josh. 'Beef tea and fresh vegetables,' Tilley told him. 'Beef in the tea and the vegetables fresh. Get 'em.'

They were got.

He was a small man with the tight, muscular body of a dancer—the result of a life spent on swaying decks—and the inclination of a tyrant. Though they scurried about more in an effort to impress him (as they had not for the Dowager), it was obvious that the days of the Four Horsemen of the Apocalypse were numbered; they didn't move fast enough.

So were Makepeace's. Bosun Tilley didn't approve of women and the more spirit they had, the less he approved of them. He was open about it. 'You can stay 'til I get my own people in here,' he said, 'then you and the moll can go.'

'Why? We work hard enough.'

'Ain't saying you don't but I can tell interferers when I see 'em.' Tilley couldn't take a rope's end to women. The twins could stay, Makepeace and Dell must go.

'What about Tobias?' She was desperate that they remained in touch with Millbay through somebody. 'He's a good worker and he won't interfere.'

'He's a blackie. Some of the men don't like it.'

There was nothing she could do; the new commandant of the prison, Captain Stewart, had given Tilley full autonomy over the hospital's day-to-day running.

Her only comfort was that while he kept to strict demarcation between black and white patients, he treated both with the same impersonal but excellent care. With the backing of Captain Stewart, a man as efficient as himself, he was able to counter the corruption of the prison staff more effectively than the Dowager; food improved, and so did the supply of medicines.

And he had one piece of good fortune not vouchsafed to the Dowager. Dr Maltby died, choked on his own vomit at a Plymouth Masons' dinner, to be replaced by a retired but capable and energetic ship's surgeon.

The women returned to attending to the slops and, as Tilley disapproved of them 'chattering' with the men, Makepeace could only snatch the occasional word with Josh during his return to health.

'They've started on the tunnel,' she muttered, sweeping round his bed. 'I'll be waiting with the coach if I know where and when.'

It was beyond them both to think how that could be managed even if Tilley kept her on: comings-and-goings between prison and hospital were strictly limited. If she were forced to leave, it would be impossible.

'I'll manage, Missus.'

'Make for Babbs Cove. Keep to the cliffs going east for about ten miles. I'll bring in some cash tomorrow.'

'Stop chattering here.' Bosun Tilley was at her side. 'Get on with your work.'

Josh reached under his pillow. 'Permission to give her this, Bosun?'

It was a ragged and none too clean scrap of paper—only God knew from where he'd stolen it or how he'd kept it for forty days in the Black Hole; he was like a magpie with paper.

Makepeace looked over Tilley's shoulder, then shut her eyes tight against tears. It was a full-length drawing in coal of Lieutenant Forrest Grayle lying as he must have lain next to Josh on the floor of the punishment block. The subject was in light, the detail of the walls around him mercifully obscured, so that he might have been a stone crusader lying on his tomb, except that this was a living, still-hopeful young man, his mouth set in endurance.

'She nursed him,' Josh said.

Tilley held it up to Makepeace. 'Like him, is it?'

She nodded.

He gave it to her. He was not an unkind man. He was also vain. 'Can you draw me, boy?'

'Get me oils, I'll do your portrait.'

'Right then. And you, woman, get going on those beds up there. We've got some Frogs coming in soon.'

Two days later the guards brought in de Vaubon and what was left of the crew of *La Petite Margot*.

Chapter Eighteen

'WILL we tell her?' Dell asked.

'Not 'til he's better, maybe,' Makepeace said, after thought.

'If he ever is, Lord love him.'

The Prince George was full but Landlord Bignall had found an attic for the two of them to share for the night. Bosun Tilley had asked that they go in the next day to help cope with the influx of Frenchmen. In any case, Makepeace wanted to make sure that all was being done for de Vaubon that could be done.

Whether he would survive his injuries was in doubt. His left leg was infected and had been so mangled from a falling mast that it was unlikely he'd walk on it again. In the hand-to-hand fighting that followed the boarding of *La Petite Margot*, he'd killed one naval officer and received a slash from the cutlass of another that had laid open one cheek from eye to chin.

'I'm right, aren't I?' Makepeace asked Tobias. 'She needn't be told yet.'

'You're right, Mithuth. Her ladyship would be motht upthet.'

'Good.' If Tobias said it was right, it was right. There was a deep goodness to the man that she used as an infallible yardstick. 'I want you to go back to Babbs Cove and tell Philippa and Ginny I can't get home until tomorrow night at least. Kiss the little girls for me.'

'I will, Mithuth.'

'It's a wicked night for the cliffs, my man, ye'd be better going by road.' Dell was at her grandest.

'I'll be safe enough, Mith Dell.'

When he'd gone, Makepeace looked out of the window. 'Leave him alone, you don't usually worry about him.' The weather had changed with a vengeance; even from here she could hear the noise of sea hurling itself against the base of the Hoe.

'Ah well,' Dell said, vaguely.

'I want to see my babies,' Makepeace said, suddenly weeping. 'I'm spending my life doing something else.'

'Think of those poor men now. They need us.'

'They're somebody else's responsibility. What have I to do with their bloody wars? He's not my Frenchman, he's hers.'

'Isn't that the pig of it? They're nobody's responsibility if they're not ours.'

'Oh, shut up.' She was tired and sad and in no mood for a Sermon from the Mount in a lofty Irish accent. She went and threw herself on the bed. 'You haven't got any children, you don't know.'

'No,' Dell said. 'Mine's dead.'

After a long silence, Makepeace said: 'I shouldn't have said that.'

'Ach, I couldn't have kept her anyways.' Dell's eyes were dry and fixed on the bedroom's door. 'Happens all the time if ye did but know it. Poor and pretty Irish girl seduced by English landlord's son. Poor, pretty girl gets pregnant. Landlord finds out. Girl's family evicted, twelve of 'em, to tramp the roads of Connaught. Girl gets the smallpox, has baby under a hedge. Girl lives, baby dies.' She shrugged. 'That's Ireland for ye.'

Philippa said it would be something like that. I never see beneath the surface.

Makepeace wriggled down the bed until she could sit next to her. 'I tramped the streets once,' she said, 'but I had people to go with me.'

'Ah well, ye see, I didn't,' Dell told the doorknob. 'I came to England where the streets were paved in gold so's I could send some of it home to the mammy. But there wasn't any gold.'

They sat side by side for a long time. At last Makepeace said: 'I never thanked you properly for Philippa.'

'Ah well,' Dell said.

When they'd got into their truckle beds and Makepeace had blown out the candle, she said: 'Why now?'

'I don't know.' Dell's voice in the darkness was reflective. 'Perhaps it's now I can bear to remember it. And you look at those men torn to pieces and you think: Will you stop skelping each other in the name of God? There's enough pain without that.'

'But they won't.'

'No,' said Dell. 'They won't.'

The weather worsened and the smuggling season began.

Along the southern coast, fast, seagoing vessels emerged from dark inlets and began battling the Channel's storms, making for France and back again in their self-imposed task of supplying the English with contraband goods.

From the oriel window, the Dowager watched the entire female population of Babbs Cove and its children line the slipway to wave off the *Lark* and the *Three Cousins* with the cheers—and a few tears—usually reserved for armies going out to do battle with the enemy.

Which I suppose they are, she thought. The sea is enemy enough.

She had not thought it proper to sanction the departure of smugglers by her presence but she offered a prayer for their safe return and, once they had disappeared into the blowing darkness, she put on her cloak.

'I'm going down to the Pomeroy, Mrs Green.'

There was no reply; there never was. The woman was getting odder and odder and looking increasingly ill. Makepeace had offered the use of Sanders and the coach so that Diana could take her into Plymouth to the doctor, but she had become so agitated, almost snarling, that they had been forced to let her be.

A few of the village women had stayed to drink to their husbands' venture but on seeing the Dowager they wished her good-night and went back to their homes. She regretted that her presence intimidated them. She had tried to be friendly: she asked after their children and enquired whether they were getting a good price for lobsters at the Newton Ferrers market, but she was not Makepeace and could not get beyond the impenetrable doin' nicely, thank you, your ladyship, fair to middlin', your ladyship.

Can't they see I am becoming as poor as they are? She met them nowadays as she collected wrack from the beach to swell the pile of firewood to proportions adequate to see her through the winter. As they passed by the rear of T'Gallants on their way to Newton Fer-rers with lobster baskets on their hips, they must see her working with Tobias in the kitchen garden to get it ready for winter cabbage. She didn't mind doing these things—indeed, she rather enjoyed them—but to be allowed some sense of fellowship with other la-bourers would be nice.

In the taproom, Sally and Jenny clamoured for her to play cards with them. Philippa called a hello from the kitchen where she was helping Mrs Hallewell. Here at least was firelight and welcoming company.

Ralph Gurney was holding forth to a florid and fat little man breathing whisky fumes. 'You just missed our lads, your ladyship. First sailin' of the season and a brave sight tew. You'll have a bumper with me to wish 'un Godspeed and fair landings, surely. This yere's Mr Chauncey.'

'I have told you before, Mr Gurney, while I do not condemn, I cannot condone. But I thank you. A glass of tea and one of your excellent pasties, if I may, Mrs Hallewell.' Chauncey? Chauncey? The magistrate. 'Good evening, Mr Chauncey. You are our local jus-tice of the peace, I understand.'

'That he be,' bellowed Gurney. 'Not for want of Nicholls a-trying to throw 'un off the bench, eh, Martin?'

'Wrote to the Lord Chancellor, the villain,' Mr Chauncey told her. 'Said I'd lost the confidence of the Revenue. Who wants the confidence of the Revenue? I do have the confidence of everybody else, don't I, Ralph?'

Sometimes she still felt that she had wandered, like Gulliver, into a topsy-turvy land that saw its illegality as a public service constantly hampered by bureaucracy.

'That you do, Martin. You see to ut that sinners be punished and free trade let to flourish. 'Twill be a sad day when the Lord Chancellor takes the word of a Revenue man against honest free traders. Shall ee come up the hill and have a bite with us, your ladyship?'

'Thank you, no.' Ralph Gurney grated on her occasionally; he made more money from delivering and selling contraband than the cousins who went to sea to fetch it. 'Mrs Hedley is away for the night and in her absence I regard myself as . . .' She had been going to say *in loco parentis* but was stopped by remembered pain. '. . . as chaperone to her sister-in-law and children.'

It was true; in Makepeace's absence the Dowager felt herself responsible for Philippa and the two little girls. Their aunt, a pleasant Northumbrian, looked after them well but she was nevertheless a stranger in a hostelry which, however companionable, was still the centre of an illegal trade. And there was no parlour at the Pomeroy to which ladies could withdraw; it was the taproom or nothing.

'Your ladyship's still making a fine old fuss about they American prisoners, I do see from the papers.'

'I write letters merely in an attempt to effect their exchange, Mr Gurney. I would wish to see all wounded men, both British and American, returned to their own land under a flag of truce.'

'I dare say.' It didn't interest him. 'That be politics, us don't concern ourselves with politics, do us, Martin?' He guided the magistrate to the door and they went out.

From his corner, Zack spoke up: 'A fine man be that Mr Chauncey. Knows his duty, he do.'

'Yes, but he doesn't *pay* any, Zack.' It had become a regular argument between them and one which Diana knew she could not win. 'How can England fight its wars if people don't pay their taxes?'

'I don't mind 'em taxing things,' Zack said, 'but why the buggers got to tax good liquor?' He looked triumphantly at the cup Mrs Hallewell was serving her. 'What you suppin' there, then?'

She sighed. 'Smuggled tea, I expect.'

She played with the children until they went to bed, then talked with Aunt Ginny and Philippa until they went to theirs.

'Don't ee forget the lantern, now,' Zack told his niece.

Mrs Hallewell looked apologetically at the Dowager. 'I do hope Mrs Hedley won't mind but she do have the front bedroom and us allus puts a lantern in that window to guide the boats back in.'

'But they have only just set out. How long does it take them to get to France and back?'

'Least a week, God an' a good wind willin',' Zack said, 'but us allus sets a light for 'un. So's they know we'm a-waiting for 'un.'

'I'm sure Mrs Hedley will not mind, Mrs Hallewell.'

They all left the inn together: Mrs Hallewell went back to her cottage and children at nights. Looking around, Diana saw that every window in the village facing the sea was lit, as if the women of Babbs Cove could ensure their men's safe return with a rushlight.

Dr Whalley, the new surgeon, finished setting the splintered bones in de Vaubon's leg. It was a relief to everybody. The Frenchman had spat out the bullet they'd given him to bite on and followed it with every swear word in the French language, as well as some that weren't, in a voice that dislodged sparrows from the rafters.

Bosun Tilley and one of the orderlies let go of his arms, rubbing their bruises.

Makepeace followed the doctor to the sink and gave him a towel. 'What he called you,' she said, 'he didn't mean it.'

Dr Whalley dried his hands. 'I hope not. My mother was a most respectable woman.'

'Will he be all right?'

'It'll never be the leg it was, always give him pain. But if you're asking me if he'll live, then, ma'am, I tell you that to kill that gentleman will require a poleaxe.'

Later in the day, Captain Stewart made his rounds on what was now a regular tour of inspection by the camp commander—something Bosun Tilley insisted on. When he went into the Frenchman's bay, Makepeace loitered outside the curtain.

'Monsewer le cappytaine, I am empowered to offer you parole if you will give me your word that you will not attempt to escape.'

Makepeace heard a weak but definite, 'No.'

'I don't think you understand, Captain. Give me your word and we can find you comfortable accommodation in the town. You may go where you please—within limits.'

'*Non.*'

'You prefer to stay in prison?'

There was a growl. '*Fous-moi la paix.*'

Captain Stewart emerged with Bosun Tilley. 'That's rather rude, isn't it?'

Tilley was protective of his patients. 'He's in pain, sir.'

When they'd gone, Makepeace slipped inside. 'You meathead,' she said. 'Why don't you give your parole?'

De Vaubon focused on her with difficulty. 'You,' he said. 'I thought you a spirit. Is she here?'

'No, she's back at Babbs Cove.'

'I dream of her. Very much.'

Makepeace smiled. 'She'll be glad to hear it.'

He kept going in and out of sleep, taking what she said with him and only responding to it later. He asked: 'Did Bilo survive? Mathurin? Félix?'

'Bilo's up the other end of the ward,' she told him, 'I don't know about the others.'

'I remember, they are dead. My brave boys.' He tried to cross himself. 'God be good to them. If there is a God.'

She didn't have time to argue theology. She put her mouth close to his ear. 'They're digging a tunnel. You'll be back in France before you know it.'

He drifted off again, uninterested. The wound on his face was terrible; he'd been lucky not to lose an eye and if the split eyelid didn't heal well his face would be something to frighten naughty children with—whoever had stitched it possessed the needlework skill of a butcher.

His good eye opened as he came to again. 'So we escape?'

'Be easier if you gave your parole.'

'I could not keep it. It would be against my honour. I have to escape.'

'She said you didn't believe in honour. You told her it was rubbish.'

He shook his head with the irritation of fatigue. 'I do not break my word. You do not understand, you are a woman.' He relapsed into unconsciousness again.

She stood for a moment looking down at the gargoyle that had been made out of his face. *Honour.* He'd cut down one man, and fired on the Royal Navy ship that had fired on his, killing more. Every patient in this ward had left a trail of blood behind him: his own, his enemy's. She could not, and never did, forget that for each man in Millbay and all the other prisons, British sailors had either risked their lives, or lost them, attempting to put him there.

And out of this unruled, mangling, burning, screaming savagery, they plucked one civilized splinter and sanctified it and called it honour and said women would not understand it.

And they were right.

Lark and *Three Cousins* came home in dawn light and weather that would have prevented any other boat getting into the cove at all. To the Dowager and all the other watching women, it seemed that they were tossed in, one after the other, as if they were not heavily laden vessels but rings in a giant game of quoits.

The collective sigh of thanks around her was whipped away in the wind. Diana found her own palms sweating and rubbed them on her handkerchief. 'That was lucky.'

'That were seamanship,' Zack said. 'Still, they'll never get the goods ashore in this blow. Us'll have to tub 'em.' He went and joined the parties of women who were pushing rowing boats into the surf to go and fetch their men ashore—a manoeuvre that seemed as risky to Diana as the one made by the bigger vessels. She watched the boats tip almost vertically to breast the grey-green waves before disappearing into a trough and rising again.

'Tub them?' she asked Philippa who stood beside her, the wind blowing her long, straight hair.

Philippa said primly: 'They weight the contraband and throw it overboard attached to a line that's got a lobster-pot on the end or something else that floats. Then they can pull it up when the weather's cleared or the Revenue's not around. They call it "tubbing".'

Such an extraordinary child. 'How *do* you know all this?'

'Mama told me. It's what the smugglers she knew in Boston did when she was a girl. She calls it "sowing the crop".'

'Your mother never ceases to amaze me.'

'Picking them up is Ralph Gurney's end of the business, I understand. He brings different men to do it and they take the tubs away on ponies. Jan and Eddie just fetch the contraband from France.'

'I hope one of those boats has your stepfather in it, for your mother's sake.'

'So do I. I should like to see him again.'

Jenny and Sally were agitating to 'go and see the big boats with Zack', and were taken back inside.

There was no Andra but there was a letter from him addressed to 'Mrs Makepeace Hedley of Babbs Cove, Devon, England'.

'Waitin' for us at Gruchy, it was,' Jan Gurney said, as the village gathered in the Pomeroy Arms to hear the news from abroad. 'Gil's man took the Missus's letter to Paris and brought this 'un back.' He poured water out of his sea boot onto the floor before taking a pull at the largest tankard of ale the Dowager had ever seen.

Eddie Gurney stretched and winked at his wife, Cissy. 'Time we went home for a liddle rest, my 'andsome.' She blushed. Eddie was the youngest of the Gurney cousins and as swarthy and black-haired as Ralph and Jan were blond. It was a phenomenon that cropped up in the village here and there; the Dowager had noticed it particularly among the children: an occasional black poppy in a cluster of daisy-heads. She had approached the matter delicately to Mrs Hallewell, suspecting scandal.

'Oh, that were the Armada,' Mrs Hallewell had said, comfortably. 'They do say a Spaniard swam ashore from one o' the wrecks. Did terrible damage among the womenfolk 'fore they caught 'un.'

Jan Gurney was telling Eddie not to rest too long. 'We'll need to get that mizzen fixed before us can go out again.'

Rachel, his wife, a tall and handsome young woman, said: 'You're never settin' out again so soon, Jan Gurney.'

'Got to while this dang wind lasts and the Revenue stays in harbour.'

As the Babbs Cove boats had been leaving the Normandy coast, they'd encountered the *Eliza* out of Thurlestone going in and had stopped to exchange information with their fellow-smugglers like two women chatting over a garden fence. 'Tom Kitto, he said as how the Nicholls have got a new vessel, a cutter. Very speedy, Tom says she is. I don't want to meet her one fine night when the hold's full. Her's patrolling from Cawsand to Bolt Head, Tom says.'

'Might you not meet her anyway?' Philippa asked.

'Not her, my lover, not in this blow. Preventives ain't got the stomach for foul weather. You'll not see them venturing out to get their wigs wet.'

The Dowager hoped he was right but Nicholls had not struck her as a coward. 'Did you meet M. de Vaubon at Gruchy?' she asked casually.

He shook his head. 'Gil's away to the war. God keep 'un.'

When, late that night, Sanders pulled up his team outside the Pomeroy Arms, Philippa was waiting at the door to hand her mother the letter.

The Dowager thought she had never seen either woman, Dell or Makepeace, look so tired. Even Tobias made for a chair, the first time he'd sat down in her presence.

'Well, we're done now,' Dell said, taking the hot rum Philippa held out to her. 'The Bosun's finished with us.'

Tilley had enquired among old shipmates and found damaged

sailors who, now their usefulness to the Royal Navy was over, were happy to serve on half-pay in any capacity rather than disappear into the pensionless void that usually awaited Britain's non-commissioned servicemen.

'Ye never saw such a patched-up lot of fellas,' Dell said. 'One had only one arm and at least two lacked an eye but wasn't your man happy with them.'

'We'll make shift now,' Bosun Tilley had told Makepeace. 'Don't need you no more.'

'*Thank you very much*,' she'd reminded him, sharply.

'Yes, well,' he'd said. 'Won't say you wasn't useful but it never was right, women nursing sailors.'

Makepeace was reading Andra's letter and pretending irritation with it. 'Him and Lavoisier are weighing air—how can you weigh air?—and he can't come right away but . . . listen to this: "I'll pack my traps soon and be at Gruchy the next time the gentlemen call in there." As if it was a damn ferry they're running back and forth. Oh, and he's relieved and pleased that Philippa has been delivered to me safe—she's not a parcel, you meathead—but condoles with me on the death of Miss Brewer. He writes like we never met before.'

She read the next page but kept it to herself, some colour coming back into her face. ' "From your loving husband, A. J. Hedley." Damn the man, he always puts that, as if I don't know who he is.'

She clutched the letter to her chest and looked round at the company. 'Just wait 'til he gets back, that's all I can say. I'll give him A. J. Hedley.'

To the Dowager, she said: 'Oh, and there's something for ladyship.' She pulled a carefully rolled piece of paper from the pocket of her cloak and held out Josh's drawing of Forrest Grayle.

Diana looked at it for a long time.

'I thought you might want to send that to his ma,' Makepeace said. 'See? Josh has given him back his hands.'

Lark and *Three Cousins* put out again and were lost to sight almost immediately in heavy sea and black, scudding cloud.

Ginny became worried that the weather would delay her and the girls' return to Northumbria. Makepeace did too; she would have liked to keep her daughters at Babbs Cove but dare not have them with her should Josh's escape miscarry and involve them all in trouble with the authorities.

'Why don't you spend a week with them in Exeter?' Philippa suggested. 'See the sights, visit the castle and the cathedral. I am told they are most interesting. Then Aunt Ginny can take them in the mail coach from there to London and on up North. You could go shopping with the girls—they are already grown out of their clothes.'

Makepeace was doubtful at first but Philippa was persuasive. 'You have spent so little time with them, Mama, and it will take your mind off things. I shall stay here in case Andra returns before you do. Dell will be here and Ladyship will look after me, won't you, your ladyship?'

It was arranged. Sanders drove them away the next morning.

'I didn't think we'd persuade her,' Philippa said, waving them off.

'Even she knows she is in need of a change and a rest.'

'It will be a change,' said Philippa. 'I don't think Sally and Jenny will make it a rest.'

Diana moved into the Pomeroy rather than treat Dell and Philippa to the discomforts of T'Gallants—but regretted it the same afternoon.

' 'Fraid so, ladyship,' Ralph Gurney said. 'Conditions is perfect. Sea's calmed some, there'll be moon enough to see by but not *be* seen. And these lads here have come along the cliffs without a sniff of a coastguard. No, we got to raise them tubs right away.'

'These lads' were as grim a crowd of men as were likely to be seen outside Newgate. There were forty of them, some carrying heavy cudgels. It didn't ease the Dowager's mind to find that these last were referred to as 'batsmen' and their job was to engage and belabour any customs men they met while their companions got away.

'Very well, Mr Gurney, but I don't want these men inside the Pomeroy; we are only women here.'

She had sent Tobias to Plymouth to post another batch of letters to newspapers and the various sympathetic organizations with whom she now corresponded on the matter of the Americans' exchange, and she didn't count old Zack and Simeon as protection.

It was dark by the time the contraband had been landed on the beach. Some of the village women went to help the men and brought the laden ponies up the slipway, pausing in the light from the Pomeroy's windows to adjust girths and the ropes that held the tubs in place. The crammed forecourt smelled of horse manure, wet, sweating men, brandy—one of the tubs had been broached 'to keep out the cold'—and, of all things, soap.

'Why are the women soaping the ponies?'

'Make 'un slippery, so's the preventives can't grab 'em,' Zack told her.

'Are they likely to? I thought the coast was clear.' She was on edge. She approached the group of men. 'I do not approve of this. I hope there will be no violence, Mr Gurney.'

'Bless your heart, no,' he said, 'but 'tidd'n the coast as got to be clear, 'tis inland. We've got a fair way to go afore dawn. Ready, my hearties?'

They began to move off, a lander holding the reins of each pony, a batsman walking by his side.

The Dowager stood in the doorway with Zack, Philippa, Dell and Mrs Hallewell, watching the cavalcade as it left the forecourt. Simeon was peering from the inn window.

With the wind dropping to a light breeze, it had become cold and the ponies' hooves were wrapped to make no noise on the hardening ground; the men wore soft boots. A sliver of moon gave just enough light to distinguish between land and sea but very little more.

An owl up on the hill screeched and screeched again, coming nearer. The Dowager heard Rachel Gurney swear. Leather creaked as the leading ponies were turned and came back to mill with those that hadn't left yet. Ralph was listening to a small, capering boy.

'What is it?' the Dowager asked Rachel Gurney.

'Trouble.'

The men went into a huddle. Rachel called the boy over. 'What's to do, Jack?'

'Preventives. Mam sent me down, saw 'un when she was shutting up the chickens. Under a bush by the gate, one was. An' I smelled another on the road down. Smokin'. Reckon there's a thousand on 'un up there, waitin'. Dad's goin' to give 'un what for.' The child was joyful.

Mrs Hallewell was wringing her hands. 'Oh my Lord, oh my Lord.'

As Gurney came up, the boy trilled: 'Smokin', he was, Dad. Smelled 'un.'

'An' not paid the dang duty on ut, neither, I'll be bound.'

'Give 'un what for, Dad.'

'Reckon we'll have to.' To the Dowager and Rachel, he said: 'Bastards.'

'Will they attack?' Diana asked.

He consoled her, thinking she was worried for herself. 'Not yere, ladyship. He's a-waitin' to follow us, I reckon. Trail us to our customers and nab they along of us. How many men's he got up there, I'd like to know.'

'Can you not go another way?'

'Cliff path? They'd see us from the hill, they ain't blind. Smell the ponies too. Stink'd travel on the breeze. And us don't want to be battlin' on a cliff drop.'

She didn't want them battling anywhere. 'Unload then. You can put the goods in the well. Put them in the cavern if necessary. Travel them another night.'

He looked around at the waiting men. 'And pay these buggers twice over? Danged if I do.'

He's going to force his way through the cordon, she thought. There'll be killing.

Beside her, Philippa said: 'Why don't we create a diversion?'

Rachel Gurney stared at her. 'Maid's right, Ralph. That's what us'll have to do.' She took charge. 'How many other ponies we got in the village?'

'Five, I reckon,' somebody said. 'That's with the one as fetches the milk, but he ain't too vitty.'

'Get 'un up yere,' Rachel ordered. 'All on 'em.' She turned to Ralph: 'Us'll need some more if 'tis to look proper. You'll have to unload a few of yourn.'

Grumbling, he ordered the contraband to be taken off four of his ponies.

'Get those tubs round the back to the well,' Rachel told him. She turned to Mrs Hallewell. 'Maggie, when we'm gone, you get the spare goods down that bloody well fast as ee can. Ralph'll have to take 'un another day. You'll need . . . how many to help ee? Joan, Betty, Tabby, you'm big strong women, you help Maggie. Now, how many've I got to come wi' me?'

'Six.' Philippa had been keeping track. 'And you've got nine ponies. I'm coming.'

For the first time Rachel Gurney was at a loss. 'Don't think the Missus would like tha-at.'

'I'm coming,' Philippa said.

Dell stepped forward. 'And so am I.'

'Grateful,' Rachel said, shortly. 'Wrap up warm in summat dark. Now then, Maggie, we'm a-going to need every empty you got. Here, you lads, go round the yard and roll me out the empty barrels.'

'This is nonsense,' the Dowager said. She caught Philippa's arm as the girl hurried past her into the inn. 'You cannot take part in this. Dell, I forbid you. There might be shooting. Mrs Gurney, please consider: there is no need to put all of us in danger.'

Rachel paused to look at her, then nodded towards the lane. 'Nicholls is lyin' in wait up there and if he don't see ponies go by, he'll come down yere to find 'un. My man risked his life for these yere goods,'tis money from they as keeps us all through the winter and that bastard ain't havin' 'un.' She came up and disengaged the Dowager's hand from Philippa's sleeve. 'If so be the maid's offered, I'll take her and thankful.'

As Philippa and Dell went running upstairs for their cloaks, Rachel tapped the Dowager's shoulder, quite kindly. 'Now you go indoors, ma dear, close the shutters and shut the door. Zack'll look after ee. This is no work for the gentry.'

She returned to giving orders. Empty tubs and barrels were being rolled out to the forecourt and strapped to the diversionary ponies.

The Dowager, going upstairs, met Philippa on the landing as she emerged from her bedroom, wrapping a cloak around her. On seeing Diana, the girl's face set like limestone. 'I . . . am . . . going,' she said.

'Me and all.' Dell had emerged from her room, swathed in a purple shawl.

'It appears that I am too,' the Dowager said, irritably. 'Where's that hooded pelisse of your mother's?'

Philippa followed her into Makepeace's room to find it. 'Are you sure?' she asked.

'No, I am not. I regard this venture as most ill advised. However, the alternative is worse. What your mother will say to it, I cannot think.'

'She'll say well done.'

'Undoubtedly she will,' Diana snapped. 'The woman has criminal tendencies.'

Her stomach was clenching and unclenching with nerves. Had she not offended public opinion enough? She thought of poor Robert when they told him his mother was locked up in a Devon bridewell for misleading the Revenue.

But for a Pomeroy to earn the contempt of a Gurney was not to be tolerated.

Downstairs the village women had taken off caps and aprons, everything white, and were wrapped in cloaks and shawls, reminding the Dowager rather nastily of the dark female figures that stood at the foot of the cross in paintings of the crucifixion.

Zack and his brother were separately and energetically commanding Rachel to take them with her as protection.

'Us'll need to be nifty,' she told them, impatiently, 'and there's neither of you two old buggers can run.'

She saw the Dowager with surprise. 'Good on ee, ladyship,' she said, 'but pull that hood up or they'll see that pale head o' yourn,'tis like a beacon.'

Diana decided that England would win the war quicker if it sent Rachel Gurney to lead its army in America.

The men with the contraband ponies had already moved off towards the bridge, ready to take the cliff path when they were sure that the Revenue was following the women. Young Jack Gurney was to be the go-between.

'Take a batsman or two with ee,' his father was saying to Rachel.

Diana stepped in. 'No. No violence, whatever happens.'

'Good luck to ee then.'

Mrs Hallewell hurried up to Rachel. 'You'll be needin' this.' It was a goad.

Rachel took her pony's reins and set off, the Dowager pulled on her pony's reins to set him going, Philippa pulled on hers and the others followed with theirs up the lane.

It was just under a mile to the farm, another mile to the brow of the hill and the turning to Plymouth, a steep, twisting climb between hedgerows and trees that shut out the light of the stars. The ponies' hooves tapped on the packed earth and sent an occasional stone rattling down the incline with what sounded to Diana like rolls of thunder.

Am I the only one who's frightened? There was no sound at all from Rachel up ahead; from behind she could hear mere excited little puffs from Philippa's mouth.

Babbs Cove women are bred for this sort of thing. She remembered Zack telling her how, on another occasion, his mother and most of the other village women had been taken to Plymouth gaol charged with possessing contraband and eventually, as was usual, found not guilty by a smugglers' jury. After their release, every jug, cup and bowl in the prison was discovered to be missing.

Virtually blinded, she found other senses coming into play. The smell of pine: they must be passing the tall fir you could see from a boat. And that was lanolin: some of Gurney's sheep. And *that* was the milk pony who always took his revenge on going loaded by farting horribly. Sudden rankness: a fox? Cow pats. The night was full of stinks. It must be like this for a dog, she thought, an alphabet of scents forming themselves into descriptions.

The heavy flap of an owl's wings overhead. Further off, something, perhaps the fox, disturbing a pheasant so that it rattled away in squawking flight.

There was a configuration on her left, a gate, just outlined against the stars, the land beyond it falling steeply down to the cliffs. Gurney had been right: shapes moving against the backdrop of the sea would be noticeable.

Tobacco. Oh God, they were passing through the cordon. Best Virginian. They were being watched.

Ahead, Rachel Gurney kept up her steady pace without a falter. Diana's ears picked up a whisper begun at the back of the line and passed forward, quieter than the breeze's rustle in the branches. Philippa lengthened the rein on her pony to move up beside her. 'They're following.'

It was then that fear left the Dowager Countess of Stacpoole. Not so much left her, perhaps, as was joined by an aggressive thrill, the excitement of the cheat, the acid invigoration of sheer spite. Was this how criminals felt? If she stood in the dock for this, it would at least be a stance. It wasn't just Nicholls, it was all authority she was trying to hoodwink; it was the stratagem of the impotent against Aymer, against rules that worked only in favour of the already puissant.

The white top of a gate pillar: the track to the Gurney farm and, somewhere under a bush, another watcher. She thought of the Revenue men rising when the ponies had passed and coming after them on heavy-booted tiptoes, like comic villains in a play. A titter rose terribly in her throat and she had to put her hand over her mouth to stop it.

I was born to this. I am a smuggler *manqué*. She was Puck, leading foolish mortals into the depth of the forest. Follow us, my dears, every step is mischief.

By the time the top of the hill showed against the stars, she was panting so hard she couldn't have heard an army if it had been behind her.

For the first time, Rachel turned to show the white of her face. 'Ready?'

She slowed, allowing the other ponies to catch up. The lane had widened to join the road, trees edging it. A fingerpost stood on an island of grass. It had been a stiff climb; steam rose from the ponies' backs to mingle with a mist that was beginning to gather round their feet. They could smell Dartmoor.

It was silent up here. For the first time, Diana looked back. There was nothing in sight behind; either they had been fooling nobody or Nicholls's men had stopped just out of sight, waiting to find out which way the ponies would go.

Suddenly Rachel pricked her pony's backside with the goad. Diana brought her hand down hard on the bony rump of her beast. Neighing in protest, the animals set off at a gallop down the road to the right, their loads rocking, followed by the rest.

The women picked up their skirts and ran like deer to the trees on their left, then dropped into the bracken and stayed still.

Diana got out her handkerchief to wipe the sweat off her face, saw how white it was, and put it away again.

A minute or two later, the night produced men: ten, twenty, thirty at least, gathering on the fingerpost island. There was a shout. 'There they go, look. I can hear 'un. Bastards is runnin'.'

'Where?' It was Nicholls.

'East. Towards Salcombe. Come on, lads.'

Even then, with the rest of his pack giving chase down the hill, Nicholls didn't move but stood outlined against the sky, a solitary hound whose nose was telling it the quarry was near.

Go, Diana willed him, *go*.

At last he shrugged and set off after his men.

'Poor ponies,' whispered Philippa.

'A worthy sacrifice.'

Rachel stood up and they followed her down, taking the field paths in case the preventives came back. Nobody said anything.

Halfway to the cliffs, they saw a moving frieze of men and animals outlined against the sea, heading west.

It was then that they began to laugh, all of them. Dell let out a wild, Celtic paean. Diana heard an eldritch cackle coming out of her own mouth that turned into a choke from Rachel Gurney's appreciative slap on her back.

When they reached the Pomeroy, Dell, Diana and Philippa were carried into the inn on the shoulders of the Dowager's cheering female tenantry.

Chapter Nineteen

IT became known as The Night We Fooled Nicholls and they were immediately punished for it.

Dawn had just broken when Nicholls himself and two dozen of his men descended on Babbs Cove like wolves on the fold, breaking down doors with musket butts in a raid that made no pretence of being anything other than revenge.

The women stood outside their houses, holding their children and listening to the sound of pots being broken and of boots kicking stools and tables to matchwood, some watching stolidly, others cursing and shouting.

The Dowager hurried down from T'Gallants to give what protection she could. 'This is unnecessary, Captain. There is nothing here.'

'I know it, madam, but how do you?' He was as collected as ever, though his boots were dirty and his chin stubbled. She wondered how far the ponies had carried the empty barrels before he'd caught up with them. Miles, with luck.

She passed him to go to Rachel Gurney who was trying to hush a baby frightened at the rampage conducted inside their cottage. Her other children stood like soldiers, though a little girl winced as a splintered wooden doll came flying out of the open door.

'Never you mind, my lover,' Rachel told her, 'us can afford to buy you another.' She winked at Diana but she was pale; a winter's supply of flour was being mixed with cider and eggs on her kitchen floor.

At Mrs Welland's front-room shop, they ripped holes in her supply of sea boots and took shelves of knitting yarn outside to tip them into the mud. They took particular revenge on the Pomeroy Arms. Gun butts were smashed into walls only just plastered since the last raid. Diana sat with Mrs Hallewell outside on one of the benches, holding her hand as a stream of ale and rum swilled out of the door and ran in aromatic rivulets towards the slipway.

'Round the back,' Nicholls told them. Mrs Hallewell's grip on Diana's hand tightened as his men disappeared round the corner leading to the well-head, but Nicholls was watching their faces so they kept them still.

Don't let them find it. Don't let them find it.

They didn't, but a shout came from Dell at a back upstairs window. 'Will you look at the dirty bastards, they're pissing down the well!'

'And now, your ladyship,' Nicholls said, 'I should be glad if you would accompany me to T'Gallants.'

She said: 'Have you a warrant yet?'

'As a matter of fact, I have, but this is a personal matter. My men will stay here.'

They walked across the bridge and up to the house. She made him wait in the screen passage while she went and warned Mrs Green that she would be bringing the captain into the kitchen; men frightened Mrs Green and set her to muttering. Tobias was one of the few she accepted.

And de Vaubon, thought Diana, *she likes de Vaubon*. She didn't want Nicholls in the Great Hall because the Great Hall contained the chair that led to the shaft and, illogically, she felt that if he saw the chair he would know that there was a secret entrance to the house behind it. *I am investing the blasted man with mystical powers*, she thought. Nevertheless, once Mrs Green had scuttled out of the way, she led him to the kitchen, and saw with relief that Tobias was working in the garden outside its back door.

Nicholls asked permission to sit down. She nodded and remained standing.

'May I have a drink of water?' he said.

'You may not,' she told him. The response was unthinking, atavistic; the least hospitality to a warlock gave him power over you. 'If you want water, I suggest you draw it from the Pomeroy's well. You cannot expect to be catered for in this house after what you have just done to those people down there.'

' "In this house",' he repeated, quietly. 'I belong in this house.'

She thought she'd misheard him. 'I beg your pardon?'

He took his hat from under his arm and laid it on the kitchen table. 'Your ladyship, let us not be hypocrites. We may confess that the likes of those women do not matter a jot to such as you and I.'

You and me. She was somehow relieved by his lapse of grammar; he was not infallible. But not human either, she thought. He's a mechanism. Because he doesn't feel for other people, he thinks nobody else does. He believes human concern is a posture. He will always miscalculate other people's reactions; he imagines that wreaking havoc in the village impressed me. It was a display of power; power is all he understands.

Tobias was at the door. 'Stay within call, Tobias. Captain Nicholls will not be long.'

He waited until Tobias had gone back to the garden. He said calmly: 'I was born in wedlock, I am thirty-two years old and unattached, in excellent health. My salary is sixty pounds a year but my reward for contraband seizures this year has been two thousand and forty-two pounds. I have been promised a knighthood should I reduce the smuggling in the Plymouth District which, believe me, I shall. At which stage I shall enter politics.'

And all your own teeth. She couldn't see where this was leading.

His eyes were on hers, like a diner's on his plate.

'I realize I should have approached the Earl first on the matter but as your ladyship is a mature woman, I felt that etiquette could be disregarded in this case.'

She felt blindly for a chairback and sat down opposite him on the other side of the table. 'Captain Nicholls, are you asking me to *marry* you?'

'It would be fitting,' he said. 'We both see that, do we not? People laugh at my mother, I laugh at her myself, but in this she is correct: the family tree she has drawn shows that our blood conjoined three generations ago. There is also reason to believe that the marriage between Jerome Pomeroy and Polly James was legal and binding. I make no claim, of course, but his lordship will see the justice of our union as well as its happiness.'

She was almost sorry for him. He had no conception that he was outrageous. She could imagine him as a little boy sitting with his mother by candlelight, her finger following the botany of a carefully drawn tree, his name on it underlined perhaps, as her own would have been, resentment poured into his ears like poison. *'You'm the true Baron Pomeroy, Walter. T'Gallants is ours by rights, the place of our ancestors.'*

How sad and how horrible; she must deal gently.

She said: 'It does not do to live by bloodline, Captain.' Good God, would she have said that a few months back? 'By your own credentials, you are making your own way—'

'You will be conscious of our ages,' he said, staring at her. 'Mother has established your date of birth, you are thirty-nine, a difference between us of no consequence. She believes you to be yet fruitful, though, again, it is of no consequence.'

She stopped being sorry for him. 'Captain, it is unnecessary for you to continue. I have no intention of marrying you.'

He'd paused for a moment, not because she had spoken but apparently to check some mental list. He began again, having found the next item. 'You can appreciate that I am careless of your straitened circumstances and am in a position to offer you the comfort your position demands. T'Gallants can be restored to its former glory—'

'The house,' she said in amazement. 'You want the house.'

'I belong here,' he said. 'We belong here together.'

Thirty-two years, she thought. He has lived thirty-two years and nobody has noticed that he is insane. Efficient, zealous, incorruptible, a most excellent customs officer—and mad as a rabid dog.

She was afraid now. She should never have allowed this . . . this *thing* to enter her house. The eyes should have told her they were windows into a blind, fixated mind.

Such a petty ambition, to own T'Gallants, a bourgeois obsession for so ambitious a man, yet to him a pinnacle. Each time he sailed past, she thought, he looked up, seeing it as rightfully his, hating the usurpers who lived in it, waiting to be rich enough to buy it, forestalled . . . He would marry to get it . . .

'*Tobias.*' Would he murder to get it?

'Your ladyship?'

The panic ebbed; she was being ridiculous. But for a moment she had been very, very frightened. 'Captain Nicholls is leaving.'

He sat where he was. 'You are rejecting my proposal?'

'I am.'

Tobias held the kitchen door for him while the list in the man's mind was folded away, its items unbought. It seemed to the Dowager that he reverted from madman to customs officer but his face had shown no change of expression at any time; it was her own perception that had seen it distorted behind bars.

He stood up. 'You asked me for my warrant, your ladyship. Here it is.' He put a hand inside his coat and brought out a handkerchief. *Her* handkerchief—she could see the Stacpoole crest embroidered on one corner above the lace; a vulgarism she had always thought. It had been a present from Alice.

How unpleasant, he had kept the thing next to his heart, imagining that was what real suitors did.

And then she remembered woods by a fingerpost and hiding in them, getting the handkerchief out to wipe the sweat off her face, while ponies with empty barrels galloped into the distance.

He knew she'd been there as part of the deception. She thought: He can't do anything, he can't; as evidence in a case against me it would be useless; I could have dropped the thing at any time.

Indeed, he was showing neither triumph nor anger. He wasn't a stage villain: *your-handkerchief-madam, you-dropped-it-and-are-now-in-my-power*. He didn't say anything. He merely put it on the table as he went.

But she knew, because he wanted her to know, that it was his warrant. She had refused him and she was now as much his quarry as any brandy-runner along the coast. He intended to hunt her down with the rest.

Makepeace didn't know which was the more surprising—that Captain Nicholls had asked the Dowager to marry him or that he was worth over two thousand pounds a year.

'What's he want with T'Gallants?' she said. 'He could buy St James's for that. For three thousand, King George'd probably let him have it.'

'It was not amusing,' Diana said. 'The man is . . . you didn't see him.'

'I saw what he did to the Pomeroy. And poor Maggie's going to have to take her water from the stream until the spring clears that well.'

'I hope you are grateful I didn't tell him that T'Gallants was yours or you would even now be the pursuit.'

'Well, I ain't going to marry him either.' Not having observed him in action, Captain Nicholls was small beer as far as Makepeace was concerned; she had other matters to trouble her. 'I'd have thought Andra and the Gurneys would be back by now.'

'If the wind in Normandy is anything like this, they won't leave Gruchy until it has blown itself out.'

Both of them were having to raise their voices in the Great Hall against the irritation of rattling windowpanes and the thunderous pounding of sea as it reared itself against the cliffs below and fell back. Makepeace went to the wreckers' window, looked out and came back again. 'What am I going to do about Josh?'

'There is nothing you can do.' The Dowager sneaked a glance towards the newspapers that Makepeace had brought from Exeter saying that there was mention of 'that exchange business' in some of them. John Beasley's help with the campaign was proving invaluable; he had virtually taken it over and Makepeace's restlessness was preventing Diana from reading about it.

She went on: 'If you would like my advice, there is nothing you *should* do. It is too big a risk. The young man's last attempt at escape proved disastrous. Better to wait until we can effect an exchange.'

'Exchange, exchange.' Makepeace started off on another circuit of the room. 'The government's never going to agree to it and if it does it'll take years. They're *tunnelling*, I tell you, they're not waiting to die of hunger and disease, they're getting out.'

'He'll only be recaptured, Missus. Forty more days in the Black Hole.' Forrest Grayle, she thought, how can you forget Forrest Grayle?

'Not if I'm waiting at the other end of the tunnel to get him away. Blast and bugger it, if I only knew *where*. And when.'

'It would be most unwise. Your duty is to Philippa and the little girls.'

Makepeace looked down at the smooth head of her friend and wanted to thump it. Instead of breaking the news gently, as she'd intended, she said abruptly: 'De Vaubon's in Millbay. He's in the hospital.'

Later, when she'd returned to the Pomeroy Arms, she was sorry to have shocked the woman—but not too sorry.

'Then it was another matter, oh yes,' she told Philippa. 'Her precious Frenchman, a different kettle of fish from some poor black lad. I said to her: "If I know him, he'll try that tunnel if he can. You going to sit on your arse while he drags his poor leg around the streets of Plymouth looking for somewhere to hide?" They'll catch him if he doesn't get help, I told her, and in his condition the forty days'll kill him. He's older than the others. They *will* catch him, Pippy. He was always noticeable but with that face of his now . . .'

'Did you tell her that?'

'No,' Makepeace admitted, 'I didn't tell her that. But I told her the rest.'

'What did she say?'

'Nothing.'

The Dowager's still figure had become stiller, as if the wind coming through the cracks of the hall's windows had done her howling for her.

Remembering it, Makepeace was sorry again. 'I was too strong,' she said. 'Andra would be cross with me for it.'

From the other side of the taproom, Zack was calling for ale.

Philippa got up and went to the barrels, turned a spigot, filled a tankard and took it to him.

Watching the contained, neat little figure, Makepeace thought how wonderful she was. Shipwreck, Susan's awful death: she had survived these things, scarred undoubtedly but not fundamentally altered nor shaken in character. She had come unstained through her sojourn in the sewers of Dock—and that too had displayed her independence, perhaps a form of insistence that her mother attend to her for once. She is a complete person, Makepeace thought.

When she came back, Philippa did a rare thing; she reached for her mother's hand. 'He'll come,' she said. 'Andra will come.'

Makepeace nodded and said: 'I looked for that book in Exeter, Pippy. The arithmetic thing . . .'

'*Arithmetica*. Claude de Méziriac.'

'They didn't seem to have heard of it.'

'It's all right, Mama. Perhaps Andra will bring me a copy from Paris. He said that I would be ready to read it when I reached twelve.'

'Oh, Philippa,' Makepeace said, 'I missed your birthday.'

'You were at the hospital, Mama. I did not expect you to remember.'

Makepeace shook her head. 'I'm not a good mother, am I?'

Philippa considered it. 'No, you're not,' she said. 'But you are an unusual person and on the whole I would not have you any different.'

Makepeace leaned across and laid her cheek against her daughter's. 'I do love you,' she said.

In the Great Hall, the Dowager sat as Makepeace had left her, arguing with a son who was three hundred miles away.

He is crippled, Robert, he will never be a combatant again. It cannot matter to the war if he gets away, it cannot hurt England.

She listened to the reply and became irritated with it.

If it was someone you loved, if it were Alice . . .

In her mind's eye, Robert hoisted Alice over a wall, took her hand and, glancing right and left, ran with her for the shelter of the trees . . . and the whole thing became so ridiculous that the Dowager pulled herself together.

Why am I bothering to justify it to Robert or anyone else? If I can get that man away, I shall do it and Hell won't stop me.

The Missus was right: he would try to get out; it was why he'd refused his parole. Years in the Bastille, then the freedom of the sea; he wouldn't be shut up again; he'd be crawling like a wounded animal through that bloody tunnel.

And the Missus was right again, I *was* dismissive of the boy Josh. Of course he will escape, the desire to be free beats as strongly in that black breast as any other. Can I help one man to liberty because I'm in love with him and deny the same to another because he is nothing to me?

All at once she was blasted, as if the hall's two great windows had blown in, allowing the wind to scour clean everything in it. A bigger vista opened before her, a greater canvas, nothing to do with the individual and everything to do with the human condition.

My God, that's what it is. That's what liberty is. It is indivisible; it can't be sliced like ham, a large portion here, a bit for some, none for the rest.

She was overwhelmed by the appalling simplicity of it. All her years she had joined in the belief held by every Englishman, rich or poor, that she lived in a free country, a democracy unique in the world. But the moment it had denied that democracy, that freedom, to America it had denied its own principle. Immediately, the thing had ceased to be freedom and become privilege. Until it was granted to everyone, American, black, white, slave, it was not freedom.

She thought: The Missus has known this instinctively all her life; it has taken me thirty-nine years.

She ran into the kitchen, calling for Tobias.

'What ith it, your ladyship? What?'

'We didn't complete it, where's my writing case?'

'Complete what, your ladyship?'

'Your freedom. If you left me, you would need to show a manumission to prove it.'

'I don't intend to leave your ladyship.'

'It doesn't matter. You must have it. *Now.*'

He fetched her writing case and shaped a quill for her—she had been wearing out point after point with her letters to the press. She dipped it in ink and was at a loss. 'What should I say?'

Eventually they worked out a form of words. 'I, the Dowager Countess of Stacpoole, do hereby declare that I have the right to declare this man . . .'

Oh God, she didn't know his surname; all these years and she didn't know what his name was.

'Laval, your ladyship. My mother wath a thlave and she took the name of her mathter.'

'. . . Tobias Laval, a free man with all the rights thereto. Dated October 28, this year of our Lord 1778.'

She shook the sand pot over it, dusted it away and gave him the paper. 'And now fetch my cloak. I am going down to the Pomeroy, I have an apology to make.'

At the bridge she met an equally apologetic Makepeace coming up. They went back to the inn together to discuss mutual business.

As they were conducted into his beautiful upper room, young Mr Spettigue greeted them with the misty politeness he extended to everybody, as if he wasn't quite sure who they were. Today he was in black-and-white-striped velvet, with a beauty spot on each cheek.

As usual, Makepeace at the first sight of him wondered if they could entrust their business to such a vacuous fop; as usual he confounded her by being as sharp as a pin.

'Oh yes,' he said. 'Knew about the tunnel. Poor fellas, diggin' away.' He put the back of his hands together and flapped them sideways in a shovelling motion and immediately resembled a striped, ineffectual badger.

'How?' Makepeace asked him. 'How did you know?'

'Froggy escaper mentioned it. Enterprisin' chap, came out in a barrel. Got returned to the brewery, waited 'til dark, hey presto.'

Diana had to ask. 'Mr Spettigue, how do the escapers know to come to you?'

'Imagine me name's passed around the prisoners, your ladyship, bit like a visitin' card really.'

'Isn't that dangerous? Someone might give you away.'

'Haven't yet, ma'am.' He nodded at her as if she'd pointed out a mistake in his reasoning. 'Good point, though.'

'If information comes *out*, can you get information *in*?' Makepeace said. 'We sorely need to be in touch. Is there someone on the prison staff who will take a message and bring one back?'

He shook his head. 'Never trusted fellas who lock other fellas up—that *would* be dangerous. Believe I told you before, ma'am, gettin' the prisoners out ain't my end of the business. Dealin' with 'em when they do, that's my job.' Wagging his lorgnette at them he said, 'Don't count on anymore comin' out for a while, anyway.'

'Why?'

'Sunday market's closed down. Too many opportunities for escape. Guards on the *qui vive*. Fellas'll wait for the tunnel. Stands to reason.'

Makepeace massaged her forehead with the heels of her palms. 'Did your Frenchman say where the tunnel would come out? And when?'

''Fraid not, dear lady.'

He had a map of Millbay Prison, minutely detailed, and spread it on a table for the three of them to pore over.

'Ask me, that's where they'll break through,' Mr Spettigue said, pointing a manicured finger. 'Beyond the north wall.'

Diana was doubtful. 'It's a long distance. They wouldn't have so far to go if they dug the other way.'

'Port's on the south side. Busy place. Risky.'

Makepeace twisted her head round to see better. 'That's it,' she said, excited. 'That's where they'll aim for, the north wall. It's where I waited for Josh. There's woodland on the other side of the road. If they know what's good for them, they'll come out somewhere along that stretch, among the trees.'

'Isn't that where Josh was shot?' Diana said.

'I know.' Then she brightened: 'But this time he'll be coming under the wall, not over it. How long do you think it will take them to dig that far?'

''Bout as long as a piece of string, ma'am,' Spettigue said. 'Tree roots, rivulets to divert, that sort of thing. Heavy clay an' gettin' rid of it . . . could take months.'

'*Months!*' She moved away from the table and sat down.

'Mr Spettigue,' Diana said, cautiously, 'did your French escaper mention how many men are expecting to come out of that tunnel?'

Mr Spettigue found a speck on his cuff and dusted it off. 'All of 'em, really.'

'*All?*'

'Well . . . think so.'

'Seven hundred men?'

'Won't be that many, in effect,' he said, consolingly. 'Prison becomes deserted, someone's bound to notice.'

She felt weak. 'I expect they will.'

She was quiet as Sanders drove her and Makepeace back to Babbs Cove.

'Scared?' Makepeace asked her.

'Of course. I keep wondering quite how I find myself in this situation, doing these things, having these conversations. A few months ago I was a stately matron and now look at what I have become: a smuggler, a potential aider and abettor to my country's enemies . . .'

'The Frenchman ain't an enemy anymore; he's too sick.' Makepeace could only think in terms of individuals. 'And Josh, he should never've been mixed up in a war anyway, he's an artist.'

'His drawing of Lieutenant Grayle was certainly exceptional. Where did he study?'

'He was apprenticed to Joshua Reynolds for a time when he was living over here with me. John Beasley fixed it up—he knows everybody. Got a high regard for Josh, has John; thinks he'll be a great painter one day. Reynolds thought so, too.'

She says these things, the Dowager thought. She throws out the name of Sir Joshua Reynolds, and says her young black friend was his apprentice. And he probably was. It is not that I disbelieve her, it's just that she regards such things as unexceptional; the astonishing is matter-of-fact to her; she is making dispositions for the escape of two men from a war prison with the insouciance with which I would go shopping. It must be to do with being American, they regard the impossible as achievable.

'See 'She this?' Makepeace was delving under her cloak for a chain that hung round her neck. She dragged out the gold locket she always wore. 'He did this. It was a birthday present. Josh sent it to me.' She opened it and passed the locket to Diana.

It was a miniature watercolour, a portrait of Philippa as a little girl, eight or nine perhaps. It was difficult to see in detail under the swaying lamp of the coach but the artist had caught exactly the gravity which, even then, suggested an unassailable common-sense.

'He is very talented,' she said, handing the locket back.

'He's even better with oils. I reckon he could make his fortune from portraiture when he's home in Boston.'

At once, they were thrown back on the question of how to get him there.

'Let us approach this stage by stage,' Diana said. 'We can assume that there will be no difficulty in getting them to France.'

'Yes. The Gurneys will take them over on a smuggling run.'

'And presumably the French authorities will be happy to return Josh to America.'

'Yes. Spettigue says they do that.' Makepeace tapped her lips with a finger. 'I wonder if Josh would prefer to go to Paris for a bit, learn from the French painters. No, I guess he'd prefer to go home; influence things through his work.'

'Missus, I think we must stick to the matter in hand; he is not yet out of prison. So then, if we assume our two men emerge from the tunnel where we think they will—a large assumption, but never mind—we are left with the real difficulty, which is transferring them from there to Babbs Cove.'

'My plan would have worked last time,' Makepeace said. 'That's if they hadn't shot him.'

The Dowager sighed, but continued: 'Very well, Sanders takes the coach and waits in the woodland to the north of the prison.' She thought about it. 'And waits, and waits, and attracts attention because not only do we not know *when* the men will be emerging from their tunnel, nor where, the men themselves do not know that they are being awaited.'

'That's right. We've got to get a message to Josh and de Vaubon and they've got to get a message out to us.'

'Which we have just established cannot be done.' Diana leaned back against the seat and closed her eyes. 'It's a game,' she said. 'We are merely throwing dice. We are gambling on a double six to come up, yet we are only allowed one throw. The chances of some other combination are vast—a hundred things can go wrong.'

She heard the Missus say: 'That don't mean we don't play.'

Makepeace had taken off her hat and her red hair, too curly ever to be totally tidy, framed a face that was all at once like a pug's in its determination. The swaying lantern shone on eyes that were the steadiest Diana had ever seen.

The Dowager knew then that Britain was not going to win the war. She was looking at the face of America, a composite of awkward, common people with all the odds against them who, when it was explained that they were already beaten by the biggest, best-trained army in the world, would merely say they were not—and go on fighting.

'I'll think of a way,' Makepeace said. 'Bribe somebody, maybe, threaten 'em. Only it can't be Sanders who drives the coach. You'd better ask Tobias.'

The Dowager sat up. 'I'll do no such thing.'

'Why not?'

'It is dangerous.'

'Well, I can't drive the pesky thing, I don't know how, you don't either. And Sanders has got a wife and children.'

Diana said: 'I cannot allow a servant of mine to put his life at risk on a venture with which he has nothing to do.' She was clear on that; to send Tobias into the front line in order to rescue her lover . . . it was David and Uriah the Hittite all over again.

Makepeace said: 'He *has* got something to do with it. He's helping a couple of men to freedom and one of them's black, same as he is. *I'll* ask him.'

'Blackness is not the question here.'

'Yes it is,' Makepeace said. 'In this case it is. He's not your slave anymore, he can make his own choices.'

And she was clear on that. Josh was the argument against those who refused to see that slavery was an evil in itself; the son of a runaway slave, a man who'd fought and suffered for the American cause, gifted, articulate. Who could look at him and believe, like Able Seaman Abell, that his race was not suitable for freedom? With Josh on their side, the abolitionists must triumph and the missing clause in the Declaration of Independence be written in. It was fitting that Tobias be one of the instruments who helped them to do it.

The two women kept an antagonistic silence for the rest of the journey. The Dowager spent some of it wondering if her ability to drive a pair in hand qualified her to handle a coach and four at speed and by night, the rest in hopelessness. Makepeace spent it thinking and thinking as she turned Josh's miniature of Philippa back and forth to catch the light.

As they reached the fingerpost and began the descent to the sea, she said cautiously: 'How would you like to have your portrait painted?'

*   *   *

'What does she want, Bates?'

'Asked for a brief word with you, Captain.'

Captain Stewart looked at the visiting card again and was wary. The fuss this female and John Howard had made over the hospital had cost poor Luscombe his post and he'd be damned if the same happened to him. However, he had to give her a hearing. One did not send away well-connected countesses, even dowagers past their prime.

'Better show her in, I suppose.'

He waited for the entrance of a beefy aristocratic old Amazon with nothing to do but interfere in other people's business.

The woman who came in was tall and slim, her skin and hair like pearl against the black of her mourning. Though she smiled, there was something tragic about her. 'You must dread to see me, Captain Stewart; I fear I caused nothing but trouble to your predecessor.'

'Not at all, your ladyship.'

'I promise that today's errand concerns nothing for which you need to scold me.'

'*Flirt*,' the Missus had said, '*and if you can't flirt, look pathetic*.'

While he rushed to find her a chair, she looked round the room. It was more bare and businesslike than it had been under Luscombe's aegis; the furniture was Admiralty issue with none of the personal touches with which Captain Luscombe had made it comfortable. Captain Stewart, obviously, was the poorer man. The walls bore nothing more than an amateur portrayal of a frigate and a walnut-framed copy of the good captain's commission—previously they had been adorned by two lush portraits, one of Captain Luscombe, another of his mother. Better and better.

'Captain, John Howard commands me to congratulate you on the improvement to the hospital. I understand it is now the paradigm for every war prison in the country.'

'Due to your ladyship's efforts, surely,' Stewart said, cautiously.

'I was not the instigator, Captain, merely Mr Howard's instrument of concern that it was not what it should be.'

She hoped it sounded as if Howard had bullied her. How like old times to try and manipulate a man by guile and flattery. She was not enjoying it.

Now that Captain Stewart came to think of it, he owed this beautiful woman rather a lot. The hospital had undoubtedly been a scandal under Luscombe and, while he himself hadn't reformed it, he was getting much of the credit for its present efficient running. And if she'd now turned her attention to the issue of exchange, it suited him very well; the sooner he was relieved of a plaguesome crew like the Americans, the better he'd like it.

Now she was congratulating him on reducing the number of escapes; he'd been rather surprised himself at the success of his methods just lately.

It appeared that, while talking to hospital patients, she had heard of a young American prisoner—'A *negro*, would you think of it, Captain'—with considerable artistic talent. Had even been shown small examples of his work. A Joshua somebody-or-other. It had occurred to her what a pleasing curiosity it might be if the fellow should be allowed to paint her portrait.

'A present for my son. Reynolds was to have done it but I am settled in Devon and do not wish to make a long journey for sittings. And have you found the local painters of any merit, Captain? Daubers all, I fear.'

A daring request, she knew, and she would abide by any conditions he thought to impose, but it would be *such* a happy reminder of her connection with Millbay, and a sign of what liberality was shown to the prisoners.

'Moreover . . .' Diana sent up a prayer. '. . . should the artist live up to his reputation, I would be most happy to commission a portrait of yourself, Captain, and have it suitably framed.'

Captain Stewart regarded the carrot dangling under his nose and found himself hungry. This woman before him, breeding and good taste in every elegant line, was sufficiently convinced of the negro's talent or she would not be so eager to sit for him. A portrait of himself, in oils and full dress uniform. At no cost. He could hear his reply to visitors: *Yes, rather good, isn't it? Same fella who painted the Dowager Countess of Stacpoole . . .*

He was stern with her. 'You understand there would have to be restrictions, your ladyship, and we will have a problem with the location . . .'

It took time to make him alight on the now empty cottage but she got him perched on it eventually.

'There must be a guard present at all times, of course. At all times.'

'My dear sir, I should be terrified if there were not. I shall bring my manservant with me, if I may.'

The north-facing upper room still had stains on its floorboards where dying men had lain but its light was good.

It was also cold. As well as the necessary painting paraphernalia, she and Tobias had brought a hamper of food, a bottle of brandy— most of it for the guard—an extra cloak for herself and firing for the room's tiny hearth. Even so, after an hour or two, being positioned by the window, Josh's hand became unsteady from cold.

The next day—she was staying at the Prince George for the duration—she brought yet another cloak but the militia guard, Corporal Trotter, a man blessed with weighty flesh but no brain that Diana could discern, refused to let Joshua wear it.

'It is not magic,' she begged him, 'it won't render him invisible.'

Trotter, however, suspected it might. He had his orders—nothing to be passed to prisoners—so sessions were interrupted while Josh thawed out by the fire.

It took three days before Trotter relaxed and succumbed to brandy, boredom and a post-prandial snooze. Even then they were cautious.

'What terrible weather,' Diana began, quietly. 'A farmer's wife I know, a Mrs Hedley, worries that the ground may be too hard to dig. She wonders when the winter sowing can begin.'

Josh looked up, stepped back from the easel, his head on one side, and approached it again. 'You helpin' this Mrs Hedley some?'

'She has asked me to advise her, but I know little about farming.'

'Bad time, ground's mighty hard.'

'Yes, she wonders when she should bring out the plough. And where.' Lord, how ridiculous; even Trotter would suspect this conversation. She looked at the man, to make sure he slept, and mouthed: *'Where? When?'*

Josh pointed his brush towards the window. *'That way. Trees.'*

Diana leaned forward from her chair and peered; he seemed to be indicating the north wall beyond which she could see treetops. It looked a long way away and there was a great deal of wall. *'Coach. Waiting.'* She glanced again at the sleeping Trotter and dared to gabble: 'There is a Frenchman. De Vaubon. He must come in the coach.'

Josh stepped back from the easel, regarded it and made another stroke. 'Different hut,' he said. 'Tell him at roll call.'

She wanted to say de Vaubon was still in the hospital for all she knew, but Trotter had stopped snoring and was making chewing motions with a mouth dry from too much brandy. His eyes were still shut.

Josh held up four fingers. *'Weeks.'*

Trotter snorted and woke up.

'At least,' Josh said out loud.

'We are discussing farming, Corporal,' Diana said. 'I suppose farmers know when to start ploughing but those with inexperience must need someone to tell them, don't you think?'

'Don't care, I'm a coffin-maker,' Trotter said. 'Light's going, Burke. Back to the pen.'

'Another month?' Makepeace yelped.

'At *least*, apparently. The sort of tunnelling they are doing can hardly be an exact science.'

'Couldn't you have stayed longer, found out more?'

'No, I could not,' Diana said. 'Captain Stewart is eager for his own portrait and kept arriving to find out how Josh was coming along. What I did do was suggest that Josh work on the hands and most of the dress without my being there, so I have an excuse for returning to collect the finished product.'

Josh himself could have spun out the sittings more by slowing his work but he had not, he would go at his own pace or not at all.

She had not found him particularly amiable or willing to please, qualities she had always ascribed to his race. It had come as a shock to be sharply berated by a black man—she had shifted her pose—but she had recognized the dedication of a true artist. While he'd worked he had been elsewhere than in a nasty little room, inhabiting a dimension of light and shade that, for him, was a greater escape than any.

The Dowager had wondered if that was why Josh had survived the Black Hole when Forrest Grayle had not; Grayle had been unable to live without physical freedom, Josh carried his own freedom in his mind's eye.

She had come to admire him. More than that, looking at the young man day after day, the sheen of light on the mattness of his skin had begun to please her. Before, she had regarded blackness as an unfortunate pigmentation cursing those who had it; now she saw it could be beautiful.

Her own painted face, when he eventually allowed her to see it, had been not altogether a pleasant surprise. 'I look like Leda after the swan left her in the lurch.'

'Swan's right,' Josh had said. 'Who's Leda?'

'Am I so tragic?'

'Yes,' he said. 'Brave, too, though.'

Admittedly, the portrait had been a subterfuge but she had hoped, as one did, that she would appear to advantage. With that in mind, she had composed her features in the (she hoped) noble mask it had worn for thirty-nine years, but the countenance on the canvas had something of the heart-wrenching endurance with which Josh had endowed his drawing of Lieutenant Grayle.

She *must* smile more.

Somewhat miffed, she'd said: 'Well, young man, I hope you will flatter Captain Stewart.'

Josh had shrugged. 'I paint what I see.'

There was nothing they could do now but wait, a condition made harder for Makepeace and the village women by the fact that *Lark* and *Three Cousins* were overdue.

Lanterns and rushlights shone out each night to an empty cove. Out at sea, every passing vessel carried expectation on its prow and disappointment in its wake. In their dreams they began to be haunted by cries for help and to see bodies twisting through water in a bubbling downward spiral.

A violent south-easterly wind swept along the cliffs as if trying to find the village, huddled in its cleft like a leveret in a forme, to sweep it away. It took off one of the Pomeroy's chimneys and brought Mrs Welland's henhouse down around her poultry's ears.

It was a relief. Rachel Gurney said: 'Explains it, that does. They wouldn't've set out in this. Blow 'em to China, this would.'

But when, after two days, the storm dropped and its place taken by a flat, viciously cold calm and still the cove remained empty day after day, there was no excuse.

'Perhaps their rigging's frozen,' Makepeace attempted. 'It's icy enough.'

Rachel's mouth was tight. 'P'rhaps,' she said.

Makepeace went up to T'Gallants to huddle by the Dowager's fire. 'It's terrible, I know,' she said, 'but I keep praying that if they've gone down, they didn't have Andra aboard.'

'That's understandable.' Diana herself was selfishly thanking God that de Vaubon was on dry land. But in what condition? He'd be so cold. She didn't know if he was alive; might never know if he were dead.

'Talk to me,' she said. 'Tell me about Andra.'

Hearing about Makepeace's marriage was a diversion from anxiety; it was so mystically different from her own. Both her husbands had made the Missus happy so that, to Diana, stories about them were like tales from a foreign country.

Makepeace never seemed to compare the two; the years with Philip Dapifer had been one thing, the life with Andra Hedley another, both different, both wondrous. The only common factor, as far as Diana could judge, was that each husband had allowed Makepeace a freedom of thought and action that her own wouldn't have tolerated. 'He allowed you to do that?' she would say about one venture or another. 'Didn't he mind?'

The Dowager never talked about her own marriage, but her questions were as revealing to Makepeace as if she had. Yon Aymer was a proper bastard, she thought. I'd have kicked him in his strawberry leaves. She didn't think the son was much better. She enquired after him.

'He takes after his father, I think,' the Dowager said, smiling with what Makepeace considered indulgence. 'Just as conservative in his attitude to women. I fear that latterly I have been a thorn in Robert's side.'

'You should stand up to him.'

Diana turned away so that Makepeace didn't see her face. 'I didn't stand up *for* him. That was the trouble; I didn't stand up for my son.'

Makepeace could see there was agony here, but she was incapable of understanding anyone who didn't assert herself against abuse. In the working-class area of Boston where she'd grown up, most women had jobs to augment the family income as well as their housewifely duties. They had barrows or stalls from which they sold fish, or they brewed ale, or ran a ferry. If they had no brothers, they took over their father's business; when their husband died they took over his, too. Mrs Hobart had been a farrier, Mrs Lidgett manufactured the pipe staves her trader husband sold to Barbados.

They didn't fit the picture of the ideal of femininity drawn in the etiquette books, they were mostly leather-lunged, horny-handed women whose husbands frequently complained of their strong-headedness, but they were generally honoured as fellow-labourers in life's vineyard. There was a comradeship among men and women there which Makepeace had expected to find when she married, and had been fortunate that in neither husband had she been disappointed.

No, she didn't understand the Dowager's marriage, nor was she allowed to pursue it because Diana changed the subject.

She has no conception, Diana thought. She was wedded to human beings whereas I was dangled from the fingers of a Cyclops who threatened to munch me up and throw away the bones. Stand up to him? He could stamp on me—and did. He would have pursued me with hounds; he would have taken Robert away from me.

Such a gentle child, oh my dearest little boy, dragged to bear-baitings and hangings by his father in order to make a man of him, terrified I would protest and we would both get a beating for being women. Of course he chose to ally himself to Aymer's world, not mine; I failed him.

But who stood up for me? Not the law. The law sanctioned every beating I received, every rape, every threat . . . What the Missus can never know, God save her from it, is the unbridled tsardom of a savage man given wealth and power with the law of marriage on his side.

'Andra's a splendid lover, too,' the Missus was saying, shockingly. 'I miss bedtimes, I can tell you. Don't you?'

'With my husband?'

'With de Vaubon. You spent the night with him.'

'We had dinner,' the Dowager said, blinking.

'Is that all?'

As Makepeace walked back to the Pomeroy, it seemed appropriate, after what she had heard, to see that the stream from the reed bed under T'Gallants's bridge was frozen and hung suspended between bridge and beach in an immobile carving of ice.

'Not even a kiss,' she told Dell, because she had to tell somebody. 'And a lusty fella like that one.'

'I know. What's the matter with him?'

'It's the matter with her,' Dell said, 'that's what it is.'

Dell had taken to going up to T'Gallants in order to help in the house: Mrs Green was becoming increasingly ill. She went up again, soon after the conversation with Makepeace, and took her specialized knowledge with her.

The Dowager paused in the act of stuffing the plum pudding into its bag. 'Lots of them?'

'T'ousands,' Dell assured her, 'and not one of them can get it up if they don't, if you'll pardon the expression. Pitiable, really.'

'Pitiable,' said Diana, musing.

'Weak in spirit, weak in body, that's what I used to say to meself. Scared they'll be found out in their weakness. They're frightened of you, so they are, I used to say to myself, and taking it out on you accordin'. Ah well, me girl, that's what you're paid for.'

'Good Lord,' Diana said. Aymer was reducing by the minute. It appeared he had not been the unique monster she'd imagined, but one of thousands. She angled the memory of him into a different position to see if it was possible that he had, in fact, used her weakness and fear to compensate for his own, like a schoolground bully. Her long struggle to assume passivity and boredom had been effective in decreasing his violence, that was certain. But the violence sprang from impotence and fear, if Dell's experience with other men was to be believed, and in this Dell must be regarded as the expert. Thousands like him, she said, a common, almost humdrum, condition.

She watched Aymer's memory scuttle round the kitchen floor, squeaking. No, she would never be able to dismiss him quite like that, but it helped, by the Lord Harry, it helped.

She looked across the table at the former prostitute. Dell was hanging the cauldron over the fire, her face a pitted moon in the light of the flames. 'Were none of them ever kind to you?'

'Kindness, is it? D'you know, I don't think so? Not what you'd call kind. If there was, wouldn't I be in bed with the darlin' this minute? A man like that, he'd be above rubies.'

They hung the pudding from a hook so that it dangled in the boiling water, then Dell walked carefully back over the ice to the Pomeroy Arms where she sought out Makepeace in the kitchen.

'I done me best,' she said.

'Good.'

There was a bad quarrel between Simeon Lewis and Rachel Gurney about the church service Rachel wanted held for the safe return of *Lark* and *Three Cousins*. In the absence of a regular parson, the slow-spoken Simeon was regarded as the next best thing, and his inclination was for a service of remembrance.

'That's for the dead,' Rachel screamed at him. 'I ain't praying for Jan's soul as if 'un were dead!'

Simeon shouted, 'Face facts, woman, they ain't a-coming back.' He and Zack had three grandsons among the missing.

The row took place in the Pomeroy's taproom and it was dreadful for everybody to see two people, usually monuments of calm, in such distress. Mrs Hallewell was in tears; her husband had been among those who hadn't returned when the *Swallow* was lost at sea.

Eventually, Simeon gave in. The weather was too bad for a priest to get to the village, so it wasn't a proper service but Simeon's deep voice begged God to return 'thy missing mariners to them as do love them, where they belong'.

Diana, as lady of the manor, was allowed to give a reading. She chose from the Litany: ' "That it may please thee to preserve all that travel by land or by water; all women labouring of child . . ." ' Eddie Gurney's wife, Cissy, was getting near her time. ' ". . . all sick persons and young children; and to show thy pity on all prisoners and captives." '

It seemed to Makepeace that the combined entreaty rose up to the ears of the Almighty with enough power to scorch a hole in the chapel roof as it went. But when they trooped out, the flat surface of the cove before them remained still and undisturbed in a quiet made more intense by the first sprinkling of snow.

Diana's heart ached for them all. We are a village of the incomplete, she thought.

A wind came up and drove the snow inland, piling it up against obstructions but scouring cliff edges and quaysides clean. The lane at the top of the Babbs Cove slipway and the T'Gallants bridge might have been swept by a Titan's brush.

The coastal path, too, remained clear but nobody came along it. It seemed to those who endured the ensuing days and days of waiting as if Babbs Cove had become an iceberg which had been calved and allowed to float away from the mainland into a featureless sea.

And then, one morning, a galloper and his horse, both of them steaming from the ride along the cliffs, reached T'Gallants with a message from Mr Spettigue in Plymouth.

Minutes later, Diana was running from the house to the Pomeroy Arms, Tobias and the galloper behind her. 'Missus, Missus, oh God help us, it's tonight. They're breaking through tonight.'

Chapter Twenty

THEY had hoped for a longer warning than this. Helplessly, almost indignantly, Makepeace said: 'We're not ready.' She turned on the galloper as if it was his fault. 'How do you know it's tonight?'

He looked anxiously around the taproom where Zack was in his usual place, listening hard, Simeon was in his, pretending not to, and Mrs Hallewell stood at the door of the kitchen, a cloth in her hand.

'You can speak out, young man,' Makepeace told him. 'Everyone here knows what we're about.' Ever since The Night They Fooled Nicholls, the village women had shown that they were prepared not only to turn a blind eye to the two escapers when they arrived but would help to get them aboard the boats for France.

Only, Makepeace thought in despair, there *are* no boats for France.

'If you say so, ma'am.' He was a slender youth, his fresh face made fresher by his ride. 'It was a French prisoner. He managed to dress up as a woman and join a gaggle of . . .' He paused, embarrassed. '. . . ladies who were leaving a celebration given by one of the guards. He came out through the gate with them in the early hours of this morning. Brave man, actually. The tunnellers had sent him ahead, as it were, to alert Aloysius—'

'Aloysius?'

'My brother-in-law, ma'am, Mr Spettigue. You see, ma'am, their intention is to escape en masse so it was necessary to let us know in order that we can make our dispositions for them.'

He finished off the tankard Philippa had put in his hand. 'With that in mind, and with your permission, I will be getting back.'

Zack hobbled to the door of the inn as the young man unhitched his horse and prepared to mount. 'Yere,' he said. 'Be you married to Spettigue's sister, then?'

'No, he's married to mine actually.'

'Family man?' Zack had encountered Mr Spettigue at Henry Hobbs's funeral and hadn't got over it.

'Oh yes.' The boy seemed puzzled to be asked. 'Devoted husband and father.'

Zack came in, brushing snow off his shoulders.

'We'll never get through, let alone get back,' Makepeace said. '*Look* at it.' Outside the windows, fat white flakes were performing an hypnotic downward dance against a background of grey.

'It may be a blessing in disguise,' Diana said. 'It will cover their tracks; it might even slow down pursuit.'

From the stables came the 'whoa-up' of men persuading horses into their traces; somebody had been acting while they havered. Sanders came in: 'Ready, Missus.'

Makepeace turned towards the stairs to fetch her cloak. 'You're not coming, Sanders.'

'No, Missus. Tobias is up.'

The Dowager hurried outside. The coach was ready in the forecourt, snowflakes melting as they touched the horses' backs. Tobias was on the driving box, muffled to the ears, adjusting the tarpaulin over his legs. 'You may get down, Tobias,' she said. 'I can manage the team.'

There was a scarf round his mouth and she saw his eyes above it crinkle with something like amusement. He pulled the scarf down. 'Not in thith, you can't, your ladyship.'

She couldn't remember him contradicting her before. 'I can't let you do it, there may be shooting. It isn't your business.'

'Yeth, it ith,' he said.

She brushed snow out of her eyes, not believing he wouldn't obey her. 'You don't even know where to wait.'

'Yes, he does.' Makepeace had come out of the inn, fully wrapped and booted. 'I showed him on the map. Anyway, I'll be with him.'

Dell had come with her and went straight up to the coach and held up her hand to Tobias. He leaned down and took it for a moment, then touched her face. 'I'll be back, girl,' he said.

Well. While Makepeace and Diana were exchanging glances, a whip cracked and they heard the squeak of wheels on packed snow. Then the coach had moved away and Philippa was holding on to Makepeace to stop her running after it. 'No, Mama! What will Andra say if he comes home and finds you shot?'

'He can't go alone.' Makepeace was struggling. 'I've got to be with him.'

'Mama, you can't drive. Ages ago, he'd decided to go alone if the call came. He told me so, he said you'd been talking to him about Josh and liberty and such; he wanted to do it.' She took her mother back into the inn.

'That's what he told me,' Sanders said.

Diana followed them, tight-lipped. 'You've been talking to Tobias, Missus?'

'Why not?'

'Because I should have been consulted. I didn't give that man his freedom so that he could put his life in danger.'

'Then it wasn't freedom, was it?' Makepeace shouted at her. She slung her cloak off her shoulders and hung it back up on its peg and let her forehead rest against it. 'He's right, isn't he?' she said. 'We couldn't do anything if we went.'

'You could get in the bloody way,' Zack said. 'Or you could make your zilly selves useful and getting summat to eat for they poor buggers when they get here. Famished they'll be, lessen they feed 'un well in Millbay, the which I doubt. Don't know about this Josh o' yourn, but Gil's a man as likes his vittles.'

It was the age-old occupation for women, to busy themselves for the return of their men, and it gave them something to do.

It had already been decided that de Vaubon and Josh should be taken to T'Gallants where, if there was a search, they could be hidden in the cavern at the bottom of the shaft. Philippa and Diana went up there to prepare beds, as well as Mrs Green, for the forthcoming arrival.

Diana still harboured resentment for what she thought of as Makepeace's interference in the matter of Tobias. 'Your mother is a meddlesome woman,' she said to Philippa. 'I cannot bear that Tobias is taking the risk for all of us.'

Philippa nodded. 'Mama's friends do tend to get embroiled,' she said, 'but he wanted to go.'

A friend? Is that how Makepeace regards Tobias? Whereas I feel this heavy responsibility for him because he is my servant.

But he *is* my friend, she thought, like Joan. This anxiety is for someone I cannot spare—and not just because he works for me but because I feel affection for him. So I must grant him the right to make his own decisions; after all, he seems to have taken this one for reasons unconnected with his duty to me. I just wish he hadn't.

They went back to the Pomeroy Arms when they'd finished to find Dell rolling bandages for the Frenchman's leg and putting out ointments for his face. Makepeace had begun chopping up half a sheep—a gift from Ralph Gurney—in preparation for Boston lobscouse, partly to relieve her feelings and partly because, as she said, 'Josh is mighty fond of my lobscouse.'

Watching the cleaver rise and descend, Mrs Hallewell said, 'Will 'un need that much?'

'Yes.' She paused. 'Time you went home, Maggie. And you should stay there. We don't know what will happen. Whatever it is, I'll say you knew nothing about it.'

'Reckon I'll stay a bit,' Mrs Hallewell said. 'What vegetables do ee need for that concoction then?'

Zack and Simeon insisted on staying as well; it's doubtful if Zack could have been dislodged if the inn had caught fire: 'Can't leave you females to manage this business on your own,' he said.

Mrs Welland came in with two pairs of patched sea boots '. . . in case they lads turn up with nothin' on their poor feet.'

Reminded, Mrs Hallewell went back to her cottage and returned with some of her husband's clothing that she'd kept like holy relics since his death, as well as a warm coat of her father's.

At the same time, and with the same thought, Rachel Gurney entered with a wool shirt of Jan's. 'I'm knittin' 'un another one,' she said defiantly.

'He'll be back, Rachel,' Makepeace said. 'And my Andra with him.'

'I bloody know he will.' She looked out of the window; it was still snowing. 'I been up the farm and told Ralph to get his oxen out and keep that lane clear.'

Mrs Hallewell set a jug of brandy in front of Zack and another for Simeon before she went home. 'That's all you're getting tonight,' she said, 'I know you.'

Sanders began to clean out the stable and put down fresh straw, ready for the return of the team.

Rachel went back to her cottage, put her older children to bed and returned to suckle her baby in front of the fire. Makepeace decided it was time the inn's pewter was polished and the rich smell of lobscouse coming from the kitchen mingled with the acidic scent of horsetail as she rubbed tankards and platters to within an inch of their lives. Dell positioned herself at the window to keep watch for the coach. Philippa took up *The Wealth of Nations* and turned its pages as if she were reading it. The fire crackled.

For want of anything else to say, Diana remarked: 'I hope that I've got in a sufficient supply of laudanum to see out the snow.'

'For Ma Green, is ut?' Rachel asked. 'Bad, is she?'

'Yes.'

The doctor Diana had fetched from Newton Ferrers had been met with shrieking violence and been forced to go away again. 'I believe her to have a canker in the breast,' he'd told Diana, 'though it is impossible to know without an examination. It may have spread to the brain.'

'Can nothing be done?'

He shook his head. 'Laudanum if she will take it.' He was a young man and an enthusiastic anatomist; to him Mrs Green was a living corpse. 'In the interest of science, I should be grateful for your permission to perform an autopsy when the time comes.'

'Poor soul,' Rachel said now. As always, when the villagers mentioned the caretaker, Diana sensed reserve.

'I asked her why she insisted on suffering,' Diana told Rachel now. 'She said a strange thing. She said: " 'Tis my due." '

'Guilt,' Rachel said, shortly. She took the baby away from her breast, put it against her shoulder to wind it, and covered herself.

'Why should she feel guilty?'

Rachel looked at the Dowager carefully and said: 'Her husband fell down that shaft of yourn.'

It was the moment, Diana realized later, when she was finally accepted into the village, or, perhaps more than that, into its female society as a woman no greater and no less than all of them who waited for a man to come back. Though Mrs Green remained the outsider she had always been, Diana became part of the sisterhood and entitled to its secrets.

'She were a Polperro maid,' Rachel said. 'They'm fey them Cornish—and her married Martin Green over South Huish. They Greens might be Cornish theyselves, so wild as they be. Dark souls, all of 'un.'

It was never a happy marriage, Rachel said. Green blamed his wife for having no children. 'But he'd'a blamed her for blinkin' her eyelashes. Beat her he would, oh, shockin'. Her never said a word but the marks was ever on her face. Good gardener, though, oh, he could make things grow somethin' wonderful. 'Twas one o' your tenants hired him for ut, years back this was, and when they left, Agent Spettigue—that were the old man, not this one—he did keep Martin on in the garden and her in the house, caretaking. Then Martin were found dead.'

It was Eddie Gurney who first saw the body, Rachel said. He'd been raising the family lobster-pots one morning when Green's corpse had come floating out of the cavern below T'Gallants and into the cove.

'Fell and drownded, they reckon. Bruises all over 'un. Could've slipped on the clifftop, though this was just before dawn and what he were doin' on the cliffs for that time o' day we don't know . . .'

Diana said: 'She pushed him down the shaft?'

Rachel shrugged. 'Lord only knows and He idd'n sayin'. But some creature do trouble her from the grave and that's a fact.'

There was never a longer night. Occasionally they would find themselves drifting into uncomfortable half-dozes from which they woke with a sense of being menaced. If the Dowager saw Nicholls's face peering into the window she saw it a dozen times. Knowing he wasn't there, she would get up and look out. And, of course, he wasn't. Just snow, getting thicker.

Makepeace began sweeping the floor. Dell continued to sit on the window seat, staring out at the snow. Diana went and sat with her. 'Tobias is a very kind man,' she said tentatively. Dell merely nodded.

'Probably hasn't even got there,' Makepeace said, sweeping hard. 'I don't know why we're all bothering.'

Their charity with one another began to wear thin.

'Can't you sit down?' Diana snapped at Makepeace.

'No.'

Philippa went to the window. 'It will be dawn soon.'

'We know that,' Makepeace said. 'Get on with your book.'

Daybreak found them hopelessly playing cribbage.

By nine o'clock in the morning, Makepeace was considering

the pros and cons of relieving the misery by throwing herself off a cliff.

At half past ten the door banged open to admit a panting little Jack Gurney. 'Coach is yere. Comin' down. Dad swept the lane for 'un.'

They tumbled out into a white world. They began running up the lane in the exaggerated high-stepping slowness snow imposed. Steaming horses with white caps between their ears advanced on them with Tobias above, outlined against the front of the coach.

The women went backwards as it came on, shouting and cheering: high drifts left no room by which they could get to its sides.

'Did it go well?' Makepeace shouted.

Tobias's mouth was set as if in concrete by the cold; he seemed to have difficulty unstiffening it. He didn't look at Makepeace. She heard him call to the Dowager: 'They didn't break through 'til nearly dawn.'

'Nobody stopped you?'

He shook his head. 'Nobody about.'

They were hindering the coach's progress. They all turned and capered back; if there had been palm leaves to strew they'd have cast them before the horses' hooves.

A small crowd in the Pomeroy forecourt had gathered to watch the coach draw up. Its curtains were closed. Sanders went immediately to the blowing horses. Tobias climbed awkwardly down from the box and then opened its door. Makepeace, going forward, was stopped in her tracks by a glimpse of piled bodies.

They're dead, she thought. It's a plague cart.

Others rushed to help with the disentanglement and slowly, through the crush, ragged men emerged. One, two, three, four . . . beside her the Dowager gave a moan of gratitude as the Frenchman was lowered to the ground . . . seven, eight, nine . . . She'd seen a comic play once, one of her brother's, in which a coach, side on to the stage, debouched an impossible number of occupants. She'd laughed and laughed. She didn't laugh now . . . thirteen, fourteen, fifteen, sixteen, seventeen, eighteen, nineteen, twenty, twenty-one.

And none of them was Josh.

Chapter Twenty-one

FOR a few minutes chaos had the Pomeroy Arms in its grip. Make-peace had Able Seaman Abell in hers; they had to drag her off him. As it was, she bloodied his nose.

'Se'gated, what d'you mean *se'gated*, you bastard?'

'Put in diff'ent shed, ma'am.' Abell wiped the blood with the back of his hand. He seemed to bear her no ill will. 'Told the commandant days back: se'gate or we's riotin', take yo' choice.'

'I'm afraid that's what they did, Missus.' Lawyer Perkins was at her side. 'Some of us protested but Captain Stewart preferred to segregate rather than have trouble in the prison.' He adjusted his glasses and turned to Diana, who was attending to de Vaubon. 'The plan was for the negroes to bring up the rear in the tunnel.'

'Why?' Makepeace demanded of Abell. 'Why'd you do that?'

He said patiently, 'I tol' you, ma'am. They's black.'

'*And what do you think he is?* He risked his life for your carcass.'

Abell looked along her shaking finger to Tobias. 'Much obliged, boy,' he said.

'Man,' shrieked Makepeace. 'He's a *man*.'

'There's nothing we can do about it now,' Diana told her sharply. 'For God's sake let us see to those we have here.' De Vaubon was semi-conscious, his lips compressed against pain.

'To hell with them,' Makepeace said. She went to a booth at the back of the room and sat down on it, covering her face.

Bilo, the only black man in the group, bent to lift his captain. 'Where, madame?'

'Up there.' Diana grabbed some bandages and the medicaments box from their shelf and followed Bilo and his burden up the stairs.

Dazedly, Philippa looked round the taproom; her mother's defection left her in command. And I don't know what to do, she thought. It was as if a multitude of scarecrows had suddenly descended on the inn, rips in their rags showing ribs and legs like white sticks strung together. They jostled to get near the fire in the way of dull-eyed bullocks, uncaring of everything except getting warm. I don't know what to do.

It was Dell, enlarged at the safe return of Tobias, who did. 'Ain't it lucky your ma made all that stew?'

Lobscouse.

They hurried into the kitchen to set it over the fire. Mrs Hallewell was already there, cutting bread. A scarecrow followed them in and stuffed a crust into his mouth. 'No need to wait 'til it's hot, missy,' he said to Philippa through the crumbs, nodding at the lobscouse. 'Smells just dandy to me.' She ignored him.

Rachel Gurney came in, looking for flint and tinder. 'Us'll have to burn their clothes,' she said. 'They'm crawling with little visitors.'

'Rachel, what are we to do with so many?'

'Don't know, girl.' Rachel looked grim. 'Let's get the buggers vitty first. Is Gil here?'

'Upstairs.'

In the taproom, Tobias sat himself opposite Makepeace in the booth and tapped on the hands that covered her face. 'I'm sorry, Mithuth.'

She looked up at him. 'All these months,' she said. 'It was all for him and they left him.'

'We'll get him out, Mithuth.'

'He's *precious*,' she said. 'He'll think I've abandoned him.' She began to weep. 'I don't know what his mother would say.'

She kept hearing King David's cry. '*O my son Absalom, my son, my son, Absalom! would God I had died for thee, O Absalom, my son, my son!*'

'Don't take on, Mithuth, I'll get him out for you.'

She wiped her eyes. 'What happened?'

He'd found the track where she and Sanders had waited on the night that Josh got shot, he told her. He'd rugged the horses against the cold and waited. To stop freezing to death, he'd got into the coach occasionally but had been frightened each time that, if he stayed in it too long, he'd fall asleep, so he kept getting out again.

There'd been traffic using the road when he'd got there but it had dwindled to nothing as the night and the snow went on.

It was still dark and the Plymouth clocks had just struck the five o'clock when he heard a scuffling sound on the other side of the road. He walked to the edge of the trees. The snow had stopped. 'Moon wath bright ath day,' he said, 'and there wath a turf lifting all by itthelf out of the ground. Eerie, it wath. They'd come up short, you thee, on the wrong thide of the road, on the verge next to the wall.'

One by one, shapes had begun to rise up out of the ground, using their elbows to lift themselves, like demons struggling out of Hell. 'I didn't know what to do, Mithuth: get their attention or wait 'til I thaw Josh and M. de Vaubon.' In view of what was to happen, he felt he'd been right to do what he did, which was to wait.

Man after man had emerged, most seeming to know where they were going, and had run off, dozens of them. 'After fifty I lotht count.' There'd been no sound from the prison.

Then, Tobias said, a peculiar thing happened. A big black man lifted himself out of the hole and stood, looking around, and in the quiet of the night had called: 'Babbs Cove.'

'Like he wath thummoning a hanthom cab,' Tobias said. 'Josh mutht have given him her ladyship'th methage. "Babbs Cove." Like that.'

'He could have woken the guards,' said Makepeace.

'He didn't care. When I thaid, "Here," he lifted M. de Vaubon out of the hole and carried him acroth the road.'

And that, Tobias said, was when the trouble began. The prison's alarm bell had started to toll and escaping men, still coming out of the hole, panicked. Some, seeing help at hand, ran over the road after Bilo and followed him to the coach. By the time they'd got de Vaubon inside and prepared the horses, about a dozen men had forced themselves into the coach with him.

'It wath a muddle, Mithuth. I had to go.'

'I know.'

The bell was clanging and more men came up out of the hole by the minute, grabbing the door handle of the coach and piling in. 'I could have beaten them off but I didn't have the heart.'

'No.' She patted his hand. 'Of course you didn't.'

'We were overloaded, any more and the team couldn't have pulled. Tho we had to thet off.' He was nearly in tears.

'There wasn't anything else you could do,' she said.

'I didn't thee Josh. That big one who called out, he wath the only nigger man came out. I'm thorry, Mithuth.'

'It wasn't your fault,' she said.

Despite the alarm bell ringing into the night, they'd encountered no checkpoints on the road, which had been virtually empty.

'I'm thorry,' he said again.

She looked at him; he'd said nothing about getting a coach through snowdrifts and bitter cold but in the candlelight his face, like his hair, was tinged with grey. 'She'll never be able to pay you,' she said. 'You go home and rest now.'

'Thegregating,' he said. 'They won't thtop it, will they?'

Suddenly she didn't know how to face him. 'I hate them, Toby,' she said.

'They don't underthtand.'

'Time they bloody did,' she said. ' "Life, Liberty and the pursuit of Happiness"? Whose? Not my Josh's, not yours.'

Tobias said: 'I *will* get him out, Mithuth, I thwear.'

When he'd gone, she sat where she was, too depressed to move.

She watched Philippa bring platters to one of the tables, followed by Mrs Hallewell carrying a pile of bread and Dell with the big pot of lobscouse. Zack was filling tankards.

Automatically, the men from the coach fell into line, a few of them helping others who had trouble standing. Most had sores around the mouth; some, despite the heat in the taproom, shivered with fever.

She heard Philippa's clear voice say with distaste: 'You *wait.*' Abell, who had been in line to have his plate filled, nodded and went uncomplainingly to the rear.

Oh well.

Sighing, Makepeace hauled herself to her feet and set about helping.

In the bedroom upstairs, the Dowager helped Bilo strip off de Vaubon's clothes and wash him. His shattered leg was withered and had pus emerging from one of the wounds where there had been stitches. His skin was hot to the touch and he kept coughing. When she needed him lifted, Bilo did it as easily and carefully as a mother her baby.

'How long has he been like this?' she asked in French.

'Two days. But he crawl through the tunnel like a snake. Nothing stop the chief, not him.' His accent had a heavy and exotic emphasis—African, she thought.

'Thank God they didn't segregate you, Bilo,' Diana said.

'Pfff. That is Americans, the specks of dirt, not French. The chief keep me with him always. I look after him. I want to stay there, he is too sick, but he say, "Bilo, we go, I have an appointment with a lady." You are the lady?'

'Yes.'

'Then you look after him good.'

She nodded. 'You go and get some food now.'

He was reluctant to go, but hunger drove him out eventually.

Diana looked at the labels on Makepeace's pots of ointment. One, less terrifying than most, said, 'Comfrey and honey. Dress it always warm.' The smell was soothing and she smeared it liberally but carefully on the suppurating leg.

The scar on his face had healed but it would always look as if someone had used a black crayon to score angrily into the flesh. Carefully, she put out a finger and ran it down his forehead and nose, across his lips to the greying stubble on his chin, as if she were tracing the line of a Praxiteles Adonis.

His eyes opened and squinted at her. 'There you are,' he said in English.

'Here I am.'

He closed his eyes again. There was icy-cold water in the bedroom's ewer and she wrung out a cloth in it to put across his forehead.

Rachel came in. 'How is he?'

'So ill.'

Rachel picked up one of his hands. 'Gil,' she said, quietly. 'Gil, you seen the *Lark* or *Three Cousins* in your travels?'

His eyes stayed closed but his forehead wrinkled. 'Missing?'

'Yes, Gil. Weeks now.'

'*Merde.*'

Rachel nodded and got up to go.

Diana followed her to the door. 'Will he live?'

'Him?' Rachel was impatient with her. 'Course he will.'

When Makepeace came in she had the same air of restrained resentment, as if the Dowager had taken some unfair advantage, but she softened when she looked at the man in the bed. 'Fever,' she said.

'His leg's festering and he keeps coughing.'

'Keep on with cold cloths, try and cool the blood.' Makepeace inspected the leg and approved of the balm. 'He's clean, he's comfortable. I'll send up some herbal tea: see if he'll take it. And pray. That's all we can do.'

'I'm so sorry, Missus.'

Makepeace went to the window and looked out of it. 'This is a fine to-do,' she said, wearily. 'Still, we can't send the buggers back, I suppose. They'll have to go to T'Gallants, we can't keep 'em here.'

'I'm not having him moved,' Diana said, quickly.

'Of course not, you—' Makepeace's temper was on the shortest of fuses. She fought it down. 'What are we going to do? How are we going to get them away?'

'I don't know.'

*   *   *

Having fallen on the lobscouse like wolves, very few of the men had eaten hugely, some very little. 'Thank you kindly, ma'am, but I reckon my belly's shrunk,' one of them said.

They were deloused in the inn's scullery, a forbidding little structure out at the back. About a pound of crushed fleabane leaves was put into its boiler, releasing the peculiar smell of cats' pee. Zack shaved the men's heads before they went naked into its steam, Simeon herded them through and handed them a blanket to wrap themselves in when they emerged like wet, sheared sheep from a dip.

In the kitchen, Dell, Philippa and Mrs Hallewell dressed weeping ulcers and sores and then sent their patients through to the taproom where Makepeace, Rachel and Mrs Welland sorted through piles of clothing that the village women had contributed to find breeks and shirts to fit each one.

'I'm grateful, Rachel,' Makepeace said when they'd dressed the last one.

'Weren't expecting an army,' Rachel said.

'Neither was I.' Makepeace looked at her squarely. 'An enemy army, Rachel.'

'Reckon they are,' Rachel said, slowly. 'Draggly-lookin' enemy, though.'

'What I mean is . . .'

'What you mean is, will us give 'un away.' She shook her head. 'Look at 'un,' she said. 'I seen pigs kept better. Near dead, some of 'em; sending 'un back'd finish the job. Us Babbs Covers are smugglers, we ain't in the killin' business. 'Sides, we owe a debt for The Night We Fooled Nicholls.'

'Looks like you're going to pay it,' Makepeace said.

Rachel was right. Faced with such need, it was impossible not to respond to it, and the men surrendered themselves to the women like grateful children. Not one of them asked what was going to happen next; for the moment it was enough that they were out and somebody was being kind to them.

In the afternoon, young Jack Gurney came running in, his face alight with bad news. 'Coastguard up on the cliffs.'

There was nothing to be done but send the escapers upstairs and pray. After a dreadful thirty minutes, the boy came back to report that the coast, literally, was clear. But it was a warning that patrols were out. The men must be moved. Philippa and Dell went ahead to light a fire in T'Gallants's Great Hall.

After dark, each man was given a guide to get him through the drifts and across the bridge. They dare not use a lantern in case a watcher had been left on the cliffs. Nearly all the escapers were in a form of collapse, as if they had used up every last modicum of energy and will to get out of Millbay and foundered now that had been achieved. Some needed help to walk.

Makepeace watched, stony-eyed, from the door of the inn as Sanders put Able Seaman Abell's arm round his shoulders and disappeared with him into the darkness.

Zack came and stood by her. 'What be going to do now?' he said. 'On ay dons la merde, as Gil would say, bless 'un. On ay dons la merde, that means—'

'I know what it means,' Makepeace told him. 'And we're in it all right.'

On the second night, Diana called downstairs in a panic for Makepeace to come up. 'He's dying.' De Vaubon's breathing was rapid and shallow, his lips were livid.

'Sit him up.' Bilo hauled him higher on the pillows. Once they'd applied more cold cloths to his head and a warm one to his left side, which seemed to be hurting him, there was little to be done. Bilo stood by the door, muttering quiet invocations, Makepeace sat on one side of the bed, muttering her own, Diana sat on the other saying nothing, her eyes never leaving de Vaubon's face, her body and mind fused in an entreaty one word long: *Please.*

Just before dawn, the patient began to sweat and each time Diana wiped his face, his skin was cooler. When light came through the window, he was breathing easily in a deep, genuine sleep and Diana was transformed into a living thank you.

*   *   *

She had to leave de Vaubon's convalescence in Makepeace's hands. Though she visited him when she could, her attention had to be directed towards the state of affairs at T'Gallants.

She would have liked to switch places with Makepeace but felt it unwise. Any soldiers who came to the village looking for escapers might think it suspicious if they saw her living away from a house that was known to be at least nominally hers. Besides, Makepeace was slow to get over her antipathy for the nineteen in general and Able Seaman Abell in particular. She had been heard to prescribe a lingering and painful death for him.

The village women were generous in supplying what food they had, but the raid by Nicholls and his men had destroyed or stolen much of their winter supplies and Diana was concerned that they were leaving themselves short.

'Don't ee worry, woman,' Rachel said, as she presented a ham and two dozen eggs. ' 'Tis only 'til we've fattened 'un up a bit, then 'un can live on pulses like the rest of us.'

Ralph Gurney led a pony and cart down the hill, bringing a salted pig and straw and clean sacks to make palliasses. 'Oh my dear soul,' he said when the Dowager took him into the Great Hall. Despite its size, it looked crowded.

Diana asked the question constantly on her and Makepeace's mind. 'What are we to do with them if Jan and the others do not come back?'

'They'll be back, oh, they'll be back, don't ee worry.' He exuded confidence. 'Havin' trouble with the boats, I reckon, and holed up in France for a bit drinkin' Calvados and toasting the *femmes.*'

'I'm making this their dormitory and day room for the duration,' she said. 'If they are all in one place it will be easier to move them in an emergency. I'd put them in the undercroft or down in the cavern right away, but it's so cold and some are still sick.'

'If that happens, why don't ee hide 'un in the shaft room, ma dear?'

'Shaft room?'

'You mean to say you an't found it?' He slapped his knee. 'You come along o' me.'

He picked up his lantern and led her upstairs to the maze of passages she had never fully explored. It was cold and dark up there, Ralph Gurney's boots woke echoes from the stone. Hearing a whisper of sound down one side passage, he called out cheerily: 'Evenin', Mother Green,' and went on.

Ralph stopped and turned to face a blank wall. 'Yere.' He was enjoying himself.

'Where?'

'Yere.' He reached out to an empty sconce, one of a series that were stuck along the passages like a collection of pipe bowls attached to a stem. He pushed it sideways, then kicked at the wall, leaving a scuff mark from his boot. A section opened slightly, creaking. 'You want to oil they hinges,' he said, and pushed the door fully open.

They went into a windowless room warmer than the rest of the upper floor. 'Chimney from the hall be that side,' Ralph said. 'Makes 'un cosy.'

It was not an adjective the Dowager would have used. It was a reasonably sized box, perhaps twenty-five feet by twenty-five with a high ceiling, but it was solely a box: no furnishings, no ornamentation, nothing to relieve the eye or spirit. The only pleasant thing about it was a faint whiff of good tobacco lightly touched by brandy and perfume.

'The stuff we used to store yere,' Ralph said fondly, then caught the Dowager's eye. 'Not now, o' course. Come over here, look.'

'Over here' was a stout, plain wooden door with a hefty bolt. He opened it and she was assailed by a blast of cold sea air. She could hear waves booming in the cavern below. The house was never quite free of the sound; she had assumed it came from outside, sea against cliff but, of course, it was internal, the beating heart of the cavern.

Ralph lowered the lantern. 'There's the entrance to the hall, look. See 'un? Bit of the way down? That door in the wall's the back of the dang great chair in the Great Hall. Further down there's an entrance to the undercroft. 'Tis possible to step on the platform there and go up or down, gettin' off at any of the three floors. Your old Pomeroy ancestors, they knew a thing or two about hiding places.'

She nodded, bemused.

'Course, you need a chap at the bottom to handle the ropes and ratchets.'

She peered but could see nothing.

'I'll row round and get they pulleys fixed up,' he said, 'then 'twill be all ready if so be we got to hide the buggers.'

The 'we' was greatly comforting. 'I'm grateful, Mr Gurney.'

She was; the escapers were none of this man's responsibility. He did not allow patriotism to interfere with business but nineteen of England's enemies—twenty-one if you counted de Vaubon and Bilo—hardly constituted free trade. The village women saw only nineteen vulnerable men in need, not what they represented, but she did not think such a feminine view was Ralph Gurney's. His help was in return for hers on The Night They Fooled Nicholls.

He confirmed it. 'You'm welcome, my dear,' he said. 'One good turn do deserve another. Though has to be said, I wadd'n expecting half Millbay to come visitin'.'

'Neither was I.'

After five days, the sky cleared, the snow stayed in sparkling, solid sculptures that the sun turned rosy at dawn and amber at evening but did not melt. Icicles like glass bunting decorated the cottage eaves.

Devon was not used to weather like this. Women took unaccustomed buckets of snow indoors to melt them and struggled with washing from the line that had to be folded by hitting it. Children slid joyfully down the slipway on trays and made a snowman, put a cracked chamber pot on its head, draped it with seaweed and called it Captain Nicholls, though it more closely resembled a rather rakish Poseidon.

Diana went into the Great Hall to find some of the younger escapers missing.

'Down there, ma'am.' Lawyer Perkins pointed to the bridge where an uproarious snowball fight was in progress.

'Would you be good enough to call them in, Mr Perkins.'

When they were assembled before her, she said, clearly: 'There are such things as coastguards. For all I know, they are walking the cliffs at this minute and have seen a group of noisy men in what they know to be an almost manless village. You gentlemen may be bent on returning to prison but I am not, nor are the families whose food you are eating and whose clothes you are wearing.'

There was a scattered chorus of: 'Sorry, ma'am,' 'Sorry, ma'am.'

She looked them over. Were they suitably ashamed? They were undoubtedly on the mend; most of their sores had cleared up, they were less skeletal and there was a sparkle to most of them which, the Dowager felt, must be dimmed as quickly as possible.

'The kitchen garden is not overlooked,' she told them. 'As long as you set a lookout, you may take exercise there—without shouting. You will also find logs and a chopping block, I should be grateful if you would employ them.'

They were chastened, though not for long. The logs were chopped virtually to matchsticks but after that there was little for them to do. And nineteen men, most of them young, with nothing to do and nowhere to go proved to be difficult guests.

Captain Totes, senior officer of the Americans, and Capitaine Laclos, senior officer of the French, found each other unbearable.

Captain Totes: 'Ma'am, I demand a room where my men and I can get away from that gamester and papist blasphemer.'

Capitaine Laclos: *'Qu'est-ce qu'il a dit? Mon Dieu, il a besoin d'un coup de pied au cul.'*

Had Captain Totes not been quite so righteous, the Dowager might have sympathized with him more. Laclos—who'd arrived wearing a woman's skirt—was an inveterate swearer and gambler, always losing his clothes in games of dice: there'd been one occasion when she'd entered the hall to find him scrambling under the bed covers to hide the fact that he was totally naked.

Totes was a Vermont Puritan who seemed to have run his ship ably but with the rigour and sermonizing of an Old Testament prophet. He would have kept T'Gallants to a similar regime—a prayer meeting morning and night, three times on Sundays, no cards, no gambling, no talking about women—but since none of the Americans had been among his previous crew, few were inclined to obey it.

The Dowager sighed. If these were the officers, what might she expect from the men? Patiently, she explained to them both that they must share what accommodation there was. 'What would happen, gentlemen, should there be an alarm and you were in different parts of the house? You must adapt your behaviour to each other's sensibilities.'

'I doubt M. Laclos has sensibilities,' Totes said. 'By the grace of God, ma'am, when can we go back home?'

The question was asked again and again by all of them, as if she could spirit sailing vessels from air. Some were eager to get back into the war, most were desperate to see their families.

She told them and told them. There would be a vessel to take them to France eventually. If *Lark* or *Three Cousins* don't arrive soon, she thought, the Missus will have to buy a boat.

She was sorry for them—and she really was—but, in the meantime, would they all be so good as to behave.

It was the invaluable Jack Gurney, having the time of his life, who first saw the search party coming down the lane and used paths that only he knew to get to the Pomeroy Arms ahead of it.

There was no time to do anything except send Zack up to de Vaubon's room to tell him and Bilo to be quiet and ask the boy to warn T'Gallants.

Mrs Hallewell met the men at the door; there were seven of them, six militia and a Revenue officer who looked at the inn sign and then at a list in his hand. 'Are you the landlady, madam? Mrs Hallewell?'

'I am.' She invited them in. 'You poor lads do look perished. This yere's my cousin and her daughter, they'm staying for a while.' Makepeace and Philippa bobbed politely.

The officer, Lieutenant Higgins, gratefully accepted a glass of ale on behalf of himself and his men. Looking for escaped prisoners along the Devon coastline was a cold and wearisome business.

'No, us haven't seen a stranger, not in this snow,' Mrs Hallewell told him.

'How many got away, Officer?' Makepeace had been dying to know.

'One hundred and nine, ma'am,' Lieutenant Higgins told her. 'They've recaptured fifty-odd so far but where the others have got to, nobody knows.'

'Dead, in this weather, I wouldn't wonder,' Mrs Hallewell said.

'That's what I think,' Lieutenant Higgins said, tiredly, 'but we've got to look.' He consulted his list again. 'Who's at the big house? T'Gallants, is it?'

'Oh, that be the Countess of Stacpoole, Pomeroy as was,' Mrs Hallewell told him and, greatly daring, added: 'But her's not likely to be hiding dangerous men, no more than me.'

'No.' He sighed. 'Got to ask, though.'

As the men trudged away, Mrs Hallewell said, 'Oh, my soul,' and collapsed amid congratulations.

The lieutenant's welcome at T'Gallants was colder. A regal Dowager was called to the door by her butler and her negative reply to the lieutenant's questions lowered the poor man's blood to freezing. He wasn't asked to come in and seemed relieved that he was not.

But the incident had been salutary. For one thing, knowledge that the military had joined forces with the hated Revenue to look for escapers stiffened the village's sinews. And it taught Diana that she must have a plan ready for another time.

That there would be another time, she was sure; she felt it in her bones like a doom. Discovery was inevitable.

To convince the nineteen of danger, however, was another mat-

ter. To them Babbs Cove was the end of the earth, a wild and successful ride away from Millbay. Soldiers had come and looked for
them; soldiers had gone away. While they paid lip service to her anxiety, they saw no need for it.

They were becoming restive; they had been shut up too long.
They had been digging their tunnel in awful conditions for months
in the expectation of freedom. Now, before them, was the sea, their
route home, but with nothing to float on it. They were brave men,
all of them; they had fought well. Yet capture had shamed them,
imprisonment had degraded them further and they wanted to go
out in the open air, walk the beach, and stroll around Babbs Cove
like free men.

Diana forbade it; she owed caution to the village, if to nobody
else. Should the escapers be discovered, the more who could say: 'I
knew nothing of them,' the better. They might be suspected but
there would be no proof on which to convict them.

Only Lawyer Perkins sensed her concern and responded to it.
'You really worried, ma'am?'

'There's a Revenue officer. Not the one who came enquiring,
another,' she told him. 'If the Revenue service are among those
hunting you, he will come sooner or later.' There was no reason to
feel that he would suspect her of harbouring some of the missing
men, but she did. Was she investing Nicholls with supernatural
instinct? No. If for no other reason, he would use the escape as an
excuse to search T'Gallants. 'He harasses us,' she said, 'he harasses
me. I am afraid of him.'

'Likely we'd better take precautions,' he said and, having been
initiated into the mystery of the shaft, began organizing a rehearsal
for the day when Captain Nicholls turned up.

Two of the youngest sailors, one French and one American,
both excellent rigging-climbers, used the ropes in the shaft to let
themselves down into the cavern.

'Haul away,' Captain Totes shouted and the platform rose to
Great Hall level for the evacuation to the shaft room on the upper
floor.

'We could take 'em all down to the cavern, ma'am,' Perkins explained, 'but if we had to stay down there too long in this weather, wouldn't matter if they found us or didn't, we'd be cold pork anyways.'

The men had been put in numbered groups to await their turn on the platform as it could only carry four at a time. They were intrigued and amused: 'Ascendin' to Heaven at last, ain't we, Cap'n Totes?'

Once again the Dowager heard the thunder caused by hoisting ropes, chains and ratchets, as she had on the night when the Frenchman had burst in on her. The chair-door was swung open. Giggling and a little nervous the first group got onto the platform . . .

It was as the third group was readying itself to go up that the yelling began, translated by the echo in the shaft into a thousand satanic screams. Abandoning the platform, everybody ran upstairs, Diana after them.

Topman Mitchell, a superstitious youth from Georgia, was backed against the hidden room's passage wall, shaking. 'Ghost! Demon. Stood right there.'

'Where?'

Mitchell pointed a trembling hand at nothing. 'Right there. Glory keep me, it was *horrible*.'

'It was my housekeeper,' Diana said. 'She's ill.' But they were off like hounds in the hunt for demons. By the time they were rounded up and the escape procedure begun again, an hour had passed before they were all assembled in the hidden room.

Lawyer Perkins stared at them over his spectacles. 'Gentlemen, I suggest we start walking to Millbay right now and give ourselves up. Cut out the middle man.'

The Pomeroy Arms, too, was being afflicted by noises.

Zack, a jack of all trades like most sailors, had cobbled a high sole to the boot which was to adorn de Vaubon's shortened, crippled leg.

He watched the Frenchman pull it on. 'Now stand on ut,' he said. 'See if it evens ee up.'

'*Merde.*' De Vaubon collapsed onto his bed, gasping with pain.

'Hurt, do ut?'

'*Putain de merde. Suis un estropié toujours, nom de Dieu, un invalide.* Yes, it does.'

'Take the damn thing off,' Makepeace begged him.

'No. Give me the looking glass.' He regarded himself. 'My God. *Quelle gargouille.*'

'You weren't no Adonis to start with,' Makepeace said. 'Anyway, she thinks you're pretty.'

'She is not to come here.' De Vaubon wagged a finger. 'You hear, Missus? Two days. Two days and I walk to her like a veritable man.'

She grinned at him. 'You looked veritable enough to me when we stripped your britches off.'

'I go to her on my two legs or not at all.'

She would never understand men. 'All right. Two days.'

'What be he talkin' about?' Zack was not sensitive to matters of the heart.

For two days a regular thumping from the upper bedroom shook bits of plaster from the taproom ceiling.

'What's he *doin'* up there?' Zack asked.

'He's marching up and down,' Makepeace said. 'Trying to get the strength back in his leg so's he can go up to T'Gallants and make love to her ladyship.'

'Don't need his leg for that, do he?'

When he was ready, they saw him off at the door. Dell was in wedding tears and the other women weren't far off. Makepeace had brushed his coat and hat (once Jan Gurney's, the only ones that fitted him). Philippa had polished his boots. One by one they kissed him, Rachel whispering something in his ear that made him tut-tut. Mrs Hallewell tucked a sprig of dried bird's eye in his buttonhole—she used the leaves for tea—for good luck.

Before he left the area of light extended by the Pomeroy's candles, he turned and waved his hat, then stepped into moonlight reflected on snow.

'Level peggin' so far,' Zack said with pride.

He made it to the bridge where he had to lean against the balustrade and take off his hat to wipe his forehead. After that it was torture to watch him as he staggered and halted and pressed on again. The women at the inn door instinctively extended wavering hands out, like mothers ready to catch a toddler if it fell.

'Does she know he's coming?'

'He don't think she does, he wanted to surprise her. But I sent Bilo to tell her. Woman needs to be ready at a time like this.'

They watched him until he reached the courtyard, then Makepeace went to her bedroom and wept for Andra Hedley.

In her bedroom at T'Gallants the Dowager Countess of Stacpoole abandoned mourning and put on a wrapping gown of blue silk, held at the waist by a fringed sash of deeper blue and hitched up on one side to show a flowered petticoat in the manner of a Sultan's favourite. *Turquerie* had been fashionable when she'd bought the dress; she hoped it still was.

I'll be cold in this. Then she thought: But not for long. She wished that Makepeace hadn't sent Bilo to warn her; she would panic, *was* panicking. It was so . . . so deliberate. Like waiting for the dentist.

Why couldn't he have taken me when I sat by his bed?

He wasn't well enough, you fool.

Dear Lord, she'd grown so thin; she had no bosom to speak of. She examined her brushed hair in the looking glass; that was one thing about being fair, you couldn't see the grey.

She piled it on top of her head and pinned it, leaving a lock to trail over one shoulder—oh help, straight as a pea stick. She rushed down to the kitchen, warmed her curling iron and turned the tress into a ringlet.

And so pale. Dell had borrowed her rouge and not brought it back. She pinched her cheeks and wished she were dead.

There were whistles of admiration from the nineteen when she went into the Great Hall.

'Going to a ball, ladyship?'

'I'm escortin' her iffen she is.'

She paid them no attention and went to the oriel window. And there he was, oh my darling, limping ferociously into the courtyard. The lamp at the archway shone on a face snarling at pain.

She ran through the screen passage to open the door to him. 'Sweetheart, you ought to be in bed.'

He hauled himself up the steps, smiling. 'I agree, madame.'

She helped him up to her room and didn't leave it for two days.

It seemed to her that they nearly drowned in love, wallowing and diving like dolphins in turquoise waters around a palm-fringed, tropical archipelago. Sometimes they pulled themselves up onto golden sand and lay in the sun to rest and talk.

'I do like love,' she said. 'It's slippery and warm.' It was as if she'd lived in arid cold all her life until now. And it was funny, love was *funny*; he made her laugh.

'I cannot go on like this without food, woman,' he told her. 'You are exhausting my reserves.'

'Perhaps they've left us some at the door.' She got out of bed and pulled on a wrap—she couldn't get used to being naked standing up.

'No.'

'All right,' she said, letting the wrap go. 'But it's chilly.'

'Come back to bed, then.'

'I thought you were hungry.'

'I am.'

He loved the contrast of her whiteness against his dark, scarred skin. 'It is a pity you are so ugly,' he'd say, kissing her, 'I have to hide my repulsion.'

'You do it very well.'

Neither of them mentioned her marriage, though his extreme gentleness when they'd first made love suggested he thought he would be countering terror. But seeing him struggle up the hill had made him vulnerable and she was ready for him.

He talked about his children and the grandchildren he hoped to have. When he mentioned *La Petite Margot* and her crew, it was with pain. Without them, he said, he would abandon the war—it was doubtful if he was strong enough to captain a vessel, in any case.

'What will you do?'

'We will take up politics. We will work for the day when Louis is toppled and the Republic of France is born. Ah, then you will see, there will be liberty for all, enlightenment, the philosophy of Voltaire and votes for women.'

When they weren't politicking and voting, they were to spend their days in his château at Gruchy. That was what he liked to talk about most, their future together.

'I shall teach you to cook, you barbarian. I will allow you some roast beef—your English beef is not at all bad when cold—perhaps I will concoct a roulade in your honour. *Roulade de boeuf à la Diana.*'

'No lobscouse?'

'No.' He had taken against Makepeace's lobscouse, though it had done him well. He'd fattened up a little on it at the inn.

He was her Scheherazade; she listened to him, enchanted by the pictures he painted of the little yacht they would sail together, the smuggling runs back to Babbs Cove when the war was over to keep their hand in and meet old friends. She revelled in him while she had him because it wouldn't be for long.

He's so complete, she thought. He didn't have to ask if his looks and the fact that he was crippled bothered her; for one thing, she showed that they did not; for another, he was too assured. They bothered him because he knew he was probably facing constant pain and would find it difficult to stand on a swaying deck again, but in essence he was the man he'd always been.

'And I will have you,' he said.

She couldn't bear to tell him that he wouldn't.

When she said that she would have to take up T'Gallants's reins again—'It isn't fair to leave all the work to Dell and Philippa'—he insisted on joining his fellow prisoners in the discomfort of the Great Hall.

'Stay in bed,' she begged him. 'You're not completely well yet.'

'It is against my honour.'

'I thought you didn't believe in honour.'

'Personal honour, woman, you would not understand. I am not a plaything, I cannot continue as your pleasure slave.'

'Not even tonight?'

'What time?'

When she returned to the cold, it was to find the Americans somewhat embarrassedly pretending she'd never been away and the French looking on her and de Vaubon with the indulgence of proud parents.

It was magical to see him playing dice with Laclos or scandalizing Captain Totes with his atheism or hauling himself up the staircase to go and talk to Mrs Green. As if he's a real person, she thought; he didn't seem real to her.

She had more patience with the other men now, encouraging them to talk to her about their homes and families. Tobias, she saw, was doing the same thing, listening particularly to the Americans, even Able Seaman Abell.

'I hope that young man is being polite to you, Toby,' she said. She had warned Abell at the start: 'Mr Abell, if you so much as forget to say thank you to Tobias when he serves your dinner, you must leave this house and fend for yourself.'

He'd been indignant. 'I got manners, niggers or no.'

Such a strange young man, she thought him, illiterate and bigoted but he could be trusted to help with the chores and to watch from a window more than the others, his eyes searching for danger as they had once looked out for water snakes when he set gossamer fishing nets in the creeks of his South Carolina home.

He begged her to teach him to read. Being busy and, she thought, cunning, she had suggested he learn from Tobias, but it appeared he could not accept the gift of literacy from a black man, so Lawyer Perkins was teaching him. 'The more advantages that

Gullah has, maybe the less he'll oppress those who ain't got any,' Perkins had said.

It was at Lawyer Perkins's feet that Tobias sat mostly, when he had time, listening to tales of the pepperbox house in Massachusetts where clients were attended to in the parlour while Mrs Perkins cooked corn hash in the kitchen, where grandchildren crawled on the floor and may-apples grew in the yard.

'I been explainin' to Tobias here about the drafting of the Declaration of Independence,' he said, when she went and sat with them one evening. 'I was telling him we New Englanders tried mighty hard on the slavery question. "All men as they are sons of Adam have equal right unto liberty," as John Adams told 'em. The Missus says we should've tried harder and maybe we should. We voted for the achievable. But abolition'll come soon. Sure as God made little apples, it'll come.'

She glanced towards de Vaubon: 'Did you never think of including women among those with the right to vote?'

Perkins smiled. 'John Adams's wife, Abigail, a real nice woman, she wrote John some such thing. But when you ladies rule our hearts, why'd you need a vote? No, ma'am, can't say we gave it a thought.'

When she and Tobias were washing up in the kitchen later on, he said: 'Mr Perkinth and Mr Abell: a funny country that'th got the two of them in it.'

'It's not a country yet,' she said, absently. She was thinking about the coming, delicious night.

'Will be, though, won't it? And all new. An old country would have thent thomeone like the mathter to Philadelphia, wouldn't it?'

The thought of Aymer framing a Declaration of Independence made her smile. 'What do you mean?'

It was the newness of America that had impressed him, that it should send a homely man like Perkins to one of its greatest meetings. 'New,' he said. 'It can thtill be shaped.'

'I suppose it can.'

'It nearly abolished thlavery in Philadelphia, Mr Perkinth thaid tho. Might do it yet.'

He had her attention now. She said: 'Just think if there was nowhere to sell slaves to. The trade would stop.'

'It will need all the help it can get,' he said.

'What is it?' she said. He was suddenly so strange. 'What is it?'

And Tobias made his horrifying proposition.

Chapter Twenty-two

'No,' she said, 'I won't allow it.'

'You gave me freedom, your ladyship.'

'Not in order for you to give it away again.'

'It'th my freedom,' he said, 'I can do what I want with it.'

He was so stupid, he had no idea of what it would entail and she did. She wanted to scream that she knew what was best for him; instead she used dirty tactics: 'It will be dangerous for me, too, have you thought of that? We could both end up in prison.'

Yes, he'd thought of that but he didn't think so.

'You think they won't notice?'

'No, they won't. They won't look. You thee'—he smiled at forty-five years of servile anonymity—'all niggerth look alike.'

Oh my God. She knew he'd won but she made one last try. 'You could speak for abolition,' she said. 'It needn't be Joshua.'

He was almost cross. 'Are you lithening to me, your ladyship? Are you hearing how thilly I thound? How can I thpeak for my people? I'd have them in thtitcheth. But they won't laugh at young Joshua.'

He rummaged in his pocket and drew out a piece of paper. 'He drew that for me. He thaw it done in a thlave market.'

It was a sketch, hastily done by the hand that had drawn Lieutenant Grayle. It showed a black man sitting in a chair while a white man fitted an iron mask over his face. The white man's face was expressionless, the negro's obscured, but brutality leaped out at the viewer.

'Do you thee?' Tobias was impatient. 'The thlave can't thpeak. I can't thpeak. But a picture like that thpeakth for all.'

'Yes,' she said, painfully, 'I see.'

That night, in bed, just before they went to sleep, Diana said: 'I must go into Plymouth tomorrow, we need more laudanum for poor Mrs Green.'

'Don't be long,' de Vaubon said.

Nobody was to know what they were going to do—except Dell. The next morning, in the kitchen, they told her. She wept, quietly, deeply, as if her heart were breaking. Diana saw that it was. So, very nearly, was her own.

Just before she left them to themselves, she saw Tobias set his black cheek against the pockmarked white skin of the Irishwoman's.

At the Pomeroy Arms, she asked Makepeace if she could borrow the coach for the day. 'Mrs Green needs more laudanum. Tobias will drive me.'

'That's good.' Makepeace was concerned with something else. 'Zack and I are going pony-back along the cliffs to Thurlestone. He's going to speak to one of the free traders there about buying or hiring a boat. We can't wait any longer, we've got to get those men to France.'

It took a minute before Diana realized what she was saying: Makepeace had lost hope for the *Lark* and *Three Cousins*.

'What does Rachel say?'

'She knows they're not coming back.'

There had been no more snow, it was even beginning to thaw a little, but Sanders, hitching up the horses for them, said that from the look of the sky, they could expect more.

As they started off, she could only think of the bereft village she was leaving behind her but, bounced and thrown from side to side as the coach skidded over packed, melting ice, she was reduced to fear on her own account, and, worse, resentment.

All very well for Tobias to widen his vision across continents; hers had been reduced to a bed and a Frenchman. And, having found them, she was leaving both on a hopeless business, a fanciful sprig of an idea from an innocent. Stupid, *stupid*.

A dozen times she raised her hand to tap on the coach glass and tell Tobias to turn back, before letting it fall because she knew she wouldn't be able to frame the words that negated everything she had learned these past months—and couldn't live with it if she did.

Damn liberty, she thought, damn it. How right she'd been to recognize its indivisibility. Once you started handing it around, there was no end to it.

And I'm in love. I'm being asked to risk too much.

So her hand would go up again and then drop as the cycle of fear, like the dreadful journey, went on and on.

Plymouth had become slushy and irritable. The few shoppers stepped warily, pausing before jumping from one duckboard to another, casting fearful looks upwards at the soft lumps of snow sliding down the roofs, cursing fast-moving carriage wheels that thrashed thick, dirty water over their boots.

Why was he stopping here? Of course, the laudanum.

He helped her down and she went into the now familiar apothecary's shop with the coloured bottles sending a rainbow through the panes of its bow window. She bought two big bottles of the opiate and fought down the desire to drink one of them.

She must think of Tobias; she bought cough drops, ointments, wintergreen, herbs for strengthening, tisanes, a pomander to keep off the noxious effect of smells, and told the apothecary to package them for her.

He was standing by the coach door, waiting for her. She handed him the package. Smiling, shaking his head, he handed it back; they would search him.

She dithered, not knowing what to do. This was their only chance to say good-bye; she wanted to hug him, tell him how noble she thought him but already passers-by were staring at them both.

'In you get, your ladyship,' he said cheerfully and handed her in. And that was that.

Fifteen minutes later, they drove through the gates of Millbay Prison.

Captain Stewart listened to the Dowager's errand with the expression of a camel regarding the last and unnecessary straw.

For all the pains he'd taken, 109 men had escaped through the tunnel and to date only 62 recaptured. Their lordships of the Admiralty were heaping condemnation on his head, as was the Plymouth Corporation. With largely the same resources, he was having to organize a search of Dartmoor and the coast for the missing prisoners and at the same time ensure he retained the six hundred and fifty-odd prisoners left to him.

Well, if she must collect her portrait now, she must, but it was not a good time. 'Thompson, tell Corporal Trotter to go to hut four and fetch her ladyship's portrait.'

'Thank you so much, Captain. I regret being a nuisance but I should like to thank the artist for his work and there is the matter of signing it . . . If he might be permitted to bring it to the cottage, I could be out of your way.'

'Very well, but it must be done quickly.'

And it was. Ludicrously quickly.

Tobias drove the coach to the cottage door and accompanied her ladyship inside. Within minutes, they were joined by Joshua, the portrait and a disgruntled Corporal Trotter.

The Dowager's attention was for Trotter. 'What a time you have had, poor man. These troublesome prisoners . . . Allow me to thank you for all your trouble. Is this the finished object? So difficult to see in this light, perhaps we could go up to the studio? No, no, Corporal, don't trouble yourself, we shall be but a minute while the boy signs it. My man will come behind to ensure my safety.'

Corporal Trotter didn't trouble himself; he sat on the stairs, nodding ruminatively at the five guineas that the Dowager had pressed into his palm.

Upstairs, Diana hissed: 'No questions, Joshua, no time.' Tobias whipped away Joshua's cap, took off his own hat and wig and fitted them on the young man's head.

'Take that jacket off, and the shirt.' For a moment, both men were bare above the waist, the dull light of the room reflected on black skin so different in shade that she knew one could never be taken for the other.

'*All niggers look alike,*' Tobias had told her; it was the premise on which they were operating. '*All niggers look alike.*'

She heard Tobias say: 'Can you drive, boy?'

She hadn't thought of that. And Joshua was saying No. He looked dazed. She watched Tobias unbutton his bright caped coat, pick up one of Joshua's arms and direct it into a sleeve with instructions. 'Whip'th in the holder on the right of the box. Flick their backthides and they'll move. Hold the reinth like thith.' While he formed Joshua's unresisting hands round imaginary reins, the Dowager knelt and buttoned the coat round the boy. As she reached the last button she came face to face with home-made thongs on bare feet.

'He has no boots.'

Tobias struggled out of his boots and tears began trickling down her cheeks. He'd have nothing, he would be so cold.

Finished. She stood up. Joshua was slightly taller but with hat, wig and the coat's high collar he would pass. Tobias, though, would not. Dell had dyed the flecks of grey in his hair but he looked what he was, a forty-five-year-old man, not a boy of twenty. Even in prison rags he managed to appear respectable.

There's no point to this; she didn't even want there to be.

Tobias was urging them both to the door. At once the enormity of what they were doing overtook Joshua. 'I ain't leaving him here.'

Diana swung back her arm and slapped the boy's face. 'Behave yourself. If I can, you can.' She shoved the portrait into his arms. 'Hold it up and get down the stairs.'

She teetered on the tiny landing, wanting to say something meaningful, loving and, because there was still a lot of Countess in her, some appreciation of his years of service. Tobias pushed her gently forward.

Corporal Trotter was looking up the stairs, heaving up his bulk so that Joshua could pass with the portrait. As she reached him, he said, 'Thank you for the 'preciation, ma'am.'

'Thank *you*, Corporal.'

They were in the open air, the failing light and moist air accentuating Millbay's greyness. The entrance gates seemed lost in the distance. Joshua had put the portrait in the coach, he was climbing up onto the box—he hadn't opened the door for her.

But here was the blessed, blessed Trotter doing it instead, earning his guineas. She got in. The door slammed; she was in darkness.

She heard the corporal call, 'Drive on, fella,' and then, more loudly, 'Open them gates.'

The coach stayed where it was. 'Drive *on*.'

He can't get the horses to move. We'll stay here. All I have done is deliver an extra man to prison.

There was a crack from the whip that startled the horse into a canter. The coach jerked forward and rolled down the track at a rate which only just gave Diana time to lean out. She had a second's glimpse through the mist of a fat militia corporal walking ahead of a black prisoner towards the hut compounds. Then the coach was rocking out of the gates and into the road, a threat to everything on it.

She kept expecting to hear the prison bell clang the alarm. Almost she wished she could; she would never rid herself of the image of Tobias trudging purposefully into darkness.

The bell still hadn't rung; he would be in the segregated but now. '*All niggers look alike,*' he'd said. '*All niggers look alike.*' Not to me, she thought. Oh, not to me.

Sanders had been right; it was snowing, and with energy. They would never get home.

Three times they were stopped by patrols searching for escapers, three times the Dowager smiled and congratulated the men on their vigilance and three times they were waved on. Nobody looked at her coachman.

It was dark by the time they were beyond the town and they had to stop while Joshua and the Dowager worked out how to light the coach lamps. Joshua was in a state of guilt and misery. 'Why'd he do that? Why?'

'He wants you to go back to America and speak for him.'

'What's he want me to say? I don't know what to say.'

'You will.'

She had to kneel on the seat inside the coach to direct him but she made mistakes. Once they were out in deep country, she called on Joshua to stop and got up on the box beside him in order to watch for fingerposts and turnings. Even then, if the horses hadn't known the way better than she did, they might have ended up at Exeter. She became so cold that she thought she was dying.

Joshua reined in and rummaged through the box under the driver's seat. He found a flask of brandy Sanders kept there along with a huge tarpaulined driver's blanket, made her drink and covered them both before driving on.

When she recovered, he told her why he'd become alarmed. When he'd been thanking her for what she had done, she'd said: 'Thank *you*, Corporal Trotter.'

It began to snow again and they nearly passed by the signpost at the top of the hill but saw its pointing finger just in time. The horses took the bend fast, scenting a restful stable, warmth and hay.

Past Ralph Gurney's farm, past his labourers' cottages, the pine tree. Through thickening flakes of snow she could see the haze of light over the Pomeroy and the cottages. Where the candles of T'Gallants should have been burning high up on her right there was only darkness.

They've all gone to bed, she thought. I'll be getting in beside him in a minute.

The Pomeroy was busy. Lanterns in the stables showed Sanders and another man coping with horses and a coach—*two* coaches, and a covered wagon.

'Coaching inn, is it?' Joshua asked.

'Some travellers have mistaken their way,' she said wearily. There would be people, she was too tired to talk but she must give explanations, witness Makepeace's joy . . .

Sanders saw them and came running from the stables. 'Afore you go in, ladyship . . .'

'Help me down, will you?'

'Don't go in yet. But it's all right, the Missus has managed it all.'

She was bewildered. He steadied her to the ground and led her to the window giving on to the taproom, pointing.

She looked in.

Their lips pursed, their backs very straight, the Earl and Countess of Stacpoole sat by the fire, apparently and unwillingly listening to Zack who had drawn a chair up to theirs. Standing with his back to the mantel, neat as ever, was Captain Nicholls.

Chapter Twenty-three

'I told 'un there weren't nobody home,' Zack said, hobbling towards her. 'Nobody up at T'Gallants 'cepting Ma Green, I told 'un.'

'And Dell,' Makepeace said, coming up behind him.

'And the maid. Only her and Ma Green, I said.' Zack was winking at Diana and grimacing, emphasizing every other word like a bad actor. 'You'd gone to Plymouth like a Christian, I said. For to get that poor soul medickyments.'

Alice swept him out of the way. 'We have had the worst journey you can imagine, Mama. A risk to life, I promise you. We stayed with the De Veres at Exeter until the snow cleared a little and then with the Grantleys at Plymouth until it cleared again. Tabitha fell ill and I've had no lady's maid for a week. And to crown all no one at T'Gallants to let us in.'

She was replaced by Robert. 'We were anxious to see how you fared, Mama. Not well, I see.' He was reserved but not unkindly; apparently the rancour of their last meeting was behind them.

Then Captain Nicholls. 'I was so fortunate as to encounter the Earl and Countess on their way and offer my services in bringing them to you.'

'And *what* we should have done without you, Captain Nicholls . . . the weather and *such* wild country, *no* indication of where one is . . . and no one to receive us when we get here!'

A florid face from the past. 'My dear Lady Stacpoole, sit down, allow me to feel your pulse. As I feared, very fast.'

Kempson-Jones, who'd inflicted extra pain on Aymer in his last throes; it seemed no more strange that he had flown down from the moon than had the others. She couldn't get used to them; their beautiful clothes looked alien in the taproom as if they'd been lit for a stage performance. She had been put in the stalls of a theatre; she wanted to get up and go, the dialogue was frightening her.

'Dr Kempson-Jones was so good as to be prevailed on, Mama. We are worried for your health.'

Behind them ordinary people went on with the only life she could understand. She saw Sanders signalling to Makepeace and Philippa. He was taking them outside, into the forecourt. Where they will find something to their advantage, Diana thought, quite clearly.

She sat where she was put while arrangements were made over her head. They travelled heavy; there were servants, talk of how to transfer luggage, mattresses and linen from the wagon to T'Gallants—Alice liked to take her own bed wherever she went; Robert had brought his favourite cook.

'If you would give the keys to Tinkler, Mama, he will see to everything.'

She stared down at her belt and then unhooked her chatelaine and stared at Tinkler, concentrating, as he took it from her. Tinkler, Tinkler, second footman in her day.

It was so strange. When she tried to remember Chantries it seemed very small and unreal as if she looked through the wrong end of a telescope at a play of manners performed by miniature actors and actresses. Now the pygmies had grown very big and were crowding about her but they were no less unreal. Time was changed by the dramatist to quicken some events and make others slow.

Robert authoritative: 'No, no, you cannot go back to Plymouth tonight, Captain. Nor tomorrow, from the look of the weather. Once we are straight we shall be pleased to accommodate you at T'Gallants until the snow clears. Ah, the landlady. You have an extra guest, my good woman, the best for Captain Nicholls.'

Mrs Hallewell, bobbing. 'Yes, your lordship. We had another staying, but he's away now.'

'And these people?'

'Relatives, your lordship.'

Philippa taking her cloak to dry it, almost dancing. Makepeace kneeling before her, tenderly unlacing her boots.

Alice wondering how to reach T'Gallants with the bridge too unsafe for a coach, not considering walking.

And in the centre of it Nicholls, the dark maypole around which they all twirled, Nicholls saying nothing, listening to every word spoken and unspoken, Nicholls's eyes glancing at Makepeace, Zack, Philippa, but always returning to her face.

'She's tired. Can't you see how tired the woman is?' Makepeace's voice shrill and doing her no favours. 'Let her rest.'

Cold and snow and the bridge.

T'Gallants already lit and bustling with servants.

Dell, coming forward, curtseying: 'Her ladyship's maid, your lordship.'

'What happened to Joan?'

'Retired, your lordship.'

'Good Lord. Very well, look to your mistress; she seems unwell.'

Dell taking her away and the voice of Alice trailing behind them. 'Robert, have you ever *seen* such a face?'

He wasn't in her bedroom.

'Where is he? Where are they all?'

'Did it work then? Has he gone, that dear love?'

Her head cleared; she was back in real life—she recognized it by its tragedy. 'It worked. Don't cry, don't cry; you should have seen how happy he was. Be proud of him.'

They sat together on the bed, tightly holding hands.

'We got the men away,' Dell said, still weeping. 'Jack, the spalpeen, was at the back door telling me not to let them in—and them at that moment knocking at the front. I wouldn't have opened in any case.'

At that time, neither Dell nor the occupants of the Pomeroy Arms had known who the arrivals were, except that there were a lot of them. 'Searchers, I thought, and likely to have the door down.'

She'd run to the Great Hall and told the men to clear the place and hide in the shaft room. 'And for a wonder, they did it. They're there now.'

'Is Gil with them?'

'No, that's the worrit. He went down to the Pomeroy to wait for you. I'd told him what you and Toby were up to and the man was worried for you; never seen anger like it.'

'Is he there now?' Her brain began to work. *'We had another staying, but he's away now.'* 'No, no, he isn't. They must have hidden him somewhere.'

They sat listening to the invasion of the house: the grunt of men carrying furniture to the bedrooms; maids talking to each other as they scurried along the passage outside; the high voice of Alice downstairs, giving orders.

'Can they do this?' Dell asked.

'Yes. I told them I had leased the house; while I am in possession they can do what they like. I have no rights, you see. A woman has no rights.'

She made Dell lie down and settled herself beside her to wait. She was saved from complete realization of what was happening by the detachment of shock, a feeling that she was a helpless twig being rushed to disaster by the waters of Fate and that Fate might as well get on with it.

'They'll be putting the servants in the bedrooms on the sea side,' Dell said. 'Dear God, they'll be near the shaft room.'

There was sudden screaming and a kerfuffle from which emerged the word: 'Ghost.' Somebody had encountered Mrs Green.

'No, they won't. They'll put them in the attics.'

'Bless her.'

Gradually, after hours, the house quietened and then fell silent.

'Time to go.'

As they crept along the passage outside, Diana heard her son's snores coming from the bedroom two doors along from hers. Not what he's used to, she thought.

She could only identify the section of wall that opened into the secret room by the scuff mark from Ralph Gurney's boot. 'Bring a cloth up as soon as you can and get rid of that. Nicholls will prowl if he gets the chance. This is his opportunity.'

'God rot him.'

They didn't go in right away but opened the other doors along the shaft-room passage. They were empty; the servants had preferred the attics.

Diana looked in on Mrs Green's room. The woman was awake and shivering. 'It's all right, Mrs Green. My son and daughter-in-law have come to stay for a while.' She paused. 'There is no need to tell them what has been happening here.'

It was supererogatory, she knew—Mrs Green told nobody anything—but it was as well to say it. Beneath the woman's nightgown one breast was noticeably larger than the other; she took her dose of laudanum like a drowning woman sucking air.

Perhaps Kempson-Jones could earn his money for once, and do an examination. Dear God, take some of these burdens away from us.

Outside, they returned to the hidden door, manipulated the candle sconce and went in, closing the door behind them. Nineteen pairs of eyes and a pair of spectacles regarded them.

'Where's the chief?'

'It's all right, Bilo. He is hiding somewhere in the village.'

They had plenty of room in which they could all lie down; they'd managed to bring their palliasses with them, as well as their cards and dice, but they were huddled against the chimney wall to keep warm. The air was thick but presumably opening the door to the shaft for air made the room too cold. They can't segregate now, Diana thought, Bilo and Abell will have to work it out. Her money was on Bilo.

'Evacuation completed successfully, ladyship,' Lawyer Perkins said.

'Very good, Mr Perkins. Gentlemen, I'm sorry,' she told them, 'but, as you probably know, members of my family have arrived and you must realize they would not look kindly on the concealment of escaped prisoners of war. More than that, they are accompanied by a captain of the Revenue who would happily have you back in Mill-bay within the hour. I must beg you to be very quiet. We are trying to procure a boat to take you to France but until that comes, or my people go, you must put up with some hardship.'

'We ain't complainin', ma'am,' Abell said, 'but we sure is hungry, we ain't had no dinner.'

Dell said: 'Grand concealment that'll be, carrying nineteen trays through the house. This isn't St James's now.'

'It ain't? Boys, we must've took the wrong turning.'

'*Thought* we was lacking dinner napkins.'

They were in good spirits but feeding them was going to be a terrible difficulty. The Missus, Diana thought, I *must* talk to the Missus. She'll think of something.

'We'll do our best, gentlemen,' she said. 'In the meantime be patient and very, very quiet.'

Even opening the door to leave presented a danger. Suppose someone in the passage outside saw part of the wall give way? She opened it a crack and listened. Then she thought of another problem. 'Mr Perkins?'

He was beside her. 'Mr Perkins,' she whispered, 'how do you manage . . . calls of nature?'

'The shaft, ma'am. Same as we did in the Great Hall. Like Tobias told us.'

'Oh. Yes, of course.' Tobias had thought of everything. How would they manage without him? She dragged her mind away from what he would be suffering in his prison.

Outside, in the passage, Dell said: 'Will you rest now?'

'I need to see the Missus. I must.' Makepeace would know what to do.

'Rest first, I'll wake you before dawn.'

They went to Diana's room and slept in her bed together, too frightened and troubled to sleep apart.

The back door was locked.

'There must be spare keys.' Diana felt the onset of panic; people would be waking up and asking her where she was going—and she had to see Makepeace. 'There *must* be. Tobias opened up in the mornings and he didn't use mine.'

They searched the silent kitchen. It was better stocked than she had ever seen it; partridge, grouse and pheasant hung in the game cupboard; hams and sausages from the ceiling hooks; pies and tarts that had been packed in snow gently thawed out in the larder; the egg rack was full, so were the vegetable bins; on cupboard shelves stood preserves, potted beef and shrimps, crystallized fruits, strawberries in wine. The pleasant smell of yeast came from under a cloth where dough had been left to rise.

Alice had stocked up in Plymouth for her stay in the wilderness.

'D'ye think they'll miss this?' Dell was holding up an enormous pork pie.

'Probably, but take it anyway.' They started purloining bits of food: a jar of potted beef; a cut or two of salt fish; the remains of some capons; a big slice of cheese. They ran with them up to the shaft room, opened the door, threw them in and ran back.

Eventually, Dell found a spare set of keys hanging inside an aumbry door.

As they scampered down the hill, they heard an upstairs window open behind them. They ran the harder.

It had snowed hard in the night and was still snowing. Each roof, each chimney, was sprouting growing white fur that copied the shape beneath exactly. As they hurried past the lane, Diana saw that it was blocked. Whatever was going to happen was going to happen here; they were all locked in together.

Nearing the Pomeroy, Diana said: 'We can't go in. Nicholls will be up.'

'He'll be an early riser, sure enough, the bastard.'

They loitered in the stables, surrounded by the reassuring smell of grains and horse manure, waiting for Sanders to come and begin the day's work on the stalls.

'This is ridiculous,' Diana said. 'I am entitled to go into an inn. I am not to be hindered by a mere customs officer.'

But she didn't move. His stillness was the fulcrum around which all terrible things swung; she felt him watching her even when he was not there.

Ridiculous, ridiculous. Nevertheless, she stayed where she was.

Dell felt it, too. 'He's a Cyclops, rot him.'

'Argus, I think. Cyclops had only one eye.'

'I'd put 'em out for him, however many eyes the bastard has.'

It wasn't Sanders who came to see to the horses, it was one of the Chantries coachmen. Callender? Challenor? A pleasant-enough man, if memory served her right.

'Good morning, Challenor. Would you be so good as to fetch Mrs Hedley out here? Quietly?'

'Certainly, your ladyship.'

That was one thing about Chantries' staff; with Aymer as master they had learned not to blink at unaccountable behaviour by their betters.

When Makepeace came nobody spoke until all three had clambered into her coach and shut its doors and windows. They huddled for a moment, their arms round each other.

'Toby's . . .' Makepeace began and ran out of words because there were none. When she'd gone outside the inn last night and seen that it was not Tobias but Josh driving the coach, she had fallen on her knees in the snow in gratitude for the deliverance of the one and grief at the sacrifice of the other.

'Dell,' she said, 'I don't know what to say to you. Or you, ladyship.'

'He wanted to do it,' Dell said, dully. 'He sets high store by that lad of yours. And I'll be waitin' at the gate when he gets out. I'll wait 'til doomsday.'

It was too painful; Diana cut her short. 'There's no time, Missus. We have to get back. Where's Gil?'

'At Rachel Gurney's. There was just time to get him through the kitchen door. Lucky Maggie Hallewell recognized Nicholls or I'd have thought they were just travellers gone astray.' She grinned. 'Manners did for the pig. You could tell he wanted to march in ahead of the rest and find the place stuffed with contraband, but he had to wait for your daughter-in-law to go first and she was a trouble to get out of the coach.'

'What's to be done about the men? How are we to feed them? Missus, I don't know what to do.'

Makepeace reached over and patted Diana's knee. 'Don't worry about the men. We'll get 'em food. We've got the shaft.'

'No, no, you can't use it, you have no idea of the noise it makes. They'll hear it.'

'Not in the middle of the night they won't.' She leaned forward; she was pleased with herself. 'And I've got us a boat.'

Diana's eyes didn't leave Makepeace's face, absorbing reassurance from it. It's the freckles, she thought.

'A lugger,' Makepeace said, sitting back in expectation of congratulation. 'Costing me a fortune, mind—those Thurlestone men are bloodsuckers. She's free trading just now but they're expecting her back in a couple of days, *when*'—Makepeace stretched—'she will sail round to Babbs Cove by night, load our perishable goods and deliver them to France.'

'Oh, Missus.'

'I know,' Makepeace said, smugly, then frowned. 'And Andra had better be there, waiting for it.' The deliverance of Josh had raised hope that everything was possible. She said: 'The trouble is there wasn't time to hide Josh. One of his lordship's coachmen saw him. In the end I took him to the kitchen. I hope they'll think he's Toby's replacement.'

Which he is, they all thought.

After a moment, she went on: 'So, ostensibly, he's your man, ladyship. Does he stay at T'Gallants or here?'

Up at the house or here? Questions about who Joshua was and the whereabouts of Tobias would require explanations which, at this moment, Diana was too confused to frame. On the other hand, to leave him at the Pomeroy under Nicholls's eye . . .

Watching her, Makepeace saw a woman at the end of her tether. She patted her knee again. 'Leave it to me,' she said.

'Thank you. And, Missus . . .'

'What?'

'Keep Gil at Rachel's; he'll be better off there than in the shaft room. And when the lugger comes, *get him on it*. Say I'll meet him onboard, put him in irons if necessary, but make sure he sails. He won't want to go.'

'Why?'

'Because I shan't be going with him.'

There was a knock on the coach door. Makepeace flung it open. '*What?*'

'Her ladyship is required up at the house, madam.'

'Let 'em wait.' She banged the door shut but Diana reached to open it again. 'I must go. This looks so odd . . .'

Emerging from the coach-house, they found Nicholls in the forecourt. 'Good morning, your ladyship.'

He watched the two women head up the hill then turned and followed Makepeace into the inn for breakfast.

Zack was already in his place. He'd hobbled up from his cottage at dawn with the intention of supporting his friend, the Missus, through her time of trial. She'd been on tenterhooks last night in case he gave something away but he'd proved himself to be an older campaigner than she was in the war against the Revenue. Nicholls, wanting to concentrate on the night's undercurrents, had been driven nearly mad by tales of how smugglers—always from other villages, mainly Cawsand—had sailed rings round past preventives. Zack was an ally of worth.

Joshua, however, was still a recruit. Horrified, she saw that instead of helping Sanders, as he should, he'd sat himself down in one of the booths with a cinder from the fire and was drawing

Zack's profile on the wood of the table, frowning as he always did when the muse was on him.

She marched over, took him by the ear and ran him to the door. 'Noughts and crosses, is it? Get to the stables and start mucking out. You can eat later.'

She'd realized that he could only forget Tobias when he was painting or drawing; the rest of the time the burden of the man's sacrifice was almost too much for him to bear. He knew what it was like to be a black prisoner in Millbay. 'Why'd he do it, Missus? Why?'

'Not so you can be miserable the rest of your life,' she'd told him, briskly. 'Paint, boy, paint.'

He was a true artist. 'I can't paint to order,' he'd said, 'I can't paint what I don't see in my head, not even for him.'

'Then paint what you do see,' she'd said, gently. There'd be unfairness a-plenty to force itself on his attention when he got back to America. The country might be new; but humanity was old, old.

When she went back into the taproom she saw Nicholls had picked up his eating irons and was carrying them to a table by the window. As he passed Josh's booth he glanced down and paused, looking at the sketch.

'Excuse me,' Makepeace shouldered him aside and rubbed the table with her apron.

In the kitchen, Mrs Hallewell stirred porridge over the fire while Philippa cut newly baked bread and ham. 'How can we feed them all if the snow lasts, Mama?' She wasn't referring to the inn's guests.

'How do I know?' Makepeace said furiously. She took a ladle to the cauldron, dolloped some porridge into a bowl and spat in it. 'Give that to Nicholls.'

T'Gallants's kitchen was busy. Diana recognized the cook but neither of the maids; Alice changed her maids with her linen. 'Good morning, Mrs Smart. It's nice to see you again.'

'Good morning, your ladyship.'

'And these are?'

'Eliza and Kitty, your ladyship.'

'How do you do, Eliza, Kitty.'

'Your ladyship.'

'And this is Macklin, ma'am. What was lent to us at Lord and Lady De Vere's. For the heavy work.'

'Good morning, Macklin. Have you been with the De Veres long?'

Old habits died hard.

When she'd left them, she said to Dell: 'Why were they staring?'

'You came through the kitchen, for a start, and, if you'll forgive the saying of it, most of them are cleaner than you are.'

She was still in the dress and cloak in which she'd set out for Millbay with Tobias; they hadn't been improved thereby, and her best calfskin boots were ruined. She didn't want to imagine what her hair looked like.

'A bath, I think,' she said. 'Eliza and Kitty can start earning their money. Tell them I'll take it in my bedroom.'

'Can I get in when you're finished? It's months since I had a proper bath.'

'You can.'

The Great Hall was empty but voices and the smell of kidneys and bacon came from the mausoleum that was the dining room; the subject of the conversation was 'she'. Diana sidled nearer the door and listened.

'. . . a certain wildness,' Kempson-Jones was saying. 'I would not wish to commit myself further without more observation.'

'There is no doubt about it.' That was Alice. 'Just look around you; she is camping out in this place like an Egyptian. She wanders the Great Hall while she eats—oh, yes, Robert; there are crumbs in every corner. Did you see her *habillement*? This is not the Mama we knew, she was always so perfectly groomed.'

'I do not understand it.' Robert's voice was grave. 'I do *not* understand it. She has lost all dignity. Tinkler saw her running down to the inn earlier, hand in hand with that freakish new maid of hers. *Hand in hand*, mark you.'

'It is all of a piece with the way she has sided with your enemies, Robert.'

There was a nasty moment before Diana remembered that, for Alice, all Whigs and reformers were the enemy.

Robert, I was never your enemy. A cowed mother and now a supporter of things in which you do not believe, never an enemy. I loved you. I love you still.

But last night, when she'd recovered from the shock of seeing them all and had hugged him, he had moved away.

She heard a maid coming from the kitchen and went upstairs, smiling despite everything. She'd lost all dignity, eh? Lost all dignity and gained the world.

She gripped the balustrade. And soon to lose that.

She kept to her room most of the day, trying to catch up on sleep yet constantly waking from nightmares. But when she dressed for dinner, she did it with care and put on the same gown she had worn for her Frenchman. Whatever they put her through tonight, she would face it without the hypocrisy of mourning clothes.

Her appearance when she swept into the Great Hall was not commented on, though her daughter-in-law's eyes gave a roll towards Robert.

Alice withstood the shock of blue *turquerie* bravely, however: 'Mama, dear, we have invited Captain Nicholls for dinner. So useful in getting us here and soon to be knighted, he tells me, so we can hardly leave the poor man to the mercies of the inn. I thought we might play a little whist afterwards, and I know you do not care for cards.' Alice loved them.

Captain Nicholls arrived and followed the Dowager and her son in to dinner with Alice on his arm.

A refectory table and some rather beautiful Queen Anne chairs had been found among the furniture in the undercroft and were now rendering the awful dining room a little less awful.

Robert himself held her chair for her; she touched his hand as she sat down but he would not smile.

The meal itself was probably the best T'Gallants had seen in years. Alice had brought her own silver, napery and glassware and Mrs Smart, while complaining bitterly at the inconveniences of the kitchen, had risen magnificently above them. The Dowager, however, ate little and joined in the conversation even less, though most of it was directed at her in the form of questions.

'By the by, Mama, did you ever discover the whereabouts of your acquaintance's son? The Grayle person?'

'Thank you, Alice, yes. He is dead.'

'There you are then.' Apparently that finished the matter.

A little while later, a question she had expected from Robert long before: 'Mama, where is Tobias?'

'He left after I gave him his freedom,' she said, languidly.

Alice tutted. 'What did I say? What can you do with these people?'

Nicholls asked: 'Isn't that your negro at the inn? I thought it was.'

All niggers look alike. 'A replacement.'

'Well, I would not have employed another one,' Alice said. 'Ungrateful and cunning, I always said so.' And the conversation turned to the untrustworthiness of black servants and the wilfulness of the working classes in general.

What is Nicholls doing here? Be sure it was by design; Nicholls did nothing through accident. He was not courting her anymore, thank Heaven, but he was courting Robert and Alice; staring at them as if they were exhibits but being, for him, positively fulsome.

Kempson-Jones was watching her. 'You must forgive an old friend showing professional interest, ma'am, but should you not eat more? In this weather one needs fat on one's bones.'

Not as much as yours, she thought. And how dare *he* inveigle himself back into the household. She'd never liked the man—an antipathy that was now probably mutual since she had dismissed him without ceremony from Aymer's bedside after it had become apparent that the leeches, the blistering, and the Venice turpentine mixed with horse dung had been mere infliction of torture at a guinea a time.

She put him in his place: 'Perhaps you would employ your professional interest on my housekeeper, Doctor; she is very ill. Please look in on her after dinner.'

It was too cold for the men to linger in the dining room after the cloth was drawn. The three men and Alice took a card table near the fire and played whist.

Diana wrapped her shawl closer round her shoulders and perched herself on the sill of the wreckers' window, trying to see beyond her reflection into the snow-flecked darkness.

Dear Father in Heaven, allow Jan and the others to come home safely. But if that is not to be, send another boat and give my men, my man, passage to France. And look to Tobias in his prison. If you put a price on these things, let me pay it, however high. In the name of Jesus Christ, our Lord, amen.

Between hands, Alice complained of draughts. 'How you abide this house, Mama, I cannot think. So cold, so *grim*. I declare I could not sleep last night for unearthly sounds and whispers. I am certain it is haunted. And that *dreadful* old woman upstairs, she will murder us all in our beds before we can leave, I know it. Our rubber, I think, Captain Nicholls.'

'You are a most excellent player, ma'am.'

'I confess to surprise that you choose to stay here, Mama,' Robert called. 'Mama?'

Diana turned reluctantly. 'I'm sorry, Robert?'

'Why do you stay here?'

'I like it.'

She saw her son glance at Kempson-Jones before she turned back to the window.

They began another rubber and their voices resumed an unheeded, half-heard accompaniment to her preoccupation, like a string quartet played in another room. Alice's querulous *tremolo*, Robert's *viole da braccio* and the bland *sul tasto* of Kempson-Jones. It was only when Nicholls spoke that her attention was caught. She could not type his voice, it had the quality of producing silence, like the snow, deadening other sound.

'. . . over one hundred.'

'I thought they had been recaptured?'

'I fear not, your lordship. We are still hunting down some forty.'

Alice was squeaking.

He knows something, he knows.

'. . . a renowned smuggling area. I suspect the inn and the entire village.'

More squeaks from Alice.

'. . . John Paul Jones has been sighted.'

'Did I not say, Robert? I begged you not to expose yourself to danger. The villain will hear of an earl in an isolated house, you will be kidnapped, it will be the Earl of Selkirk over again and the rest of us murdered in our beds.'

'My dear, the Earl of Selkirk was not in residence and . . .'

Gratefully, Diana relaxed. Nicholls was *frightening* them. He thought the house was still theirs and, having failed to get T'Gallants by marrying into it, he was hoping to scare Robert into selling it cheap. Poor, bourgeois little man; he wasn't hunting, he was shopping.

You should have enquired of Mr Spettigue, Captain. It doesn't belong to any of us here, it's the property of the woman who served your breakfast this morning.

She saw her reflection smile and then stop smiling as Kempson-Jones's loomed up behind it. He addressed her indulgently as if she were a child. 'What is out there that pleases you?'

'Nothing.'

'Ah.' Again the exchange of glances between him and Robert.

He went back to the game.

Little shards of cold found cracks in the glass and penetrated the thick shawl. Outside the snow blew in gusts, sometimes allowing a glimpse of the cove, obliterating it the next.

Tinkler was beside her, bowing. 'Your ladyship, Challenor found this in the coach you were using last night. He asked me to give it to you.'

It was her portrait. She had forgotten it.

'What is that, Tinkler?' Alice, from the other end of the room.

'A painting, your ladyship. For her ladyship.'

Alice came bustling over. 'A painting? Let me see. My goodness, it is *you*, Mama. How unusual. Rather primitive, is it not?'

They all followed her, taking it in turns to hold the canvas at arm's length to the light, cocking their heads, commenting. 'It has caught you in a certain mood, Mama, no doubt of that.'

'The brushwork is good but, as the Countess says, unusual.'

Robert, very cold. 'Is this the famous portrait painted in prison?'

Alice, very high. 'In prison, Robert?'

'I did not mention it to you, my dear. George Grantley took me aside to tell me: my mother sitting for a black man in Millbay Prison.' Her son had dropped his reserve now. 'I wonder that did not get into the papers, like all the rest.'

'A black man,' said Nicholls, softly. 'An artistic black man.'

She told Tinkler to take the portrait to her room. They resumed their cards, she sat on at the window.

She was awake very early the next morning so that she could go to the kitchen and find food for the men in the shaft room. She took her holdall for the purpose. When she looked for Dell to help her, she found the Irishwoman's bedroom empty and there was no sign of her anywhere else. First she went to the Great Hall and looked out.

Nothing. Ice cliffs, ice fields and houses frozen into an ice-blue sky empty of birds, like a scene in glass; Babbs Cove seemed suspended in a space of its own. Sheep were a dun-coloured, immobile huddle in the pasture just below Ralph Gurney's farm. A tiny figure that could be seen carrying fodder to them along a track cut deep in snow was the only moving thing in the landscape.

She went to the kitchen. As she gathered up scraps and bread, taking a slice from this, a cut from that, so as not to leave gaps, she tried to work herself up into a fury that she was being forced into thievery in her own home.

Instead, she knew she was frightened; there had been something ominous about Nicholls, after all. Why the portrait had alerted him to something wrong, she could not imagine, but she had seen the change. By the time he'd left to return to the inn, he had reverted to being a hunter.

She put the food in the holdall and hurried through the sleeping house to the shaft room. The men were irritable from hunger and she didn't blame them—what she and Dell were managing to provide was little enough for twenty toddlers, let alone grown men. 'I am sorry,' she told them, 'but with luck the boat will come tonight. Just a little longer.'

She fetched them water and left to go to Mrs Green. Kempson-Jones had looked in on the woman and had diagnosed that she was dying—something Diana could have told him—and that there was nothing to be done but continue with increased doses of laudanum.

Alice, not an unkind woman, had instructed the two maids to take turns sitting with the patient and when the Dowager entered the room Eliza was dozing in a chair by the bed. Mrs Green was in a drugged sleep.

Between them, they saw to her. 'I will relieve you in a little while, Eliza. First I must go down to the village.'

'Ooh, your ladyship, you're not supposed to go out.'

'I beg your pardon?'

The girl was flustered. 'His lordship said. You was too poorly, he said, and to tell him if you wanted the keys to the doors. For your own good, he said it was.'

'Nonsense.'

She fetched her cloak, realized that nobody had given her back her chatelaine back, fetched the keys from the kitchen, unbolted and unlocked the front door—to see Makepeace hurrying towards her across the courtyard. 'Has anything happened?'

'Yes.' She was out of breath. 'Is there anyone about?'

'No. The maids were up with Mrs Green, so everyone is late rising.'

They went into the Great Hall and sat near the still-warm ashes of the fire. 'Is it Nicholls?'

'Partly. He's been questioning Josh, asking all sorts of questions:

where did he learn to draw, how long has he been in your employ, things like that.'

'What did Josh say?'

'Not much, you know Josh. I sent him off to the stables and gave Nicholls a piece of my mind but the bastard's suspicious, no doubt of that.'

'He's got instinct. He's like a dog. Missus, that boat must come soon. Is Gil all right?'

'Yes, Rachel's taken his boots away, but that's not the thing.' Makepeace took Diana's hands in both of hers and held them tight. She was very pale. 'You've *got* to sail with the boat when she comes. They're going to put you in a madhouse.'

Chapter Twenty-four

DIANA laughed. She said: 'It would be a rest after T'Gallants.'
Makepeace bounced their joined hands up and down in irritation. 'Sanders was drinking with Challenor late last night and he came and told me this morning. They're going to put you away. That's what they've come down for, to have you certified.'

'Servants' fantasies.' She was still smiling.

'Servants know things; you aristocrats talk in front of your footmen as if they were sideboards—I saw that when I was married to Philip. I tell you, they are going to have you put away.'.

Diana said: 'Dear Missus, listen to me. Robert wants me to live in the Dower House on our estate so that he and Alice may keep an eye on me; he's a man who wants everything ordered, and I have proved disorderly. That is what the servants have heard, if they've heard anything. It is why T'Gallants was sold over my head, so I would have nowhere to go but the Dower House.'

She raised Makepeace's hands and put them to her cheek. 'What Robert does not know is that he sold the place to you and that you are allowing me to stay on.'

'Are you sure?'

'Yes. It has been bad enough for his reputation to have his mother putting up hospitals for enemy prisoners, but I assure you that to have it known that she's in Bedlam would be worse.'

'What a noodle.' Makepeace appealed to Heaven. 'It wouldn't, don't you see? It would explain *why* you put up hospitals for prisoners.' She blew out her cheeks. 'What have they brought a doctor with them for then?'

The first twinge of doubt crossed the Dowager's mind. Why had they? With troubles coming from all directions, she hadn't questioned it.

She said, because it was true: 'Alice always fancies herself ill with this or that; she likes to have a doctor on hand.'

Makepeace didn't believe a word of it. 'Go to France with Gil anyway,' she said, earnestly. 'Have a happy life.'

'I can't.'

'I didn't believe it when you said that yesterday; I can't believe you're saying it now. Why *not*?'

So difficult. Diana got up and walked away from her to the wreckers' window. 'It would be dishonourable.'

Behind her, Makepeace sagged with frustration. 'He'll marry you. First chance he gets, he'll marry you.'

She turned round. 'I don't mind if he doesn't. Missus, if my marriage was virtue and Gil and I are sin, then the world is upside down. I am prepared to shout that from the dome of St Paul's itself.'

'What then?'

So *very* difficult.

'Dishonour's the wrong word,' she said. 'Betrayal is a better one. I failed Robert. What he is today is not just his father's fault, it is mine. How I could have done differently, I don't know, but I should have found a way. I failed him when I was a prisoner in that marriage and I've failed him since I've been free of it. Instead of the noble Roman matron he would have liked me to be, I have shamed him before his King and his party.'

And, Hokey, don't they need shaming, Makepeace thought, but she kept quiet. Let her talk it out; I'll find a way around this.

'I have associated with people and causes Robert despises, I've been what Shakespeare called a hissing and a byword. And, though my son wouldn't believe it, I've done it for his honour and the King's because they were *wrong*. Treating those prisoners as she did, England was dishonouring herself. She is still dishonouring herself by refusing to exchange the Americans.'

'Ye-es,' said Makepeace, cautiously.

'Eccentric, wild, mistaken, rebel, even traitor, they can call me all these things. The Tory press already has.'

'Ye-es.'

'The one thing they have not been able to call me with any truth is a whore. But the moment I run away with a Frenchman, our family is shamed forever. There would be jokes, cartoons; they'd sing songs. The Depraved Dowager, they'd call me. I have inflicted a great deal on my son, but I will not subject him to that. Don't you *see*? Worse even than that, the scandal sheets will say: "That is why she did what she did. She is merely a trollop; the hospital was her excuse to parade among naked men." '

She came down the Great Hall towards Makepeace, wagging the keys to the house, like a female St Peter sent to teach humanity manners.

'I will not do it, Missus. It would negate everything that has been achieved. John Howard would be made a laughing stock, called a procurer, his work set back years. Any woman raising her voice on behalf of men left to bleed to death on an earth floor would immediately be howled down.'

She stood over Makepeace for a moment and then went back to her window. 'I won't do it,' she said.

And she won't, Makepeace thought. She breathes a different air from other people.

Diana was looking at the stone-set floor of the Great Hall and seeing a battlefield dotted with strategic positions she had held and abandoned and which now, seen from the rear, had not been worth holding in the first place.

Pride in her family—lost. Honour and riches because a man had once waded in bloodied foam to rob the dying.

Faith in England's infallibility—lost.

Belief in the inferiority of other classes, other races—lost, and well lost.

Conviction after conviction lost, overrun by a superior and wiser army, until she was driven back to this redoubt. And this last ditch she would hold because to surrender it would mean that all she had learned in these last months, everything she had tried to put right for her country, would be soiled.

She could not live with that knowledge, even with a Frenchman who was more to her than her life. Tobias had given up his freedom in order to better the world; she could do no less.

'I won't do it,' she said again, quietly.

Makepeace thought: I don't know if she's right or wrong—thank God, I don't deal in principles, only people. But I've come to love that skinny piece of bloodstock over there and she must be saved from herself.

She said: 'You realize that what you and Gil have found together doesn't happen every day.'

'Yes.'

'And at our age especially, it's a gift from God.'

'Yes.'

'And he won't go without you.'

Diana looked up quickly. 'You've got to make sure he sails on that boat, Missus. Another spell in prison will kill him.'

Yours is going to be a different prison, Makepeace thought, but they'll shut you up in it—and it'll kill you, too. She got up and turned to the door. 'Well, all I can say is I agree with Robert, you're as mad as a March hare. Oh, hello, Robert.'

The Earl of Stacpoole stood in the doorway. She felt he was not pleased to see her. 'You have just taken my name in vain, madam. May I ask what you are doing here?'

She'd been looked down on by a lot of nobility in her life but not, she thought, by as big a piss-pot as this one.

'I've come to inspect my property,' she said. 'Now get out of my way.'

She pushed past him and went out.

Robert stared after her. When he turned round his jowls were streaked with red. 'That female bought this house?'

'Yes,' Diana said. 'That lady is Mrs Hedley.'

'And what was she doing here, may I ask?'

'She came to impart some servants' gossip. They say you are planning to commit me to a madhouse. Oh.' His face had changed; she was suddenly very cold. 'Oh, Robert.' She slumped down on the windowsill and buried her face in her hands.

He was blustering. 'Nonsense, Mama. It is not like that at all; of course you will not go to a madhouse.'

He advanced on her, reasonable and solicitous. 'My only concern is for you. You must see that your behaviour these last months can only be interpreted as deranged. I realize it was brought on by Papa's death but others . . . well, others, people I respect, our sort of people, have frankly called it mad.'

Yes, she thought. Mad people do not do what they are told, therefore if you do not do what you are told, you are mad. *Quod erat demonstrandum.*

The more he justified himself, the angrier he became. 'Perhaps you have not seen the papers lately. I can tell you the storm you have raised rages ever higher. Each time the matter of prisoners' exchange is brought up your name is mentioned, *our* name. Well, it must stop. I have done my best to persuade you, even forbid you, yet you have persisted. Dr Kempson-Jones is prepared to say—in court, if necessary—that for your own good—*your own good*—you must be restrained.'

He was squatting beside her now. 'I don't blame you, Mama. I blame the company you have kept. That person just now, my dear, surely you can see that she is not a suitable friend for you.' Gently, he took the keys from her fingers. 'I would prefer it if you did not go out and mingle with the people at the inn. Only last night I had to dismiss the creature you took on as maid—it appears she has been stealing food from the kitchens.'

The chatelaine jangled as he stood up. 'You must rest in your room now and when it has thawed we will take you home. Alice has found a nurse, a most reputable woman, who will stay with you in the Dower House until you are better.' He kissed her cheek. 'There, we will soon have our dear Mama returned to us, won't we?'

She nodded and, with the utmost tenderness, he led her out of the hall.

' "And lucky you are not to be prosecuted with full rigour of the law," ' Dell said in a fair imitation of the Earl of Stacpoole. 'I nearly told him, the number of times the law's paid me to get rid of its rigours . . . Anyway, he'll have that damn kitchen under lock and key by now. She'll never get food to the lads; they'll be famished.'

The women had to choose their moments to get together. One or other of the Stacpoole servants was always around. Even now, Philippa was sitting in the taproom playing cribbage with Zack, ready to warn the conference in the kitchen of any approach.

Outside the thaw was turning the air into grey gauze and it would soon be dark.

'When are those Thurlestone buggers going to turn up with that boat, that's what I want to know,' Makepeace said. 'We'll have to row food round tonight. Go in through the cavern and up the shaft. What do you say, Rachel?' They were the only strong rowers in the group.

'He's been up on the cliffs again,' Rachel said.

They joined her at the kitchen window. They could just see the dark blue figure coming down from the headland opposite T'Gallants and the stitching of footsteps he left behind him. 'He's got his bloody eyeglass under his arm. What's he been looking at?'

Makepeace said: 'He senses something's up, I know he does. I've stopped being relieved when he goes out. I'd rather have him here, under my eye.'

There was triumph in the taproom. 'Fifteen two, fifteen four, fifteen six and one for his knob and I won. Let's have another brandy, Maggie.'

'She lets 'un win,' Mrs Hallewell said. 'Well, that's one thing. Nicholls can't impound the brandy—Zack'll have drunk the lot.' She called, 'Coming,' but stayed at the window, watching.

Dell shuddered. 'Ladyship says he's a dog, he can sniff the air and smell people out.'

'He'd sniff twenty fathoms of saltwater if I had my way,' Rachel said. 'All right, we'll row round to the cavern tonight. Give me something to do.' Grief made her restless.

Makepeace was suddenly doubtful. 'Perhaps you should stay with the children. I'll go on my own. We might be caught.'

'Gil can stay with 'un. He's good with little 'uns.'

'How is he?'

'Fidgety. I told 'un, sneak into T'Gallants and you'll put her in danger. But I don't know how long that'll hold 'un.'

'You didn't tell him she won't be going with him?'

'Course not, never heard such silliness in all my life.'

Makepeace wiped her face with her apron and said again: 'When are those Thurlestone buggers going to turn up, that's what I want to know.'

Every time the tiny, wasted talon squeezed her hand at the onset of pain, Diana got up, poured some of the laudanum into a spoon and trickled it into the little gasping mouth.

Like a mother bird with a fledgling, she thought. Except that you won't get big and strong.

'Don't you be leaving me now,' Mrs Green had said, the last time.

'I won't.' There is nowhere to go; I would rather be with you. And even you are leaving me.

The world had narrowed down to this dour room and the skeletal little woman in its bed. Beyond was numbness. There were things she supposed she should be doing; seeing to the other suffering creatures in the shaft room, making arrangements, but she didn't have the will to do them.

She had challenged something too big for her. The establishment of England had looked down with its unwinking eye, seen the troublesome ant, lifted a colossal foot and crushed the life out of it.

You and me, Mrs Green. Two madwomen together.

There was a twitch on her hand. Mrs Green's eyes were suddenly bright and sharp in her skull, like a blackbird's. 'I'm paying, idd'n I?'

'No. My dear, you are only ill.'

'I'm paying.' There was another tug on her hand and Diana leaned down to bring their faces close together.

'I pushed 'un down the shaft,' whispered Mrs Green.

Diana leaned even closer. 'Good,' she whispered back.

The blackbird eyes widened in astonishment until the entire iris was exposed, then they crinkled. Wheezes came out of the mouth in what Diana was terrified might be penitential sobs, but Mrs Green was laughing.

Well, there goes my hope of salvation. She felt better for it.

She sat on, administering to the pain when it was necessary, through the ensuing sleep and the quiet death with which it finished.

In the end, it was considered best that Zack and Rachel should row the food round to the cavern. Makepeace had never handled the shaft platform whereas Zack and Rachel had helped to use it often while hiding contraband at T'Gallants at times when the Revenue had been expected to search the inn. 'Us can make that dang thing go up and down, quiet as a zephyr,' Zack said.

Makepeace was uneasy about it but Rachel said: ''Sides, they Stacpoole servants like ee.'

'That's because I buy them drinks,' Makepeace said.

'Well, buy 'un plenty tonight then. Make sure the buggers sleep tight.'

Diana, sitting at the wreckers' window, saw the darker shadow that was a rowing boat enter the thin gleam cast on the water below by the many candelabra with which Alice insisted the Great Hall should be lit to make it warmer and less forbidding. The long thin shape of the boat was there and then it was gone into the darkness, heading for the cavern.

The Missus, she thought, with love. You can depend on the Missus.

Makepeace would wait until the light was snuffed and then the men in the shaft room would be fed.

She hadn't dined with Robert and the others. Robert seemed to think she was sulking: 'Now Mama, we must start as we mean to go on. Dr Kempson-Jones says you must eat.'

But she had stayed without answering where she was at the window and eventually they had left her alone. When they finished eating, they came into the hall and began playing whist by the fire. She barely noticed their presence any more than she had their absence. They had moved beyond her mental pale; she was aware of them like encircling trees; as individuals she no longer found them interesting.

Nicholls had made Alice nervous by telling her something over dinner and was now reassuring her.

'You are perfectly safe, your ladyship. I walked to the coast-guard's hut today and sent a signal to Plymouth. I expect reinforcements tomorrow.'

Robert was behind her. 'I think it is time you went to bed, Mama, you look very tired. Kitty shall sleep in your room tonight—to make sure you are not disturbed.'

Rachel and Zack returned to the Pomeroy in a temper; Rachel, particularly, was raving, and had to be hushed in case they heard her in the taproom.

'Slipped into the cavern, didd'n us, and what was there when we got inside 'un? A Yankee and a Frog, bold as bloody brass, sitting on they bloody rocks dangling a home-made fishing line in the bloody sea. *And the cover to the cavern open, so's they could see by T'Gallants's lights.*'

Zack nodded. 'Strung the netting back they had, only a crack mind but still . . .'

It was too appalling for comment. Makepeace asked the only question worth asking. 'Had they moved the netting earlier?'

Zack nodded. 'Reckon they had. Them lads been up and down that shaft rigging all day, catching fish and crab and eating 'un raw. Said they was hungry.'

'I'll give 'un hungry,' Rachel said. 'They moved that bloody cover sure as eggs to give 'emselves daylight to see by. And now we know what Nicholls was looking at through his bloody telescope, don't us?'

Unaccustomed sea air made Alice tired. Though worried about being murdered in it, she was eager to get to her bed and did some prodigious yawning to prove it.

Nicholls, taking his cue, said good night and left for the Pomeroy Arms.

Alice retired. Robert and Kempson-Jones smoked a last cigar over their port before following her example.

Tinkler put a cover over the fire, snuffed the candles and went to bed himself.

Nobody at T'Gallants saw the moon cast a silver path over the sea from the Sound to Babbs Cove nor the tiny white dot that appeared in it.

Makepeace opened her bedroom window and dodged as another snowball hit the casement. '*What?*'

'Open up. Open *up!*'

In their beds, Philippa and Dell sat up. The three women had been sharing a room since the arrival of Nicholls and the Stacpoole men. As supposed relatives of Mrs Hallewell, they could hardly command separate accommodation in the face of paying guests.

'What is it, Mama?'

'Rachel. Somebody behind her . . . oh God, it's Gil.'

And Nicholls was asleep thirty feet away at the end of the passage. At least, she prayed that he slept.

They threw on shawls and wraps and went downstairs in their bare feet so as not to make a noise.

Rachel fell over the threshold in her haste to get in. 'They're *yere*, they've come, oh God bless 'un, there's a sail, a *sail*.'

'The lugger? Oh, thank you, Lord, it's the Thurlestone lads.'

De Vaubon limped in. 'It is not,' he said. 'She's too big for a lugger.' Quietly, to Makepeace, he said: 'Not the *Lark* or *Three Cousins* either.'

'Don't see nothing,' Dell said.

'There, *there*. Far out.'

'Warship.'

'Too small. And she keeps going about.'

Straining her eyes, Makepeace managed to make out a speck which might have been a mere sparkle of the moonlight except that, as Rachel said, it was slowly, very slowly, moving back and forth on the water.

'White sail, ain't it?' she said. 'Can't be a free trader then.'

'Revenue?'

'The bugger's *signalling*,' Rachel said in exasperation. 'Let me at that bloody lantern.'

She ran for the stairs, but Makepeace got there first. 'Quietly, girl, or you'll have to explain Gil to Nicholls.'

The inn door opened and the room went still, but it was Zack. 'There's a vessel out there,' he said.

Josh came in, smelling of the stable, where they'd made him up a bed in its loft.

'Does nobody sleep around here?' Dell asked.

'Let's hope Nicholls does.'

Everybody tiptoed up the creaking staircase and crammed into Makepeace's bedroom.

Rachel counted. 'Flash, flash. Pause. Flash, flash, flash. *All right to come in?* Thank ee, Lord, oh thank ee. It *is* them, it's my Jan.'

She picked up the lantern but Makepeace stayed her arm. 'They can't come in, Rachel.'

'Bugger to that, they're coming.'

'Rachel, they can't. Nicholls could wake up any time and see them. And if it *is* Jan he'll have goods on board.'

'Take 'un a long time to come in anyways,' Zack said. 'Tide's against 'un.'

Scrubbing the tears off her cheeks, Rachel began sliding the lantern's shutter back and forth. *Stay off.* 'But I'm bloody rowing out to 'un,' she said, 'Maggie's looking to the kids.'

'You're not going without me,' Makepeace told her. 'If it is Jan, he's maybe got Andra with them.'

'And me,' Dell said.

Makepeace patted her shoulder. 'You can't row,' she said. 'And who's to get the breakfasts if we're not back by morning? You stay.'

'What'll I tell them? Where are you supposed to be?'

Makepeace was at a loss. That Andra might be waiting for her beyond the cove drove every other thought out of her head.

'I'm coming,' Josh said, 'I'm the only one in a regular navy.'

'Mama,' Philippa said, quietly.

'Tell 'un Cissy 's having her baby,' Rachel said impatiently. 'She's due to pop any minute.'

Philippa pulled at her mother's sleeve. 'You do realize there may be danger. That ship could be anything.'

'Vessel,' Makepeace said automatically. 'Whatever that thing out there is, she ain't square-rigged.'

'Vessel, then. I wish you would not go.' The girl's face was as composed as ever but her eyes were stricken.

Makepeace laid her hands tenderly on her daughter's shoulders. 'Been worth it for you and me, hasn't it, Pippy? Bad as it's been.'

Philippa nodded.

'And you know if it's pirates out there, they'll be sorry once I get aboard.'

Philippa nodded again.

'Then you keep that lantern filled and guide us back in. And tell Nicholls we're birthing a baby. Something.'

De Vaubon came away from the window where he'd been looking out. 'Don't worry for the pirates, Philippa. I shall protect them from your mother.'

'*You* can't come,' Makepeace said. 'Not with your leg.'

'Damned if I go without it,' he said. 'And I tell you something. That boat out there? She is French.'

'I don't care if she's Chinee,' said Rachel. 'Are we going?'

They took the heavy longboat, Zack rowing with Josh, Makepeace with Rachel, de Vaubon taking two oars. Its bottom scraped loudly on the shingly sand as they pushed her into the water and they all glanced back at the Pomeroy, which remained silent.

As they went under the dark loom of T'Gallants, they heard a quiet cackle from Zack. 'Want to wave to your sweetheart, Gil?'

Makepeace heard Rachel muttering, 'Poor woman. John Paul Jones went after the wrong earl, I reckon. He could have this 'un, and welcome.'

Once they were in open sea, the moon seemed to shine on them as if it had picked them out for special illumination. The only sound was the quiet, rhythmic clunking of rowlocks and the hiss of blades. The tide was with them but Rachel was setting a rate that caused Makepeace to doubt whether she herself could keep up with it for long. It was over ten years since she'd rowed her small boat around Massachusetts Bay and she was no longer as muscular as she had been then. Or as young.

I'll get there if it kills me.

The heat from their mouths rose as steam into the air as they leaned back in a pull.

Andra. It was just possible. Might be.

She risked looking behind her and missed her stroke, making Rachel swear. They'd come a long way but there was as much to go again. She could make the boat out now even though it had lowered its sails. She'd dropped anchor. She was bigger than either the *Lark* or *Three Cousins*, bigger even than de Vaubon's *Margot*. A cutter, rigged fore and aft, very swift by the look of her.

And eight gun ports: sixteen cannon. She could blow Nicholls out of the water.

She prodded de Vaubon in the back with the toe of her boot. 'Recognize her?'

He looked behind him. 'A year ago I ordered a cutter like her from the Gruchy boatyard.'

'See!' Rachel said, rowing harder.

'Is that her?' Makepeace insisted.

'Perhaps. But I do not like the white sail.'

No smuggler worth his salt put his vessel under white canvas: it was too noticeable by night.

It could be, though, Makepeace thought. And Andra could be aboard.

The wish was so intense she became angry.

I've never been first with him, never. Put me beside some alchemist with a plan to stop fire-damp and see who he'd choose. Blast him, he was so . . . admirable. His miners had better housing, better pay, better conditions than any in the North-East.

And who was the first down the mine with a dog on a long leash to check for gas? Never a thought for her and his children if he blew himself up. Haunted by the death of his brother, shredded by an explosion years before.

Dear God, he was a lovely man.

The skin was coming off the cushions of her palms; she arched her hands so that she could keep on rowing. And, blast him, he was a magnificent lover. Oh, Andra.

A hail came over the water. 'Who are you?'

Rachel gave a sob of gratitude. 'Who d'you bloody think?' she called.

Boarding nets came rolling down the cutter's side. Men were clambering down to help them up. Makepeace saw Rachel and Jan Gurney entangled in netting and each other before somebody's helpful hand under her backside hoisted her over the side onto the deck.

The mast lantern swayed in the gentle swell so that light swept over a bewildering press of faces and then left them. Somebody, she thought it was Eddie Gurney, was shaking her hand; an unknown Frenchman was kissing her on both cheeks; de Vaubon was being embraced by other Frenchmen; Zack was chattering to his grandsons . . .

'Howay, pet,' said a voice behind her.

She stood where she was. 'Where've you been, you *bastard*?' she said and heard her husband laugh. Then she turned.

A grim, stocky man, like a pugilist with his breadth of shoulder and his broken nose. Curly hair grizzled at the edges, dark eyes set deep under black eyebrows. Whatever the quality of his coat it was always reduced to the same shape by papers, tools and plans stuffed into the pockets, as they were now.

One part of her mind asked what all the fuss was about, even while her breath was snatched away. She wanted him so much she dare not touch him.

'Got the cure for fire-damp yet?' she asked him, nastily.

'Na, pet,' he said, 'but we're nearer doon the road to findin' it.'

'And the Paris women are pretty, I suppose?'

'Bonniest I've evor seen,' he said, 'but there wasn't one it'd be etornity to stay away from.'

'Like me.'

'Like you.'

What was it about him that could melt her into liquid? 'I've missed you so much,' she said. 'We've got ourselves in a fine old mess without you.'

She leaned her head against his shoulder and felt his arms go round her. He was here. He would manage things now; he always did.

Jan Gurney came up to hustle them below for a conference. 'Dear goodness, what you women been up to? Got your voolish selves into a might of trouble, seemingly.'

'Voolish?' she said, happily. 'Who're you calling vools? Where've you *been*?'

Rachel, euphoric, slapped her husband hard and asked the same question.

Men were left on watch while the Babbs Cove contingent went below, fitting themselves round the long table in a cabin that smelled of new wood and bilge. Light from a single overhead lantern showed tired, russet Devon faces. Jan Gurney broached one of the barrels lashed in tiers to the bulkheads, and beakers were handed round so that the company could drink to its reunion in brandy of horrific proof.

Jan had aged. 'We lost the *Lark* and the *Cousins*,' he said. 'And Davy Salmon and Tommy Crabbe and young Sammy Kingcup.'

Rachel's eyes closed tight.

'Storm it was, done for *Cousins*. Just out from Cherbourg. Sleet and snow come on sudden. Never seen the like of 'un. Blow, blow, blow, fit to tear your hair off, swept young Sammy overboard—he were gettin' down the tops'l. She started to fill. We got all the rest off somehow—an' if ever there were a miracle, it were then. *Lark* weathered the point.'

He looked across at de Vaubon. 'That's a wicked coast of yourn, Gil.'

De Vaubon nodded.

It had been an appalling storm and appalling luck. They'd glimpsed the light at Gruchy, always kept burning by de Vaubon's retainers for their master's return as well as the smuggling fraternity they served, but as *Lark* was about to drop anchor she was holed beneath the waterline by a mast from a vessel wrecked further down the coast.

'Worse nor a bloody batterin' ram,' Jan said. 'Started sinkin' there 'n' then we did, and I thought it was up with the lot of us but your Gruchy lads, Gil, they got us a line and we went ashore one by one holdin' on to the bugger. My soul, I never seen waves like 'un.'

That was when Davy Salmon and Tommy Crabbe had been swept away.

Eddie said: 'Found 'un both two days later when the wind dropped, lyin' in deep water just outside the harbour. Strangest sight I ever did see, you could tell their faces as they lay on the bottom, it was that clear.'

'In your churchyard now, Gil,' Jan said.

A swing of the lantern showed their faces and compassionately hid them again. Rachel shook her head, spraying tears. 'How to tell Sammy's ma, I don't know.'

'How to tell any of 'un,' Jan said, heavily. 'Nor how to tell Ralph us've sunk both the bloody boats. That's us ruined.'

They'd been marooned in a country at war with their own. It

could have been worse; they were in a lonely area and sheltered by people of their own kind who would no more have dreamed of giving them up than would Babbs Cove if the position had been reversed. The European union of smuggling kept them safe—but boatless.

'So you took my nice new cutter,' de Vaubon said.

Jan looked at him. 'It was either that or take out French nationality. I ain't saying your Norman maids ain't pretty, but, well, Rachel may be a ugly old crow but I'm used to 'un.'

Rachel hit him.

They'd had to wait, Jan said. The cutter was still being built—under difficult circumstances. 'If King Louis'd seen 'un, he'd have commandeered her for his bloody navy. Boatbuilders mostly had to work o' nights.'

'Bloody cold it was, too,' Eddie said. 'They couldn't use the metal without the skin came off they bloody hands.'

'Then Andra turns up,' said Jan. 'Tells us he's married to the Missus, and can we help 'un.'

'More like he helped us,' Eddie said. 'Wunnerful with his hands, Andra. Got that bloody mast stepped in a lick.'

Makepeace patted her husband's hand. The honorary smuggler. Send him anywhere and he fitted.

It hadn't been easy to persuade the Gruchy people, complaisant though they were, into allowing Englishmen to sail off with their master's brand-new boat. 'Some of 'un's come with us, Gil, to help ee sail 'un back and see we didn't steal 'un,' Jan said. 'We couldn't let 'un wait to tan the sails. Nor christen her.'

It was a measure of the Devonians' desperation and courtesy that they had set sail for England in a nameless, and therefore unlucky, boat. But to christen her themselves meant de Vaubon would have been stuck with what they called her for all time; changing a vessel's name was the unluckiest thing of all.

Jan had finished talking. What he and his men had endured: their losses; the weeks of frustration and waiting, being hidden from the watchful eye of French authorities; the long and arduous tack home in bitter weather—the account of these things would have to wait.

'So our women been acquiring men, seemingly,' he said, looking around.

Makepeace's and Rachel's account of the situation at Babbs Cove took longer, and the discussion on what was to be done about it longer yet.

As she talked, Makepeace realized that she might have expected disapproval, even anger, from these men on hearing that their wives and daughters were helping to conceal twenty-one runaway prisoners of war.

There was none. Surprise, some jokes showing slight sexual suspicion, perhaps, but no condemnation. It was accepted that their women had become enmeshed in the Missus's and Ladyship's concerns as much as she and Ladyship had become enmeshed in their women's.

As for helping de Vaubon, their mutual past was so entangled with favours done and received that there could be no accounting of who owed what to whom in the generalized debt. It would be another venture in the chore of their lives. Dealing in contraband, outwitting the Revenue, overcoming their greater enemy, the sea: this was everyday business to them. The abnormal was their normality.

Flip a metaphorical coin with the King's head on it, Makepeace thought, and on the obverse you would find the face of Jan Gurney, or Zack, or Eddie, or any of them, men who felt as free to break the law as the great landowners of England considered themselves free to make it.

Muscled arms gleamed bronze in the lantern's swing. Callused hands, hard features, were illumined and darkened. Josh, sitting on Makepeace's other side, was tracing cut-throat silhouettes on the wood of the table in spilled brandy. Without thinking, she rubbed them out with her sleeve.

But he's seen it, she thought; Josh always sees. These men could kill if it came to it. Given the choice between killing and capture, they'd kill.

The question was: If they were resisted by one of their own; if one of their women, say, was disobedient, mutinous, displeased them, would they dub her mad and condemn her to the long death of confinement? Or was that a refinement only of England's ruling class?

That was the question and it was time to ask it.

Chapter Twenty-five

KEMPSON-JONES certified Mrs Green's death as natural and returned to his breakfast.

Diana remembered that there was a process called laying-out which must be gone through; when Aymer died a woman had been fetched from the nearest village to perform it.

'Can you lay people out, Kitty?'

'No, I can't, ma'am. It ain't my place.'

'Run down to the village and ask Mrs Hallewell at the inn if she knows someone who can do it.'

The girl was flustered. 'I can't, your ladyship.'

'Why not?'

'I'm not supposed to leave you alone, your ladyship. In case you need anything, like.'

It had begun; she had acquired a keeper already.

'Then ask the Countess to come to me here. One presumes you can leave me alone while you go downstairs and up again.'

She was putting on the old disguise, she could feel it stiffening on her face, hear her voice adopt boredom. Dignity was the only resource they'd left her.

Not again, she thought. I can't go through it again.

Alice was surprisingly helpful. 'I'd forgotten the poor soul was still lying here. Presumably there's someone in the village who can build a coffin and make the arrangements. I suppose it is for us to pay for the funeral.'

'I suppose it is. Zack Lewis in the village can turn his hand to everything. He would know who could lay her out.'

'I'll get Tinkler to send for him. He can do the measuring or whatever it is one does.' Alice looked at the sheeted figure in the bed and shuddered. 'Where do we put her?'

'The undercroft, I suggest.'

It was a normal exchange and Diana was grateful for it; everyone else—the servants, Robert, Kempson-Jones—now treated her with the cautious solicitude accorded to the very young, the very old and the witless. Alice would support Robert's intention to make her behave, verbally agree with him that she had lost her mind, and yet, deep down, retain the old resentful admiration for her mother-in-law and know it to be a stratagem.

She thought: I am becoming thankful for being treated as a normal human being.

Run away. Go to de Vaubon, take one of the rowing boats and set off for France. If we die at sea, it cannot be worse than this.

Yes, it would. Survival would be worse. You would have to live with what you had done, the abandonment of your last ditch of honour. Her decision had been right; she *knew* it was right. She just wondered how she had been able to overcome its pain sufficiently to deliver it in reasoned, consecutive sentences.

Kitty had to follow her down to the undercroft when Tinkler and Challenor took the body down there and wait, shivering, while she saw it was properly disposed.

Dawn had hardly deserved the name, being merely a lightening of black into grey; the thaw had brought fog which pressed against the house like a besieging enemy and made the undercroft more eerie than ever.

The body was put on a table, covered with one of Diana's shawls and a candle left burning at its head. Under the low-vaulted ceiling, the impression was of a catafalque and Diana was reminded of her introduction to the late Mr Henry Hobbs.

Kitty saw the smile and widened her eyes; the Dowager's madness was being confirmed by the minute.

T'Gallants was afflicted by unease. The fog gave a vagueness to the candles that had to be lit everywhere; some sounds were intensified, others misdirected so that it was difficult to identify them.

There was no point in staring out of a window into nothingness, nor could she do anything for the prisoners in the shaft room, dogged as she was by Kitty. Diana went to her room in order to try and read, putting her trust in the Missus to see the men fed tonight.

No boat from Thurlestone, from anywhere, could risk the narrow entrance to the cove in fog like this. Bilo and Abel, Totes and Laclos would have to endure each other's company another day.

'If you wish to be sure of me, Kitty, you may lock me in.' The girl kept fidgeting.

'No call for that, your ladyship, I'm sure.'

'Then employ yourself outside the door.'

A bored and anxious Alice joined her. 'The entire French fleet could be in the bay this minute and we should know nothing of it.'

She hovered over Diana's dressing table, taking bottles and vials out of the *étui cosmétique*, studying them and putting them back again—an exercise that caused a nerve to twitch in her mother-in-law's cheek. 'Orange flower water, I see . . . hmm . . . when we are back at Chantries you shall have some of my Suave. It is more up to date.'

'When is it your intention to leave?'

'Tomorrow, if it clears. Challenor is uneasy about travelling in fog on these out-of-the-way roads. So easy to miss the route completely. I think you would find *pomade à baton* easier to apply than the oil, if I may say so.'

Tomorrow. If I went to Robert, begged him: give me a keeper, set a guard, but allow me to stay. I would at least have the village, Rachel, Zack, people I could talk to about him. Aeneas might sail away but Dido could live on with her memory of him in her draughty, damp, enchanted house.

'Is Nicholls coming to T'Gallants again today?' She dreaded leaving the place empty for him to conduct a search that must inevitably uncover the shaft and the men in it.

'Later,' Alice said. 'He has taken a rowing boat out this morning to examine the cliff below the house. I suppose customs officers have to go out in all weathers.'

Diana's head went up. 'Why?'

'It is their duty, Mama.'

'Why is he examining the cliff below the house?'

'Apparently, he thinks that when he was on the headland opposite yesterday he saw a cave on this side that he had not seen before. He so concerned me on the subject, I could only peck at dinner. I said, "Would smugglers be using it, Captain?" And he said, "Perhaps." '

He had found it. She didn't know what had led him to it, but at this minute he was rowing through the tiny gap in the rock that led to the cavern. He was looking up, seeing the shaft . . .

'Mama!' Alice was concerned that she had gone too far in disseminating alarm. 'Don't look so frightened. It is unlikely that there are smugglers in the cave this moment . . . I cannot understand why the captain should think there are . . . They are not a threat to us up here. Robert says so. Captain Nicholls walked to the coastguard hut yesterday and signalled to Plymouth to send men. They will be here today, he says. And Robert has called for his fowling pieces to be got ready in case . . .'

She couldn't move.

I don't know what to do, I don't know what to do.

'Come, Mama, we must be brave. Oh dear, I should not have mentioned it, Robert said I should not tell you in your weakened state. But perhaps now you will see how easily one courts disaster when one steps into the commoners' world. It will be a lesson to you. Mama, I beg you . . .'

The Dowager had stood up suddenly and was looking down at her. If ever Alice had seen a madwoman it was at that moment.

Then she had gone out of the door. Kitty, who had been standing outside it, was flung aside.

She would not give way. The Missus would not give way, nor would she. There was still time. Blast and bugger Nicholls's eyes, he should *not* have them, not Gil, not any of them.

A boat, that was it. Tell Missus and the others. Get them to take a boat to the cave. Be ready. In this fog they can row the men away, anywhere, anywhere, Thurlestone. I shall go to the shaft room and start evacuating them, that's what I shall do. Start evacuating them. The platform will be heard but it doesn't matter, it is all over in any case. That's it, that's it, send the biggest men down first. If Nicholls stops them they can throw him into the sea.

The front door was locked and had no key in it.

She strode into the kitchen. Tinkler was in there with the cook. 'Where are the keys to the front door?'

'His lordship said—'

She picked up a bread knife from the table. 'Give me the damn keys.'

Tinkler handed them to her and she took them to the front door and unlocked it.

Nicholls was coming up the steps, smiling. 'Your ladyship really should not be venturing out in this weather.' He took her arm and led her back inside.

Makepeace was watching the clock. 'Are we going to live through this day, Andra?'

'Reckon we will, pet. The Frenchie's the one taking the biggest risk. But tha's not coming. Nor Philippa neither. Lasses stay here.'

He was the best of husbands but there were still things she had to fight for. She said: 'It started with me and I'm going to see it through.' She kissed his ear. 'You know I had to get Josh out of Millbay.'

'Ay, you did. Let's hope the experience comes in handy getting the two of us out of the Tower.'

She'd won.

'The three of us,' Philippa said.

'God save us from independent women,' said Andra.

And God save men who let us be independent, Makepeace thought. She looked at Philippa and realized how hard it was to relinquish the power to protect. 'Just stay in the background, that's all,' she told her.

'Now then.' If thing did go wrong, she had dispositions to make.

She turned to Dell. 'There's a letter to Mr Spettigue on my table upstairs—just in case. Maggie Hallewell's selling me the Pomeroy and I'm putting it in your name. Toby'll make a good landlord when he comes out.'

'Missus . . .'

'It's a little present,' she said, firmly. 'A thank you for Philippa. Oh, and Andra and I have decided to go into the free-trade business. We're buying a boat for Jan. Try and recoup our losses; freeing people is a very expensive business.'

Young Jack Gurney put his head round the door. 'Just beaching the boat he is, the bugger. He's alone. Reckon he's left the other two in the cavern.'

'Thank you,' she said, 'and you watch your language.' She went up to Josh who hadn't taken his eyes off her all morning, as if engraving her on his mind for later. 'Have you got the pasties? It'll be short commons 'til you get to France.'

'I got 'em, Missus.'

'He'll press you, you must look scared. Don't smile, whatever you do.'

'I won't, Missus.'

'And when you get to Boston, look up Sam Adams. He'll help you get set up. Give him my love. You've got the money belt on?' She couldn't think of anything else and started picking lint off his coat.

'I love you, Missus.'

'Don't, don't. I love you, too. Betty would be so proud of you.' She clung to him for a moment, then wiped her eyes to look over his shoulder at the clock. 'Better be getting ready.'

The entire household had to assemble in the Great Hall.

'Is this necessary, Captain?' Robert disliked drama, especially in front of his servants.

'It is. Somebody in this house is a traitor and I do not want him'—he looked straight at Diana—'or her alerting the enemy before I am ready.'

'Enemy?'

'Yes.'

He looked at Diana again. She saw total victory in his face and knew there was total defeat in hers. Her legs were giving way. She moved to the throne-chair and sat in it, gripping its arms so that she could sit upright to face what was coming.

'With your permission, your lordship, I have appropriated Challenor and your other coachmen. For the moment, they must regard themselves as Revenue men. I took them with me in the boat and they are in the cave now awaiting my instructions.'

The rest of the staff had lined up with Macklin against the far wall; Kitty and Eliza scared, but with their hands politely clasped; Mrs Smart cross and protesting that she had bread in the oven; Tinkler hovering, like the good footman he was.

Alice, now genuinely frightened, gripped Robert's cuff in her little plump hand.

'Did you collect all the arms you have?' Nicholls asked.

Robert pointed to the pile of pistols and fowling pieces stacked by the oriel window.

'Break them out, if you please. Those two men to be armed.'

'Captain, I shall do nothing until you explain yourself.' Robert was trying for control but losing ground to Nicholls's command.

'Very well. I believe there to be men hidden in this house.'

'*Within* the house?'

'Yes. They may be smugglers, though I believe it more likely they are escaped prisoners from Millbay.'

'That is impossible.'

Nicholls strode across to where Diana sat and stood in front of her. Everything had combined for him; his career was to be enhanced; this representative of the family that had tormented his mind all his life was about to be destroyed.

Not *in* control, she thought, looking at his eyes, out of control.

He spoke to Robert but he regarded Diana. 'There is a negro at the inn who draws with skill,' he said. 'Her ladyship had her portrait painted by a negro of equal skill. What odds would your lordship give against two artistic black men cropping up within the same ten-mile radius? He is an escaper and I suspect that there are others'—he leaned forward—*'who have been succoured by a resident of this very house.'*

She was the link between T'Gallants and Millbay; he knew it could be nobody else. She looked back at him, expressionless.

He turned round; he was having a lovely time. 'Yesterday, I saw a cave in the cliff below this house where previously there was no cave. Believe me, your lordship, I have sailed in and out of this cove too many times to have overlooked it.'

Robert inclined his head. 'I am sure you have, Captain.'

'This morning I took a boat to examine closer and I found that it had been concealed, cleverly, by a drape of netting woven with gorse, almost impossible to distinguish from any other section of overgrown rock. Yesterday it was out of position, which was how I saw it. Today it was weighted in place and, though I knew it must be there, I had difficulty finding it. You understand me, your lordship? Somebody had put it back.'

'But it's still just a cave,' Alice pleaded.

'No, it is not. It is a cavern with a vertical tunnel, a shaft, leading upwards from its roof directly through the foundations of this house.' He was suddenly in a hurry. 'A measure, I need a measure, Tinkler. And a plumb line.'

Without a glance at Robert, who didn't even notice the *lèse majesté*, Tinkler left the room to do as he was told.

Robert was still challenging evidence he did not want to admit. 'These ancient houses are often riddled with tunnels and hidden rooms, Captain, priest holes and suchlike. There is no reason to suppose someone is using it to enter T'Gallants, there has been no sign . . .'

'There is. There are droppings in the cave.'

Robert's nose went higher; this was becoming not only alarming but unpleasant.

Kempson-Jones said, 'Could it not be birds?'

'These do not come from birds. These are human, a considerable amount, suggesting many people. And fresh, very fresh.' He looked down at his boot.

He stepped in it, she thought hysterically, he stepped in it.

Tinkler came back with a measure, a ball of string and a fire-iron.

'Very good,' Nicholls said. 'Now, break out the arms. *Now*. I have left my pistol in the cavern with Challenor.'

The Great Hall became a war room, filled with the smell of gunpowder and the click of ramrods as they were pushed down barrels. Kempson-Jones was quicker than the rest, he held out a musket to Robert, who shook his head. 'I must be convinced first.'

Nicholls had opened the wreckers' window and hung his line from it, positioning it by some point he could see below; he kept consulting his cuff which had measurements written on it. 'Yes, yes, here or next door. This floor? Perhaps the undercroft.'

For the first time Nicholls the Obsessed became apparent to everybody in the room. He had snatched the tape from Tinkler's hand and begun crawling along the floor with it, looking at his cuff and back to the measure.

Kempson-Jones and Robert exchanged glances. Robert put his arm round Alice. 'Captain . . .' he began, and then fell silent.

Nicholls didn't hear him. 'The chimney, it must come off the chimney.' He picked up a poker and began tapping the blackened stones of the fireplace, the flames reflecting red on the pale skin of his face. 'Clear this grate,' he said. 'I want this grate cleared.'

Diana had a feeling of *déjà vu*, a suspension of time as if she were present at something she'd seen happen before without remembering what it was. He will find it, she thought, quite calmly. He is as excited as if he were making love; this is sex to him.

He crawled on towards her and then looked up and met her eyes. She sat still. You kept very still before animals with bared teeth.

There might have been no one else in the room for him; he looked at her hand gripping the arm of the throne-chair and his face became gentle.

'Yes, I know,' he said, as if she'd told him something. 'There is a chair like that at Dartmouth. Get away from it.'

It was almost an expression of love.

She didn't move.

He stood up. '*I said get away from it.*' He pulled her to her feet and swung her so that she staggered.

'Captain!' Robert protested.

He'd gone down on his knees again, pulling the rug away. 'Do you see? See here?' His fingers traced the scratch marks in the stone like a beloved's skin. 'Now then.'

He sprawled on the floor to explore the chair legs. Nobody else moved.

'Yes. *Yes.*' He'd found the bolts. He got up, dusting his hands and knees, then positioned himself so that he stood with his back to the wall by the chair, his hand on its arm. He swung it outwards, not looking behind him, watching their faces like a fairground magician waiting for applause. 'And that is how it is done.'

They stared at him, they stared at the black rectangle behind him. His smile widened.

'Let us see what we shall see,' he said and turned to the hole to call down it. 'All right, Challenor, raise the platform.'

Makepeace and Philippa, tightly holding hands, walked out of the door of the Pomeroy Arms with Josh beside them and began the march up the hill to T'Gallants, with a gun trained on their backs.

I could ram the chair at him, Diana thought.

Nicholls had his left hand on the rear of the chairback and the right hand flat on the wall on the other side of the shaft entrance, supporting himself as he leaned forward into the hole.

She envisaged his two sets of fingertips as they were squashed, one above the chairback, the other making tiny sausages against the wall. She would ease the chair away then, releasing the broken fingers, and he would fall.

The ropes began to move in the shadows of the shaft; they heard the deep rumble of the platform coming up. Nicholls put out a hand behind him. 'A light, if you please.'

Robert shook himself as if from a dream, took up a branched candlestick and put it in Nicholls's hand.

Nicholls stepped onto the platform, holding the light high. When he spoke his voice was distorted by echo and happiness. 'There is a room up there. I see the door.' There was a sudden flare of flame as he held the candelabrum downwards. 'And another down there, on the floor below.'

She had reached the level beyond which terror loses its effect. Would he shoot them? No, he'd left his pistol with Challenor down in the cavern. Perhaps they would kill him. I beg you, God, don't let anybody kill anybody.

'Lower away.' He was drifting downward; he was going to try the undercroft first as the more likely hiding place.

Her body seemed to be bloodless; she was very, very cold.

The Great Hall had become a gallery of sculpted figures in which nothing moved nor, it seemed, even breathed. They could hear the faint sigh of sea against rock. Outside the windows, the fog drifted more purposefully than it had—a light breeze was getting up. A seagull yelped, seeming a long way away.

Nothing continued to happen. Mrs Smart looked anxiously towards the kitchen from which the smell of baking bread was becoming very strong. Alice decided to collapse and Eliza had to light a taper from a coal and waft the charred end under her mistress's nose.

Squinting, Macklin started aiming his fowling piece at the stone apples carved into the ceiling and Tinkler took it away from him. Robert's foot tapped.

After a while, he went to the shaft. 'Have you found anything, Captain?'

The reply came back garbled by distance. 'Nothing.'

Robert grunted. 'Didn't I say?'

Tinkler said, almost to himself: 'He's still got to try up top.'

The platform was coming back up the shaft. They waited to see Nicholls transported past the hole and up.

Instead, the platform stopped at the Great Hall level. Nicholls lurched out of it with a gag in his mouth, his hands tied at his back and de Vaubon behind him, pushing a pistol against his spine.

'*Allons.*' The platform began a descent.

'Good afternoon,' de Vaubon said, over Nicholls's shoulder. He looked around the room. Tinkler was still holding Macklin's fowling piece. 'Put down the gun or I shoot this one where he stands.'

Tinkler stood for a moment, looking at the weapon in his hands as if he hadn't seen it before, then knelt down and placed it on the floor.

'Move away from it,' de Vaubon said.

Tinkler moved away from it.

Weakly and very slowly, Diana edged to the wreckers' window so that she could hold herself up against a mullion.

Only then was there a reaction. It was Alice's. '*It's John Paul Jones!*'

De Vaubon tutted. 'Madame, please. I am French.'

He shifted so that Nicholls's arms were hooked backwards in one of his own. 'All of you to that wall.' He waved the pistol towards the oriel window.

He's come for me. She couldn't think of honour, of country, of anything. They had done that for her with their doctors and their keepers, their locked doors; they had left her the only option: to go with him. I can spend the rest of my life with him.

Even in that precious moment she knew she was wounded; everything done undone, every gain of her fight for betterment lost, her allies deserted and their work made harder by her defection.

I'm so sorry, she told them, but they made it too hard for me. And I love him very much.

The man she loved very much was pointing a gun at her. 'Did you hear? To that wall.'

Blinking, she went and joined the small crowd by the oriel window. The cook was shuddering. Diana put her arm round her. 'It's all right, Mrs Smart.' Alice had her face hidden in Robert's coat. Robert himself stood like a pillar of salt, unmoving, his eyes staring straight ahead.

The platform had gone down. Now it rumbled up again; out of it stumbled Challenor and his fellow-coachman, both with their hands tied but apparently otherwise unharmed. Behind them came two men, red stocking caps on their head, each with a cutlass at his belt and a pistol in hand. In French, de Vaubon said: 'Tell them to begin.'

One of them nodded and shouted down the shaft. *'Allons-y.'*

The room vibrated as the platform went upwards.

The other man went and gathered up the arms from the oriel and carried them across to the shaft entrance, putting them beside it on the floor. Then he crossed the room and went down the screen passage. They heard him open the front door—nobody had locked it since Nicholls came in.

De Vaubon took his arm out of Nicholls's and made him sit down on the floor. The man's face above his gag was white and blank, his eyes made slow blinks which closed them completely for a second or two before they opened again.

'Alors.' De Vaubon settled himself comfortably on the sill of the wreckers' window, the boot of his bad leg on Nicholls's shoulder. 'Which of you is the earl?'

The question was answered by Alice who flung herself on Robert, shrieking, 'No! No, don't take him.'

'Madame . . .' de Vaubon began and then stopped as the door opened and Makepeace, Josh and Philippa were pushed into the room. 'Who are these?'

The man ushering them in with his gun said in painful French: *'Les gens de l'auberge, mon capitaine. Ils essayent aller pour . . . pour le garde-côte.'* He had a red handkerchief tied over the lower half of his face.

'Uh?' For a moment de Vaubon was off his stride. 'They try to go for the coastguard, is that it?'

'Oui.'

He's seeing they don't get any blame for this, she thought. Oh *Lord*, I love him.

'Look from the window all of you,' de Vaubon said. 'You see my men occupy all the village.' His mouth twitched as he added: 'It is useless to resist.'

He's always wanted to say that, she thought.

Everybody turned to the oriel. Armed men lined the track at the top of the slipway, their backs to T'Gallants, guns trained on an opposite line of women. Diana saw Zack, miming terror, being held up by one of his grandsons, the enormous figure of Jan Gurney pointing a pistol at a grinning Rachel.

They're home. She looked across at Makepeace, who was looking back at her. Makepeace gave a slight nod.

The platform was coming down; Diana had a brief glimpse of familiar faces going past before the Frenchman who stood by the shaft pushed the chair back into place. She was left with an image of Bilo, winking at her.

That too. My lambs are escaping—and Robert will never even know they were there.

Perhaps there were days like this, when every good thing in Heaven was poured onto a trembling soul below. There couldn't be many; this was hers.

Makepeace thought: We're late, we've missed the best part.

It had worked amazingly well. Once de Vaubon had a pistol to Nicholls's head it was bound to. But she would have liked to see his entrance. There he was, bless him, the largest and ugliest thing in the room, and still the most vivid, one foot up on the sill now, dominating everything just as he had at Henry Hobbs's funeral feast—and what a long time ago *that* was. The plump daughter-in-law was carrying on and clinging to her plump earl who was very pale and considerably less pompous. Dignified, though, she had to give him that.

He dumped his wife into the arms of the doctor and stepped forward. 'I am the Earl of Stacpoole. I protest at this outrage. What do you want, sir?'

'To begin, food.' De Vaubon nodded at his men. 'The kitchens.'

As the men went past them on their way out, Diana heard Mrs

Smart mutter: 'Froggy devils.' Then professionalism got the better of her. She shouted: 'And take my bread out the oven.'

Vibration tickled the soles of their feet as the platform came up and went down, up and down, rattling like a giant tinker's cart as it went past the closed chair-door.

'I wish better treatment for prisoners of war,' de Vaubon was saying. 'I wish Americans exchanged. I wish the French exchanged quicker. You will tell this to King George.'

'I shall do no such thing.'

'Yes,' said de Vaubon. 'You will. I take a hostage to make sure of it. One of your women, I think.'

Alice began to moan.

De Vaubon put his head on one side, apparently considering. 'I take the thin one.'

'That's the Earl's mother,' said Makepeace, helpfully.

And then Diana knew what they were all about. With guile and infinite care, they were removing her from the hook on which she had been speared.

'Pack some clothes, madame. And be quick or I miss the tide,' de Vaubon said to her. 'That woman can help you. Yes, you, red hair. André, watch them.'

The man who'd brought the women and Josh up from the Pomeroy gestured with his gun at the door and obediently Diana went towards it with Makepeace. As they went out, Diana heard Robert begin to beg for her.

Going upstairs, Makepeace said: 'This is Andra.'

'How do you do, Mr Hedley,' she said, politely. 'I've heard so much about you.'

'And me about you.' He pulled the handkerchief down from his face. 'Tha'll have to hurry, pet. I'm sorry, I'd have liked to chat.'

In her bedroom, she and Makepeace wrapped their arms around each other and then stood back.

'Your idea?' Diana asked her.

'Rachel's really. She mentioned John Paul Jones and I thought:

Well, why not?' She jerked her thumb at her husband. 'The old alchemist here supplied the finer points.' She gave one of the grins that made her momentarily and astonishingly beautiful. 'Everybody gains. Gil gets you, the Millbay lads go home, Robert gets rid of a mad mother and everybody's sorry for him.'

'They will be, won't they?'

'They'll weep in the streets.' Makepeace's tone suggested that she would not.

'Might it actually help, Missus? If they think I'm hostage, will they improve prisoners' treatment?'

'Oh, stop it,' Makepeace said, 'it's nothing to do with you any more. Of course they won't. The rest of us will have to take up the banner, I suppose, me, Andra, Beasley. Now then . . .' She knelt down by Diana's clothes press. 'You won't want all this black. Are you taking the blue?'

'Mr Hedley?'

He looked at her squarely. 'No, pet,' he said, 'they'll not raise a finger. They'll use the excuse that they can't give in to blackmail. Like the Missus says, it'll be up to us agitators.'

'I won't ever be able to come back then, will I?' Diana said.

Makepeace paused in her packing but didn't look at her.

'Do you want to?' Andra asked.

T'Gallants, Babbs Cove, an English spring, Tobias. 'You'll look after Tobias as well as can be, won't you?' she said.

'He and Dell are going to run the Pomeroy when he comes out,' Makepeace said, delving into a wardrobe for a valise.

If he comes out, Diana thought. She said: 'I would have liked grandchildren.'

Still with her back to her friend, Makepeace grimaced at the children the Earl and Countess of Stacpoole would produce between them. 'You'll just have to borrow some of Gil's,' she said.

Andra was watching Diana's face. 'Gains and losses, pet,' he said, 'gains and losses. Always the way.'

'Yes.'

'And a big, ugly, attractive gain it is,' Makepeace said, throwing a bulging valise on the bed. 'And it's going to miss the tide if you don't stir your stumps. I've gone to a lot of trouble for this. So's he. And he's committed now, he's got to take somebody hostage. You want him to sail off with Alice?'

They had to stop laughing before they went down the stairs in case they were heard in the Great Hall.

Andra and Makepeace watched her go in. More Frenchmen had come up the shaft; the room was becoming crowded. One of them came forward to take the valise from her.

'I'll be off then, pet.' Andra had to take off his disguise and become a chance guest at the Pomeroy Arms.

'Take care, they might see you going down.'

'Not them, they'll all be watching her. They won't notice me.'

'I'd notice you. I always notice you.'

Andra smiled. 'I know tha would,' he said. 'And in case you were wondering, you're my life's length and its breadth and its height.'

She watched him go. 'Now's a fine time to tell me,' she said and went into the Great Hall.

He was right; every eye was on the Dowager Countess as she walked towards her son. Robert's argument trailed away . . . 'Mama.'

'It's all right, Robert.' It was dreadful; he was crying.

She wondered what to say to him and realized that in these last days she had come to think of him not so much as her son but as 'Them', one of the faceless members of the cabal that fought so hard to keep itself in charge of an unchanging nation.

An innocent really, she thought. He believes that ruin comes from change yet, without change, England will be ruined. It was inevitable that he would deny her liberty; he was too entrenched in a class that had gone to war to deny it for others.

'I'm so sorry, my dear,' she said and when she kissed him, she was kissing the child he had been.

De Vaubon was beside her. 'Also I need more crew.' He limped along the line of people under guard by the oriel. 'Too fat,' he told Kempson-Jones. 'Too old.' That was Tinkler.

He stopped in front of Josh. 'You.' His men pushed Josh towards the shaft. Just before he stepped onto the platform, the boy looked back. 'Good-bye, Missus.'

Makepeace sobbed. Hopeless, she said to herself. I told him not to smile.

'Good-bye, Alice.'

'Mama, Mama . . .' Diana saw that, oddly, it was Alice who would miss her the most. Her daughter-in-law's face was stricken. She tried to tell her: 'Don't mind, my dear. Believe me, I am happy to do this.'

True to her breeding, she would have gone along the line of servants to say good-bye but de Vaubon was looking at his timepiece. 'We waste time,' he said. *'Allons-y.'*

As she went towards the shaft, Nicholls moved towards her feet. Looking down at him, she thought: He knows this is a charade, his instinct is telling him. Or if he doesn't know now, he soon will.

'What are you going to do with Captain Nicholls?' she asked clearly. Above the gag the man's eyes were promising to kill her when he could.

'He is coming with us. He is being impressed into the navy of King Louis. It will be good for him.'

How nice for Babbs Cove and free trade. She smiled down at the Revenue man. Not today, I'm choosing life today.

Most of the Frenchmen had gone down the shaft, leaving two to bring Nicholls and cover their captain's retreat.

Makepeace, watching, saw de Vaubon pick up his hostage and sling her over his shoulder before stepping onto the platform. You Frenchmen, she thought. She's a lucky woman. You're both lucky.

As they went down the shaft and with her head hanging against de Vaubon's leather coat, Diana said: 'This is the equivalent of being carried over the threshold, is it?'

'It looks well for a kidnapping. Not so good for my leg, you're heavier than you look.'

Bilo was waiting for them in the cavern, already in the rowing boat with oars unshipped.

'I'm so happy, Bilo,' she told him. 'Are the others away?'

He grinned at her. 'Yes, madame.'

For the last time the platform went up and came down with the rearguard and Nicholls. He was put in the bottom of the boat between the thwarts and she couldn't be bothered to look at him anymore. One of the men started hacking at the platform's ropes with a knife.

'*Allons-y,*' de Vaubon said again, and held the netting up so that they could be rowed through.

There was a general rush to the wreckers' window as if, somehow, by watching her go, the poor hostage might still be saved. Makepeace found herself next to Alice.

The breeze had blown away the fog to reveal a smart white-sailed cutter just outside the groyne of the cove. Men clambered in her rigging, unfurling sails.

Robert was raving, calling on a navy that wasn't there.

'I fear for her.' Alice's tears plopped onto the windowsill in correspondence with the last drops from the thawing icicles outside it. 'I fear that dreadful man may ravish her.'

'Yes,' Makepeace said, watching the Dowager Countess of Stacpoole raise an arm, and waving back to it. 'Yes, I'm afraid he will.'

Diana looked one more time behind her, at the red dot that was her friend's head. Losses and gains, gains and losses. But one of these days, Makepeace and that nice man she'd married would arrive at Gruchy in Jan Gurney's boat. In the meantime, she must just trust England to the Missus's care.

God help it, she thought, lovingly.

And now I can write to Martha.

De Vaubon pointed to the cutter they were nearing. 'My new boat,' he said.

'She's lovely. What is she called?'

'In view of everything,' he said, 'I thought perhaps . . . *La Liberté?*'

'A good name,' she said.

Author's Note

THOUGH the conditions in which captured Americans were kept in Britain during the War of Independence were undoubtedly bad, the report by John Howard (of the later Penal Reform League) of his visit to Millbay in 1778 seems to indicate that—the hospital apart—they were not much worse than in ordinary prisons of the time. That was bad enough, of course, and my fictional Dowager Countess represents those among the British public who were shamed into protesting and raising money to alleviate the suffering.

Such aid, along with the political sympathy for the American cause expressed by men like the Marquis of Rockingham and Edmund Burke, was taken further by some and there is evidence from diaries kept by American escapers who made a 'home run' that they received help from ordinary English men and women.

The captive 'rebels' were at last given recognition as prisoners of war in 1782, thereby becoming eligible for exchange, after the British defeat at Yorktown the previous year decided American independence—although the war itself was not concluded until the Treaty of Paris in 1783.

The mass escape from Millbay took place, as in the book, in December 1778. One hundred and nine men broke out of whom seventy-seven were eventually recaptured. John Paul Jones's attempt to kidnap the Earl of Selkirk took place in the same year. Sadly, the segregation of black prisoners by the white is also a fact.

★   ★   ★

It is almost impossible to exaggerate the extent of smuggling in the eighteenth and early nineteenth centuries. Despite desperate attempts by the Revenue Service, 'free trade' thrived with the connivance of the general public as well as many magistrates. For instance, in 1817 two Revenue men were arrested by the Mayor of Deal for having tried to stop a band of smugglers from bringing brandy kegs ashore. At their trial they were sentenced to gaol for having wounded some of the gang during the struggle. They were later released by the intervention of a higher court but the case was not untypical.

Coastguards weren't given the name until 1822—until then they were members of the Waterguard—but since they performed much the same service, I have used the more familiar and modern word.

READERS GUIDE TO

Taking Liberties

Taking Liberties is a novel about two women who help to bring liberty to others. Discuss the ways in which Makepeace Hedley and Diana Stacpoole are opposites. How do they complement each other? Are there qualities that they share?

• • •

In the course of this novel, Diana is transformed from a prisoner of propriety to a liberated women of spirit. It could be said that the same sense of honor that kept her in an unhappy marriage is ultimately the source of her liberation. Discuss this.

• • •

While Diana is enslaved by British aristocratic traditions, Makepeace Hedley is an enormously successful businesswomen and outspoken American with a passion for all. How does the author use her two main characters to illustrate the differences between the rising new world and the old empire?

• • •

Diana and Makepeace reach a turning point in their relationship when Diana treats Josh just as she would a white man. What is Makepeace able to gather about Diana that wasn't apparent to her previously? And how does Makepeace's lease of the house to Diana shatter Diana's misconceptions about her?

• • •

How are each of the characters in this novel motivated to become political because of the personal? Do you think that this is often the case in real life?

• • •

In this novel, Diana and Makepeace—though normally upright citizens—have a great disregard for the law. Is this pardonable? Why? Is the lawlessness of Babb's Cove justified by its long tradition?

• • •

Nicholls and deVaubon are virtually polar opposites. Discuss the differences in their characters. Why do you think the author intends us to cheer on deVaubon and deride Nicholls?

• • •

Makepeace has to overcome her own inner snobbery toward Dell, despite the fact that she probably saved Philippa's life. Why is this and what lesson does she learn in overcoming her antipathy? How has she changed by the novel's end and what has most influenced her attitudes?

• • •

A free man at last, Tobias makes an extraordinary sacrifice in taking the place of Josh. Why is he willing to do this, after so many years of forced servitude? What kind of burden does this place on Josh's shoulders?

• • •

Even at the end, as much as Diana loves deVaubon, she cannot imagine going with him because of the disgrace it would bring on her family and her feeling that running away with him would be used to discredit all the good she had accomplished. How does deVaubon demonstrate the depth of his understanding of Diana and liberate her completely?